Praise for Ava Miles

Nora Roberts Land
"Ava's story is witty and charming."
—Barbara Freethy #1 *NYT* bestselling author

Selected by *USA Today* as one of the Best Books of the
year alongside Nora Roberts' *Dark Witch* and
Julia Quinn's *Sum of all Kisses*.

"If you like Nora Roberts type books, this is a must-read."
—Readers' Favorite

Country Heaven
"If ever there was a contemporary romance that rated a 10
on a scale of 1 to 5 for me, this one is it!"
—The Romance Reviews

"*Country Heaven* made me laugh and cry...I could not
stop flipping the pages. I can't wait to read the next book
in this series." —Fresh Fiction

Country Heaven Cookbook
"Delicious, simple recipes... Comfort food, at its best."
—Fire Up The Oven Blog

The Bridge to a Better Life
Selected by *USA Today* as one of the Best Books of the
Summer.

"Miles offers a story of grief, healing and rediscovered
love." —*USA Today*

"I've read Susan Mallery and Debbie Macomber...but
never have I been so moved by the books Ava Miles
writes." —Booktalk with Eileen Reviews

The Gate to Everything
"The constant love...bring a ~~~~~~~~~ ion to
this appealii

D1378051

More Praise For Ava

The Chocolate Garden
"On par with Nicholas Sparks' love stories."
—Jennifer's Corner Blog

"A must-read...a bit of fairy magic...a shelf full of happiness." —Fab Fantasy Fiction

The Promise of Rainbows
"This is a story about grace, faith and the power of both..."
—The Book Nympho

French Roast
"Ms. Miles draws from her experience as an apprentice chef...and it shows...I loved {the} authenticity of the food references, and the recipes...looked divine." —BlogCritics

The Holiday Serenade
"This story is all romance, steam, and humor with a touch of the holiday spirit..." —The Book Nympho

The Town Square
"Ms. Miles' words melted into each page until the world receded around me..." —Tome Tender

The Park of Sunset Dreams
"Ava has done it again. I love the whole community of Dare Valley..." —Travel Through The Pages Blog

Also by Ava Miles

Fiction

The Friends & Neighbors Novels

The House of Hope & Chocolate

The Dreamer's Flower Shoppe

The Merriams Series

Wild Irish Rose

Love Among Lavender

Valley of Stars

Sunflower Alley

A Forever of Orange Blossoms

A Breath of Jasmine

The Love Letter Series

Letters Across An Open Sea

Along Waters of Sunshine and Shadow

The Dare Valley Series

Nora Roberts Land

French Roast

The Grand Opening

The Holiday Serenade

The Town Square

The Park of Sunset Dreams

The Perfect Ingredient

The Bridge to a Better Life

The Calendar of New Beginnings

Home Sweet Love

The Dare Valley Series (cont'd)

The Moonlight Serenade

The Sky of Endless Blue

Daring Brides

The Dare River Series

Country Heaven

Country Heaven Cookbook

The Chocolate Garden

The Chocolate Garden:

A Magical Tale (Children's Book)

Fireflies and Magnolias

The Promise of Rainbows

The Fountain of Infinite Wishes

The Patchwork Quilt of Happiness

Dare Valley Meets Paris Billionaire Mini-Series

The Billionaire's Gamble

The Billionaire's Courtship

The Billionaire's Secret

The Billionaire's Return

Non-Fiction

The Happiness Corner: Reflections So Far

Home Baked Happiness

Country Heaven Cookbook

Reclaim Your Superpowers

Courage Is Your Superpower

The Dreamer's

Flower Shoppe

A Friends & Neighbors Novel

Ava Miles

ISBN-13: 978-1-949092-33-2
www.avamiles.com
Ava Miles

To my old neighborhood in Del Ray and all the wonderful friends and neighbors who brought me so much joy and showed me what true community could be, especially Julia and Danilo, Colin, and my little tree-climbing buddy, Luke.

She was the luckiest girl in the whole world.

Bundles of colorful flowers filled the entire back seat where she was sitting, and roses and peonies, her favorites, scented the air. Her papa's thirteenth birthday present—a trip into New York City to visit the famous flower market—had made her squeal so loudly a cab driver had stopped to see if they needed a lift as they reached the market on foot.

Her papa had said her gift was all the flowers she could buy with the crisp bills he'd made yesterday at his barber shop. There'd been enough for a sea of flowers, plus she'd gotten some good deals from the shopkeepers because it was her birthday.

They had the best job ever! If she could be surrounded with flowers all the time, she'd be crazy happy.

No question about it. Today was one of the best days of her entire life.

Already she couldn't wait to go back. Or to give her mama and her friends some of her flowers.

"Gather what you can, Rosie," her papa said as he stopped the car in their driveway. "I'll bring the rest. I know you're eager to tell your mama about our adventure. But let's keep it quiet with your brother. You know how jealous Al gets of our special days together. But he doesn't love flowers like you do."

"No one likes flowers like me, Papa." Flowers and plants were her special connection with her papa. She and Mama shared cooking. Al made fun of everything good, in her opinion, and he drove her and everyone else crazy by doing it.

"Mama's going to be so happy to see them," Rose

answered, overloading her arms. Thank goodness the roses had been wrapped tightly in butcher paper to keep the thorns from scratching her. She gave a deep sniff and nearly melted. This was heaven.

The distinct dribbling of basketballs had her craning around in her seat. Vinnie and Hank were walking down the middle of the street on their way to the schoolyard. They might be in Al's class, but they were nothing like him, thank goodness.

"Vinnie!" she shouted from inside the car.

"My Rosie's got it bad," she heard her papa say with a chuckle. "Here, I'll get the door."

"Thanks, Papa." She raced off, flowers falling to the ground in her haste.

"Vinnie! Hank! Come see what my papa got me for my birthday."

The dribbling ceased, and they both turned around, the basketballs tucked to their hips. She nearly dropped all her bundles when Vinnie smiled at her. Oh... He was so gorgeous, from his curly hair, which she'd never found this appealing on another boy, to his dreamy brown eyes. Tons of Italian guys had brown eyes but on Vinnie they looked different. Friendly. Playful. And yes, dreamy.

Everything about Vinnie Scorsese was dreamy.

She was so glad she was wearing the new yellow dress that her mama had let her open before their trip as an early birthday present. Maybe he'd think she looked as pretty as a flower.

Hank's mouth tipped up. "Happy birthday, sweetie. Looks like your dad got you your favorites and then some."

"You left a trail of beauty behind you, Rosie. Happy birthday!" Vinnie said, and then launched into the birthday song.

He was singing to her! Her arms went lax, and more flowers spilled down as her cheeks heated. Oh my God!

Sure, he did it all the time at his family restaurant, but he wasn't working now.

When he sang her name, she couldn't meet his eyes anymore. If only she were older and filled out. It wasn't fair that he was three years ahead of her. She was sure he was going to find a girlfriend in Chicago when he went to go work in his uncle Angelo's plumbing business for the summer. Oh, she was going to miss seeing him around.

"Your mama is probably making you a special birthday dinner tonight," Vinnie said when he finished, "but if you swing by the restaurant afterward for dessert, it's on the house. I know you love my mama's tiramisu."

Vinnie always remembered everyone's favorites, but it didn't keep her heart from bursting in her chest.

"I'd say my dad's shepherd's pie is on the house," Hank said, "but I can't imagine you'd want to eat it."

She liked Hank, but she'd never stepped foot in his dad's Irish pub. As her mama always said, the Irish weren't known for their food. Vinnie's family restaurant was different. They went to Two Sisters for his mama's famous lasagna. Every Italian in town, her mama included, swore it was the best they'd ever eaten.

"Thanks, Hank, but you know my mama is cooking up a storm for my birthday. Only cake though. Not tiramisu. Maybe she'll bring me in to Two Sisters for some, because Vinnie's right. It's my favorite."

Hank sent her a knowing wink. He'd found out about her crush on Vinnie three years ago, but he'd promised he'd keep it to himself—and he had. He was so much nicer than her brother, who had turned into a complete jerk when he started high school.

"No tiramisu for Al though, okay?" Vinnie gave her a conspiratorial wink.

"Don't worry," she said with a hefty sigh. "He'll cut out early after dinner. He and Tony Grasiaca go off God knows where at night, Mama says. Since he's gotten his *driver's license, she prays a rosary for him every day."*

The two boys shared a look before Hank said, "He's not a sweetheart like you."

That was a kind way of putting it. Al complained all the time. About everything. Including helping out at Papa's barber shop now that he was sixteen, even though Papa paid him good money. Sometimes he was so nasty about it she wanted to whack him upside the head. Worse, he didn't even show up for work every day! Papa and Mama would yell at him, but he never listened. Not even to the local priest!

She couldn't wait until he graduated next year and left the house. Papa was trying to get him to join the military to learn some discipline. Rose thought Uncle Sam should run the other way if he saw Al coming—presuming he showed up at the recruiting office at all.

"I can't wait for dessert, Vinnie. It's going to be so great!" Her face burned. She'd totally yelled.

He didn't seem to notice she was gushing. He just smiled.

Oh, how she wished she could marry him when she grew up.

"Here!" On impulse, she selected a rose, flicked off the thorns with her fingernail, and gave it to Vinnie. "I want you to have one of my birthday flowers. May roses always smell the best."

Vinnie lifted it to his nose. "Wow! They do smell incredible. Maybe we should start filling the restaurant with these. We can give them to our female guests on special occasions."

"You would think of that," Hank said, chuckling.

"It would make the ladies happy," Vinnie said. "I mean, look at Rosie. She's glowing."

She flushed again and thrust a dethorned rose out to Hank. "Flowers make people happy. When I'm in the garden or Papa's greenhouse, the whole world feels perfect."

"That's a pretty special place." Vinnie sniffed the rose again. "I feel like that in our restaurant. Especially the kitchen when Mama and Aunt Alessa are making sauce. Or garlic bread."

Her stomach gave a delighted gurgle.

"I'll give this rose to my mom if that's okay, Rose," Hank said. "My dad would probably beat me up if I came home and put it in a vase or something."

"That's all you need from your pops," Vinnie said, tucking the rose behind his ear. "Thank God my dad isn't like that. He might be tough, but he always says the more a man cries, the bigger his heart."

"Your dad is one of the nicest dads ever." Rose started walking backward. "Well, I'm keeping you from the court. I'll see you later, Vinnie. Bye, Hank."

They waved and started walking off, the boys' basketballs pounding the pavement in time with her shoes as she ran back to her house, smiling as the sunlight caught the glass of the greenhouse in their backyard. One of Papa's best customers had given them that greenhouse. It was a sign that even the most impossible dreams could come true.

Rose had a dream or two. She wanted to be surrounded by flowers, maybe even work with them like those nice people at the flower market. And she wanted to marry Vinnie Scorsese. It seemed like a tall order, but maybe God listened extra special on birthdays. She bowed her head and said a prayer.

Please God, help me find a way to work with flowers. Also, I need to grow up super fast so I can marry Vinnie. Thanks for listening.

If that last dream came true, she would make sure their wedding was loaded with the most beautiful flowers she could find in the entire world.

CHAPTER 1

EVERY BRIDE NEEDED FLOWERS.

Rose might be single with no prospects, but even she knew that. She'd dreamed about her wedding flowers ever since she was a flower girl at her cousin's wedding on Long Island years ago. Throwing rose petals on the floor and being patted on the head for it had been one of her best childhood gigs ever.

Nothing said celebration and good fortune like flowers, and if she had anything to say about it, her friends Alice Bailey and Hank O'Connor were going to have them at their upcoming nuptials. She'd casually asked around, and to her horror, she'd discovered the only flowers they planned on having were for Alice's bouquet. Now that the town's holiday festival was over, and everything was settling down, she'd asked to meet them at Alice's chocolate shop so she could offer her services.

Helping her friends would be a good trial run to see if she could arrange flowers with enough verve to make a run at a real business. In her wildest dreams—the ones she let herself get lost in every time another job rejection showed up in her inbox or she listened to Pink sing about being empowered—she was running a floral business. She'd done the research, so she knew it was possible to do such a thing from home. People did it all the time with e-commerce and home delivery, although she didn't know how successful they were.

Covid had hit the florist industry hard, but Rose's research suggested online orders for houseplants and flowers had gone through the roof, what with people being home so much. Plus, everyone had gone crazy for growing their own food gardens early on in the pandemic. Every catalogue Rose followed had sold out of their stock in a single week. Surely, with the right marketing plan and stock, she could dip her toe in.

She had to do something positive, and flowers had always made her happy. Even if she didn't make a ton of money, at least she'd be doing *something* with her life. Living like she was, barely making it from one day to the next, would break her before long.

When she arrived at the chocolate shop, Alice and Hank led her back to the Chocolate Bar. She got straight to the point as they started to fix cups of hot chocolate.

"I'd like to do some flowers for your wedding. As a gift."

"That would be totally awesome!" Alice shrieked, and the chocolate pieces in her hands scattered across the counter.

"That's great of you, Rose," Hank said as he helped Alice gather up the scattered pieces. "Can't imagine anyone doing them better."

"Oh, stop! You'll embarrass me."

"With the town's florist gone, you and your greenhouse have been a lifesaver. I've appreciated being able to buy some flowers and plants for my girl."

His dad had also bought a few arrangements for Vinnie's mom, Mama Gia, and praised them for their beauty. Mr. O'Connor was no pushover. He wouldn't have complimented them if he hadn't meant it, and if he liked them, she imagined others would too.

"I loved the houseplant!" Alice added. "And the yellow roses. Oh, and some white flower."

Rose's lips twitched, not that Alice could see them through her mask. "Good. We'll find ones you'll love for your wedding too. Preferably ones you'll remember."

"I wish I could bear hug the heck out of you right now." Alice's big brown eyes gleamed with tears over her mask. She was always wearing fun masks, and this one—a dinosaur in a Santa hat eating chocolate—was no exception. But that was Alice, the woman who had brought hope and community back to their small town of Orion, New York. She was nothing if not a go-getter, and she'd managed to get her guy while saving their town.

Maybe if Rose spent more time with her, some of the woman's positivity and good fortune would rub off on her. Like Alice, she wanted to open her own business. Then there was the guy she'd always wanted, Hank's best friend, no less, who'd visited her greenhouse a few days ago to make a promotional video for Old World Elegance. They'd made half a dozen videos to promote the town's holiday festival, and they'd drawn so much attention a few shopkeepers had contacted them about making more.

Working with Vinnie. Spending time with him...

It was what she'd always dreamed of. Then there was what he'd said to her in the greenhouse: *You look more beautiful standing in this greenhouse than anywhere in the world.* She might have repeated that to herself a dozen times a day. It had awoken old dreams in her heart, both that she might use her love of flowers to create the job she couldn't seem to find and that Vinnie Scorsese might finally be ready to see her as something other than a de facto kid sister from the neighborhood.

"We'll save our hugs up," Rose said, excited to think about hugging Vinnie at some point.

"Since when are you a hugger?" Hank asked with a

bemused glance.

"Since Covid," Rose answered carefully. "I might be tough, but I'm still Italian enough to miss touching people."

Of course, in her old world that usually meant kissing cheeks and occasionally grabbing or nudging someone's arm to emphasize a point. All of that was gone, save for with her parents, whom she was living with, although they were all so down at times that there wasn't much of their usual exuberant hand gesturing.

"We need to have a hug party when Covid is over." Alice pulled out her phone, as she often did when an idea struck. "The whole town can come, and we'll have a hug mob instead of a flash mob."

Hank put his arm around her. "I'd come to that."

"Me too, especially for the dancing," Rose said. "Before we hug, let's burn all our masks in garbage cans in the town square. I'll hurl mine into the fire and say, '*Addio a qualcuno che non ti piace.*'"

"Oooh, that's a good one," Alice said in Italian, one of the many languages she spoke fluently. She loved to flex her language muscles, as she called them, and so did her multilingual business partner, the distinguished Clifton Hargreaves. "I'd say '*Ciao, testa di cazzo.*'"

Rose sputtered out a hearty laugh. "Salty," she said in English since Hank was patiently standing by. Of course he was used to it, given Vinnie had grown up slipping in and out of Italian with his parents, like Rose did with her family. That connection wasn't one every Italian American family had since some of the immigrants from the Old Country had chosen not to speak the language with their descendants. But Rose would always be grateful to know and speak the language of her ancestors, and it felt special to share this with Vinnie.

"I won't even ask what she said," Hank said, laughing. "Come on. Let's finish making these hot chocolates. Rose, yours is on me, and I won't hear otherwise."

She blew him a kiss. "You're the best."

"The bestest," Alice agreed, dotting Rose's hot chocolate with a thick dollop of whipped cream for punctuation and pushing it across the counter to her.

"You have a minute to chat flowers with us first?" she asked, calculating she had less than a month before their wedding, which was scheduled for the first week of January. "What other arrangements have you made for your wedding? Getting a better idea of your plans will help me figure out which flowers to use."

"Vinnie's mom has cooked and frozen more pans of lasagna and chocolate cannolis than we have guests," Hank said with another hoarse laugh. "She told me to put the rest in the freezer so we can give ourselves a break from cooking during the work week."

"You're a son to her, and she needs something to fill the time," Rose said, her heart tearing a bit. "Sure, she's seeing your dad now"—and hadn't that been a shock to everyone in town—"but that's not enough to fill the day. She's used to keeping busy in the restaurant."

But Two Sisters was gone, and so was Vinnie's aunt.

"Time drags," she finished softly, thinking about how true that was for herself. Her job and life in the city had been fun and exciting, filled with travel and social engagements. But then the pandemic had hit, and everything had changed. Now, here she was, laid off and living with her parents. She helped out around the house and worked in the greenhouse, but there was still too much downtime, and there was only so much Netflix a girl could watch. She wanted—*needed*—more for herself. She had to dig her way out, even if it meant digging herself into her greenhouse.

"Talking about Mama Gia's dating life with my dad is like listening to nails on a chalkboard." Hank rubbed his forehead. "Heck, Rosie, why don't you just take a tire iron to my head and bash it in?"

She laughed. "I don't have a car, or I might take you up

on it. You and Vinnie need to chill about the whole thing."

"You seriously don't think it's weird?" Hank asked, his dark brow furrowing.

She wanted to tease him more, but it was too easy. If Vinnie had been here instead, she would have gone for it.

When they were kids, she'd always hoped Vinnie would look at her differently one day. That she'd fill out, and he'd suddenly realize she was a woman. But that transformation had happened years ago, and he hadn't seemed to notice. Until he'd told her that she was beautiful in the greenhouse. She was hard-pressed to think of a more promising turn of events.

"Sure," she told Hank, "it's a little weird, but they used to like each other back in the day. The whole Irish-Italian thing got in the way. Nothing against your mom or Vinnie's dad, but nobody should be kept apart because of ethnicity or color or anything else for that matter. If you love someone—"

"You should be able to be with them. Hank and Vinnie are still getting used to the idea of their parents getting so serious so fast."

Hank shuddered. "I can't see a red-and-white-checkered tablecloth and a dripping candle from a Chianti bottle without breaking into a sweat."

She wanted Vinnie to take her on a date like that. But she just shrugged. "Mama Gia always knew romance. That's why Two Sisters was the go-to date destination in town."

Maybe she could encourage Vinnie in that direction by using those props in their next marketing video for Old World Elegance. Apparently, the shop owner, Aunt Gladys, so called because she was an aunt to the whole town, had a new video in mind. She wanted to promote a mix of formal and loungewear—a tuxedo dinner jacket over a bare chest with easy lounging pants.

Now *that* was a look Rose could get on board with,

especially if Vinnie's bare chest was involved. She hadn't seen his bare chest since she was in high school at the community pool, and boy, had it made an impression. She'd gone under in the deep end, swallowed a whole bunch of disgusting pool water, and popped up coughing her brains out, only to be rescued by a lifeguard who thought she was drowning. That day still ranked in her top five most embarrassing.

Now that Vinnie lifted weights, she couldn't imagine how his chest would affect her. From the cut of his clothes, he was bursting with muscle. Hot. So hot. She needed to make sure she wasn't holding anything or operating any heavy machinery if and when she saw it again.

She tucked that image away for later. "And what colors will you be using for the wedding?"

"All I know is my dress is white," Alice said.

"*Oh, honey,*" Rose said as Hank spurted out a laugh. "I know you're busy but that's downright sad."

"Let's sit outside. It's not too windy out, and my new heat lamps rock," Alice said, finishing Hank's hot chocolate and then grabbing a bottle of water from the small fridge behind the counter. "Let me just tell Clifton I'm stepping out for a moment."

Moments later, Rose sat at the adjoining table across from the couple in the House of Hope & Chocolate's outdoor dining area, sipping Alice's fabulous hot chocolate. If she were being a serious professional, she'd think of this as her first consultation. The thought gave her a little thrill.

"Why don't you run me through the nuts and bolts? I know it's going to be a small gathering due to Covid and the regulations."

"We're only having the closest of the closest," Hank said, "otherwise we'd have to think about who in the neighborhood and town businesses."

"Good plan," Rose said. "You don't want anyone getting upset."

"We're going to close the chocolate shop and have it here," Alice said. "There's better light than O'Connor's."

"Irish pubs aren't supposed to have great light." Hank rolled his eyes. "So long as you can reach for your Guinness…"

"Oh, Lord," Rose said, giving him a return eye roll. "It will be lovely here, Alice. Now flowers. Any ideas?"

"None, and I'm not sure my brain can even drum up any." Alice turned to Hank. "You had no say in your first wedding. Got any preferences here?"

"Flowers. Hell, no. But on color, Alice loves red—"

"I don't just love it. I adore it. He loves green."

Rose took a drink to hide her smile. "That will make things easy. Red flowers have green stems."

"Smart aleck," Hank said companionably. "Rose, what would you suggest?"

"Also, I am so paying you," Alice said, pointing at her like a good Italian. "It's sweet to offer it as a gift, but I won't take anything but a yes on this one."

"I was only offering as a friend," Rose said, cringing. "Seriously, I thought it might be an opportunity for me to up my game a bit—"

"Paying," Alice repeated, her eyes narrowing. "So. Flowers. What about those giant red blooms you decorated a few of Orion's shops with for the holiday festival?"

"Poinsettias," Hank said.

"No—"

"Amaryllises," Rose finished for her. "The stems are a bit thick for a bouquet. It can be done, of course, but if you just like the colors… What about ranunculi? They're a cross between a daisy and a floribunda rose, and in season."

They both blinked at her. "Ra-what? I mean, I bought flower arrangements working for Francesca, but they came finished. And you'll remember that until recently, all house plants around me bolted like they were engineering a plant prison break."

"The heart fern I got for you from Rose is still alive."

Yeah, that was one of Rose's favorite houseplants, both for its heartiness and the shape of its leaves.

"Thanks to our consult," Alice said, patting herself on the back. "Whew! Let me look up this flower." She pulled out her phone and started typing. When a wistful smile broke across her face, Rose knew they had a winner. Now Alice had a lovely "bride glow."

"Oh, Hank, I love them. Look at how cute they are." She thrust her phone at him.

His mouth tipped up on the right. "They're perfect. Can you put some of those amaryllis flowers on a table for the reception? If she wants them, let's include them too."

"Absolutely, we can," Rose said as Alice gave him an effusive kiss on the cheek.

Rose had a dozen amaryllis blooming in her greenhouse, in fact, ready for the holidays. Might be smart to offer them year-round in the store she fantasized about starting. A lot of people couldn't get them to rebloom themselves.

"Any other colors?" Rose asked. "White to contrast the red? Or cream?"

"What about purple? I love purple."

"Ranunculi come in purple," Rose said.

Alice held up her phone proudly. "I know."

This was going much better than Rose's last professional meeting—an airline marketing presentation she'd given in Ames, Iowa, about drumming up regional air travel beyond college football season. "Okay, we have a winner. How about something with a scent? Ranunculi don't smell. Say winter jasmine? They come in white—"

"Jasmine and I go way back. It's Francesca's favorite, and she's my matron of honor. I bought it for her every chance I got because it reminds her of home in Lebanon. I love it, but it can have a strong scent."

"It would only be accent," Rose said. "If I can find some, I'll keep it discreet."

"I know it's not always easy to find the flowers you want right now," Alice said, "so why don't you go with the red, white, and purple palette and see what you can find beyond ranunculi and amaryllises? Honestly, I never much saw myself having a lot of flowers at a wedding, but I really like the idea of delegating it to you. I trust you, Rose."

Those three words were every marketing person's goal. Client trust almost always led to success. She was feeling so juiced. "I appreciate your faith."

"We'll be grateful for anything you can do to make our day brighter," Alice said, a smile lighting her face. "And sweet-smelling."

Hank jerked his thumb at his fiancée. "What she said."

"I still wish you'd let me give this to you as a wedding present—"

"No," they both fairly shouted at her.

Her heart hurt a little at that, but they weren't wrong. She knew how much she'd have to make to move out of her parents' house and cover things like health insurance, which they were paying for her right now. While she could draw unemployment benefits for another four months, they wouldn't last forever, and given all of the rejections she'd gotten over the past months, she wasn't confident she'd find a new job until the pandemic ended. Besides, she'd much rather be out doing something than sitting in her room applying for jobs. Which was why she'd made those videos with Vinnie and sold some bouquets for the greenhouse. That was small-scale stuff though, not a busines. Not a full-time job. If she wanted to make a go of this, she needed to scale up. "Fine, since you insist. Any budget?"

Alice picked up her phone and typed some things in before naming a figure. Rose had to invoke her old corporate game face. It was higher than she'd expected. For that figure, she could make up some nice arrangements in addition to the wedding bouquet.

"That will work great. Hank, what about boutonnières for you and Vinnie? Maybe your dad? Warren? Clifton?"

Alice's father had passed, so her business partner was giving her away, dear man.

"I think flowers for the men would be sweet," Alice said. "Make sure Warren's is especially quirky since he's marrying us."

Individual boutonnières would be more interesting, but also more expensive. Oh, but if she included that in her flower portfolio...

Okay, she was apparently doing a flower portfolio.

"But no ranunculi for Hank," Rose said, winking at the guy. "Any manly flowers come to mind?"

"You pulling my leg, Rose? You've known me your whole life. Have I ever struck you as a flower guy?"

They shared a quiet look. "I have known you that long, haven't I? It's been pretty great, O'Connor."

"Yeah, it's nice having you back in the neighborhood."

Hank had lived in New York City too, for a time, but they'd never seen each other there. They'd led very different lives. Just like her life now felt impossibly different from the one she'd had last year.

Her old life in the city was gone. She knew that. If she went back, it wouldn't be the same. Orion felt more familiar, safer somehow, and she had her friends and neighbors here. And Vinnie...

"Can't deny our roots are in the old neighborhood," she said softly.

"It's the 'new' neighborhood to me and I love it," Alice said. "Hank, maybe we can have Rose work with Vinnie on picking flowers you men can stomach to pin on yourselves. He's your best man, after all, and that man knows how to wear a suit."

Did he ever. Vinnie dressed like a man about town as a matter of course, and goodness, how he made her mouth go dry.

Hank and Alice shared a long look. "Good idea, babe."

When they turned their gaze to her, she could sense something in the air. "The boutonnières should be easy to make," Rose said, trying to keep a straight face. "I'd be happy to work with Vinnie on them."

She was proud her voice sounded professional. She couldn't very well say that spending time with Vinnie lifted her spirits as much as it inflamed her senses, although they both knew she had it bad for him. Privately, Rose thought they were both hoping their wedding might cast a little magic, and Vinnie would finally see her as a woman.

Alice gave her a mischievous grin. "In fact, I'm thinking these men's boutonnières are going to take a whole lot of time. I mean, Hank wants something *crazy* special for our wedding. Right?"

Hank's eyes suddenly widened as the implications struck. "Oh, shit. Yes, Alice. If there's one thing I'm looking forward to, it's the men's boutonnières at our wedding."

Alice punched him lightly in the shoulder and started laughing. "You should see your face."

"Glad you're amused, babe. Jesus, I'm going to need help from both of you to sell this to Vinnie. Boutonnières! Never in my wildest…"

Rose knew he wouldn't have to sell it. Vinnie would do anything for Hank. "Honestly, you could ask him to dress up as the flower girl and he'd do it for you."

"Please! You'll give me nightmares."

"I'll ask Warren's three-year-old, Madison, to be the flower girl. She may hurl them instead of gently scattering them and ask a million questions in the process, but that's my kind of girl."

Rose didn't mind a kid who wanted to hurl rose petals. "That sounds like pure enthusiasm to me."

"Oh!" Alice exclaimed, linking her hands and putting them under her chin. "I can't wait for them to arrive. It's going to be so much fun to have my old pal and his family here. I'm so happy he and Amy were ready for a new adventure."

"Well, Warren will have his hands full getting Orion's Friends & Neighbors Trust off the ground," Hank said. "Still, I bet he'll come in before too long to volunteer at the House of Hope & Chocolate."

"Doing what?" Rose asked.

Hank sent her an amused look before turning to Alice. "Warren told me he used to be their primary chocolate taste tester when they had their chocolate stand back in the day."

"And Amy backed him up?" Alice scoffed. "He's exaggerated that point ever since we closed up shop ten years ago. Even as a kid, he was tricky, but as an adult, he's downright wily."

"He sounds like trouble in the best way," Rose said, smiling. "By the way, I'd volunteer to chocolate taste for you anytime."

"You can join Warren when they arrive. Whew! It's been a mad rush helping them move."

"If he weren't your oldest friend, I'd be suggesting more balance," Hank said. "But I'm excited to have them here too. You always give one of your famous yawps after seeing him."

"He's one of my happy places," she said, pinching his cheek teasingly, "and so are you."

Oh, they were too cute! Rose knew Alice had helped the Anderson family move heaven and earth to find a home in Orion only a few weeks after Warren had been hired to administer the newly formed trust for Clara Merriam Hale, Clifton's former boss and an incredible philanthropist. Rose hoped to meet her someday. She sounded like Aunt Gladys but with a ton of money she liked to help people with.

"I'll make sure Warren has the best boutonnière ever," Rose said. "Something befitting a man of trouble."

"If you can make a flower squirt water like those clowns do in the circus, he'd go crazy," Alice said, making them laugh before cracking her knuckles. "Well, I think we have the makings of a good plan. How about you, Rose?"

She'd just received her first commission for wedding flowers after coming in to offer her friends her services free of charge. Her floral business was suddenly underway. *And* she'd been handed a reason to spend more time with Vinnie.

Good fortune might be starting to smile on Rose Fiorni once again.

CHAPTER 2

ESPRESSO.
    Frank Sinatra.
Acqua di Parma Colonia.

The Italians always say *La vita inizia dopo il caffe*—life begins after coffee—but lately Vinnie Scorsese needed other boosts before facing the day. Today was a prime example. Instead of listening to his usual Louis Prima or Dean Martin, he needed the Chairman of the Board's "My Way." Like Frank Sinatra, Vinnie had some regrets, but he was keeping on. As he sang along with the man himself, he slapped Colonia on his face, eyeing his diminishing supply.

He only had a quarter bottle left. He'd promised himself that by the time it was finished, he'd have charted a new course for his life.

His family restaurant had closed months ago, and he wasn't anywhere close to figuring everything out yet.

He sipped his espresso, closing his eyes to inhale the dark roast and let the nutty flavors saturate his mouth. Life was a bit dark right now, but with the right perspective, anyone could appreciate it. Like espresso. It might taste overly bitter in the beginning, but with the right music and atmosphere, it grew on people.

That's how Vinnie viewed life with Covid. It was like espresso—dark and bitter—but it was a taste that could be acquired. He was doing his damnedest to acquire it, because otherwise his entire life would become bitter, and he wouldn't allow that.

Covid had taken his precious Aunt Alessa, his mother's twin. Thankfully, by some miracle, it hadn't taken his mother, too, although her illness had scared twenty years from him and driven him back to kneel in church after a long absence. Then, in the wake of that awful loss, they'd sold Two Sisters—the one place he'd always counted on.

He no longer had a purpose, and worse, he was alone. For years, he'd felt complacent about his love life, figuring he had plenty of time to find the right woman, but Covid had made him feel alone in an aching way.

He wanted a wife and a family, badly enough that he'd lit a candle in church, asking for help.

Still, focusing on the things he didn't have wasn't going to make him happy or fulfilled, so he tried counting his blessings as he dressed. His best friend, Hank, was employing him at his Irish bar. His mother was finally rallying after months of ill health and depression. He had a roof over his head. Sure, he'd given up his town house to move into the garage apartment in his mother's house, both to look after her and save money, but he counted himself lucky to have it. He had his health, thank God, which he rigorously took care of by lifting weights every day, and health insurance, thanks to working at O'Connor's. He had wonderful friends and neighbors.

But mostly, he had himself. He was doing it his way, every day. Finding light. Uplifting his thoughts. Preparing himself to find the good in every day.

His phone pinged, and he eyed the text from Aunt Gladys.

Vinnie, my boy, I've got an absolutely tantalizing new

idea for a video. Swing by the store when you have the chance. I'd like you to try on the outfit before we arrange the filming. I'll see if Rose can come by for the consult.

He texted her back after finishing his coffee.

Can't wait to hear. Be there in ten.

Talk about a new possibility he'd never foreseen. He'd starred in a few videos promoting the Orion holiday festival, and now he was a sought-after actor for social media videos promoting the Friends & Neighbors Shoppes in his hometown. He'd done a video for Alice's chocolate shop, but he especially loved working for Aunt Gladys. Her store, Old World Elegance, was one he believed in down to his soul.

Vinnie had always enjoyed the classics, like Colonia, and fashioned himself after his father and grandfather. Men who'd dressed with respect. Who'd put family first. And who'd treated women and older people especially well, in addition to any strangers on the street. Sometimes he didn't recognize the world today. Where had kindness and good manners gone?

He finished his espresso and eyed his phone when it chimed again. Rose Fiorni's message had him smiling.

I hear you'll be at Aunt Gladys' in ten. She already told me what she has in mind, and this new video is a doozy. Better bring your game face. See you soon.

Game face, huh? That was Rose. Always talking smack. He'd known her for almost his whole life, going back to the days when she'd ridden her yellow tricycle around, pigtails flying in the wind.

She'd had a crush on him when she was a kid.

He'd always known.

Heck, he'd been *tempted*, but they wanted different things. He'd only ever wanted to stay in Orion, and Rose had moved to the city the first chance she got. Within months she'd started straightening her gorgeous black hair and wearing all black. Besides, she was Joe and Carlotta

Fiorni's daughter and Al Fiorni's younger sister. A girl from their neighborhood. A guy didn't mess with that unless he was sure it was going to lead somewhere.

Now she was back. She was struggling, but her black hair had been allowed to run wild again, curling in luxurious locks that rained down her back. She was still tempting, even more so than she had been when she was eighteen and blossoming.

The other day he'd gotten swept away and told her so. He blamed the magic of her greenhouse and the sheer radiance she emitted amidst her treasures. Still, their situation hadn't changed: she was going to leave at some point, and she was still a girl from the neighborhood from a family he respected.

He glanced in the mirror, still singing softly, and took in the strands of gray threading his black hair—a new addition since the pandemic. Usually he'd be sporting a healthy tan from the summer spent on the beaches outside the city on his day off. Not this year. He was pale, with new lines around his eyes. He wanted to say it was age, but he knew it was stress.

It struck him that he and Rose had a lot in common right now. Both of them were living with their parents, their careers jettisoned, and needed to chart a new course for their lives. He hoped he could help her somehow. Maybe the videos, which benefited them both, were a start.

Finishing the song, he put on his outerwear and let himself out. His mama would be watching from the window, and he was always upbeat with her. She had enough worries on her plate. When he came down the stairs, he headed to the house to wave to her.

She opened the window, drawing the white handknit shawl Aunt Alessa had made for her around her now thin shoulders—Aunt Alessa still managing to keep her sister warm from heaven. "Vinnie!"

"Mama, close that window! It's freezing out."

"I spoke with your uncle in Chicago," she called. "He said he'll think about bringing you on if you want. Uncle Angelo thought you hated plumbing, but I told him he was remembering wrong."

It wasn't like Mama to stretch the truth. Clearly she was more worried than he'd realized if she'd called Uncle Angelo.

Plumbing was a trade his parents had thought might be a good profession for him, so they'd decided to send him to Chicago for a few summers to learn the business. He hadn't taken to either Chicago or the plumbing. He was an Orion boy through and through. Plus, his uncle might be a Scorsese, but they hadn't liked each other much either. The man had a chip on his shoulder from hard work and hard times—something that had skipped Vinnie's more upbeat father.

Worse, Uncle Angelo had thought Vinnie's deep affection for all things classic Italian both impractical and frivolous. They hadn't spoken much. Vinnie had done what he was told, all the while missing his family and Hank and their restaurant like crazy. He couldn't deny the knowledge he'd gained was useful, but little else could be said for the time he'd spent there.

"Business is going real good if you can believe it. With so many people working from home, they're stopping up a lot of toilets and kitchen sinks."

"Mama, I wish you would have talked to me before calling him."

"He's still family, and you helped him those few summers your dad and me sent you as a teenager. He knows you're a good worker."

He regarded her through the window. "Mama—"

"Vinnie, he has no son to take over his business, and he's only five years younger than me. He could also catch Covid. Look what happened to your beautiful aunt, God rest her. It's a good business to keep in the family, and it will give you something for yourself and your family, when you have one, which I pray for daily. I wish I could have given you the restaurant, but it wasn't your calling."

He bit the inside of his cheek to keep from correcting her. He'd loved being the host there, making people's evenings by remembering their favorite dishes, offering a kind word, and singing to them. "I might not have cooked the meals, but I made people feel at home too, Mama."

She put her palm on the window, looking every one of her sixty years. "I know you did. But with Alessa gone, there was no heart in the kitchen, and food is what keeps people coming through the door." She shook her head. "The restaurant is gone now and you have to move on. The whole industry is struggling. You know what Hank's going through to keep his doors open."

He did, and every day, he tried to lift up his friend's spirits. Now he had an ally in Alice, Hank's lovely fiancée. The days weren't always better, but they seemed easier when you had someone to love.

"You can't work at an Irish pub forever," his mama said. "It might be a restaurant, but it doesn't have enough heart for you. I know my son."

He bit his tongue, because he could hardly tell her that working with Uncle Angelo, plumbing toilets and sinks while his uncle griped at him, would have even less heart. He didn't want to move to Chicago. He wanted to live here and take care of his mother. But maybe such thinking was naïve.

Still...Covid couldn't last forever.

He thought of his Acqua di Parma bottle. He had some more time.

"Is Mr. O'Connor coming over for dinner tonight?" Vinnie asked, hoping to change the subject.

"Yes, and don't think that will distract me." Still, her face softened.

"You sound like your old self when you say that. Mama,

I need to run. Aunt Gladys has another video idea. Have a good day."

"Vinnie, I love that woman, but she's putting ideas in your head. Videos! What respectable man sells things online? We didn't need videos to advertise Two Sisters. It's no way to make a living."

"Bye, Mama!" he simply said, not wishing to engage.

She said goodbye with a frown, and he headed off. As he turned the corner, he spotted Mr. O'Connor walking toward him with Mutt, and he lifted a hand in greeting. He'd hoped that would be it, but the older man slowed to a stop, and Vinnie reluctantly did the same.

Hank's father had never been a kind man, and although he'd undergone a remarkable transformation—one that had improved his relationship with Hank and led to his reunion with Vinnie's mom—it hadn't done anything to allay the awkwardness between them. Thankfully, though, the man didn't seem quite as giant now that Vinnie was no longer a kid. A bulky Vietnam vet with a military-style buzz cut, Paddy O'Connor had always been intimidating as hell.

"Hello, Vinnie," Mr. O'Connor said, his mouth moving into what looked like an uncomfortable smile. "Not too windy out, is it? I was just going to see if your mama wanted to go for a walk. The doctor said short walks would be good for her, and it seems to improve her mood to get out of the house."

Vinnie couldn't fault the man for his treatment of his mama. "You do right by her. I know she appreciates it. So do I."

"I know it's only been a few weeks, but being with her has changed my life," the man said, ducking his head. "Every day I light a candle for her in church. She's a good woman. I'm grateful we've finally stopped being so stubborn around each other. How are you doing, Vinnie?"

He nodded cautiously.

"I mean," the older man said, "if you need anything, you

let me know. You were always there for my boy. It would be nice if I could do something for you. I know I have a lot of making up to do."

He'd be able to knock Hank over with a feather once he got a load of this. "I'm good, Mr. O'Connor. But thanks for asking."

Mutt gave a quiet bark and nudged the man in the thigh, almost as if encouraging him. "I don't like knowing you're living above the garage to keep your mama safe. She said it isn't much. She sometimes gets tears in her eyes when she talks about you with nothing but a cold plate, a microwave, and a tiny shower barely big enough to fit you."

Vinnie blamed the cold wind for the tears burning in his eyes. "Mama's a sweetheart, and she knows I'm happy to have somewhere to stay. It's no secret times are tough. I'm grateful to have that place over the garage."

"You're a good man for that, Vinnie." He patted Mutt on the head. "I respect it. But I mean it. If I can do anything to help, you tell me. I know Hank is determined to stand on his own two feet, and I imagine you are too, from what your mother tells me, but if I've learned one thing lately, it's that we sometimes need to let others help us. Anyway, that's all I wanted to say."

His speech was starting to make Vinnie sweat. "Thank you, Mr. O'Connor. I appreciate it. I need to get going. Have a new video with Aunt Gladys in the works."

"Your mama mentioned those videos are becoming more regular. Gladys helped me pick out a few things I liked so I could look a little more respectable for your mama."

Hank's father had shopped at Old World Elegance? Maybe Vinnie was the one who could be knocked over with a feather.

"And for Hank and Alice's wedding, of course. Got a long ways to go before I could stand next to you without looking like an idiot. You two being fitted for tuxes or anything? I don't want to wear the wrong thing."

Vinnie's jaw cracked as he worked it before saying, "With money tight, we're bringing out the best from our closets. I'm sure whatever you bought at Gladys' will more than do."

"That's a relief, right, Mutt?" the older man said, stroking the dog under the ears. "I didn't do anything to support Hank's first marriage. Didn't care for the girl much."

Neither had Vinnie, but he'd backed his friend regardless.

"This time, everything will be different, both for my boy and for the wonderful woman he's marrying. Alice brought hope back in my life and helped show me a better way. I owe her."

The man suddenly had tears in his eyes, and Vinnie got an answering knot in his throat. "She doesn't expect anything. That's how she is."

"I know it. Well, I'm keeping you. You tell Gladys hello for me. Have a good one, Vinnie."

With a final nod, he and Mutt started walking. Vinnie remained rooted where he stood. He looked up at the sky. No, it wasn't falling. "You have a good one too," he called back over his shoulder.

Vinnie kept walking, waiting until he was well out of range before he expelled a big breath. He shook off the encounter, waving at a few more neighbors he came across on the rest of the short walk, and let himself enjoy the holiday decorations and holiday spirit in the air. He loved this time of year.

As he reached the hill where Aunt Gladys' two-story Victorian store sat, unmistakable in a classy deep pink, he put on his mask. A chime sounded as he let himself in through the black double doors.

Rose sat in her usual chair on the other side of the counter, a black mask covering her face, which blended into her outfit of a baggy black sweatshirt and loose yoga pants. Still her green eyes caught him, especially the way they glowed when she saw him. He'd always thought she had beautiful eyes, with the most alluring shape—almost like a cat's eyes—and they popped against the black. Her beautiful cheekbones were hidden, much like the rest of her. Still, seeing her always brought a smile to his lips.

"Ladies," he said, taking a moment to savor the luxurious clothes in front of him, everything from Valentino to Gucci to boutique Italian brands. Aunt Gladys' store was a clothing paradise, and he got to model some of it. His mama didn't understand the kind of pride that came from dressing like a distinguished man, someone people respected.

"Vinnie, my dear!" Aunt Gladys called, standing up from her chair beside Rose with her trademark verve. Despite being in her early seventies, she'd had auburn hair as long as he remembered. The gold bracelets on her arms, clad in long yellow gloves, clanged pleasantly, in harmony with their wearer's good humor. "The sight of you always makes me give a fashion purr. I love the turquoise scarf with the gray fedora. Dashing as always."

"Dashing is right," Rose agreed, purring out loud, God help him. "I never knew turquoise could work on a guy."

"*Sprezzatura,*" he said, opening his arms and owning the word Italians had made famous in fashion. "A man's gotta have his own discernable style. Aunt Gladys, you look as bright as a bird of paradise."

She raised up her hands, the long sleeves of her tropical print muumuu flapping like large bird wings before settling to her sides. "I found myself missing the beach when I heard we might have a truckload of snow coming."

"I've resigned myself to a few hours of shoveling," he answered. "Looking on it as exercise."

Rose made a sound he didn't recognize. "Given what Aunt Gladys has in mind, keeping yourself in shape is a good idea."

She and Aunt Gladys shared a knowing look. *Oh, brother.* Like he hadn't had enough of a morning.

"Videos or not, I always keep myself in shape," he said, shrugging out of his outerwear and hanging his things on the coatrack by the door.

Every time he came into Gladys' shop, he promised himself he'd be in a position to buy one of her specially tailored Italian suits someday. When he'd patroned her shop in the past, it had usually been because she was having a sale. Hank's upcoming wedding to Alice was going to require some invention on Vinnie's part, since he couldn't afford anything new right now. Not that Hank cared. But Vinnie wanted to look his best when he stood up for his best friend, a sentiment he apparently shared with Hank's father.

He took the seat on the left of the counter. "I'm eager to hear your idea, Aunt Gladys."

Her eyes sparkled over her yellow mask as she leaned on the glass counter. Aunt Gladys' eyes were a light green, while Rose's were almost moss-colored. Not that he'd ever say that to Rose. She'd kick him in the shins for saying her eyes reminded him of the stuff that grew on trees.

"I have Clifton to thank for this new idea," Aunt Gladys said. "On our last day off, he emerged from doing his normal routine of tai chi and Qigong in nothing but his loose white gi pants and a black velvet Valentino tuxedo jacket. He wore it all day in complete and dashing comfort. Except, of course, when I persuaded him to take a 'nap' with me."

Vinnie was glad the mask covered his smile. Aunt Gladys loved to talk about all the "naps" she was taking with her fiancé. "I've never worn gi pants, but I've seen people in karate movies wear them."

"Ralph Macchio, here we come," Rose said with a laugh. "Can you do a crane kick? I'm just kidding, Vinnie. What Aunt Gladys really wants to know is whether you'd feel comfortable doing a video without a shirt on under the jacket?"

"So long as I have pants, I think I can pull it off," he quipped. "My mama is having a tough enough time adjusting to these videos. I'm a model. Not a stripper."

Aunt Gladys clucked her tongue. "I love your mother, but she was still wearing black lace on her head to church less than a decade ago. She gives you any lip, you tell me. There's nothing untoward here." She tilted her head. "Also, Mama Gia and her beau are *quite* serious. Did you know he bought two new suits to wear on their date nights? The fearsome O'Connor has turned into a romantic."

"*Two suits?*" Rose pressed a hand to her mask.

"Could have knocked me over," Aunt Gladys said.

Vinnie didn't mention that he'd had a similar reaction on the way here, when he'd found out from Mr. O'Connor himself.

"Any mention of a wedding suit?" Rose asked, whipping her head to stare at him.

Today might as well be nicknamed "smack Vinnie upside the head" day. "Did you have to go there?"

"Hmm," Aunt Gladys said. "Let's get back to the video. The jacket needs to be something a man would wear while working from home or on a casual sexy date."

"Like the kind with checkered tablecloths and candles in wine bottles?" Rose asked.

He cut her a look, knowing she was referring to his mama's dates with Mr. O'Connor. "You enjoy making my skin crawl?"

"It's hard not to tease when you get so worked up," she responded with a laugh. "You won't be wearing a shirt soon, so I'll get to see how much it crawls."

Aunt Gladys put her hands on her hips and studied him. "Perhaps we should do a separate video selling pants, no jacket needed. What do you think, Rose?"

"It would be a holiday gift to the women of the world."

Heat radiated from her gaze.

Holy hell, had his slip in the greenhouse caused this? She'd always been sharp, but their exchanges had never felt this charged. "Let's focus on this video. Can we do pants in cashmere or soft cotton?"

The older woman came around the counter and walked toward the changing rooms, gesturing for them both to follow. "I'm already ahead of you. I picked something out. See what you think."

He waited for Rose to precede him and then joined them. Sweeping the black curtain aside dramatically, Aunt Gladys gestured to the two pieces hanging there. "I chose a dark blue velvet jacket from a new and rising Italian brand that isn't as well known or expensive as Gucci and Valentino. I thought it would go well with your black hair in the right light."

"It sure will," Rose said, giving him another thorough glance.

Stop that, he wanted to tell her. First, they were only friends—or supposed to be. And second, they were making a video with Aunt Gladys around, for Pete's sake. "I like going with something other than black. When I see it now, all I can think of are funerals."

"Nice to know I look like a mourner to you," Rose said, crossing her arms over her outfit. "After living in the city, I still feel more comfortable in black."

Vinnie decided to keep his mouth shut. "The cream pants seem casual enough. Ah... Aunt Gladys, those aren't lined. Did you expect me to go commando in the video?"

She snorted out a laugh. "Oh, my dear boy, wear whatever works. Or don't."

"Funny," Vinnie said. "You two want to get serious or keep treating me like a piece of meat?"

"Any video I do is serious," Rose said, this time giving him a more impartial directorial glance, thank God.

With a last name like Scorsese, people always joked

about him being related to Marty. There wasn't any blood between them, but he was starting to wonder if Marty looked at people the way Rose did. It could be very unsettling. She saw everything.

"Let's see about the fit," Aunt Gladys said. "If you don't mind, Vinnie."

He shook his head but headed into the changing room anyway. Usually they muttered while he tried on the clothes he was modeling, but today it was eerily silent. "You two are making me nervous."

"Good," Rose answered. "Keep you on your toes."

He decided to keep his underwear on, but he took a moment to appreciate the sensuous fabric of both pieces of clothing. "Boy, these are nice, Aunt Gladys. Makes me wish I could wear them at home."

"You're never home," Rose said from behind the curtain. "You're always working. Even more now that Hank's engaged to Alice."

Staying later at the restaurant so his friend could go home to his woman was a happy thing in Vinnie's world. Hank would have done the same for him. Besides, what did he have to go home to? Nothing.

Despite what he'd told Mr. O'Connor, the place above the garage was small, and if he spent too much time in it, he felt like the walls were closing in on him. Spending more time at O'Connor's meant talking to their new chef, Derrick, who was a pretty stand-up guy. He didn't have anyone to go home to either, and they often stayed late at the restaurant to hang out.

"What do you think?" Vinnie pulled open the curtain.

Rose's unguarded gasp had him fighting a smile. She was staring at him like he was a plate of tiramisu, and he was man enough to enjoy it. Funny how it made him think about that time he'd shown up at the pool, and she'd gone under, requiring the lifeguard to rescue her. Someone had teased him that his body had made her flounder, and while he'd never told a soul, he suspected the guy was right. Good thing there was no pool around right now, or she'd be underwater for sure.

"Earth to Rose," Vinnie said, waving his hands to distract her. "What do you think?"

"I think Aunt Gladys is going to sell a whole bunch of velvet dinner jackets," Rose said slowly. "You have these in other colors?"

Aunt Gladys made a motion with her finger for Vinnie to turn around, so he did. "Yes, I do," the older woman said. "Red as well, in fact. This is what I call a hit. I owe Clifton for giving me the idea. Kids, I can't tell you the kind of click that happens when you find the love of your life. Everything starts to make sense in a whole new way."

Vinnie couldn't wait for that. Both to find the woman, and for everything in his life to snap into place.

"That sounds pretty nice, Aunt Gladys," Rose said with some whimsy. "I could use that right about now."

Her response surprised him. He'd never seen her as the settling down type—she'd worked for an airline, for goodness' sake, and she'd always seemed eager to get out of Orion. But from what she'd just said, she wanted the same thing he did.

He couldn't help glancing at her.

Her eyes were trained on him, like he was the link to her secret formula.

What was she doing? She knew the rules. They were from the same neighborhood. They could only see each other if it was serious—serious as in "could be the one I've been waiting my whole life for" serious—and she probably didn't plan on staying past the pandemic. If they did anything else, anything involving a state of undress more than what he was currently rocking, he wouldn't be able to hold his head up in town. Or her, for that matter. She knew that. So why the hell did she keep looking at him like this? Why was she perpetuating a schoolgirl crush?

He stared back at her, daring her to break away first, but her eyes only gleamed brighter. She might as well have been caressing his skin. He shifted, glad he had underwear on.

"Care to open the jacket?" Aunt Gladys asked, interrupting his thoughts. "Give a girl a thrill."

"Aren't you engaged?" he shot back, his patience wearing thin.

"I meant Rose!" Aunt Gladys gestured rudely at him. "Oh, you idiot. Go change, and then off to O'Connor's with you."

He took some time putting his clothes back on, gathering himself. When he emerged, Rose was standing where he'd left her. Awkwardness stole over him.

"Aunt Gladys is gathering up a few more props for us to use. We'll probably do the filming tomorrow."

"Great." He answered short and sweet, hoping she would get the message.

"Alice and Hank are having me do the flowers for their wedding," she said, looking down at her feet. "They're going to talk to you, but as best man, they were hoping you might help me with the boutonnières. You know how to wear a suit like nobody's business, Vinnie."

Hank could give a flying leap about boutonnières, but maybe Alice liked them. He scratched his head. "At Two Sisters, I'd use a rose or a flower from one of our arrangements for my lapel. I'm not sure how much I can help, but if it's for their wedding, I'll try."

"Great," she said a bit too brightly. "Who knows? You might discover you have a knack for it."

"Flowers are *your* calling, sweetheart," Vinnie said, wishing he could tap her nose like he used to when she was a kid.

But she wasn't a kid anymore. Her schoolgirl crush couldn't be sweet or endearing anymore. Not when it made him want to feel her fingers caressing his skin for real.

The stress and fatigue from this year were getting to him. That had to be the reason for his slip. Usually he could block out her beauty and humor. Stand firm in his conviction that she was off-limits.

Maybe her own fatigue and stress were causing this resurgence in her interest as much as his compliment, and for that, he couldn't be upset with her. He was familiar. Comfortable. They'd always gotten along great. Yeah, that was it. Who didn't want a safe harbor right now?

But he had to find the strength to keep ignoring her interest, the way he always had.

If it didn't work out, too many people could get hurt, his friends and neighbors as much as him and Rose. His conscience couldn't stand for that.

He'd walk by her papa's barber shop on the way home and make a point of saying hello to the older man. Light a candle at church. Take cold showers. Wear a hair shirt.

Anything to remind him that he had to keep away.

CHAPTER 3

A NEW TOWN MEANT A FRESH START, AND WARREN HAD HIS best friend to thank for it.

He removed Taylor from her car seat and jostled her in his arms, making her laugh, while his wife released Madison on the other side. "Well, sweetie," he said to his one-year-old daughter, "what do you think of our new home?"

Personally Warren thought he and Amy had done pretty well in such a short period of time. They'd been so done with their old house. After being in it nonstop since the pandemic hit, they'd felt the walls closing in on them. They'd wanted to break out even before he got his new job last month. Managing the Orion's Friends & Neighbors Trust for small businesses for Clara Merriam Hale and helping this community and the other communities Mrs. Hale wanted to help gave Warren renewed purpose, something working in banking with the same businesses hadn't. There were so many rules and red tape. He hadn't always been able to help the people that needed it the most. He would now.

They could have stayed in their old house, near

Chicago—most people worked remotely these days—but they'd been hungry for a change. Alice had sent them this listing the minute it went up after Thanksgiving. She was a roller coaster on human legs, he liked to say, and he'd always matched her speed when it was right.

This house, this move, was all the way right.

Sure, the two-story house was a little overpriced and needed some work, but it was vacant, sadly due to a Covid death, which had allowed for a ten-day closing. They'd jumped on it because the view of the Hudson River was spectacular from the four-acre property. Their suburban home outside Chicago had just gone under contract to a couple who wanted to move out of downtown due to Covid and work from home. Their new house was a thousand square feet larger, which was going to be awesome. He was totally getting his man cave.

He expected he had Alice to thank for turning on the front porch light. She'd seen to the movers on her day off, following instructions delivered via Zoom. Moving during Covid hadn't been easy but they'd gotten it done in record time. No one moved around the holidays, apparently.

"Aunt Alice did a great job, didn't she, Taylor?" He nuzzled her little neck, and she giggled.

"She sure did," Amy said, "and I can't wait to tell her when we see her."

"Me either." He'd mastered the art of holding a kid and playing with his phone. "Let me text her and let her know the Andersons have landed in Orion, New York. Whoo-hoo!"

The small town had always been a special place. He and Amy had come here to visit Sarah, the third chocolate maverick, before Covid hid. But Sarah was gone, struck down by Covid, a loss Warren was still processing even though he'd decided not to let grief hold him back. He and Amy both needed a new beginning, and this was it. He'd been withering in his job and she'd been withering from a lack of purpose.

That was all about to change.

It had to change, because he worried for his marriage otherwise.

"Are you ready to see Aunt Alice, sweetie?" he asked Taylor as his phone immediately signaled a text. "She said she's doing the cha-cha and coming for a quick drive-by with Hank. You good with that?"

"It would be nice to see familiar faces," Amy said, her face lighting up with a smile. "Tell them to drive on by."

"What about you, pumpkin?" he asked his young daughter as he gave Alice a thumbs-up emoji to swing by.

"Daddy, why do you keep asking Taylor questions when she can't talk?" Turning three a few months ago had apparently made Madison into the questions police. She literally asked him questions *about* questions. He was hoping this was only a phase. If it went on longer than a year, he was going to crack. He shot a conspiratorial look at Amy, and she grinned outright.

Good. She already felt lighter here. Some of the worry about this impetuous move lifted from his shoulders.

"Why do I talk to plastic dinosaurs, dolls, or teddy bears?" he shot back.

"Because you're *crazy* funny," Madison said with a giggle as she dramatically put her mittens to her cheeks. "Right, Mommy?"

"Right." Amy gave Madison a high five.

His girls did like to show their solidarity, and now they would have Aunt Alice to join their troupe. "You got an easy question, honey," Warren said, crossing to where Amy stood beside the SUV. "Shall we go inside?"

"I'd love to," Amy said, rubbing her hands together. "I'm glad we made it before the snow. Oh, Warren, it's so beautiful here."

The drive from their former house had been a little long, at just over twelve hours, but thankfully the girls had been happy with family song time, naps, and a few videos. If he'd had to listen to episode after episode of *Bubble Guppies* like he had on one trip to the Black Hills, he would have poked his ears out.

"The view is going to be even better after it snows," he said, setting Taylor down.

In another sign, Taylor had taken her first steps two days ago. The little one they used to call the Toothless Wonder was ready to move forward too. He'd decided that very moment to retire the nickname, tearing up as he watched his baby girl hold out her hands to him and teeter toward him in her snowman onesie.

"Hey, Madison, can you help your sister inside? Daddy has something he needs to do."

"Why you need to do it right now?" she asked, her big blue eyes staring him down. "Because Aunt Alice is coming?"

"Take your sister's hand, and I'll show you." When she did, he swept Amy up into his arms and started for the front door.

"Yay, Daddy!" Madison called out, and Taylor gave her own excited gurgle.

Amy kissed his cheek and then laid her head on his shoulder. "You sure are kicking off our new life with a bang."

"I'm only reestablishing one of my most important roles in life," he told her, ducking his head to meet her eyes. He needed to see them right now.

The moment he'd looked into those tropical blue eyes, he'd fallen hard. Six years into their marriage, her eyes still got to him.

"What is that?" she asked softly.

"Being your hero."

Her eyes gleamed with tears, but she smiled. "That's very nice... It's good to meet you again."

The pandemic had been rough on their relationship,

and they both knew it. They'd pulled the girls out of the daycare they'd gone to three times a week, and Warren had shifted to working at home. It had been hectic and often overwhelming, but Warren had done everything he could to make Amy and the girls laugh, going so far as dressing up in a dinosaur costume once.

But he knew there was something deeper going on. His own unhappiness had been rooted in the job he'd left. Amy hadn't been as happy since she'd stopped working when Madison was born, something he'd known her mother had put a lot of pressure and guilt on her to do. While Amy hadn't loved her marketing job at the bank he'd just left, it had kept her focused and given her confidence, which her own mother chipped at with every word she uttered.

Motherhood hadn't completely filled that void, and it hadn't helped that Amy's mother became the biggest busybody in tarnation, always criticizing their parenting and Amy in particular. Warren was glad she couldn't show up to "help" anymore. Moving had put some serious distance between Amy and her mom, which was one perk he was definitely going to enjoy.

"Think I can match your hero ways?" she asked softly.

Warren set her down in front of the door on their deeply covered porch, casually noting the wrapped presents stacked in front of it, and put his hands on her shoulders. "I think you can do anything you set your mind to, babe."

She touched his face, and that's when he could see her. There was a new part of Amy wanting—needing—to emerge. It was going to happen here. The way everything had fallen into place for them these past few weeks was a sign.

"Look! We have presents."

Madison was already pulling the tissue paper out of the robin's egg blue bag that read The House of Hope & Chocolate. So much for going inside.

"That's from Aunt Alice," Warren said, plucking out

the envelope tucked inside and opening it.

"What does it say, Daddy?" Madison asked.

Taylor grabbed his leg, and he made a face at her to make her laugh. "It says, 'Welcome Anderson family. We're so excited you're here. There are groceries in the fridge as well as a dinner you can heat up. We thought we'd give you a little dessert too. The brownies aren't your mom's, Warren, but I know they're your fave. Love, Aunt Alice & Uncle Hank.'"

"Oh, Warren, I'm so glad they're driving over. That's so sweet."

"The sweetest. You remember that horrible pot roast your mother brought over when we moved into our last house?"

Amy didn't bother to respond. She understood what he meant. She hated pot roast. Who cooked something for you that you didn't like? Amy's mom, that's who.

"I want a chocolate!" Madison pulled out tissue paper from the next bag. "Oh, here's some wine like you and Mommy drink. The kind that pops so loud it makes Taylor laugh."

Amy gave a downright heartfelt chuckle that reminded him of old times. They had, indeed, drunk their fair share of wine during the pandemic when they were exhausted after a long day. "It's champagne. Wait, there's a note in this one too. 'To our new friends and neighbors. From all of Orion's Friends & Neighbors Shoppes.'"

Those were the people he was going to help with the trust, and he got choked up at the kindness.

Warren suspected he knew who the last package was from before he even picked it up. The wrapping was too elegant for it to be from anyone else. "It's from Clara. 'To Warren and the Anderson family. May your new home and time in Orion be everything you could ever dream of.'"

"That might be the nicest sentiment I've ever heard," Amy said, wrapping her arms around herself.

His own throat was raw with emotion now. Hell, he'd expected Bailey to do something because that's who she was, but the rest of this? Totally unexpected. He opened the box and drew out the small stained glass panel. Holding it up in the light, he heard Amy gasp.

"Oh, it's beautiful," she said, tracing the bluebirds of happiness resting on the Celtic tree of life.

"Let me see," Madison called, and she and Taylor touched it gently when Amy held it out.

"The card says it's from a shop in Manhattan," Warren told his wife. "The more I get to know Clara, the more I love her." He'd already thought an eighty-one-year-old female philanthropist was the hottest thing since Britney Spears in "Baby One More Time," but with a gesture like this, he was thinking about asking Clara if she would adopt him as a grandson.

His own grandmother had passed before Madison was born, and he still missed her. Man, she would have loved this place. Like him, she'd always loved rivers, and they'd taken long walks along the Chicago River.

"Oh, we have so many presents!" Madison twirled in a circle, making Taylor clap. "People must love us."

"They sure do," Warren said, his voice a little raw. "Man, it feels good to be here."

"Who's ready to go inside for our new adventure?" Amy asked.

Madison started to jump up and down, yelling her excitement, while Taylor grabbed his leg again and gurgled.

"I was born ready," Warren said in his best superhero voice.

She unlocked the door, and Madison raced inside, exclaiming in delight. Taylor let go of his leg and started after her, weaving a little but mostly solid. Their former Toothless Wonder was growing up. Like the rest of them.

"Thanks for bringing us here, Warren," Amy said, turning to him in the entranceway of their new home.

He kissed her softly on the lips. "Thanks for wanting to come, babe. Orion is going to be so good for us."

Then he heard the sound of a car honking in excited beats.

"I love that we're moving to a place where we already have friends," Amy said while the girls ran back onto the porch as the honking grew closer.

"Friends make all the difference, babe, and we're going to make a whole bunch more. Just wait and see."

They both waved at Bailey, waving and honking like a mad goose, with her beau laughing beside her. Yes, they had made one hell of a decision coming here, personally and professionally.

He was going to help a lot of people with his new job.

But first and foremost, he was going to help his wife.

CHAPTER 4

ROSE WAS GOING TO SEE VINNIE'S BARE CHEST TODAY.

The prospect of filming him in a velvet tuxedo jacket, loose pants, and little else was *the* best damn thing she had had to look forward to since the world had fallen apart.

Usually she had to drag herself out of bed in the mornings. Not even the smell of her mother making cappuccinos for breakfast could bring a smile to her face. She knew her mom did it to lure her out of bed and away from fussing over the plants she kept in her room. They'd made a habit of having breakfast together as a family before her papa went to work.

Today she sprang out of bed and raced to the mirror over her bureau. She wanted to look good today—*actually* good. Her personal care spark had died with the pandemic. Her papa had cut her hair a couple times, but her riotous curls were back and driving her crazy with their tangles. She traced her eyebrows, which hadn't been waxed in nearly a year. God, they resembled overgrown hedgerows. And when was the last time she'd shaved her legs? She might gag if she checked.

Then there was her figure to consider. Between depression and inactivity, she'd put on twenty pounds. Walking in the city had helped her in the past, as well as being away from Mama's cooking. Now all she did was sit around, sample what they were cooking, and eat a plateful of comfort. Hazelnut biscotti had become her best friend.

She didn't recognize herself anymore.

The black she wore wasn't all about retaining a city style. Vinnie had said it reminded him of mourners, and when she thought about it, Rose realized she *was* in mourning. For her former life.

But God, she didn't want Vinnie to think about death when he saw her. Everyone had had a belly full of it. She pulled open her drawer and eyed her sweaters. Most of them were black, but she had a few in other colors. Eggplant was one of her favorites, and she pulled out a cashmere top before she could chicken out.

She needed an intervention, and she needed to give it to herself.

Jumping in the shower, she got down to business and shaved her disgusting legs. Afterward, she plucked at her eyebrows until a thin arch covered each brow line instead of a jungle. On impulse, she grabbed her mascara. The wand was dry from age and lack of use, but she wet it under the faucet and made do. Makeup had gone away as surely as cocktail hour. But today she wanted to look pretty again. But foundation, blush, and lipstick? Forget it. The mask either smudged it or covered it.

All she had these days were her eyes, and she tried to appreciate their green color and their cat-eye shape. Did Vinnie ever notice her eyes? Did he think they were beautiful too? Oh, how she wanted to hear him say it.

Dropping her towel and looking in the mirror was painful. There was nothing she could do about the extra weight and the thicker curves, so she ignored them as best she could as she dressed. She tried to tell herself she would walk more, but that was total bull in wintertime. She hated freezing her ass off. Eating less biscotti might be the ticket, but she feared she might be too weak to ignore the hazelnut scent that called to her from the cookie tins Mama had stashed around the house.

She focused on happier thoughts. The purple sweater reminded her of a purple lisianthus. Those vibrant three-inch flowers made the cutest little posies. When she was a kid, she'd pick them and give a simple bouquet to her mama. Wedding posies were so popular right now. Would Alice like something like that? Ranunculi were the perfect flowers for it.

"Rose!" her papa called. "You finished dressing yet? Your mama says it's time for breakfast."

She patted down her curls and crossed to the door. "You caught me daydreaming," she said when she opened the door.

His lined face softened, and he smiled as he kissed her cheek. His silver hair had thinned out more since the pandemic, and he'd shed weight he could barely afford to lose, being so slim already, but he still seemed larger than life to her. "You look beautiful, my Rosie. Was this daydream about flowers or Vinnie?"

She gestured in the air. "Both. I'm probably crazy."

"You've always been crazy about both, and it looks good on you," her papa said, chucking her under the chin. "Is this new Rosie I see ready for a haircut? I could work you in before my first customer."

She was too eager to start prepping for the video. Plus, a new haircut might be too obvious. She was praying the redness from plucking her brows would be gone by the time he met her at Aunt Gladys' shop at nine. "Maybe later. I'll let you know. Thanks, Papa."

"You're welcome. Now, come down before your mama tracks us down with a knife. You know how she hates her cappuccinos to get cold."

When they arrived in the kitchen, her mama put her hands on her ample hips and regarded her. God help her, Mama had her black hair twisted up in a bun like she meant business. "Finally! Something other than black. And from the redness at your brows, it's clear you finally got the Weedwacker out and took care of those eyebrows. Rosie, you were starting to remind me of Cousin Madolina, God love her. We used to joke she didn't need sunglasses because her eyebrows were so thick they acted like sun umbrellas to shade her eyes."

Her papa burst out laughing, but Rose only shook her head. From what she remembered, Cousin Madolina had died a spinster. "I shaved my legs too, Mama, in case you want a play-by-play. Now, can we eat?"

"Thank God for that," Mama said as they all sat. "I didn't want to mention that your legs were starting to remind me of that horrible shag carpeting we had in your grandmother's house growing up."

"Thanks, and you'll be happy to know I didn't clog the shower drain." She reached for the bread on the table but stopped short of the butter and strawberry jam. God, did she need to go on a diet? She'd *never* gone on one.

On second thought, giving up butter and jam felt like too much of a sacrifice right now. She stopped short of slathering them on, but still, she coated the bread well. She would have to walk more. That was it. Her biscotti friends couldn't take a diet betrayal.

Maybe she could ask Vinnie to be her walking partner. They could talk about video ideas—for her business.

Was she really starting a business?

"I'm doing the flowers for Alice and Hank's wedding," she announced. "I decided I need to do a practice run."

"Oh, that's a marvelous idea," her mother said. "You can take photos of the arrangements and bouquets and put them on a website. When are you going to set up one of those?"

"You're talking to me about websites?" She shoved a piece of bread in her mouth. A website made things official. Was she ready for that? She had a greenhouse and one wedding.

"Your mother has a point," her papa said after sipping his coffee. "In my day, you opened your business and people came if you did right by them. Now you can sell most everything online."

"Except haircuts, thank God," her mama said, passing her the jam. "You didn't put enough on your bread."

Her mother might as well bring out a dish of biscotti. But the jam pushing confirmed one thing. Carlotta Fiorni wouldn't support a diet in her home.

"Rosie, you've always been good at making plans," Mama continued, grabbing her bread and adding the jam to it. "So different from your brother."

She and Papa shared a look, their brows knitting, and Rose's inner Al alarm clanged. He'd been calling their parents more often, which only happened when he needed money. God, she wasn't going to ask.

"Mama? You were saying."

She shook herself. "What was I— Oh, do you remember the plan you made when you were thinking about college? It was as thick as our family Bible."

"I like to be thorough," she said, and in the past it had worked out pretty well for her. She'd gotten a scholarship to college, and it had been exactly the experience she'd hoped it would be. Educational and fulfilling.

"Be thorough here," her mama said, drilling the table with her finger. "It's time, Rosie."

The quiet seemed as soft as the morning sunlight shining into the kitchen. Her papa took her hand. "You kept expanding the greenhouse, even when you lived in the city. You took it further than I ever thought to. I'd like to think your guardian angel knew something you didn't about what was in your heart."

"You weren't named after a rose accidentally," her mama said. "Whenever your papa and I lit a candle at church for your safety and mine and an easy labor, there would be fresh roses at Mary's feet. So sweet-smelling."

"It was a sign," her papa said, rubbing the back of her hand before releasing it. "I agree with your mama—you're made for the flower business—but you're grown now. Your own woman. You need to decide because it's you who has to do the work."

Her mama passed her another bread roll. "Not alone, Joe. If you need help, you ask. Family always helps. I'm not as good with the flowers as you and your papa, but I get things done, and you know it."

She bit her lip as her throat filled with emotion. "Oh, Mama."

"Your papa and I have been praying for you to move forward with your life."

"Every week, we light a candle for you," Papa said, his eyes wet with tears. "While we love having you back home, you deserve a home for yourself with a wonderful life to go with it. Including a family. Everything that's been happening, all of this madness...it's shoving you to a new nest so you can fly."

"You shove the baby bird *out* of the nest, Joe, so it can fly." She gestured with her hand to him. "This is why you're the papa and I'm the mama. But I get your point. Rose, your old nest is gone. Time to build a new one."

"And fly," Papa said, gesturing to the sky.

"Of course she'll fly. She's our daughter."

They started sparring back and forth about the nest analogy and flying, and Rose took a moment to swallow the lump in her throat.

"Also, we're giving you a little money," Papa said.

"No, Papa!" Especially not if Al was asking.

"You'll take it or break my heart."

Talk about a choice. "You know I couldn't do that."

He smiled. "It's not a lot, but it will get you started. You'll need to do a few promotional videos with Vinnie, after all. He'd do it for free, of course. The boy would give you the shirt off his back."

"But he needs the money too," Mama said, tapping the table for emphasis. "And he deserves to be paid for his work."

"You don't have to—"

"It's done," Mama said. "And we won't hear another word."

"We believe in you, Rosie," Papa said.

Mama took her hand and squeezed it. "We always have."

They believed in her. It was time for her to believe in herself. Again.

"I'll start my marketing plan today." She rubbed the tightness in her diaphragm.

"After you make your video of Vinnie wearing nothing but a velvet tuxedo jacket and loose pants," her mama said. "Need an assistant, Rosie? We'd have fun."

"I'll ask Gladys if I can borrow the outfit, Carlotta, if you want to see it that bad."

Her mama laughed. "Please do, Joe. I'd love to see you in it."

Rose tried not to think about that. She was living in the same house, for Pete's sake.

"Doing those videos with Vinnie helped pull you out of your shell," her mama said, her expression serious again. "You've wanted that boy your whole life. Seems like you two are being brought together on these videos for a reason. Think about it. Your papa is going to hire him to do a video for his shop, you know."

"*I am*?" He tore off a piece of bread and waved it in the air. "After buzzing his hair that one time, I'm amazed the boy ever came back."

Mama laughed. "That was the day. But you'll do the

video, Joe. To support Rose and Vinnie."

He patted her waist. "Anything for my women. You'll tell Vinnie when you see him. He stopped by the shop yesterday and poked his head in to see how I was doing. Always a nice boy."

She leaned over and kissed his cheek. "You're the best, Papa."

"And what am I?" Mama asked.

"Pretty smart," she said, giving her cheek the same affection. "Thanks, Mama. Thanks, Papa."

"We Fiornis stick together, especially when the going gets tough," Mama said, sending Papa another look. This one spoke volumes about her brother and whatever he'd called for help with this time. "You remember that and who you are. There will be no stopping you."

"Just like always," Papa said.

She pushed back from the table and stood up, excitement spreading through her. "Please excuse me. I have a plan to get started on."

"And you're gonna get a treat better than biscotti when you get to Aunt Gladys' place," Mama said. "I might love your papa like crazy, but even I can appreciate a handsome man like Vinnie Scorsese."

"Turn your head, Rosie," her papa called. "I'm about to kiss your mama and remind her who she married. Then I need to head to work."

Rose smiled and waited until her papa was free so she could say her own goodbye to him. After kissing his cheek, she laid her head against his chest. She'd always been so grateful to have loving parents, and never more so than right now.

Before he left, Mama lifted the cross she wore from around her neck, and Rose silently watched their morning ritual. Since Papa had returned to work after lockdown, Mama would take off her confirmation cross and place it around his neck and whisper a prayer of protection over him. In the beginning, the gesture had made her flee to her room to hide her own fears for Papa and her sorrow for herself and the state of the world. Now she saw only love and devotion.

She wanted a marriage like this.

The way she and Vinnie had both been raised, the boy needed to make the first move. Had him telling her she was beautiful been it? Was it her turn to say something to encourage him?

All her life she'd been keeping her feelings under wraps. She was tired of it. He either liked her or he didn't.

It was time to discover the truth.

CHAPTER 5

SHE WASN'T WEARING BLACK.

Vinnie knew Rose's purple sweater was significant. Had he hurt her feelings the other day when he'd said the color reminded him of mourning?

"Hey, Rose," he said as he closed Aunt Gladys' shop door, grateful the woman had made herself scarce for the videomaking—even if it had been a lame ruse about her washing her hair—since he was about to go all personal. "You didn't drop your city look because of what I said before, did you? I wouldn't want that. You look good in black."

Of course she looked good in deep purple too.

"I realized you were right about needing a change up," Rose said, letting her hands fall away from the tripod she'd been adjusting for their shoot.

"You're perfect like you are," he said, removing his outerwear and hanging them up. "It's just I remember you wearing bright colors when you were younger. Like you were a wildflower running around. The city changed that."

Her deep moss eyes studied him over the black mask covering way too much of her face. God, he missed seeing people's faces, hers especially. Sometimes he even missed his own face when he caught sight of himself in the bathroom mirror at O'Connor's or a shop window as he walked to work.

"The city changed a lot of things for me," she responded, grabbing a fistful of her hair. "Straightening this awful mess made it more manageable and..."

Her abrupt silence had him shifting on his feet. "What?"

"Pretty." She turned her back and begun to play with the tripod again.

He stood there. If he said what he wanted, how would she interpret it? Things had already changed between them because of the comment he'd made in her greenhouse, and the way she'd looked at him the other day...

Screw it. He couldn't let this one lie. "Rose, didn't I tell you how beautiful you were the other day in your greenhouse? Doesn't matter what you do with your hair. Heck, I bet you'd look pretty bald. Did you have hair as a baby? I don't remember."

"You were three," she said quietly. "And I had tons. Thanks, Vinnie. It's nice to know you think that. I've been a little down on myself."

"Who hasn't?" He wanted to pull her into his arms and comfort her, but he forced himself to stay put. "Some days I think I look a decade older, and that pisses me off. This should be my prime."

Those cat eyes of hers seemed to curl even more, and he knew she'd smiled. Her eyes looked different today. More open. Bolder even. Heat broke out over his body as he kept staring.

"Vinnie, trust me...and all the women in Orion and beyond. You are most assuredly in your prime. In fact, you've never looked better."

Given the way she'd looked at him recently, he knew she thought that, but the man in him liked to hear it. To keep it light, he sent her a playful wink. "*All* the women, huh? That's good company."

She raised her eyebrows playfully. "You ready to strip?"

He laughed. "If I must—for all those women." *And for you.*

When he emerged from the dressing room, her gaze was as erotic as a caress. Flirting and sex had always been tactile for him. Some guys liked to watch, whether in a bar or a bed. Not Vinnie. He wanted his hands all over his woman and hers on him, even if it was only for one night.

But this kind of watching? Its power swept over him. There was a new stillness in the room as she stood near the tripod fitted with her camera phone. Before one of their shoots, Rose was usually busy setting up, moving a mile a minute. Not today.

"Didn't I say prime?" Her voice was so soft and sensual it was unrecognizable to him. "You look incredible, Vinnie."

He grew hard, and it was as unwelcome as it was unstoppable. His briefs weren't going to hide anything. So much for the cold shower he'd taken this morning. Maybe he should have asked Aunt Gladys to show up, after all. Being alone with Rose was like the electricity in the air before lightning struck.

"You up for some music?" He reached for his phone, turning his back to her so he could take some deep breaths. "I think Aunt Gladys has a docking station."

"You'll just have to turn it off in a moment when we shoot."

Even a few minutes would make a difference. The air was thick with heat, and he was desperate to break it. "I like setting the mood. You want me to be charismatic, right?"

"You have charisma in your DNA."

What to play? He couldn't do Louis Prima or Dean Martin. Too romantic. He scanned his playlists and smiled. Yeah, this would work. It wasn't a hair shirt, but it was as close as he could get. He crossed to the docking station and turned the playlist on.

"'Ave Maria'?" Rose asked, putting a hand on her curvy hip. "Seriously?"

Surely a guy could fight arousal with church music as a beautiful woman looked at his body. "You got something against it?"

"I was hoping for your usual Italian classics. But if this works for you..."

He started humming under his breath to convince her since skepticism didn't begin to describe her look.

"I want you over here," she said, pointing to Aunt Gladys' gold velvet chair in the corner of the anteroom. "I think a simple close-up video of you would be the most powerful approach. If you're sitting down, it'll convey the casual look of the outfit yet keep the jacket in focus. The pants don't matter."

He thanked God for that. Standing might be indecent if the church music didn't do its job. Sitting down, he regarded her. She met his gaze and his heart started pounding. *Holy hell.* They should have gotten a chaperone. Or videoed this in the back of the church.

"How are your mom and dad?" he asked as he lowered into the chair. "I haven't seen them in a while."

She dropped her hands from the tripod. "You nervous, Vinnie? You see my parents all the time. Dad said you popped in just yesterday. Why don't you rest your arms on the chair's arms? Relax. This is going to be a piece of cake. Like always."

Except somehow this was different than the other videos. He was aroused, and everything suggested she was turned on too. But this wasn't how a guy kicked things off with a girl from the neighborhood.

Was he kicking things off?

He started singing, loud enough to make his old school music teacher, Mrs. Kirkpatrick, proud.

"Your voice truly is incredible," Rose said between refrains as she moved the tripod and tested the lighting. "I prefer your usual playlist, however. I feel like I should be kneeling in front of Mother Mary when you sing this one."

That was the idea, sweetheart.

"Could you...ah..." She gestured with her hands.

"What?"

"Give me a more man's position in the chair. Open knees." She cleared her throat.

As he did her bidding, he was aware of the velvet against his skin. Tough to ignore the sensuality in the room. He sang louder. *Mother Mary, don't fail me now.*

"Chin up. You're going to look straight into the camera like usual. Like you're looking at me and only me. Wrists soft. Casual. Vinnie, take a breath."

His diaphragm contracted, unusual when he was singing. His lungs weren't cooperating. He missed the next note.

"Unbutton the jacket," she said softly.

He slowly undid the button and was aware of her gaze on the middle of his belly. This was turning into a striptease.

She lifted her gaze from the camera. "How do you feel about baby oil?"

A million kinky thoughts came to mind, but he decided the best approach was to pretend he hadn't heard her. He belted out the next verse and winced as his voice trampled the notes in complete flatness.

"I think that's a sign that we're good on the music." She walked over and clicked it off. "You don't want to lose your voice."

He was losing his mind. Not his voice.

When she produced a small bottle of baby oil, his mind got good and lost. Holy shit. For the first time, he thanked God for Covid because she couldn't be the one to rub it on his chest. If she had, he'd be a goner all the way.

"Do we really need that?" He was grateful his voice didn't squeak. "I'm only showing a little skin here. It's not like I'm in nothing but swim trunks."

"More's the pity," she murmured.

He ignored that and breathed a sigh of relief when she shoved the bottle back into her bag. "We'll try the video without the oil."

"I'd hate for it to ruin the velvet."

"You're always so considerate." She stepped behind the tripod again. "You're best when you just talk into the camera. So, I'm going to count down from five and then point to you when you're on. Give it a few seconds before you start, for the editing."

"I've got this, Rose." It would be easier if he couldn't smell the soap she'd used for her shower. At least he was pretty sure it was hers. It smelled of flowers.

She held up her hand and did the countdown. When it was time to speak, he stared into the camera and said, "Tired of looking too casual around the house these days? Interested in being comfortable and still having your woman look at you like she did when you first met? I've found the perfect combination. It works great during the day or for those long winter nights. I'm wearing nothing but a blue velvet tuxedo jacket and fine cotton pants from Old World Elegance in Orion, New York. Check it out."

Rose made a slashing motion with her hand and then hit the Off button. "Good. I like the combination of day and night. But let's do one ad for day and another for night. That way you can make the most of the evening angle. Talk up date night. Maybe be a bit more sensual. Got it?"

He snorted. Sensual was an unwelcome friend right now. "Let's do the evening one first." They could finish with the daywear one, and then he'd get the hell out of here before he crossed a line he couldn't uncross.

She gave him the motion again for filming to begin.

His brain went blank. "Sorry, Rose. Give me a minute. I'll be right back."

He headed to Aunt Gladys' bathroom and stared himself down in the mirror. *Pull it together, Scorsese.* He wet the back of his neck, careful of the jacket, and took a deep breath before emerging.

"You need a script for this one?" she asked. "Been a while since you've had a date?"

He detected her usual banter, but there was genuine curiosity in her voice. "It's been almost a year. I might have forgotten how to behave." *Be nice to me, Rose. I've known your parents my whole life, and your asshole brother will kill me if I make a single wrong step.*

She tucked her shoulder to her chin. "So practice with me. It's been about that long for me too, but my mama's always said two brains are better than one."

"Unless one of them is an idiot, my mama would say," Vinnie said.

The crinkling of her eyes told him she was smiling, and he found himself smiling back.

Her moss green eyes brightened, and seeing that, his chest lightened.

"I know this isn't something we ever imagined doing together, but it's nice. Vinnie, I miss people, and you're one of my favorite people. I've enjoyed spending time with you."

"I feel the same way." He knew they should continue with the shoot, but he didn't want to move. His whole life, he'd known when to stand still with a girl, especially one from the neighborhood, and this was one of them. Something was happening, and he was going to let it, he decided. There was a feeling of rightness he couldn't ignore.

"I know my life is a mess, and the whole world is off-kilter, but I'd really like to hang out with you more. It makes me feel good. You know?"

He was a goner. Tough-as-nails Rose Fiorni was showing her vulnerable side.

She clenched her fists at her sides. "I mean, who knows what's going to happen? Some days I get up and I wonder if I can take another day of not knowing when things are going to get back to normal. Vinnie, I miss going out to dinner and having drinks and eating way too much popcorn during movies. I know we have to be careful, but I thought even watching a movie together with masks on might be nice. Or taking a walk outside. I need to do something to get back into shape."

He loved her curves, but he wasn't sure that was the thing to say. From what he was hearing, she wanted them to be friends. *Friends.*

But that wasn't the way she looked at him...

"Did I weird you out?" Rose asked, her green eyes flickering to his in brief passes before shooting away. That she couldn't met his gaze like usual told him everything. He finally got it. She was hoping they could go from friends to lovers. And she was giving them both an out by calling it "hanging out."

"We've always been friends," he said, his voice deeper than usual. "You know that. I'd do anything for you." *I don't want to screw anything up either.*

"I know that," Rose said, turning away and going to the tripod.

"You want to hang out, we'll hang out." His throat grew thick. "I miss a lot of things too, although I try not to think about them. Only stirs me up. But a movie or a walk would be nice."

"I thought with Hank getting married, you might—"

"Miss seeing my best friend? Nah. What kind of friend would I be if I were jealous of him spending time with the woman he loved? Nothing could change things between us, even when he moved to the city and we didn't see each other as much. We're brothers for life."

"I've always loved that about you two," Rose said quietly. "I've heard people talk about you being an unlikely pair, but I always thought you fit. You're the talker, and he's the strong silent type."

His mouth curved. "Talker, huh? Haven't been doing

too much of that this year. I've been alone more often than not."

"I've been more blue than I've ever been," Rose admitted, rubbing the space between her brows. "And I'm tired of it. I need to make some changes. Vinnie, I'm going to start a flower business out of our house."

"That explains why you started dressing like a flower again. The purple looks nice. Good for you, honey. Nothing makes you shine like flowers."

"So you said, and it meant the world to me. You can't know how much."

His heart hurt for her. A woman like her—strong and beautiful and big-hearted—should never have to doubt herself. "I meant every word."

She ducked her eyes again. "Flowers have been a love my whole life, but they've saved me this year. They keep growing, whatever weather comes, and I need that reminder. Plus, caring for them fills the hours so I don't lose my mind."

"I've had those moments," Vinnie said, buttoning his velvet jacket. "When you have them, it feels like the sun is never going to rise again."

"Exactly, and with this damn virus staying around, I need to move forward with something. My dream of working with flowers might be crazy, but it's exciting. It feels good to be excited about something again. My parents are going to give me some seed money to start out."

"Sounds like you're planning on staying in Orion," Vinnie said, feeling emotional at the hoarseness in her voice as much as her revelation. If she was staying, they had a chance.

She nodded slowly as if knowing what he was thinking. "The city will never be the same, I don't think. Not for me. I love being back here with my friends and neighbors. Like you... And Hank."

He noticed she'd rushed to add his best friend's name.

"It's good to have you back, Rose. You've been missed."

"Yeah." Her voice was whisper soft. "And I've always wanted to work with flowers, since that first visit to the flower market."

That day was clear in his mind. "For your thirteenth birthday, right? You were so excited you lined the street with roses chasing me and Hank down."

"You were dribbling basketballs, and later I came to Two Sisters for tiramisu because you'd invited me specially. Mama let me have two desserts that night."

He hadn't known that detail, only knowing he'd lit the candles and sung to her like he normally did on such occasions, and it got to him. "Your parents are good people. I'm glad they can help you. If I can do anything, you let me know."

Her head lifted, those green eyes alight with what looked to be joy. His breath caught. God, she was so beautiful. He'd give anything to see her whole face now.

"I'm glad you said that. You're so good in the videos, and I'll need a major social media presence to become successful. I'd like to create a marketing campaign centered around you if that's okay."

"Anything you need, Rose, and I'm there. Just remember, bare-chested videos won't work as well with plants."

She laughed out loud, and it was as sudden and refreshing as a shot of grappa on a hot summer day. "Don't be too sure. My creative powers are unlimited. Especially with you as my subject."

Their eyes met, and hers wandered down his chest again. He let his wander over the curves under her purple sweater since she was otherwise occupied.

"Haven't you ever heard of the *Naked Chef*?" she asked, flirtation as hot in her eyes as it was in her voice.

He grew aroused again. Images of them in the kitchen without a stitch of clothing on filled his mind. He'd boost her onto the counter and run his hands all over her glorious curves. "Sounds like a good way to get burned."

Her laugh caught him again, in the belly this time. "Not if you're careful."

Was there wisdom or a warning buried in that remark?

"I remember what you told Alice about flowers a few months ago. In fact, I haven't been able to forget it."

His brows shot to his hairline. "What did I say?"

"I said something about not being able to imagine trying to sell flowers during Covid, and you basically said that we need flowers now more than ever. And that if you had a woman, you'd give her a flower every day to tell her how glad you were that she loved you and that you were going through this crazy time together."

His throat thickened. "It's true. If there's one thing Covid has taught me, it's that I don't want to be alone forever. I've always wanted a wife and family, but I thought I had plenty of time."

"I know what you mean," Rose said, making a gesture with her hand. "I was so happy in the city, working and traveling and going out. While I miss it, I'm still a little amazed and scared by how quickly it all fell away. I used to go out with friends and people from work almost every night, and now it's like no one's around. We tried to text and Zoom, but the more time passes... Maybe we all can't handle the news about each other's lives. Everyone has lost so much."

He caught an alarming gleam in her eyes and had to force himself to stay put. If it weren't for Covid, he'd have wrapped her up tight and held her. "The same thing happened to Hank when he moved home after his divorce. In the end, he said relationships in the city aren't like the ones in our neighborhood."

She cleared her throat. "Sure, but you're not allowed to change here much. I'll always be Joe and Carlotta's daughter and Al Fiorni's younger sister, although I do my best to forget that last part. Sometimes I don't think anyone sees me as I really am, not even my parents, although they probably come the closest."

That tore his heart open. Hadn't he been forcing himself to think of her in those terms to keep his distance? "I've been doing you an injustice, Rose, and I'm sorry. I don't want you to think I don't see you. I promise to do better."

She fingered one of her curls. "Thank you."

He let out a shallow breath. "And I know what you mean. I've felt like that too. Just the other day my mama said something about me that didn't feel right. To use your words, it was like she wasn't seeing all of me. I guess that's why I used to go down to the beach a lot, before all of this. I could meet people who didn't see all of the baggage, and it felt pretty damn great." He was just another guy having a time-out, talking to girls, eating and drinking, and hitting the ocean every chance he could get.

"I hope *I* see you," Rose said softly. "But I'd like to spend more time with you and find out who you are now. We're all different after what we've been through this year."

They sure were. Here he was talking to Rose Fiorni about things he'd never imaged saying out loud. "You like *Lord of the Rings*?"

"Do Italians like spaghetti?" she shot back.

Comments like that showed how well they understood each other, but he found he wanted to know her, all the way. Forget the neighborhood rules and who she was. She was right. The world was different, and they were different because of it. Hell, he wanted to see more of the vulnerable, unsure Rose as much as he wanted her to blast him with her toughness and wit.

And deep down, he wanted her to know him too. He was lonely, but that wasn't why he was drawn to her—she saw him as a man, appreciated him as one, and he liked that. He liked it a lot.

"Why don't you come over tomorrow night, and we'll

watch the first movie? I won't have another early night for a week. Right now, I'm working six nights a week and grateful for it." The holidays had increased their foot traffic as much as the hiring of the new chef. O'Connor's was finally boasting a menu people wanted to savor.

"I'd love that," Rose said, blowing out a breath so big her mask moved.

"I'd offer you some food and a drink, but it's too cold to eat outside."

"I can drink something outside," Rose said, her moss green eyes bright now. "Don't worry. And I'll eat at home. You don't need to go to any trouble."

Maybe not, if they were truly just hanging out, but Vinnie wouldn't ever not go to trouble for a date. Especially if it were with her. They would likely both know after one night of hanging out if they had what it took to move to the next step.

"It's a strange, strange world," he finally said. "My place isn't much—"

"When did you start thinking you have to impress me?" There was fire in her voice.

Good question, he thought. But he knew the answer. Today had changed things.

"Come on, let's wrap up these videos. Aunt Gladys wanted to see them before I do the editing. I imagine she'll give you a hard time, but that's only because she loves you."

"You didn't give me as much of a hard time as I thought you would," he commented as he sat down again in the chair and faced the camera.

"If I'd known you were looking forward to it, I'd have delivered." She smiled with her eyes and then fiddled with her camera phone. "My mama wanted to come along with me, but I thought you might balk. She's suggesting you in swim trunks holding a sunflower for one of my videos."

"I suppose I should be grateful you'd consent to swim trunks after that *Naked Chef* comment."

"The Naked Gardener *does* have a nice ring to it."

His mama would faint dead away or knock him with a wooden sauce spoon. "Am I nothing but a piece of meat?" he joked half-heartedly.

"Prime," she answered with a laugh. "Some people have let themselves go during the pandemic. I'm one of them, so I get it. Why bother? But, Vinnie, my dear, you look positively delectable. Like always. But there's so much more about you to like. When you need reminding, let me know, and I'll list your best qualities. Besides your body, which you take good care of for a reason, I might add."

Amusement and arousal seemed to take hands, and Vinnie realized he rather liked the feeling.

If this was how hanging out with Rose was going to be, he was already looking forward to it.

CHAPTER 6

AMY DIDN'T MIND THE EMPTY WALLS OR SPACES.
The new house was like a blank canvas, and if
there was one thing she'd learned from all that time at
home with kids during Covid, it was that a space needed
to feel bright and happy. Those four walls, so to speak, had
become one's whole world, and if they weren't quite right,
they'd feel like they were closing in on you. Hers had.

To pacify her mother, she'd agreed to a neutral color
palette in their last home. Warren hadn't said anything,
knowing she was angry at herself for going along with it.
But this time she was painting the rooms whatever the
heck she and Warren wanted.

"You're up early," Warren said, wrapping his arms
around her and kissing her neck. "I was hoping to wake up
with you."

They'd put the kids to sleep after having a quick chat
with Alice and Hank through the car window, and then it
was dinner, more running around, and baths. Their bed
had been made, and Warren had tugged her onto it, saying
he'd heard a rumor about needing to christen one's new bed
in New York. Otherwise, disastrous events would ensue,

like the giant meteors that had sent the planet into the Ice Age, ending dinosaurs for all time. "Life and death, babe," he'd said, but she'd seen the vulnerability and question in his eyes.

Their sex life had been spotty before the pandemic, with the kids being so little, but during lockdown, they'd been listing. She hadn't much felt like sex. Ongoing exhaustion and worry about the world and the kids and how they were going to navigate it all had been a serious passion killer. He'd been stressed too, and he'd understood her feelings. That was Warren.

Instead, they'd watch late-night movies, and he'd tease her into making out like they were teenagers. Sometimes it had led to passionate sex on the couch, and other times, she'd simply cried from the stress. He'd held her, and she'd held him. Especially after Sarah died. Sex had been far from his mind then, and that was okay. They loved each other, and that was all that mattered.

Last night, the fire had blazed between them like it had early in their marriage. Thank God. She'd held him in relief afterward, and he'd clutched her longer than usual, conveying the same feeling. They weren't giving up on that part of their relationship, but they had some leaks to plug. "I wanted to see the sun rise before the kids woke up. Make some coffee. Take it all in. We had a dusting of snow."

"Yeah, it's nice. Maybe the kids will sleep in an hour since they're on central time."

She ruffled his hair. "Here's hoping. I was thinking about bringing coffee back to bed. Along with myself."

He slid his hands along her belly and then up her chest, cupping her breasts. God, feeling passion again was incredible. She pressed into his hands.

"I'm thinking about keeping our bedroom exactly as it was last night," Warren said, caressing her. "Nothing on the walls. As bare as our bodies last night. Nothing to distract us from each other. You rocked my world, babe."

"You rocked mine." She put her hands over his. "Been a while. I've missed this."

"Me too," Warren said, kissing the side of her neck.

"How do you feel about bright colors for the walls?"

"Paint them fluorescent if you like. You know I'm good with bright colors. We could do a hot pink room with flamingos for Madison. She'd love it."

"And a blue or green room with baby dinosaurs for Taylor?"

"With cute cartoon eyes, of course."

His imagination had delighted her from their first date in college, where he'd made up a tall tale on the spot about a beautiful blond co-ed saving a bored and listless wannabe prince in disguise named Heinrich from the toils of finance class.

He'd told her that his first ambition, to be a chocolatier in Paris, had shifted to archeology so he could sport an all-season tan, which had struck her as terribly funny, living in Illinois. Over pizza, he'd gone on about archeology being a sadly expensive hobby, which was why he'd resolved himself to getting a finance degree to support his passion for antiquities.

When he walked her back to her dorm, he'd asked her if she might someday want to take a cruise with him on the Nile. She'd broken her three-date rule and kissed him on the spot. They'd been inseparable after that.

"Have I told you how much I love it that you always make me laugh?"

His hands slowed. "Not always. But I do my best. Been hard to laugh this year, but a new year is coming. Up for having a private party with me in our newly christened bedroom? I figure we can have New York pizza tonight and a bottle of wine and make out for hours."

She wanted to do more than make out, especially right now. But he'd started couching it that way to give them both an out if they weren't in the mood or couldn't sustain it. "We can compare it to Chicago deep dish."

"Good idea." He resumed his stroking, and she moaned aloud. "I love it here already. I love how you feel here already. Let me help you feel even better. We'll be able to hear Madison thundering down the hall upstairs."

He pressed her against the back of the couch and took her in a way he hadn't in years, and she returned the favor a little later by pushing him onto the couch and riding him hard. God, the wildness of it made her want to yell her pleasure through the house. But those days were gone now that they had kids.

When the running of small feet sounded as predicted, she rolled off him with a smile. "Perfect timing."

He grinned, reaching for their discarded robes. "We're already finding our rhythm. Get dressed. We've got about fifteen seconds. New stairs and all."

"Ten," she said, shoving her arms in the terrycloth and laughing. "I feel a little reckless. I like it."

"Me too. Incoming."

Sure enough, Madison burst into the family area, her blond hair tousled. "I love our new house. Taylor's up, and she has the stinkiest diaper *ever*."

"I'll take that since I'm reestablishing being your hero," Warren said, caressing her waist tenderly. "Then I'm making blueberry pancakes and sausages. Alice stocked an Anderson fave. I find I'm starving this morning."

Amy glanced over at him. "Me too."

"I want a giant stack of pancakes, Daddy." Madison ran over, and Warren swung her up. "Do you have to work today?"

She'd wondered too since he'd already started receiving grant requests from some of Orion's businesses. Some of them were more organized than others, Warren had told her, so he'd asked them to submit the information they'd given for government support along with their applications to the trust. He also planned to visit businesses and owners to get a better sense of the way they operated now, something he'd done with the bank. Given he'd just started, he had a good gauge on what needed to be done.

Then again, that was Warren. Always on top of things. Maybe being here, in this new place, she would find a sense of direction too.

"I'm only checking email today," he answered, making Madison cheer. "Your mother wants to start painting. Right, babe? Mommy might be the master with the paint, but Daddy's good with the tape."

"Tape?" their little quiz show host asked. "What's that for?"

"So the paint won't smear on things you don't want," Warren said. "What color do you want for your room? I was thinking hot pink with pink flamingos."

"That would be so cool!" Madison took Warren's face in her little hands. "Daddy, you always have the best ideas."

"That's what *I* always tell *you*," Warren said, starting a game of butterfly kisses and making her giggle.

Warren *did* have the best ideas, and moving here had been one of them. She couldn't wait to put their house in order. Then she would turn to putting her own house in order and figuring out what came next. Sarah had always told them good things about the people in this town. Alice too. When Amy had first heard about their new Friends & Neighbors' motto, she'd been deeply touched. This year the world had turned scary, and she wanted to do her part to keep goodness and decency alive. She was so happy Warren was going to help this town.

Hopefully she could do the same in some capacity.

CHAPTER 7

RAINSTORMING AND A CUP OF HOT CHOCOLATE WERE THE perfect combination.

Rose opened the door to the House of Hope & Chocolate, enjoying the trilling of the welcome bell as much as the sight of Clifton Hargreaves holding up his hand in a greeting.

"Hello, Rose," he said over the soft holiday music playing in the background. "I hope this morning finds you well. I was looking forward to seeing you, in fact."

"You were?" she asked, her curiosity spiked. "Did Aunt Gladys show you the final videos from yesterday?"

He gave an uncharacteristic laugh. "I inspired the look, it seems. She sent the videos to Clara, who immediately called to FaceTime. They both laughed so hard they cried, but not before Clara suggested Arthur start wearing that outfit around their house."

She only knew about the older couple from others' stories. Personally, she thought it was outstanding that Clara and Arthur had reunited after nearly sixty years and married. They both sounded like pistols, and she hoped they would visit more, now that Clara was helping their community through the small business trust. "How did Arthur respond?"

"With his usual bluster," Clifton said, "and some fine ribbing directed at me. But that is the nature of our relationship. I did hear from Alice that you will be doing the flowers for her wedding to Hank. She's in the back tackling paperwork and some marketing should you wish to speak with her."

"No, I'm only here for a cup of hot chocolate," she said.

"Fine then. I hope you will allow me a moment before Maria sees to that in the Chocolate Bar. Gladys and I would also like to engage you for the flowers for our wedding."

"You would?" She pressed a hand to her soaring heart. "That would be wonderful." Two weddings already. It felt like a sign. She was gaining business, which was essential for success, and it would give her the chance to showcase more flower offerings in her portfolio. Win, win.

"When would we be able to meet and discuss what we have in mind?"

"Anytime you want," she said. "Just text me. I didn't know you and Aunt Gladys had set a date."

"We have been speaking of various scenarios, given the state of the world. I vetoed her idea to elope via Zoom *immediately*."

Rose couldn't help but laugh. Aunt Gladys was so hip sometimes. "It's becoming widely popular." She wondered if those couples bought flowers to set the stage for their online ceremonies. She made a mental note. *Market to the Zoom elopement industry*. Who would have imagined that a year ago?

"I'm more traditional, while Gladys would be happy marrying on a beach with a piña colada in her hand—or so she tells me. I suspect she's only throwing out wild ideas to tease me. She swears that it's to keep my spirits up. But I remain firm. I would like something more traditional, surrounded by friends, especially as it is my first and only wedding."

And at eighty-one too. "You might see about being married in the Union Church of Pocantico Hills. It's in Tarrytown near the Rockefeller Estate and not far from Orion. Do you know it? It has stained glass windows by Marc Chagall and Henri Matisse, the famous painters."

He cocked his head. "I did not know that. Thank you. I am a great fan of their work. Even without a date, we will engage you with a retainer, of course. Now, I have kept you long enough. I'm sure Maria is eager to assist you."

She nodded, but truly she wished she could raise her fist and give a good yell of delight. She hadn't even officially opened up shop yet, and she already had two weddings. She strode into the Chocolate Bar.

Maria lifted her hand in greeting, and once again Rose admired her perfectly straight black hair. Maria had the hair Rose wanted. Oh, how she missed her hair straightening appointments in the city. "Hi, Maria."

"Hello, Rose. There's a powerful air about you today."

She didn't feel comfortable sharing her news. First, until there was ink on the contract, it was hardly official, and second, it was Clifton and Gladys' business. "I'm laying claim to my life. Today, I'm sketching out marketing plans for my online flower business so I'm going to need all the spice I can get. A Mexican hot chocolate, if you please."

She thought of the two weddings she was doing. Her mother had helped her take inventory in the greenhouse yesterday, after she'd finished editing the videos for Aunt Gladys. She and her father had accumulated a lot of plants, definitely enough to give her a good start. Now she had to sell them. "It will suit your mood," Maria said. "This is the most fire I've seen from you."

She looked down and patted her clothing. "Do we need to call a hot fireman to put me out?" How would Vinnie look in that outfit? Combustible, she decided, mentally adding it as a video idea.

"No, but that would change the day up." Maria chuckled and began to make her drink, selecting chocolate pieces and then stirring them into the warm cream before finishing it with a dollop of crème fraîche.

"It looks like a sensuous swirl," Rose commented, craning to watch. "Forgive me. I'm—"

Horny. Like she could say that.

Maria added a sheen of chili powder and salt. "Yes?" she asked with amusement in her voice before pushing the drink toward her.

"Preoccupied a little." By Vinnie. "Thanks, Maria."

"Of course," the woman responded. "I continue to pray for your job situation, but I feel like it's starting to come together."

"My whole life seems to be, and I couldn't be more grateful. Thanks for your good thoughts." Her good thought for the day was about going over to Vinnie's place tonight for a movie. They both knew what "hanging out" meant. Sweat pooled at the small of her back just thinking about being with him.

Sitting down at one of the tables, Rose took off her coat and got down to work. She drank her hot chocolate and let her mind center on Vinnie. Most online businesses focused around a person and a storyline. The Squatty Potty commercials had done it with medieval wit and a unicorn, and they'd pulled in one hundred and seventy million views. And for good reason. Their marketing was hilarious. Dr. Squatch was also targeted and funny with its soap-for-real-men marketing.

She needed to give Vinnie a storyline, and she let her mind fill with old daydreams. He would sing under her window with fresh flowers, like Romeo to Juliet—forgetting that Romeo didn't sing in the play, to her recollection. Suddenly she knew where Vinnie was from.

Romeoville.

He was a modern troubadour in a pin-striped suit or midnight velvet tuxedo jacket. A man who serenaded women, and yes, gave them flowers to show adoration. He was a man who'd do anything for you. One who'd run you a bubble bath on your worst day and pour you a glass of wine just because. He'd remember everything about you, from the way you took your coffee to your favorite dessert.

"I've got it!" she exclaimed, throwing her pen down.

"You've got what?" a male voice asked. "Rose, sweetheart, you look downright triumphant. And you're not wearing all black for once. What's the occasion?"

A quick glance up revealed the newcomer was Baker, owner of Orion's very best—and only—coffee shop. A smile broke out across her face. She couldn't even summon the energy to be annoyed by his comment about her wardrobe. "Baker! You are looking at a woman with a winning idea. Love the T-shirt."

He pointed to the bold white letters over the black. *Do the World a Favor. Spread Kindness.* "It's part of my walking billboard for humanity. Another video? You've been killing it. I need to hire you to do one for my coffee shop. *Hola,* Maria."

The woman nodded and said softly, "*Hola.*"

"Are you two going to start speaking Spanish?" she asked, marveling at the way Baker's voice had gone all soft when he'd used that single word. She knew she always sounded louder in Italian.

"It's nice to speak it with someone who speaks it so elegantly," Baker said, gesturing to the woman.

"I wondered why the owner of the coffee shop would be coming over here," Rose said, watching as Maria began preparing his beverage.

"It makes me feel better to speak Spanish and have Maria's incredible hot chocolate." He opened his hands, his dark eyes a bit haunted. "This is my touchstone to traveling. Man, I miss it. I miss a lot of things."

"We all do," she said, the emotion in his voice pinging her own.

She knew Baker usually visited a half dozen foreign countries each year to meet with the local coffee farmers he partnered with. He and his recently ex-wife would sometimes go together. Other times they took turns while one of them ran the shop. That was all gone now, like so much else.

"Back to positive thoughts," Baker said, strolling closer. "What's your winning idea?"

She kicked back in her chair and buffed her nails on her shoulder. "I've created a personalized brand for my business that's going to rock."

"I heard from your dad that you were going into flowers. Good for you, honey. We need as much beauty as we can get right now. Count me in for a houseplant."

Another sale. Talk about a red-letter day. "How are you on care? Easy or regular?"

"I planted coffee plants in the Peace Corps, and later I grew one in our family room out of nostalgia, but Meg killed it when I was out of town." He huffed a laugh. "Hell, I sound bitter. Sorry. I'm still working on my crap."

"You're getting divorced," Rose said. "It's allowed. Maria, Baker's hot chocolate is on me."

"That's sweet, but no way. You're rebuilding, and I'm—"

"Sometimes we need to be reminded we have friends and that there are good people in the world. Spread kindness, right? Let me do it. Don't make me put on my Rosie-the-Riveter act."

His throat worked. That was obvious even with his mask on. Finally he said, "Thank you, Rose. When you need a reminder, you come by for a cup of coffee or treat on me. I'd better get back to the shop. I'll see you later. Maria, *como siempre, gracias.*"

"*Es mi placer.* I put some extra magic in it for you today."

"I'm surrounded by goodness suddenly," Baker said, tapping his chest. "Maria, you come by for a cup on the house anytime too. Ladies, you made my day. Have a good one."

He strode out much like she imagined he'd walked in. "He's always been a sweetheart," Rose said, "but I hate how much he's hurting."

"His heart is mending, but there are many emotions yet for him to sift through. He will get there. He's a good man."

The woman was staring at the doorway he'd just exited, her eyes brighter, Rose noticed. "You like him."

"Everyone likes him," Maria said quickly.

Rose stood up and walked closer to the counter. "True, but you *like* him like him."

She put a finger to her masked mouth. "Please say no more. He's a customer, and he's still going through pain from his divorce. I would have no one be uncomfortable."

"I wouldn't say anything," Rose said, wishing she could pat Maria on the arm. "Believe me. I know what that feels like. Hank's kept one of my crushes secret for a lot of years."

"Vinnie," Maria answered. "I remember how you used to look at him when you'd come home for the weekend and your family would come to Two Sisters when I was the hostess. Later when I started working in the kitchen with Mama Gia and Mrs. Alessa, I would hear them mention how sweet your affection was."

They had?

"But don't worry," she continued, placing her hand on her heart. "I won't say anything."

"Hopefully, it won't need to be a secret for much longer." Except now she was thinking about creating her entire brand around him, and her idea was a winner.

If they got together and broke up, it could screw things up.

Well, she simply couldn't allow that to happen.

CHAPTER 8

THE VIDEO OF HIM IN THE MIDNIGHT BLUE VELVET TUXEDO jacket, pants, and little else already had over three thousand likes and over four hundred comments.

They'd filmed it yesterday, and it had only been out for an hour. So far it was breaking all their earlier video records.

His own social media account followers were skyrocketing. Most of them were women. Some of them had asked if he wanted to hook up. Others had made some frank comments about his body.

Holy shit.

"Your mama is going to have something to say when she sees it," Hank said from a table in the bar area in O'Connor's.

Vinnie grabbed his towel and scrubbed the bar for the third time. "She isn't online."

"Doesn't mean someone won't call and tell her about it." Hank kicked back from his paperwork. "You seem more nervous about this one."

"Did you see some of the comments?" Vinnie asked. He had ignored the few that had said he looked a little fat or pretentious. He had no truck with haters.

"Let's see." Hank pulled out his phone. "Whoa! 'Hey, Vinnie, you're hot. Wanna fuck?' Okay, that's... But this one is nice. 'You're so handsome. I love your videos. Can't wait for the next one.'"

"Are you laughing, man?" Vinnie asked, turning to polishing the bar glasses.

"Me? No way. There were comments like that on the first video we made for the holiday festival—the one with Alice as sexy Mrs. Claus. I didn't know until I got a social media account and looked, but plenty of guys talked about Alice and her outfit."

"Does that make you uncomfortable?" His best friend wasn't the jealous type, but this was the woman he loved.

"Alice and I talked about it." He spun his pen around like a compass needle searching for true north. "She told me you can't control what people say. Some comments are great. Some aren't. We don't focus on the shitty ones. But we agreed that if anyone says something too weird or creepy, they get blocked and reported. You have to draw a line. Also, Covid has messed with a lot of people's heads."

"Loneliness can do that, I suppose," Vinnie said, humming "Return to Me."

"We were both pretty lonely in the early part of the pandemic," Hank said, leveling him with a look. "Neither one of us would write a comment like that. I figure it's not so different from talking to the person directly, but that's just me. It's amazing what people think they can say online."

"You and I were both raised to believe that you shouldn't say anything behind someone's back—or behind a computer screen—that you wouldn't say to their face. It's sad that principle seems to have fallen by the wayside. Like good manners."

Hank stood up and gestured to them both. "We've got them, so they're not lost. This talk is depressing. Why don't you call Aunt Gladys and see how many orders she has for this jacket? It's like I reminded myself when we did that first video. We're doing this for our businesses and our community. For that, you can take a few women making comments you'd usually only hear on *Girls Gone Wild.*"

"Thanks, man. I needed that. Calling Aunt Gladys now."

When he dialed her up, he immediately got her voicemail. So he texted her. She was into texting these days. It only took her a few minutes to respond.

Vinnie, my boy, you're a wonder. I've sold out of every velvet jacket in stock in less than an hour! I've been asked to create a waitlist. Some impatient customers went ahead and bought jackets I suggested as an alternative. The phone and online orders are incredible. Thank you! More videos for you, my boy. I've already texted Rose.

His heart was so full it pressed against his chest bones. "She's getting orders right and left," he told Hank, who was sitting again, bent over his papers.

"That was fast. Good for her. See! You're helping another Friends & Neighbors Shoppe and a good friend."

He nodded crisply, his emotions tangling in his throat. "Did you know your dad has been shopping there?"

"He might have asked Alice for her opinion on a few of his purchases," Hank said. "I decided to stay out of it. What do I know about fancy clothes? Plus, it's his business how he wants to dress. I remember him dressing in a suit to take my mother to dinner and a dance when I was a kid. It's their deal, Vinnie."

Yeah, it sure was. Since he was bringing uncomfortable subjects up, he might as well push through and go the rest of the way. This was his best friend, after all. "I need to talk to you about Rose."

Hank looked up from his inventory list. "Shoot."

"She likes me. Like, she likes me now. Not just when she was a kid."

Hank snorted. "I know that."

He gestured in the air. "So how come you didn't say anything to me?"

Hank rolled his eyes so hard he could have sprained them. "Because she told me years ago not to tell you, and she's continued to say so."

"But you're my best friend." Now he sounded like an idiot.

"Vinnie, if you'd seen her crying—"

"Crying!"

"She was so upset about you calling her a little girl. I guess that's why she fooled her dad into giving you the buzz cut."

He came around the bar. "Wait. When the hell was this?"

"The summer after she'd finished up fifth grade, remember?"

Whistling his shock was out of the question. He had no spit in his mouth. "That long ago? She was ten, and I was thirteen."

"She didn't like you pulling her braids—"

He couldn't believe they were talking about this. "They were cute."

Hank shot him a look. "What girl likes having her braids tugged? Come on, man. This is Rose Fiorni we're talking about. She used to give you flowers, remember? A girl only does that if she likes you."

"But that was years ago. We were kids. Besides, later she started to throw things at me. Her face would turn red, and she'd hurl a book or a rock at me."

"Good thing her aim sucked, or I'd have had to come down on her." Hank walked to the bar and motioned for Vinnie to give him more room. "You need an espresso? We can go outside for a minute."

He cursed under his breath. "Or grappa. You said she continued to ask for your silence. When was this?"

"A few months ago when she started to come around

more after moving home. Vinnie, what's this about? Is she making you uncomfortable? Oh, wait! I'm so slow sometimes." He slapped his forehead. "You realized this when she videoed you with your shirt mostly off, right? Alice thought she might not be able to hide it. She's been slipping for a while now."

He motioned Hank away from the coffee machine and began to make them both espressos. With the dinner crowd approaching, it was best not to go for the grappa, although it *was* tempting. "So Alice knows too?"

"Vinnie, I think everyone knows," his friend said softly.

"Excuse me a sec," he said, going out the other end of the bar and heading to the kitchen.

Derrick was chopping a mound of onions when he opened the door. When the man looked up, he blinked hard to dispel the tears in his eyes. "Damn onions get me every time. What's up?"

"Did you know Rose Fiorni likes me?"

"Nope, but then again, I just started working in Orion."

"Thanks." Vinnie closed the door and headed back to the front. "Derrick didn't know. That's one person, at least."

Hank poured two espressos and jerked his head toward the front door. "You're going to make me freeze my balls off over this. Let's cool you off outside. What's got you so upset? That she likes you or that people know?"

He did need to cool down, he realized. "I've known she's liked me since forever. I've always ignored it."

Hank cut him a look, but he followed him out into the cold. "Why didn't *you* tell me?"

Vinnie gestured with a hand. "Because I didn't want to talk about it. She's from the neighborhood. Al's younger sister. The Fiornis' little girl. You don't go there."

The cold wind was a smack to the face, and Vinnie welcomed it. Hank put the appropriate distance between them and lowered his mask to sip his espresso. "Plus, your best friend got decked for asking out a girl in the neighborhood to the junior dance."

"I enjoyed punching Tony Grasiaca for you," Vinnie said, "but yeah, I understood. That was his baby sister. Plus, he had some crazy ideas from his parents about Irish and Italians not mixing. I thought his dad might have put him up to it. Or expected it."

"I hate that crap," Hank said. "Glad you and I were never that stupid."

He toasted him with his espresso cup. "Me too."

They both drank for a moment, gazing out toward the Hudson River. Without the leaves on the trees, the surrounding hills looked downright barren except for the snow. God, it was going to be a long winter. Why in the world would he keep going it alone when he enjoyed being with Rose so much? Because he *did* enjoy being with her. A hell of a lot, in fact.

"Rose wants to hang out," he finally said, watching the steam rise off his coffee. "It's her softball way of seeing if I like her and want more. I might have slipped and told her she was beautiful, and then she threw out a few curveballs of her own, so to speak."

Hank pursed his lips as if thinking, then said, "Smart. Gives you both a way out. Vinnie, what do you want here? All you've talked about is Rose liking you. Do you like her back?"

He'd never been able to hide anything from Hank. "I got turned on when I caught her staring at me while we were doing the video. Jesus, is this too weird to talk about?"

"Did we or did we not say that it shouldn't have taken a goddamn pandemic to get us to tell each other things that mattered? I'm becoming more Italian, expressing more of my emotions. A terrible time for you to become *less* Italian."

Vinnie snorted out a laugh. "You know, Alice likes the more emotional you."

"So does Rose. Remember when she saw us having a

moment after your mom left the house for the first time since she came home from the hospital to see me?"

"That was a day," Vinnie said, tearing up at the mere mention. "Mama seems to get more worried about me the better she feels herself. Your dad mentioned she's upset that I'm living over the garage, and she called my uncle Angelo in Chicago to ask him about hiring me and eventually having me take over his business."

"You hate that guy, plumbing, and Chicago." Hank's face fell. "You aren't really thinking of leaving the neighborhood?"

His heart pained him. "I don't want to, but she's not wrong. I have to figure out my life. I can't keep working in your bar, Hank." If he and Rose did start dating, what could he offer her?

His friend planted his feet. "Why can't you keep working here? I'm finally able to pay you from the books and not my personal account. Business has been better. I thought we were past this."

Vinnie gestured to the sign above them. "This is an Irish bar, and while I'm a good bartender, server, and host of sorts, it's not my calling."

"And being a plumber is?" Hank shot back.

He gripped his cup. "Hank, I don't want to do it, but I need a career. I need to be my own man. I want to be a man a woman can be proud of. A man my kids can be proud of. My dad was like that, and I respected the hell out of him for it. Especially when he let my mama and Aunt Alessa do their thing with the restaurant. Mama wanted to handle it on her own, but she knew he'd be there if she needed him."

"But she never did, of course," Hank said, kicking at the ground. "Your mom and aunt ran that place like they wanted."

"When I was a part of it, I loved it. It was home. An extension of my family in this community and beyond. But that's gone now."

"And O'Connor's isn't Two Sisters," Hank said softly, in a way that crushed Vinnie's heart.

"I wish it were, man."

Hank looked off, fighting emotion. "What will you do?"

"I'm giving myself some more time to work it out." He thought of his cologne bottle. "I was thinking these videos might become a thing."

"You're good at them," Hank said.

"And despite the weird comments, I like doing them. I get to ham things up and wear nice clothes, which is fun. Plus, I like helping people I care about make money. You can't know how good it felt to hear that Aunt Gladys is selling jackets like hotcakes."

Hank looked over. "Yes, I can."

Silence stole over them again, and the wind seemed to howl loudly without their voices to drown it out. "You freezing your balls off yet?"

Hank sputtered out a laugh. "Like I'd say. Vinnie, whatever you do, I'm with you. All the way. Anything you need. But if you're thinking about leaving, you need to be extra careful with Rose. You could break her heart, and I know you'd hate that."

He bit the inside of his cheek. "You're right. Maybe I need to tell her about this stuff too. Seems like the fair thing to do. She told me she thinks she's going to be staying in Orion, especially now that she's starting her flower business. Funny...the only reason I never thought about her this way before was because she was in the city and seemed to want different things. Now, *I* might have to leave."

"Doesn't seem so funny to me." Hank gave him a tight smile. "Won't be the same here if you leave."

Despite what he'd said to Rose, his friendship with Hank hadn't been the same when Hank was in the city— and they'd only been a short train ride apart. Vinnie sometimes wondered what would have happened if Hank hadn't divorced and come back to the neighborhood. Would they have fallen out of touch completely?

He liked to think they'd be brothers forever, but he didn't want to find out he could be wrong.

"I understand being your own man," Hank continued, clearing his throat. "You keep talking to me whenever you need it. Even if it's about leaving town. I can take it."

Suddenly he realized he would break Hank's heart too if he left, and the ache in his chest intensified. Just recently, they'd renewed their promise to have their kids play together at Sunday BBQs while they watched the Jets play football.

Truth was, if he left, his heart would break too.

He simply had to find another way.

CHAPTER 9

TONIGHT WASN'T A DATE.

But Rose was sure as heck going to approach it like it was. "Mom, can I look at your sweaters?"

Her mother came out of the kitchen, holding a wooden spatula covered in the marinara sauce they'd made earlier. "Thank God you've stopped wearing all black. Rose, you know I love you, and I understand they wear it in the city, but you've looked like a mourner since you moved home."

She made a face. "So everyone says. Did anyone consider that maybe I felt like a mourner? But I don't now, and I don't have many clothes in other colors."

She didn't mention that her budget didn't run to buying new clothes at the moment. God, she missed the days when she could walk into a shop anytime she wanted, no planning, nothing, and buy something. Who would have imagined that something so simple would ever feel like a luxury?

"My red sweater would look nice on you," Mama called. "Are you planning to wear perfume for your date?"

Yanking open her mother's dresser drawer, she pulled

out the sweater. "It's not a date."

"When a boy asks you over to his place to watch a movie, it's a date. That might not be what you're calling it, but everyone knows better."

"He's not feeding me, so it's not a date. We're eating the pasta you and I made this afternoon, remember?"

"He's not feeding you because of Covid," her mama bantered back. "Make sure you wear some perfume since Vinnie won't be able to see your lipstick. Perfume will travel six feet at least."

Scent and social distancing. Somehow Rose hoped it wouldn't catch on. "I'm not wearing lipstick because of the mask," she called, trying the sweater on. Even with the extra twenty pounds she'd put on, it fit.

"Perfume!" her mama ordered.

"Oh, for heaven's sake," she said, emerging from her mom's room and spying her still in the hallway. "It's not a date."

"You waited your whole life for an opportunity with Vinnie. Treat it like a date, will you? Otherwise, it won't go anywhere. Your father took me to a movie and a walk in the park before we made it official. Didn't make it less than a date. Please tell me you shaved your legs."

She gestured to her mother. "What does that have to do with anything? It's not like I'm taking my clothes off."

Mama thrust out the wooden spoon she was holding. "I would hope not. Your papa and I taught you to have more respect for yourself. You shave your legs because you're a woman. And make sure you wear a nice bra and panties."

"Anything else? Maybe I should wear crazy high heels even though it's going to snow."

"It's like your grandmama said. An Italian woman shows her curves. Not her skin."

Rose patted her hips. "I've got plenty to show."

"So you've gained some weight." Mama patted her right hip to mime the same was true of her. "Who hasn't in these times? Your papa tells me I've never been so beautiful, and he means it."

"Funny, but Vinnie told me the same thing in the greenhouse."

"See," her mama said victoriously, "it's a date!"

"What do I mean?" Papa asked as he stepped up next to Mama, his cheeks red from the short walk home.

"That I'm even more beautiful now," Mama said, crossing to him and kissing his cheek.

He cupped her cheek and kissed her softly. "You are, my Carlotta."

"You see! This is the kind of man you want to marry. Joe, Rose doesn't think tonight is a date."

"You've got to be kidding," he fired back, shrugging out of his coat. "A man doesn't invite a woman to his place in this neighborhood—"

"Exactly what I said," Mama interrupted.

"These young people! Rosie, you listen to your mama. You wearing her red sweater?"

"I have it on, don't I?" She smiled at them both. "You done smacking me around?"

"You have on good underwear yet?" Mama asked.

Papa sputtered out a reluctant laugh.

She gave him a look, which he returned. "No."

"Then get to it. Unless you need your mama to pick them out for you."

God help her if it came to that.

"Gladys popped in to tell me how much she owes you for that video. Her sales have been through the roof. She couldn't say good enough things about you. And Vinnie too. She said you two were a hell of a pair. Made my heart happy to hear about her good fortune, especially since my daughter helped."

Warmth filled Rose's chest. "That's nice to hear, Papa. I'm so glad the video is doing what we'd hoped."

"Better than anyone hoped, I'd think," Papa said.

Rose nodded, excited to think about what a few carefully planned and executed Romeoville videos might do for her own business. *Her own business!* Who'd have imagined it? She'd thought her life was ruined, but she was making a go of something she'd loved forever and finally going out with the man she'd loved forever. Even better, they were helping each other. His online following was skyrocketing. She had every intention of helping him keep it that way, and of letting him help her sell flowers and houseplants. But she didn't want it to be just business, please God!

"No more talk of business," Mama said. "Jump in the shower and shave. I need to call your brother back, and I might need more wine."

"I'll do it this time," Papa said without enthusiasm, studying Mama's tight expression as she poured a glass to the rim.

Rose was so glad Al never called her. Sometimes she felt guilty about not liking her brother. A few years ago she'd called him on his birthday, hoping for a different kind of relationship. They were adults now. He'd only said, "Why the fuck are you calling me?" She'd shut down immediately, muttered happy birthday, and never called again.

She strode down the hall to her room and showered. After putting on some light makeup, she selected a lacy underwear set in dark blue she'd gotten on a business trip to Paris that had always been a bit big on her until lately. Sure, they were a bit tight now, but she wasn't going to think about that. She had to wear something pretty underneath on her first date with Vinnie.

Before she could chicken out, she dabbed a little perfume on her wrists and eyed herself in the mirror. Her green eyes looked darker because of the brown shadow she'd used, and the eyeliner made the cat-eye shape more pronounced. She looked saucy again. Like she would have on a night out in the city.

Rose Fiorni was back in business.

Alone, she admitted to herself that it was a date. She fully intended to have the time of her life.

Papa's head was bowed when she walked into the kitchen, as if the weight of the world was on him, but as soon as he saw her, he looked up and whistled. "My God, Rose, you're beautiful. If Vinnie doesn't start singing 'That's Amore' when he sees you, I'll have to give him another buzz cut for being an idiot."

Her mama gave her a slow smile. "Now that's our Rosie. Come and eat. Then I'll send you with some leftovers for Vinnie, and you can get along with your evening."

The phone rang, and when Mama answered it, she cupped the receiver and said, "You and Papa start without me. It's Al again. He must have needed to talk to his mama."

"Papa just talked to him. Tell him it's suppertime." Rose grabbed their plates and dished up the pasta. "Does he have no respect?"

She knew the answer. The entire world centered around him and his problems. He liked to be babied, and for God knows what reason, her mama still babied him.

"He's been having a hard time too," Papa said tiredly, sitting down at the table in front of the plate she'd served him. "It's a tough time to be a provider for your family. Especially with Christmas coming up."

Call her uncharitable, but Al's wife's desire to be a real-housewives celebrity didn't help matters. She'd just posted a photo of her new Prada handbag, which they couldn't afford, on social media. Their three daughters, ages five to eleven, were anything but angels, and Rose had a hard time being around them.

"I thought they were going to Paulina's family this year for the holidays, Papa, since they were here at our house last year."

He sighed. "Paulina's parents decided not to invite anyone this year."

"Because of Covid," she said, getting fired up, "and they were right to. I've seen Paulina posting photos of their family without masks on practically everywhere. They're not being responsible, Papa."

"Hush now," Papa said, ripping off a piece of bread and chewing it, his jaw cracking.

Usually that meant the discussion was over, but Rose couldn't let it lie. "Papa, I live here too. I don't want you and Mama to get Covid from them, but I sure as hell don't want to get it either. If they want to come, they'll have to take a test fast. Christmas is next week. They'll have to quarantine—"

He muttered and shook his head, reaching for his wine.

Rose looked down at her plate, her appetite gone. She didn't understand why they allowed Al to treat them like he did. Boys in Italian families possessed an almost godlike status, but her brother had only ever let people down. "Saying he's family doesn't work anymore, Papa. Not when they're acting so irresponsibly."

"I said enough, Rose." But he took her hand and squeezed it. "He's still our son and your brother. I know Paulina is difficult, and so are some of their children, but they're our grandchildren. If they want to come for the holidays, they can come."

"Mama has to put away Nonna's plates from Italy whenever they come, Papa. Angel broke three last Christmas, remember?" She hated thinking her nieces were hellions, but they were already mini versions of Al and Paulina.

"Money is tight for them right now, what with fewer people getting their cars fixed. Have some compassion. They need to put bread on the table too."

Rose's eyes shot up. He might have less business than usual, but she had no doubt Paulina was still running up their credit cards. The purse proved that. "Has he asked you for money? You've already paid off their credit card debt once. Don't do it again, Papa. That's your retirement money."

"Your mama and I just gave you some money too, and you're living here," he said softly. "You're our children, and we support you both."

She jolted in place. "I don't want the money then. Papa, I don't want to be a burden. It's hard enough letting you pay for my health insurance."

He grabbed her hand and kissed it. "You're never a burden, and you need health insurance and a place to live. You're our child. We love you. Just like we do Al, although he tests us. God knows how many rosaries your mother has said for him. Please, let us not talk about this anymore. It will only cause more hurt."

Hurt? Yeah, she was aching with it. She pushed back from the table. "I didn't realize the time. I need to get to Vinnie's."

"You didn't eat," Papa said, gesturing to the food. "Don't leave the table angry, Rose. Wait for your mother."

So she could see the grayness that came over Mama's face after talking to Al? Feel the weight of knowing she was a burden too? Before she hadn't felt that way. Today she did.

"Papa, I love you, but I'm going to go." She was going to start crying soon, which was awful on its own, and it would surely ruin her makeup. "Only...please remember what I said about Covid. Surely we can go one holiday without seeing them. I don't want to risk you or Mama or me."

"I'll speak with your mama." He hung his head. "You go on then. Have a good time."

There wasn't the usual energy in his voice, and her heart ached. Damn Al and his family. They were users and reckless to boot. What would she do if they came for Christmas?

She left the room, resisting the urge to stomp her boots. Damn Al for intruding on her date night. She finally got a date with Vinnie, and her stupid brother was going to spoil it. Well, she wasn't going to let him. She studied her face in the hall mirror, then opened her purse and swiped on her lipstick, determined to put on her best sexy date strut to walk to Vinnie's.

Her resolve lasted all the way to the door, but before she stepped out, she could hear Mama arguing with Al. She laid her forehead against the door for a moment. Here she was, just starting to get her act together, and now Al was going to sweep in and screw things up like he always did.

She let herself out, her mama's voice ringing in her ears, and reminded herself that there was only one thing she could do.

Protect herself like always.

CHAPTER 10

HE WAS ACTING LIKE IT WAS A DATE.

"This isn't a date," he told his reflection.

Except hadn't he dabbed on a little more of his dwindling supply of Acqua di Parma after coming home from work? He'd combed his hair twice. And wasn't he wearing his favorite date apparel, a black suit jacket with the barest of white stripes? Under it, he wore an off-white shirt unbuttoned at the collar. A siren red pocket square added some panache, while the simple yet tailored black trousers lacked a belt. Because hello, *sprezzatura*. His look would have turned heads, most notably his date's, and that gave him a powerful sense of male satisfaction.

His heart was pounding, and his belly was tight with nerves.

He was done lying to himself.

He only felt like this on a first date—and only then when the prospect particularly excited him.

"Shit," he muttered, checking the living room one more time before Rose arrived.

Eyeing the attic space he called home, he tried not to be critical of himself. He was grateful to live here, but having a girl over was different. There was little to impress her or recommend him as a possible partner. He needed to make more—consistently—so he could get a better place. Not an apartment or town house. But a real home with a yard. One his kids could play in.

Right now, given Covid, the freezing temperatures, and his limited space, he couldn't even offer Rose an antipasti platter. She deserved better.

His talk with Hank had been helpful but heartbreaking. He didn't want to think about leaving Orion. Aunt Gladys had hired him for four more videos, and a few other shops in Orion had reached out to ask for details, namely how much it would cost. Part of him still wished he could do it for free, but a man had to live and so did Rose. He planned to talk to her about it tonight.

"On our first date," he said out loud and checked his watch yet again. She was a little late, which was unusual.

Her hesitant knock sounded, and he strode over to open the door, instantly noting the turmoil in her eyes. "What happened?" he blurted.

"You weren't supposed to notice." She made a frustrated sound. "I stomped around the neighborhood a few times hoping to put it all behind me so we could have a good night. I even threw a few snowballs. I'm so angry and sad I could just kick something. So much so I didn't even eat dinner. But I'm not letting it ruin our date."

The fire in her tone didn't completely assure him—even if she had confessed to thinking it was a date like him—especially when he noticed the snow on her gloves. "You always did like to throw things when you were angry. Except flowers. How about you tell me what's wrong, and if it doesn't make you feel better, we can go outside and throw more snowballs?"

She gave an anguished laugh. "My brother called, and since you know what a great guy he is, you can only imagine. I'll get my good humor back. At least by the time

Frodo and Samwise Gangee leave for their quest. Here. I brought you some pasta."

"How about we table the pasta for a sec?" He narrowed his eyes at her. "Let me guess. He and his family are coming for the holidays even though they're a Covid shitshow."

"How did you know?" she asked, stepping inside when he motioned her to come in.

"He's always been irresponsible. He drank and drove a lot in high school."

She blinked in horror. "I didn't know that."

"A few times, Hank and me intercepted a few girls who were getting into the car with him. We drove them home instead."

Her outraged breath was audible. "That was nice of you. These days he swears by his PBA card, which his wife's cousin got him. Personally, I think it's made him even more reckless."

"That's only supposed to get you out of speeding tickets," Vinnie said, familiar with the Police Benevolent Association cards he'd been offered a time or two.

"Al is good at hiding being drunk." She waved the pasta container for emphasis. "Fooled my parents all the time in high school. Or maybe they just saw what they wanted to see. They'd lay the law down. He'd ignore it. They'd punish him sometimes, but it never stuck. He's always gotten away with everything."

"He's the only boy in an Italian family," Vinnie said, giving her a look.

"So are you, and you're not a leeching jerk." Rose gestured to him. "Why is that?"

"My dad's older brother got the royal treatment in their family, and it made it tougher for him to make his way in the real world. While Uncle Angelo works hard—he got past the babying—my dad always said it soured his outlook on life. Made him feel resentful when life suddenly stopped giving him what he wanted. My mom and dad raised me to take personal responsibility. Be kind. Not to expect handouts."

"It looks good on you." Rose looked him up and down, her gaze sending a spark through him. "So does your wardrobe tonight. I should take a picture and send it to Aunt Gladys. Maybe it will inspire another video idea, although I should tell you that she's mentioned you selling pants this next round. No shirt in sight. After today, her inventory is heavy on pants, not so much jackets. It's kind of funny."

He couldn't help but laugh. "I've created a monster. And a fashion imbalance, it seems. A store with only pants."

"After the next video, she'll have only shirts."

The light was back in her eyes—she'd put on makeup for tonight. A hint of perfume touched his nose, and he realized she'd treated tonight as a date too. Happiness shot through him, and he wished he could put on Louis Prima and whirl her around.

"The video has over five thousand likes, which is incredible, but the real magic is that it translated directly to sales. Trust me, our winning formula involves a successful marketing plan that leads to monetization. Otherwise, we're only entertaining people the way funny cat videos do."

"Hey, I like a good cat video. I expect you're hungry since you didn't eat your dinner, and we can't take off masks in my place. Do you want to run back to Hank's? I can open up. The air circulation system is up to Covid standards, and we're using some spray right before we close that's supposed to fumigate the air."

She tugged at her purple scarf. Hell, what kind of host was he that she still had her coat on? "That's really sweet, Vinnie, but I can eat something on the steps outside."

He gestured to the window, where the moonlight highlighted the snow on the ground. "It's twenty degrees out!"

"How were you planning on having us drink anything? Straws under our masks?"

He lifted his shoulder. "I brought a couple home from the restaurant in case. Rose, I don't know exactly how to do all of this."

She opened her arms, her uncertainty a becoming picture. "Sometimes this whole situation seems impossible. Maybe we shouldn't do this."

No way was she leaving. "Don't get down. If you keep thinking about what's wrong, everything starts to look that way. How about we try something else? Starting right now, we'll pretend we aren't wearing masks. Let's have an adventure. We'll walk to O'Connor's and have a bite." Why hadn't he thought of it sooner?

"I like that idea," she said. "I've started going to the Chocolate Bar for hot chocolate because Alice told me about their new air units. And they're fumigating with the same kind of spray that's supposed to kill viruses. Boggles the mind, but it makes me feel better."

"Everything helps," Vinnie said. "How about I make up something in the kitchen? Unless you want to bring the pasta."

Oddly, he was pleased by the thought of feeding her.

"No, you keep it." She scanned his place. "My first apartment in the city was a studio, and while it was barely bigger than my parents' family room, I loved it. It was all mine. I enjoyed having roommates in college, but there was freedom to having your own space. You really have a smart setup here."

He was oddly moved that she didn't see anything lacking. "Thanks, Rose. I plan to have a house with a yard soon. Not sure when, but it's going to happen."

"I hear you." She met his gaze. "For now, this is perfect. A corner for your kitchen. Half fridge, microwave, hot plate, and an espresso machine, of course. A few cabinets for storage. The dresser by your bed. Do your feet hang over?"

"They do," he said, feeling heat rise as an image of her feet hanging over with his came to mind. "The closet is big enough to hold the clothes I'm feeling. When I want a new look, I go into my mom's house in the back bedroom, where we're storing more of my things."

"The bathroom looks pretty small. Do you fit in the shower?"

He laughed. "I've learned not to knock my elbows on the tile."

"I did that when I was shaving my legs today."

Her eyes got wide, and she put her hand over her mouth, as if her mask weren't already covering it. He found himself grinning. Under other circumstances, he might have asked to inspect. He knew she had great legs.

"Of course, you had to keep your big-screen TV," she said hastily.

He didn't have to walk far to rest his hand on it. "My baby. I figure I can use it as a shoji screen for privacy if I ever have the need."

"Shoji screen?" Rose laughed out loud. "Where did you hear about those?"

"I won't lie. Probably in *The Last Samurai*."

Funny how the masks made them look like ninjas. Maybe that's how he should start seeing the world. Ninjas were taking over. Good would prevail.

"Oh, no, Vinnie. Not that movie."

"I like it," he said, extending his hand to the door. "You know what? I like the idea of taking you out to eat. I don't know why I didn't think of it before. I mean, I work at a restaurant. I can open it anytime I want. Let me check with Hank, though. It's his place."

He texted his friend, and Hank's response was near instantaneous. "All clear. He says hi."

"Hi back. I'm excited to do their flowers. I'm still ruminating."

He liked the way her eyes narrowed. "I'll text you some of my ideas for the boutonnières. I did some searches. My favorite for Hank is this frosty assortment of burgundy berries with greenery."

She stared at him. "Didn't it come with the plants' real names?"

He closed his fingers and gestured at her with his hand. "Jeez, don't bust my balls. I don't know plant names. That's your job."

"My job is right," she said, the flower sparkle returning to her eyes. "Vinnie, I got going on my own business idea, which I wanted to talk to you about."

"Let's go. Do you want to drive?" His car didn't allow for social distancing.

"I was thinking we could walk. It's cold, but it hasn't started snowing like crazy yet. Might as well get out while we can."

"Gearing up for our first big snowstorm," Vinnie said, girding himself for all the shoveling it would involve, time taken away from other pursuits. "I'm good with walking."

When they reached the street, he took the road. "Stay on the sidewalk, okay? I'll run if a car comes. No need for a pretty lady to hustle."

Her head swung in his direction. "I know what I said earlier, but I'm really glad we're doing this. I mean, if I'd stayed home I'd be holed up in my room with my babies, listening to Boyz II Men. Pretty pathetic."

"We're all allowed some TLC." He suddenly wished he could see the moonlight on her face, but the mask prevented it.

Instead, he enjoyed his neighbors' holiday decorations as they headed toward downtown. The blinking reindeer noses and happy snowmen made him feel like a kid again. He'd always loved Christmas. The four-foot lights Alice had installed by the Christmas tree up the hill by Aunt Gladys' store shone brightly. Walking home from work every night, they filled his heart. The words she'd selected had even greater meaning this year. *Hope. Love. Joy.* He wanted to bottle those feelings up and bring them out in the moments when he felt blue.

"It's quiet," Rose said softly, as if she would wake someone.

"I like it, but I miss seeing my breath in the cold sometimes. Weird, right?"

"I find I miss the oddest things the more time passes," Rose said. "I mean, I miss what used to be normal, of course. No masks. Going where I wanted. Seeing people's faces. Traveling."

"Having someone over for dinner, drinks, and a movie?" he asked, scooping up some of the remaining snow on Main Street and making a snowball, which had her rolling her eyes before he threw it aside. "Like tonight."

"Exactly. But the other day my dad was watching some movie with Denzel Washington and John Travolta set in the city. The plot centers around a madman on the metro, and I found myself missing being on the train at rush hour and having people crush you on the way out. How about that for weird?"

"You sound pretty sane to me. Here, let me unlock the door."

Once inside, he fought the impulse to help her with her coat and hang it up for her. But perhaps that was a good thing since seeing her rooted him to the ground. She wore a red sweater that fit her curves and tight black leggings with knee-high black boots. Hot.

He gulped. "You look real good in red, Rosie. Like those big flowers you have blooming in your greenhouse. Now that's a flower that attracts attention."

He was aware of her regard as he shrugged out of his coat. Even though he was fully clothed, her gaze reminded him of the other day, when he came out of the dressing room and all but felt her fingers caressing his bare skin.

"Let me turn the heat up and flick some lights on." He headed to the bar and plugged in his phone. It was tempting to play more church music, if only so he could get himself back under control, but he settled for one of his peppy Italian playlists.

She walked over to the bar but kept her distance. "There's something luxurious in being the only people in a restaurant after hours."

The skin on the back of his neck grew hot. "Not if you're looking for a full dining experience. What would you like to drink? Tonight, everything's on the house."

"I don't want to put anyone out. Do you have a bottle of something open?"

He did, but he wasn't giving it to her. "Red wine good? I have this terrific Montepulciano. We should celebrate. We've made a few successful videos, and other businesses in town are interested in hiring us. Aunt Gladys is making bank. You're finally starting a flower business. My best friend is getting married to one of the sweetest girls ever. My mama is feeling better. Your parents have their health. Our town is coming together like a community should. Let's toast all the good things in life."

She studied him in the soft light of the bar. "You didn't mention yourself much."

"Sure I did." He opened the wine and poured them both a glass. "I have a lot to be thankful for."

"You're downplaying your needs, but I'll let it go for now." She raised her glass and swirled it. "I miss drinking wine in a restaurant. I used to go to wine tastings all the time in the city."

"I didn't know that." Her life there was probably much like Hank's had been—part of another world. "Do you miss it?"

"Sometimes, but then again, I'm living with my parents. If I said I wanted to stay with them forever, I'd need my head examined. I mean, I'm thirty-two."

He'd judged where he was living earlier, and yet hearing her say it, he realized he was being too hard on himself. "We're both making do. If living at home for a while frees us up financially, all the better. To us, Rose."

She lowered her mask when he did, and his breath caught. After years of blocking her out, telling himself he couldn't take notice, he let himself study her face. Her lips were touched with red, her cheekbones a striking slash on either side of a bold and assertive nose. Her rich cat eyes softened the intensity of her features. Her beauty was strong and a touch exotic, and it went as deep as her soul. "It's good to see your face. You really are beautiful."

She smiled softly. God, that smile had the power to slay him. "I suppose I've missed seeing the whole of you too. Every time I see your face, it still hits me. Vinnie, you are one handsome man."

Heat radiated in the air as if they were on the beach with a summer storm coming in. Yeah, they were going to be doing this again, and next time, it would officially be a date. He was already looking forward to it.

"I kinda wish we could touch glasses." Her voice held a whisper of something he'd never heard from her. "It's our first toast together."

Tenderness was in her voice, he realized, and his own heart knotted up. "I'll always remember this toast."

Sipping the wine after looking away, she said, "It's a nice wine. Thank you, Vinnie. Perhaps this is a good moment to give us something else to celebrate. I figured out the marketing campaign for my new business. In fact, I'd say, modestly speaking, that it's a winner."

"That's wonderful. What are you thinking?"

Her smile was so breathtaking he gulped his wine.

"It's about a modern troubadour, like Romeo from Verona."

He laughed and gestured to himself. "My family is originally from Verona."

Her gorgeous cat eyes curved at the corners as she sat in a chair by the bar and crossed her legs. "Talk about a sign. I want you to be my online Romeo. From Romeoville."

He set his glass down. "Your online what?"

The full blast of her smile caught him across the bar. "I want you to be the face of my business."

"You're kidding."

"Today's video of you is going gangbusters, and your online presence is getting stronger with each video. Did you check to see if any businesses have contacted you about sponsoring their products?"

He actually had done so earlier, during his break, and the number of emails had shocked him. "Yeah, I had fifteen of them, but their products weren't personal. I don't know them like I know you and Aunt Gladys."

"See!" She gestured to him. "I told you. We'll get back to that in a moment. But you're right. It's easier to support something you believe in, and I know *you* believe in the power of flowers. Which is why you're perfect for me."

She said it with a certainty that made his heart catch. Was he? A part of him was beginning to believe they were perfect for each other.

"You're romantically inclined," she continued. "I mean, listen to your music."

In the background, Dean was singing about love and life and a beautiful woman. "I can't deny that—"

"Vinnie, you're every woman's dream."

Her exuberance echoed through the restaurant. Their gazes locked and he could see the truth in them. He was *her* dream. His heart started pounding. There was something growing between them, and it was time for him to call it out.

"Is it a good idea for us to hang out like this? We live in this neighborhood, but we're also working together."

Her fingers turned white as she clutched her wineglass. "I've thought it over, and I think we can handle our personal relationship well enough to ensure our professional one stays, well...professional. Unless you feel otherwise."

Suddenly he knew it was the moment to tell her. "What if I got a job somewhere else?"

Her mouth twisted immediately. "Are you applying outside the area?"

"My uncle Angelo in Chicago has a thriving business. Even now, if you can believe it. He has no son to take it over for him. My mama called him about taking me on, and he's considering it. You know how mamas are."

"Didn't you go to Chicago to work with him for a few summers in high school?" she asked.

"How did you—"

"I remember everything." She tapped her head. "Isn't he a plumber?"

"Yes, he is."

She started laughing. "Vinnie, you came home miserable from those summers. I remember because I wanted to give you some sunflowers to cheer you up, but I thought you or some other kids might laugh at me."

A hard ball of emotion lodged in his throat. "High school was all about being cool, but I'd like to think I would never have laughed at you."

"Maybe not, but other kids aren't always kind. Growing up isn't for the faint of heart. We're getting off-topic though. You're so not a plumber. In fact, I can't imagine you ever having a plumber's crack, and I think that's absolutely mandatory for a plumber's success."

He winced. "My uncle has one, but I'm sure some do just fine without them."

"Not the point." She swept her hand in his direction. "Do you want to go to Chicago and do this?"

Her directness was downright disarming. "No. I want to stay here."

"Good, because I'm staying, and I might have to kick you if you decide to leave now, when I only just got back."

Her moss green eyes held a special entreaty. "So stay and be the face of my business. Do more videos for Aunt Gladys and others. Keep working with Hank. You'll make enough to live on."

But that didn't address his problem. "A man needs to make his own way, Rose. He needs—"

"To take over a business he hates and move away from a home he loves? Orion needs you. I can't imagine it without you."

"I have to figure out something permanent. Something settled."

She stared him down like they were back on the playground. "Why?"

"How could you ask me that given your own situation?" He picked up the bottle of wine and pointed to the label. "Because, like this picture, I want a home with a wife and a family. I want to be able to provide for them. Make them proud."

She rose and stalked over to the front windows of the restaurant. "What if I helped you become a social media influencer? You've already been contacted by over a dozen businesses, and it's only going to grow from there. You would help businesses like mine and others make money. People would give you their products for free and pay you to promote them to your followers. We're talking good money, Vinnie."

That's what some of the people who'd contacted him had said, although he hadn't read all of their messages. What did he care about dinner plates or haircare products? Yet, he came around the bar to be closer to her. "How much are we talking?"

"The ranges are pretty wide, but I'd say anywhere from fifty thousand a year to one hundred and fifty after a few years. Later, it could be a lot more. More than enough to take care of a family. Plus, you get to do it all from Orion. Your hometown."

It seemed impossible. "I'll need to see—"

"Give me three months to show you what I'm talking about," Rose said. "I'm your friend. Hopefully more. I care about you and your life."

He thought of his cologne bottle. Up until now he hadn't told anyone about his bargain with himself, but he wanted to tell her. "You know, it's funny. My favorite cologne has about a quarter left, and I decided to let it be like my hourglass for getting my life in order. I probably have about three months left before it runs out. Interesting, no?"

She sniffed and sighed. "You always smell good. What kind is it?"

"Colonia," he answered.

"Classic, but that's the kind of guy you are. Well, my mama would call this a sign. Do you trust me?"

"I do. Straight down the line."

Those beautiful lips curved, and he found himself grinning. Her arguments were ones he'd make himself.

"All right. We have a deal."

CHAPTER 11

GLADYS GREEN WAS A PISTOL IN A LEOPARD PRINT VELVET caftan with matching hot pink gloves and a face mask.

Warren found himself wishing they made more women like her as he sat across from her in a chair in her store and listened to her talk about her recent video sensation. He'd seen it, of course. Amy had even smacked his butt and told him to consider wearing the look at home. He'd reminded her that their youngest still drooled like a fountain—spit was hell on velvet tuxedo jackets.

When Gladys finished, he nodded. "They do say sex sells. Has Clara seen it?" In fact, his moneymaking buzz was starting to sound in his ears. He wanted to see if this kind of advertising might be something the trust could help fund. So long as Vinnie kept his clothes on.

"Clara thought it was a hoot and encouraged me to put that boy on retainer." Her bawdy laugh was pure Mae West. "They've certainly convinced an old lady like me. Personally, those kinds of ads have never worked for me. I look at Italian fashion magazines ad nauseum. It's one handsome unaffected man with pouty lips after the other. Once you've seen one, you've seen them all."

"I can't stand handsome unaffected men either." He was grateful for his mask, which covered his silent mirth. "I'm glad it worked for you in the sales department, however." It was also encouraging to know that Clara approved.

"I'm doing so well that I'm wondering whether I need a grant from the trust, after all," Gladys said, "which is why I asked you to meet with me. I know you only arrived, but I don't let grass grow between my toes."

"Difficult to weed-whack," he responded, making her cackle. "This fresh infusion of sales does change your business model, correct? You have more online orders now, which necessitates shipping. Who is doing your shipping?"

She opened her arms, her massive sleeves like something out of *The Last Emperor*. "You're looking at her."

"What about social media? Who is responding to all the comments on your videos?"

Snorting, she said, "You mean the ones from people who want to lick Vinnie like he's a plate of pasta?"

"Pasta, huh? People do have some imagination."

"Or they're horny or perverted." She waved a hand. "Usually I give those a thumbs-up or ignore them altogether, sticking to the serious comments from people who want to buy from the store. But honestly, there are so many comments. I'm lucky to like even a quarter of them, what with the phone ringing off the hook for orders and packing stuff to ship."

He pulled out his phone and brought up her social media account. "I'm checking the recent video. It's gotten another two thousand likes since I last looked and probably a whole bunch more comments. Yep. I didn't see this one. 'Hey stud. Call me.'"

"Vinnie is hot stuff," Aunt Gladys said, "and he's the nicest boy. Have you two met yet?"

"Briefly, at the chocolate shop's opening a few weeks ago," Warren said. "Anyway, back to social media. You might consider hiring someone to handle the comments. If you respond, it boosts your profile."

"That algorithmic stuff," she said with a slight edge. "Yes, Rose and Alice explained that to me. Goes over my head mostly. Good business is responding to customers. I couldn't agree more. But I don't truck with responding to crazy. Those women—and some men, I might add—who find Vinnie appealing aren't likely to buy anything. He's just another online piece of meat."

Warren cleared his throat. "A technical term. I expect you're right, but still, it might help to hire a social media assistant to work a few hours a week. Make graphics to showcase the store and its collection. Take some artful photos of what your store looks like, along with its incredible merchandise. I would also add that you personally would be a welcome addition to the videos. You're as much of a character as Vinnie. I'd personally love to watch a video of you talking about men's fashion."

"Can I swear?" she asked, her green eyes dancing with mischief.

Yeah, she was a pistol. "Right now?"

"No, dammit!" She came around the counter. "In the video. When I talk about fashion, I sometimes get worked up. Never mind. I'll talk to Rose about who she would recommend. She's the one doing the videos behind the scenes, but her new business will probably keep her too busy to do it herself. Rose Fiorni. She's the daughter of—"

"Joe, the town barber," he responded. "She's doing the flowers for Alice and Hank's wedding."

"Ours too since Clifton won't agree to get hitched over Zoom. I thought it would be funny for a couple our age to do it, but he nixed the idea straightaway. Not that I expected anything different, but it *was* fun to rile him up."

He imagined she could ruffle anyone's feathers and enjoy it. "Yes, Alice mentioned Rose is starting her own online plant business." They'd had another nice chat when she and Hank had come over to offer babysitting—and she'd caught him up. "I understand Orion lost its only florist." He liked to buy flowers for Amy and his girls, so this was personal.

"Yes, we did, and I hope Rose's venture is a huge success. Always been a dream of hers, and with her job situation in the crapper, it feels like now or never. Plus, she's smart as a crackerjack when it comes to marketing. I expect she'll find a way to use Vinnie's sex appeal to sell peace lilies and whatnot. Probably not a mother's tongue. Be a bit Oedipal with the name."

Warren couldn't help but laugh. Keeping up with Aunt Gladys' wit was a fun challenge. He wondered how Clifton managed it every day.

"You planning on giving grants to new business owners too?" she asked.

He rested his ankle on his knee. "So far it's only for established businesses, but let me think about it and do some research. Clara would get the final say, of course."

"Getting a loan as a newbie entrepreneur would be next to impossible, and it's not like Rose has collateral. No house, for example. Not even a car since she lived in the city."

"You're absolutely right," he said with a nod. "It isn't easy for new business owners to receive loans. Most people put their startup costs on multiple credit cards." Time and again, he'd heard people talk about running up credit card debt to the tune of a hundred thousand plus. Failure was disastrous, to their lives and credit history, and he hated that there were so few mechanisms to help.

"We're glad you're here, Warren. That Clara is one hell of a woman. It's good to have someone like her with this kind of a vision to help our community. Not too many like her."

"She is one special lady," he agreed. "Aunt Gladys, how about we do this? You track how this next month goes, especially with the social media help. We can meet again at the end of January to see how things are going."

"Sounds good," she said. "I don't want to take money if I don't need to. I know some of the people who took the PPP loans didn't need the money, and I'm not good with that. And that's enough pontificating from my soap box for today."

Her phone rang, and he lifted his hand. "I'll let you get back to it. If you need a new model who's average-looking but very affected, I might be available."

She looked him up and down. "I'll keep that in mind."

"I was only kidding," he said, getting to his feet. "No one wants to see this dad bod."

"I bet you'd get some 'hot stud' comments online," she called back before picking up the phone.

He shrugged into his coat and let himself outside. After the holidays he'd come back and look into buying a few items for himself. It didn't feel right to spend money on anything other than his girls right now.

Heading down the hill, he grinned at the light display Alice had arranged. That girl knew how to spread hope and cheer wherever she went, and it heartened him to know she lived so close to him now. He also loved seeing the Friends & Neighbors Shoppe logo emblazoned on every storefront. That kind of unity choked him up.

Making the rounds to greet new clients as much as to thank them for their welcome gift, he popped into Lala's West Side Boutique, the Merry Widow's Gift Shop, Antiques Anonymous, Reardon's Jewelry Store, and Urban Vintage.

Other storekeepers weren't experiencing the same kind of uptick as Aunt Gladys. The holiday festival had brought some traffic in, but their sales were still down forty to sixty percent from last year at the same time. They all knew about Gladys' success, and everyone wanted Vinnie to do a video for them. Antiques Anonymous' owner Lucia Tesoro was even hoping to feature Vinnie in a gold Speedo on a fainting couch, according to Lala.

The empty storefronts he passed only drove home the town's losses. According to his research, Orion had lost a third of its businesses. The trust would hopefully stop further losses, but Gladys had raised an interesting point about supporting new businesses. They *did* need new businesses to come in. No one wanted to see a thriving business next to a bare empty building lined with dust bunnies and spiderwebs. Also, few people would travel specifically to Orion for a couple of stores, unless they were super loyal or the shop had unique offerings. This town needed to save its current businesses, but for long-term survival, it also had to bring in new ones.

The desperation was suddenly as harsh as the cold air, and he felt his spirits sinking. He looked up to the lights on the hill and fixed his gaze on HOPE. Everyone needed it, himself included.

He needed caffeine and hadn't yet introduced himself to the owner of the local coffeeshop, so he made a beeline to the Coffee Roastery. When he stepped inside, the smell of dark cocoa and toffee gave him a boost as much as the powerful voice of David Gray singing "Heart and Soul." He'd stopped by on a previous visit to town, so he knew this was his kind of place. Amy would love it. They'd have to take Alice and Hank up on that babysitting offer and come down here for coffee sometime.

"Welcome!" the man behind the counter called out. "You're Warren Anderson, right? I got a text you were making the rounds. I don't remember if you've visited the store in the past, but in case we haven't met before, I'm Baker Malloy, the owner."

"Let's start fresh and say it's good to be acquainted. Love the T-shirt. *Gratitude Changes Lives*. I couldn't agree more."

"Sometimes people need the reminder. You'd be amazed how many people don't give a simple thank you anymore for a basic service. The state of the world keeps me up at night. Can I get you something or are you only coming by to introduce yourself?"

He liked the direct approach of the man. "Alice said you were a good egg. Doing your part to spread good vibes with the T-shirt campaign. I might join you. The state of the world keeps me up too, and I have two young girls."

"Brave of you," Baker said. "Although maybe I just feel that way because I'm recently divorced."

"I'm sorry to hear of your divorce," Warren said.

"Don't be. We're hardly the only couple to split during the pandemic. Something like this teaches you about the people in your life. She couldn't understand why I wanted to offer financial help to our coffee farmers, and here I'd thought they were like family to both of us. It was the last straw."

"Since we're sharing philosophies," Warren said, shaking his head a little in commiseration, "I've told Alice the pandemic has put people into two solid categories for me. You're either a humanitarian or a sociopath."

Baker coughed out a laugh behind his mask. "Isn't that the saddest truth around? You're clearly the former, and we're all grateful to have you on our side. Clara Merriam Hale is one hell of a lady."

"She is, and I'm excited to be working with the trust on her behalf. How's business?"

"People still need coffee, but the commuter traffic is gone with people working from home mostly. People don't stick around like they used to. Back in the day, they'd hunker down at a table and stay all day. Breakfast. Lunch. No more. And forget music nights, dates, or the odd group meeting. The coffee shop used to be a community meeting place—one of the reasons I started it. I believe in the whole people-to-people thing. Former Peace Corps."

"You work in a coffee-rich country? Guatemala perhaps?"

"Got the coffee bug there, yeah, with our farmers," Baker said. "Some of the best, most hardworking people you'll ever meet. Anyway, community meeting spaces like coffee shops have taken a real beating. Now it's buy your coffee and take it outside. But I'm grateful to be selling hot beverages in winter. Plus, you can drink it on the street whereas you can't with alcohol. Always find the positive."

"Yeah, but you gotta call a spade a spade, otherwise, it festers inside," Warren said. "I miss going to coffee shops like your place. My wife, Amy, and I used to spend our Saturday mornings in one when we first got married. It was nice to see the usual suspects, there every Saturday just like we were. It felt like a home away from home."

The man gave a gusty sigh. "Yeah, I miss my people. Some of them will be back, I know. Covid got others. Like your friend, Sarah. Damn, I really miss seeing her bright and smiling face every morning. She always had a good word for everyone."

Grief clogged Warren's throat as her sweet face rose in his mind. "Yeah, we all miss her."

"Glad we had her while we did, though," Baker said, coughing to clear his emotion. "That's what I tell myself whenever tragedy strikes. Have to appreciate everyone and everything in the moment because you never know what might happen."

"True that," Warren said. "How are your online coffee sales?"

"Up, thank God. I'm doing well with coffee box sets, surprise bundles, and gift sets with beans and my favorite gold filters and press pots. My customers remember how good the coffee is here, although a few have messaged me that they can't get it to taste the same at home. It's a beautiful thing, that. There's something special about a person putting their energy into something, even a cup of coffee."

"Plus, there's your place," Warren said, gesturing to the

wooden beams, brick walls, and hardwood floors along with the large burlap bags of beans propped up in the corners. "Amy and I had a favorite pizza place in Chicago, and we got so excited when it started selling ready-to-bake pizzas. We'd just had our first daughter. We lit candles and got out some good wine that first night. The excitement popped our sleep-deprived eyes open. But when we cut into that pizza and took our first bite, we were both crushed. It didn't taste anything like our favorite place. Left an impression, let me tell you."

"I hear you," Baker said. "How are you and your family settling in? You need anything, let me know, although I'm sure Alice and Hank have got you covered."

"They do." He pulled out his wallet. "Before I go, I'd love to try your favorite coffee."

"They're all my favorite, depending on my mood, but given our conversation, I'd suggest this grand reserve from El Salvador. Not only does it have coffee notes of dark chocolate, candied lime, and orange blossoms, but it's a true success story in terms of a family company, female leadership, and a bold belief in quality over quantity. Also, it was one of Sarah's favorite, and I thought you might like knowing you were sharing something with her."

Their eyes met, and he noted a sadness in the other man's eyes that he knew was mirrored in his own gaze. "Thank you."

After that, he was too choked up to speak. Baker wouldn't let him pay for the coffee, and they had another silent moment before he lifted his hand and got the hell out of there. In the street, he lowered his mask and inhaled the coffee's fragrance. He could tell why Sarah loved it. He could smell the dark chocolate straightaway.

God, he missed her.

He was suddenly acutely aware of walking the streets she used to walk. He remembered some of the stories she'd told him, about Vinnie singing to her and other patrons at

Two Sisters, and how Hank's place had some of the best chocolate beers imaginable. Of course, he recalled how much she liked Baker. She'd told him that he bled for people in a good way, what with him being a former Peace Corps volunteer and all. That sure was true. He was the kind of guy who made you think good was still trying to hold its own in the world.

When he arrived in front of the House of Hope & Chocolate, he simply stood there and finished his coffee. He would go in and see Alice and her crew in a moment. The family would love it if he brought home some chocolate. They'd already eaten everything Aunt Alice had brought.

Clifton waved from behind the counter, and Warren returned the greeting. He gave a moment of thanks to Sarah for drawing Alice here and now him. The pact they'd formed long ago, when they first started their chocolate stand—to bring community spirit to their neighborhood—had never left any of them. Already he owed a lot to this town. His wife was different since they'd come here. Heck, being in Orion was helping them find their way back to each other.

He was going to pull out all the stops to bring hope and prosperity back to this town.

CHAPTER 12

DIRT WAS THE EARTH'S MAGIC WOVEN TOGETHER.

Rose had always loved it, from the days when she used to sit on her papa's knee while he started seedlings after Valentine's Day. They'd plant them in the garden when they were ready, and her little knees used to sport familiar dark smudges from kneeling down next to him and picking flowers or pulling the weeds choking them.

He'd taught her plants were like people and had their preferences and comforts just like anyone did. He'd always used pasta as the example. There were a million shapes, but her true love would always be orecchiette because shaping those funny little ears with her mama had always made her laugh. Plants were like that too. Some liked sandy soil while others preferred dense, rich earth. Know a plant, know the secret to growing it well.

She sifted her hand through the potting soil she'd made for her new amaryllis bulbs, a mixture of peat moss, compost, and perlite. Trusting in their selling power, she'd bought the Black Pearl variety in bulk online. Her plan today involved some smart multitasking. She was going to pot a hundred of them while Vinnie came over to talk business.

If she didn't focus, she was going to daydream all day about them dating because that's where they seemed to be going. Hot damn! He was her own personal Romeo.

She turned on some Pink music to help her focus. It suited her mood. Empowered. A little emotional. Edgy. She was about to help Vinnie become a sensation—and he was about to help *her* make her business one. After their talk last night, they'd eaten a quick dinner and then headed back to his place to watch the movie.

She'd sat on his couch while he'd kicked back in the single chair in his small space. The storyline hadn't transported her the way it did him, and she'd grown bored since she couldn't get away with stealing looks at Vinnie all night. She'd decided they were never watching another movie again. She wanted to *talk* to him. Soak him in. Look into his beautiful brown eyes. Enjoy him. Not watch some quest about an indestructible ring entrusted to guys with hairy feet. Today was going to be different.

"Rose!" her mama shouted. "Put your mask on. Vinnie is here."

She put it on as she looked up at the clock she'd hung in the greenhouse. Gone were the days when time could stand still in this magical place. She was a business owner now, which meant making the most of her time. She also needed to start gauging how long it was going to take her to do things for the business. Like potting a hundred amaryllises. She was estimating two hours, but she wouldn't know until she finished.

"Hey, Rose," Vinnie said, opening the door and shutting it quickly to keep out the cold wind. "Remind me who gave your papa this greenhouse? I was a kid when a semi-truck brought it. He could barely fit down the street, and the whole neighborhood was shouting over how beautiful it was."

She'd been three, and it had looked like a glass castle to her. Still did. "My papa had a longtime client who left it to him when he died. Mr. Palladino had a big estate in Irvington and knew how much my papa loved gardening. He'd always said unused greenhouses went to wrack and ruin if someone didn't love them. He wasn't going to leave it to anyone in his family when he died. They didn't love gardening like him. Papa cried for weeks not just from his passing but from him coming through on a promise like that. People say things sometimes in passing—"

"But they don't always follow through even when they mean well." He looked up at the glass ceiling. "It sure is pretty and warm. That surprised me when we made our video in here. That, and all your plants."

"Mr. Palladino arranged to have everything brought for the greenhouse, including the heaters and the fans. Papa had to run electricity out here, but it was well worth it. He also got all of Mr. Palladino's plants. You know, he brought that lemon tree in the corner in his suit pocket in 1901 when he came to America. It's from Sorrento, the town known for the best lemons in all of Italy."

"I think I had one when Mama and Papa took us for vacation. You can eat it like an orange, right?"

There was a look of wonder on his face, and she decided she'd save him a lemon when the fruit came in. Maybe they might even eat one together if things went like she hoped. "Yes, the skin is softer and the pith isn't bitter. Every year, Mr. Palladino's tree produces a good crop starting in the spring. Papa makes limoncello and sorbet, and the rest we eat raw. It's one of our favorite plants in this whole place. The blossoms are intoxicating."

"You're intoxicating today," he said, taking out a small robin's egg blue box she immediately recognized. Her heart sped up at the gift.

"It's so nice not to have to block out how attractive you are."

She leaned forward, staring at him. "You were blocking it out? Since when?"

"Since you grew up, but you were a neighborhood girl and then went off to the city. So... Blocked. But not anymore. I'm going to take everything in. Like your ponytail. It's cute. Almost reminds me of the braids you wore when you were a kid."

"Keeps my hair from going crazy from the humidity and also out of the dirt. I always seem to get it all over me. Did you bring chocolate?"

He lifted his shoulder. "When you pay a girl a call, you bring a treat."

She melted in her chair like chocolate on a warm day. "That was very nice of you. Thank you, Vinnie. How are you today?"

He certainly looked good enough to eat as he shrugged out of his outerwear. Under it, he wore a wine-colored sweater under a gunmetal corduroy jacket with sleek designer jeans and black mid-cut boots. She certainly hadn't dressed up to match his look, but these days, she wasn't sure she could. Most of her wardrobe ran to black, and much of it was too tight from the extra weight she'd put on. Also gardening... Fleecy yoga pants with a green hoodie her papa had bought her that said *Plantaholic* surrounded by spring flowers seemed more practical and fitting.

"Energized after shoveling for a couple hours." Vinnie walked down the center aisle toward her potting station. "Heck of a snowfall last night. But that wasn't the worst part of my morning. I checked my voicemail before I came here. Lucia Tesoro of Antiques Anonymous wants me to lie down on one of her fainting couches in nothing but a gold Speedo for a promotional video. She said that since I showed a little skin for Aunt Gladys, I can do the same for her. Can you believe that?"

Rose rested her hands on the pot as that image of Vinnie took root in her mind. All those muscles and olive skin. She imagined he had a goody trail running down to...

"How did you answer her?" she asked, interrupting her

inner fantasies.

"I called her back and told her you were the creative director. She didn't like that much. Said Aunt Gladys was boasting the bare chest idea was all hers, but you know Lucia Tesoro."

"She likes her way, like most people from the city."

"Except she's lived here for thirty years." Vinnie pointed to the chair she'd set aside for him. "That for me?"

"No, it's for my gardening fairies. Please don't sit on them. You'll crush them."

He laughed, the sound boldly masculine. God, she was getting hot. Must be the combination of her proximity to him and the dirt. So much primal energy. She could lay him on her potting table and feast on his body right now. Last night with him had given her ideas, especially the way his eyes had settled on her—and kept looking.

"Let me scoop them up to a safer location then, since I want to sit by you. Or at least as close as possible. I had a nice time hanging out."

Her fingers curled into the dirt. "I'm glad. Me too. Next time let's just talk, though. I like talking to you."

He sat down in a mouth-watering male posture, with his legs open and his elbows on his knees, giving her his whole attention. The pose reminded her of him in that velvet jacket, and fire raged in her belly. "I wish I could see you without your mask on, like at O'Connor's. You always smile when you're around flowers."

"I always smile around you. Even when you can't see it."

His brown eyes danced under the longest and thickest eyelashes imaginable. "Except when I remind you of your braids and talk about you being a girl. I promised to see you as you are now, and I will. Only, I really liked that girl. Not in a weird way—"

"Of course! I know that, Vinnie. And I might have had a crush on you, but it wasn't weird. You were my version of

Prince Charming."

He tilted his head to the side. "Am I still?"

She thought about shooting him a Rosie-the-Riveter look and then decided to be honest. "Yes, even though it scares me a little to admit that. Vinnie, I really like you. I always have."

"This is where I would scoot my chair closer and take your hand."

"But there's Covid, and I'm dirty."

"Looks good on you. Like your curly hair. The straight look never suited you, in my humble opinion, although it's your hair. But it was like you'd flattened out the Rose I knew and loved. She's not the kind of person who likes everything straight and flat. She likes twists and turns and edges and bumps. You like complications, Rose, and the kind of variety you have in this greenhouse. That's why Orion bored you sometimes and likely still does."

"I already told you I plan to stay." She took her hands out of the dirt and set them on the table.

"It's still the neighborhood. There are rules."

"I hate the rules sometimes." She leaned her elbow on the table and gazed into his steady eyes. "This is where *I* would scoot my chair closer and put my hand on yours. Or maybe your thigh. Then I'd ask if it's possible that you could come to care that much about me."

He put his hands on the table palms up, almost like he was offering himself to her. "I wouldn't be talking about it if I didn't think so. Rose, I want to kiss you. I wanted it last night. I want to go out with you—although it's not like it used to be—and hold you and cuddle up with you and a whole lot more. It's more complicated with Covid, and it takes commitment. We need to figure that out if we're going to do this."

The urge to tear her mask off was a wild idea she had to fight off. "What about Chicago?"

"I'm trusting you to help me work this social media

thing out, so that's not on the table."

She flopped in relief like one of the fronds on her maidenhair fern. "Good. You really *would* ruin your image with a plumber's crack."

"Maybe I could redefine it. Start a new craze."

If anyone could, it was Vinnie. She couldn't help but imagine how nice his butt must be. "So you really are going to do a video in a gold Speedo?"

He gave her a wink. "For you, perhaps, and only you. If you ask nicely."

She gulped. "Christmas *is* right around the corner."

"It is." He seemed to lean more on the end of the table, as if he was getting as close to the six feet line as possible. "Rose, I think we should take the Covid test that gets results in two to four days. I've looked at the options, and it doesn't seem like the one that can take up to ten days is any better. I want you to be safe, but it still feels like there are no guarantees. I work in a restaurant, after all."

"I know that," she said softly. "My dad works as a barber. We can only do the best we can."

"Then we're getting tests."

It wasn't a question.

She crossed her arms to contain the energy she felt bursting within her. She was finally going to be with Vinnie. Her, Rose Fiorni. "We're kissing the moment the negative results are in. Got it?"

"Agreed." His gaze warmed. "I'm glad we're doing this. It feels right in a time when so little does. You know?"

"I know."

"Since I can't touch you, how about I help you with what you're doing? Just tell me what to do."

The intimacy of sharing her love of plants stole over her, and she couldn't find words for a moment. To cover, she slid a dirt-filled pot his way, along with a bulb, and then demonstrated what to do in silence.

"Seems simple enough. Is it always this easy to grow

things?"

"I think so." When she thought about their relationship, how they were finally transitioning from friends into something more, she marveled at how easy it had been. Once she'd provided the right soil. Honesty.

He'd brought the sunlight.

She craved that sunlight like her hothouse flowers did.

As they potted up the amaryllis bulbs, she turned to business matters. "I think you'll want to set up a business account on Instagram, TikTok, and YouTube. They lean more toward videos, which you're showing great growth in early. You might consider posting photos of your morning wardrobe laid out on your bed, plus videos of you drinking a glass of wine or singing behind the bar. We can go through more ideas, but you'll want to keep it on point. I'd suggest charging three hundred per post for a product to start."

"For one post?" His eyes went wide.

"We can sit down and go through your services and prices."

"I want to do this with you, Rose." He gestured widely. "You're the magic in our partnership."

She surveyed the stack of empty pots she still needed to make up. "I can do it now, but as my business grows and your demand grows stronger, we might need to think about another solution."

"I want you."

Oh, how she wanted to soak in those words, preferably when they were both in a state of undress.

"I don't know that I'd be as good without you. Plus, I love doing them with you."

Her heart warmed. "That's one of the sweetest things you've ever said to me."

"Then I need to up my game." He patted the dirt around the bulb he was planting, his movements careful and methodical. What would she give for him to touch her like that? "Have I told you how beautiful you are today?"

She couldn't hold on to the warmth as her self-consciousness rose up. "I'm curvier than I've ever been, which I'm not thrilled about."

"You're being too hard on yourself. I love your curves just as much as I love your gorgeous curly hair, but again, it's your body," Vinnie said, his hand twitching like he wanted to reach for her. "Just wait until I show you how much. After that, I hope you won't have another thought like that. But you should feel good for you."

"I've read self-help," she growled, frustrated that he couldn't show her *now*. "Why is it sometimes so hard to love yourself?"

Vinnie reached for another pot, added some soil, and then tucked the bulb in like she'd shown him. "Maybe it's because people start cutting you down early, when you're impressionable."

Al had been her biggest bully on that front, pulling her hair and calling her fat when she was a kid. She didn't have any good memories of him. Mama said he'd been jealous of her from the moment she was born. That he'd bitten anyone who'd tried to hold her at the dinner after her baptism. She'd never understood it.

"Kinda like a young plant being attacked before it's well rooted," she said, pointing to the far-right table. "Like that Swiss cheese plant I just took a baby from to make into another plant. I've been thinking I took a cutting too early." Better to talk about a plant than Al, although she did wonder why he was so hostile and full of resentment.

"I'm sorry if I ever said anything that made you think you were anything less than beautiful." Vinnie hummed a few bars of music. "I'll have to serenade you like Romeo from Romeoville to tell you how beautiful you are to me."

Her chest wasn't simply warm now. Her heart knocked hard against her ribs. "I can't sing well, but I've never had a problem telling you you're handsome."

"Sounds like a good deal," he said, setting aside a

finished pot and reaching for the next. "I like doing this. It's kinda like folding napkins or putting candles in the Chianti bottles at Two Sisters before dinner. There was something peaceful about the repetition, especially when you worked with someone in camaraderie. I feel like this polishing glasses while Hank's doing paperwork at a nearby table."

Nostalgia laced his words in a way she was newly attuned to. "Vinnie, do you like working in a restaurant?"

He lifted a shoulder. "I liked getting ready for the dinner crowd. Seeing people come in, especially regulars, and making them feel good. Remembering what they liked. Hearing how their family and job is. Singing to them if the mood struck. Giving the girls and ladies flowers. Hearing Mama and Aunt Alessa singing and smelling the garlic and tomato from the kitchen."

Everything he described was in the past, memories from Two Sisters, and she mourned the loss with him. "Two Sisters was a special place."

"It was." He coughed. "It hurts to think about it, like it does Aunt Alessa being gone, but my papa always said the more you remembered, the more you loved. Love makes the memories easier to bear, and in the end, it's all that's left."

She hadn't lost anyone close to her from Covid, but God, how it must hurt. "What about O'Connor's? Does it feel good to be there?"

He rubbed his eyes with his sleeve, and her heart clutched. "I've got no words to talk about how Hank's saved my life, giving me a job. If I'd known he was paying me out of his savings in the beginning, we'd have had words. But he said I'd have done it for him, and he's right. It's what friends do. Seeing him every day gets me out of Mama's garage apartment. It gives me purpose. I'm glad I can spend time with him and help him and his place. But it's not my place or food, although he's been good enough to let me add little touches. You know…"

She paused in her potting, hearing something passionate and strong in his voice now. "But if it were your place?"

"Mama said the heart of a restaurant is the kitchen, and I don't do that part. I'm the floor show. Not the main event. Kinda like the videos, I guess. Besides, opening a restaurant is never easy, mind you, but in these times, it would be flat-out crazy."

She gestured with her closed right hand. "Opening a flower shop is pretty crazy too. Hence why I decided to call it The Dreamer's Flower Shoppe."

She could only see the crinkling at the corners of his eyes, but she could imagine the wide grin on his face. "I love it, Rose. If I had a bottle of Prosecco, I'd toast the name and its beautiful proprietor."

She could feel herself beaming. "I've still got loads to do, but I registered the company with the state today and got a bank account. Now that I've done all that, I can set up the website and social media accounts. Oh, Vinnie, sometimes my belly feels like I ate too much pasta, and other times I feel like I do when an airplane takes off and you reach the clouds. Like everything ahead is going to be incredible."

Their eyes met. "Even with the mask on, you have your flower sparkle. Those gorgeous eyes glow when you talk about them. It's nice to finally look into them without fearing you'll smack me upside the head for impudence."

She laughed. "I'd do it only because I liked you, you know. Tough girl stuff."

"I like you retiring her with me." He traced a line of dirt on the potting table and then looked up. "With everything you have to do, I want to be clear about you putting your business first over helping me figure out mine."

"My fingers are starting to itch to smack you all of a sudden. Vinnie. I told you I'd help you. Plus, you're helping me with the videos for my store."

"So we'll help each other. Like today. You got more of

these balls to stuff into soil?"

"Balls?" She laughed with gusto, and boy, did it feel good. "I can almost hear my plants laughing with me. They're not mozzarella, Vinnie. They're bulbs."

"Okay. But you know what I mean. I'm going to help you however I can. Got it?"

She thought about the quiet camaraderie he'd mentioned earlier. She liked it too. Helping each other was what couples did. "Got it. Now let's talk about these videos the other shop owners want, Lucia included. I'm vetoing the gold Speedo straightaway as an artistic choice, but if you'd like to do a private one sometime, only for me, you'd find a rapt audience."

"I'll send away for the outfit when we finish potting these plant balls up."

Was he serious? Didn't matter. She took in the image he made, dressed to the nines, hands coated in dirt— completely at ease in her most cherished place.

Life couldn't get much better.

CHAPTER 13

DATING A GIRL FROM THE NEIGHBORHOOD MEANT DOING things differently.

Vinnie had a list of the ways, and as he came down the freshly snow-covered stairs after his morning routine to find his mama waiting at the open window, he was ready. "Mama! How are you this morning? Can you believe we got another five inches on top of the fifteen the night before? I'm afraid our shovel is going to break."

"So you buy a new one," she said, ever practical. "And you let me give you money for it."

He didn't want to get into that today. "You hear the snow? It pinged the windows something fierce for a while."

She glanced over her shoulder for a moment before turning back, a soft smile on her round face. "No, I slept good. Paddy was here late after eating my cannolis. He's such a nice man, Vinnie. All his bark is gone."

Vinnie sure hoped so because Mr. O'Connor's bark had been infamous. Their conversation the other day had been nothing short of astonishing. "I'm glad he makes you happy, Mama."

"He does," Mama said. "It's nice not to be alone

anymore. Getting old alone was easier with the restaurant to fill my time, but I was so lonely after being sick and losing Alessa. Having a companion gives my heart peace."

He studied her, taking in the changes. Her gray hair was secured in a bun like she preferred, but her posture held a strength he hadn't seen since the pandemic had started. "Peace is a beautiful thing. Mama, I wanted to tell you that I'm starting to date Rose Fiorni."

She gestured in the air. "Like I didn't see her going to your place above the garage the other night. She's a good girl, from a good family. But you be careful with your heart. She always wanted the city life—"

"Not anymore, Mama. She's opening her business in Orion."

"Good, because city life isn't what my boy wants."

Yet she was encouraging him to go to Chicago? He didn't want to discuss these intricacies with his mother right now. He only nodded. "I'm going to shovel—"

"You forget about that," Mama said. "Paddy said last night that he's happy to use his snowblower. You have enough work on your plate."

Mr. O'Connor taking over duties at her house meant a serious commitment. "That's nice of him. I'm glad you two are getting along so well."

"He's quickly becoming a permanent feature of my life," she said. "I hope you're good with that."

He studied her face again. Before, lines of stress had threaded their way through the normal wrinkles from age. Now they were gone. "I'm happy you're happy, Mama. That's all I've ever wanted. Well, I'm going to go talk with Mr. Fiorni now since I don't need to shovel. You tell Mr. O'Connor thank you for me. Have a good day, Mama."

"Vinnie, I'm glad you're talking to Joe like your papa and me taught you. Tell him hello from me—and to give my best to Carlotta."

"I will, Mama." He waved and took off toward

downtown, more than a little heartened by the extra time Mr. O'Connor had given him by taking over the snow shoveling. The sidewalks downtown were freshly shoveled and salted after last night's snowfall, and his boots crunched the grains as he waved to the few early shopkeepers.

It was nine o'clock and most shops opened at ten. But Mr. Fiorni would be open. He had always opened early, taking a couple of hours for lunch so he could eat at home before going back. The new regulations and reduced clientele hadn't altered his routine much. But he'd decided to stop offering old-fashioned shaves and beard trims.

As Vinnie opened the glass door to Mr. Fiorni's Barber Shop, Mr. Fiorni set his copy of *The Times* down and stood. "Hey, Vinnie! You need a haircut? I have some time until my next client."

He was stretching his budget between haircuts. "I'm good for the moment. No one has complained about my hair being too crazy in the videos yet."

"Yeah, I hear you're a hit. Good news, eh? I told Rose you'll have to do a video for my shop sometime. I'll throw in a free haircut."

He suspected Mr. Fiorni was making the offer to support him, and likely Rose, as much as to drum up more clients. "Mighty nice of you. How's business?"

"Better around the holidays but not like old days." Mr. Fiorni shifted on his feet. "You here about my Rose?"

Suddenly he felt like he was back in high school, picking up a girl at her house. He hadn't talked to anyone's papa since then, and it wasn't something he missed. "Yes, out of respect. Rose and I are starting to date, and I want you to know I'll be good to her."

Mr. Fiorni's gaze was steady, and since the rest of his face was concealed by a mask, Vinnie realized Rose had gotten her eye color from her father. But he imagined their unique shape had come from her mother.

"Your parents raised you right, Vinnie." Mr. Fiorni

patted his chest. "It makes a papa feel better to hear that kind of reassurance. Those boys in the city don't have the same respect, and it's given her mama and me some bad moments. It makes us feel good to know you'll take care of her. Times haven't stopped being rough, and she's going to need— We're glad she'll have you."

Mr. Fiorni had cut himself off. Vinnie wondered if he'd almost let slip something about Al, especially given what Rose had told him, but he couldn't come out and ask. "She does. Well, that's all I came to say. I won't keep you."

"Vinnie, you need a haircut for the other videos, you come in and I'll do it. On the house. It's not only because you're dating Rose. I know you helped her pot up the amaryllis bulbs. Not every boy would do that."

His throat was choking up a bit at the kindness. "It was nothing. Besides, she's helping me. I'll do what I can to help her too."

Mr. Fiorni rested his hand on a worn barber chair. "Helping each other is a good start to a relationship. You need anything from me and Carlotta—for you or your mama—all you have to do is ask."

Their neighborhood was a close one, and they'd always help each other if push came to shove, but Vinnie and Mr. Fiorni both knew things had changed now that Vinnie and Rose were involved. "We appreciate that. Mama sends her best to you and Mrs. Fiorni. And speaking of helping each other, sounds like Mr. O'Connor is doing our snowplowing from now on."

Mr. Fiorni swiveled the chair in his hands, almost speculatively. "That's big news."

Everyone knew a man shoveling snow for a woman meant serious business. "I'm sure it will be all over town by lunch."

"It's a good story," Mr. Fiorni said, his eyes crinkling above his mask. "Love can change every heart and every situation. Don't think I haven't noticed my Rose taking better care of herself and starting to wear colors again. Growing up, she used to dress in the colors of the flowers, she used to say. Moving to the city, she set that aside. I'm hopeful it's back—that our Rosie is back."

Hadn't Vinnie had that very thought? He'd promised to see Rose as she was now, and while she was wearing some brighter colors, she still dressed half in black—almost like her mourning wasn't fully over. "She's finding her way. Like all of us. Well, I need to get to the restaurant. You have a great day, Mr. Fiorni."

"You too." The man's eyes shone with warmth. "Thanks again for coming in and talking to me. I'll be sharing it with my Carlotta."

He nodded and left the shop. As he reached Kelly's Hardware, Mr. Kelly appeared in the doorway. "Hey, Vinnie! Heard Paddy O'Connor has his snowblower at your mama's house. When's the wedding?"

That was fast, but then again news like this traveled fast. "It's nice of him to help out. How's business? You got any Christmas lights left?"

"A bunch of people put them up early this year, so I sold out before Thanksgiving. I got more though, and that new Anderson family that's come to manage the trust just bought a bunch the other day. A good sort, Warren. He's lucky he's used to the snow, being from the Chicago area. Judging from the snow we just had, we're in for it this winter. Not that we ever close up shop. Snow doesn't slow us New Yorkers down."

Vinnie thought of his uncle. If he was going to be crazy enough to leave Orion, he should at least pick someplace warm like Florida. "Warren must be a good egg since he's Sarah and Alice's friend from way back."

"You think you can make my hardware store sexy?" The man wiggled his large waist. "Maybe do a scene with a power drill like Channing Tatum did in *Magic Mike*?"

He snorted, having expected this kind of ribbing from

the community. "When did you ever watch that movie, Mr. Kelly?"

"My wife was trying to show me what real moves were a few Valentine's Days ago. Almost popped a disc in my back."

"Way too much information for me." He gave a mock shudder. "I've gotta get to the restaurant. See you around."

Only three stores down, Lucia Tesoro stood outside her shop door in a vintage fox fur coat, clearly waiting for him. Even at five foot nothing, she resembled a terrier with a short cut of black hair. "Hey, Vinnie! Heard about Paddy O'Connor shoveling snow at your mama's. Every time I think of those two together my eyes cross. They've acted like mortal enemies all these years."

He held up his hands. "You know Mama's brother stopped them from dating when they were kids because of all the Irish/Italian stuff. It would make anyone angry, I guess. Nice to have warmer feelings around these days. Times are tough enough."

"They sure are." She flicked her gloved hand at her store. "Business is awful, and I need you to do that video for me. When Rose called me and quoted your joint fee, you could have knocked me over. Like I have that kind of money. Gladys might be willing to pay that, but I'm not. Vinnie, you and Rose should be willing to help everyone out for free. Aren't we friends and neighbors like we have written on our windows?"

He knew a trap when he saw it. "Everyone's gotta put bread on the table, Lucia. Rose and me included. Maybe you could use some of the money you receive from the trust."

"That's not the point, Vinnie. You and Rose shouldn't be making money off us in times like these. We're supposed to help each other."

His belly knotted at her attack. "Mrs. Tesoro, we aren't taking advantage of you. Only trying to make a living ourselves. Come on. You've known me and Rose our whole lives. We wouldn't do that."

Her dark eyes turned hard. "I don't know anything anymore. The world is ending, and our businesses are in danger, and Rose is quoting me an outrageous price for a video that could save my business. That doesn't sound very neighborly to me. Where's your holiday spirit?"

He felt eyes on his back and wondered if her raised voice had brought others out from their shops. She was being dramatic, unfair, and a bit cruel. But arguing with her wasn't going to change her opinion. Certainly not now.

"I'm sorry you feel that way. It couldn't be further from the truth. You might remember that we lost my family business and Rose lost her job, so we more than understand that times are tough. I'll leave you now. I need to go to work."

To make my own living.

His heart was pounding as he resumed walking. How dare she say those things? He wished he could turn around and march back to tell her what he thought of her insults, but that would only make things worse. Plus, he didn't like to be unkind to people. On the rare occasion he'd have to handle an upset or irate customer at Two Sisters, he'd always shoved his own anger aside and treated them with kindness, even when it killed him. Sometimes it had even turned the situation around and made the person a customer for life.

Yet moments like this tested that conviction. Lucia Tesoro had just maligned his character and, worse, Rose's. He would need to tell Rose because Lucia was going to spew her opinions about town. They needed to head off any further bad feelings.

He had two more store owners stop him and mention the snow shoveling. He supposed he should be relieved they hadn't mentioned Lucia's loud words moments before.

By the time he reached O'Connor's, his shoulders were

stiff as boulders, although his thoughts had shifted from Lucia to the man whose name was on the sign.

His mama was serious about Mr. O'Connor. Were they thinking about marriage? They'd only been dating about a month, but she'd called him a companion. He supposed time didn't govern the heart. Later he'd go to church and light a candle for her happiness and let God sort out the rest.

Using his key, he let himself inside. A quick look around told him Hank hadn't arrived yet, but that wasn't a surprise since Vinnie was early. Heavy metal music was spewing from the kitchen, and Vinnie plugged his ears and kicked the door open.

"Jesus Christ!" Derrick said, a butcher knife raised in his hand. "Warn a guy. What are you doing here this early?"

Vinnie didn't have to ask Derrick. He had a mound of peeled potatoes on the cutting board in front of him. "Long story. Potato soup?"

"Yeah. We had it as a special a couple of weeks ago, and someone mentioned loving it in a review. Seemed a good day for it with all the snow. Plus, it's cheap and keeps well."

That was one thing Vinnie liked about their new chef. He might be from a tony restaurant in Brooklyn, but he'd grown up on soul food, the kind that tasted good and wasn't expensive to make. He understood what the restaurant was up against in these times, what with his former restaurant having closed due to Covid.

"I'll look forward to a bowl later on," Vinnie said, wincing as the guitar screeched. "What coffee do you want today?"

Every day he made Derrick a cup, and it had forged their bond. "Cappuccino. Thanks, man. I'll turn down my music now that I'm not alone, but you keep that Dean Martin stuff at a reasonable level, or I'll have to use my cleaver on you."

"You're holding a butcher knife, you idiot."

Derrick laughed. "I save my cleaver for the scary work. Now get out of here. My potatoes don't like when I talk violent."

He closed the door to the kitchen, chuckling, and breathed a sigh of relief as the music ceased. Pulling out his phone, he decided to do Hank a favor.

Walk the back way to work today. If you haven't already heard, I'll explain when you get here.

His phone immediately pinged.

Marty already hit me up. He says my dad must be thinking about giving your mama an engagement ring for Christmas. I knew they were serious, but this... See you soon.

He was already looking forward to talking to his friend about it. They would share their views and settle on wanting their parents to be happy, even if it was still a little weird and fast. He delivered Derrick's coffee, and his phone pinged when he came back to the bar. He smiled for the first time all morning, seeing Rose's name on his screen. He opened the text.

Hey! You doing okay? Heard you stopped by to tell my papa we were dating. I told them last night. It was sweet of you. Moving on... Heard about Mr. O'Connor at your mama's with his snowblower. If you feel faint, put your head between your legs.

That prompted a reluctant laugh. He texted her back.

Terrific way to greet customers. I'm reminding myself of her happiness. Waiting to talk to Hank. On another note, Lucia Tesoro was a real pain today, complaining about the price you quoted. She said some other things that made me real angry, but I kept a lid on it. We might need to do something about it though. I don't want her opinions to go any further.

He waited for her to respond. It only took a moment.

She can be a real bitch when she decides to be. If you're on her good side, she'll kiss your ass, but otherwise she'll slice you up with her box cutters. We quoted her the same price Aunt Gladys paid, what we're charging. If she doesn't like it, she can jump off a cliff. Not very nice, but I'm so sick of people acting mean and unfair. Don't we have enough going on with Covid?

He texted back a simple, *Amen.* Her new text came in immediately.

I'm going to my greenhouse to play with my babies and calm down. Let me think about next steps. I'll call Aunt Gladys. She won't like Lucia Tesoro talking like this either. So much for Orion's Friends & Neighbors push. See you later. I promise to be in a better mood.

Funny how Lucia Tesoro had used the Friends & Neighbors theme to press her own argument. But in his mind, she'd perverted it. A friend and neighbor wanted everyone to be paid what they were due. They wanted others to be successful. He texted Rose back.

Me too. Have a good day, sweetheart.

She sent a single red heart emoji, and it struck him. Hard. Did he want to send a heart back? Somehow it felt like a big decision. People threw emojis around all the time, but it was different now that they were on the verge of something. He brought up the image of her potting up those plant balls, wearing the cute green hoodie that said *Plantaholic.* She'd looked more approachable and young than she did in her usual black veneer.

He was excited to see those facets of her personality blossom again. There was no way he'd let anyone stunt her regrowth. Certainly not Lucia Tesoro. Come to think of it, how was he supposed to make a living as an influencer if people balked at paying for promotion? He needed this to work to stay in Orion.

Although he didn't have an answer, he wouldn't let any ugliness blunt Rose's growth. Or his.

CHAPTER 14

AMY HAD A PLAYDATE WITH ORION.

Warren had sweetly offered to watch the girls so she could spend some time downtown to make friends with their new community. Her first stop was at the Coffee Roastery since Warren had said it was their kind of haunt.

She parked the car on the street and counted four holiday shoppers walking into the House of Hope & Chocolate, which she'd make her last stop, for dessert. She planned to have lunch at O'Connor's, and Old World Elegance was also on her list, not just to meet the so-called Aunt Gladys but to pick up a last-minute holiday gift for Warren.

Most of the storefronts were red brick. Some had awnings with their names on them. Holiday wreaths with red bows winked white lights while others had displays of snowmen, trains, and Santa Claus' helpers in their windows. All sported the new Friends & Neighbors logo, which really touched her. If you let the news paint reality for you, you wouldn't believe there was a single decent human being out there anymore, which was why she and Warren had decided not to watch it anymore.

When she walked into the coffee shop, she inhaled the scent of roasted beans as much as she could through her mask. The music grabbed her throat as she heard, "Welcome."

"I haven't heard 'What a Wonderful World' by Louis Armstrong in forever," she told the tall, broad-chested man behind the counter. Baker, she guessed. "I'm Amy Anderson, Warren's wife. He told me this place was our jam."

He brightened immediately. "Yeah, we had a great chat. I'm glad you like the music. Someone just complained about me not playing Christmas music. Personally, I was trying to remind myself the world isn't ending."

"That explains the hoodie." She eyed the navy block letters that read *Kindness and Compassion: Don't Let Them Go Extinct.*

"On a very dark night some months ago, I contacted my merchandising supplier and we got to talking about the world. He lives outside Washington D.C., and you can imagine what a picnic that is right now. We were both feeling down, and I said people were so thickheaded that maybe we all needed T-shirts reminding us of important values like kindness, justice, unity, and compassion."

"I could get on that bandwagon," she said.

He pointed to his clothing. "The next day he said he was printing up some merchandise and putting them on his Zazzle store. He shipped me a bunch of them for free. His way of doing something positive. I sent him a coffee box set in thanks and have been wearing them ever since."

"I'd love to support his store. My girls are little, and I love dressing them in positive messages."

"I'll write down his store name on your receipt. Gotta teach people early, but that's no guarantee against bad manners or racism." He pointed to himself. "Jaded former Peace Corps volunteer speaking. But forget that. What can I get you?"

She looked for a holiday portion of the beverage menu and found none. Somehow, she imagined Baker might be a traditionalist. "I'd love a whole milk mocha with whipped cream."

"Coming right up," he said, starting to make her drink.

The door opened and the four holiday shoppers came in. She squeezed to the end of the counter to give them room. When Baker slid her the mocha, he extended her receipt with the handwritten information for the Zazzle store.

"You take care, Amy. And happy holidays."

"Keep spreading those good vibes," she answered with a smile she hoped he could see in her eyes, and let herself out.

Making sure no one was around, she pulled down her mask and sipped her drink. The rich creamy brew had her eyes fluttering. That was some good coffee underneath the enhancements of cream, chocolate, and sweetener. Righting the mask, she walked along Main Street, looking in windows, some of them vacant eyesores. Warren was right. They needed to bring new businesses in as well as shoring up the surviving ones.

Maybe the town needed to create a city marketing plan to attract new business. Already Warren was talking about how the trust could do more to help with advertising online, much like that very hot video had done for Aunt Gladys' store. Amy had dived into research to help him and watched a few of the New York State tourism commercials online. The scope was impressive. Maybe they could do something like that for Orion. The Friends & Neighbors angle would attract like-minded people.

Now that was something she would be interested in working on. Something that made a difference. Something driven by good values. Something that helped bring in prosperity and innovation.

Her old marketing muscles began to stretch. She

wandered around and made more mental notes, taking note of which sorts of businesses the downtown area lacked. She walked into a few shops—spoke with the owners and browsed—but she wasn't buying. She was researching.

By the time she climbed the hill to Old World Elegance, she was feeling empowered. Alice's light display of *Hope, Love, Joy* gave her stomach a warm feeling. The hot pink storefront charmed her as much as the classy rose-colored sign with the elegant black letters.

As she reached for the door handle, it opened and a man hurried past her, his multiple shopping bags making scratching sounds. She entered, and it was like walking into a boutique in Paris. Warren had taken her there for their two-year anniversary, and they'd had a ball and done a load of shopping.

"Aunt Gladys, I presume," she said, smiling broadly as she took in the red-haired woman who stood behind the counter, remarkable in her red sequined scarf over a cream caftan. "I'm Amy Anderson, Warren's wife."

She had a moment of self-reflection after delivering that intro the second time in an hour. Was this how she wanted to introduce herself here? Certainly her mother thought that was all she needed in her life, and for a time, she'd gone along with it, quitting her job to stay at home when Madison was born. She'd let herself believe she'd be a bad mother if she kept working. Worse, she'd been wrapped up in gaining her mother's approval.

By God, how had she allowed herself to get to this place? What were *her* merits? It only brought home what she'd already known: she needed something of her own.

"Hello, Amy! Good to meet Warren's other half. Are you doing some holiday shopping or scouting for your husband? Alice says you have a heck of a marketing brain, and trust me, we could use it."

That rocked her back on her feet. Was this woman psychic? How had she known that Amy's trip into town had unexpectedly changed direction?

"Have you met Rose?" the woman asked. "She's coming by later to help me look for someone to help me with social media. Our last promotional video is generating a lot of traffic, and I can't keep up. Nor do I really want to sift through any more provocative comments about Vinnie, although he's the cat's meow, for sure."

Who said 'cat's meow' anymore? "What are you looking for? I used to do the social media for my old job, so I have a sense of what's required and the kind of skill set you'd want."

Aunt Gladys propped her elbows on her glass counter, staring at her with very intent green eyes. "What's your situation these days? Clifton showed me the video of Warren playing golf in a dinosaur outfit in your backyard with your girls—pee my pants funny, by the way—so I know you have two young ones."

Her mouth gaped for a moment—she hadn't come here for a *job*—and then old business training kicked in. She ran with it. "I've been thinking about the next thing, honestly. Walking around town gave me some ideas. I want to do something in addition to taking care of the girls. Not that I don't love it."

"You don't have to justify anything to me, honey." The older woman tapped the glass with a turquoise fingernail. "I didn't have children. Wasn't possible. But I respect it, although I also know everyone needs to have something for themselves. Have you ever noticed how no one ever asks a man if he feels bad about wanting to have a career after he has kids? The double standard only hurts women, and we have plenty enough to deal with without pointing that knife at ourselves. Don't you think?"

"I've been having thoughts along those lines recently." She finally shrugged out of her coat. "I've always trusted in timing and, honestly, walking in here today right when you're looking for someone with my skill set seems—"

"Heaven-sent," Aunt Gladys said, gesturing to the ceiling. "Best things in life work that way. Amy, I like the idea of someone invested in this community helping me and my store. Let me run you through what I'm thinking, and you can tell me whether you're interested."

She grinned, happy in a way she hadn't been in a while. To work with this exuberant, no-holds-barred woman would be a gift beyond the work. Aunt Gladys was a firebrand. A woman like this wouldn't let her mother talk her into painting her whole house neutral tones. Or feel like moving away was the safest way to escape her bullying. Or even dread the inevitable holiday FaceTime call.

"That would be wonderful, Aunt Gladys. Can I call you that?"

"Be a shame to call me Aunt Beatrice," the woman bandied back with a twinkle.

The mocha she'd drunk may as well have been laced with whiskey because she was feeling a little tipsy. "Right. Do you have a jacket Warren might look good in bare-chested? He's a 44 Long."

Aunt Gladys shook her head. "Not anymore he's not. The man who visited me was a 42 Long, and I have just the jacket for him."

As the older woman blazed by her, Amy clenched her fists in her hands as her excitement bottomed out. She didn't even know her husband's size anymore. How had that happened?

She had a lot of transforming to do, and she needed to do it fast. Warren and the girls—and herself for that matter—were too important to her for her to stay lost.

CHAPTER 15

SHE WAS BACK TO WORKING LONG HOURS.

After months of listlessness, the delicious grind of working hard for something she believed in had shattered Rose's remaining fears. She was doing this. All in. Fully committed. Her marathon two-day focus on her website had paid off. As she punched the button to make it live from the worktable in her greenhouse, she stomped her foot in triumph. "It's official. The Dreamer's Flower Shoppe is now open for business."

Vinnie popped the bottle of Prosecco he was holding, looking positively dashing in another one of Aunt Gladys' borrowed tuxedos. "Way to go, Rose! If I could kiss you, I'd plant a good one on you."

They'd done their tests but were still awaiting the results. She put her hand to her masked mouth and blew him a kiss. "This will have to do."

He mimed the action back and sang a few bars of "*Buona Sera*." Her toes curled. He was singing to her more and more now that they were dating, and she couldn't get enough of it. The tenderness and heat in his dark brown eyes made her breathless.

"After we toast," Vinnie said when he broke off the song, "we'll do The Dreamer's Flower Shoppe's inaugural video. But first, I'd like to be your first official paying customer. I'd like a lemon tree for Mama from Mr. Palladino's, if that's possible. She'd love the story as much as the tree. Things like that make her homesick for Italy in a good way. Plus, I thought she could cook with it when it produced fruit."

She went all soft and gooey at his thoughtfulness. That was Vinnie, through and through. He'd brought her little gifts the past couple days. She'd loved the single chocolate in one of the House of Hope & Chocolate's gift boxes as much as the cup of Derrick's tantalizing potato soup from O'Connor's. They'd gone through his influencer offers and chosen the ones he liked that she thought were the best fit. He'd already agreed to promote three products—pasta, olive oil, and a line of men's watches. He'd said he was looking forward to giving his mama the olive oil and pasta. She'd told him it was only the beginning.

"I suppose I could graft a baby tree for you, Vinnie, but it's going to take a few years to mature."

"Everything worthwhile takes its time to grow," Vinnie said. "Like your papa said. Plants are practically people. I don't expect a baby tree to be an adult. There's no rush. Mama will like tending it and watching it grow up."

His presence in the greenhouse was putting him in touch with his green thumb, or so he said. His ancestors had farmed in Italy before immigrating, and he often commented that it was nice to feel close to them, saying he'd gotten his Italy nostalgia from his mama. Comments like that, as much as his ongoing support and thoughtfulness, had her falling hard. She'd always "loved" Vinnie, but now she was starting to *love* him. And they hadn't even kissed yet!

"I'll graft one straightaway. Were you thinking about giving it to her for Christmas?"

With Christmas Eve five days away, she'd intentionally

created extra work for herself to keep her away from her brother and his family. Her parents had grown stiff and silent when she'd asked them again to insist that Al and his family take rapid Covid tests. Mama had said they'd tried and left it at that. Rose was in a quandary. To eat their traditional Christmas meal, she'd need to take off her mask, and she frankly didn't want to.

Vinnie wasn't sure if he was going to have Christmas Eve dinner with his mama either. He hadn't been around her unmasked since her bout of Covid, and besides, she wouldn't be alone. She'd invited Mr. O'Connor to join her.

Meanwhile, Rose's sister-in-law had just posted another photo of herself at some under-the-radar Pilates class without a mask on, in a room full of equally unmasked women. The whole notion was terrifying, and having just taken her Covid test so she could be with Vinnie, she didn't want to up and get Covid from her brother's family.

She wasn't sure what to do. If she stayed out in the greenhouse all day, it would upset her parents, although she doubted Al's family would care. But hell, she felt caught between a rock and a hard place. Then there was her worry for her parents' health...

"Mom and I agreed to only exchange two gifts this Christmas," Vinnie said. "And I've already gotten them. Her birthday is in February though. Maybe the tree would be a little taller by then."

"February would be perfect," Rose said. "That will allow for it to take root better. Maybe I should do up a few more to sell in my store."

"You ought to tell them the story about Mr. Palladino. Maybe you could do a video to tell people how your papa got this greenhouse in the first place and special plants like that lemon tree. Put it on your website and on social media. It's kinda a dreamer's story. Like a plant fairy tale."

Her mouth twitched as she watched him feather the flowers of her white winter camellia. "A plant fairy tale.

That's a good one."

"I've been thinking about what to say in your videos. Given who you are and what you named your business. To my mind, The Dreamer's Flower Shoppe is *your* version of a plant fairy tale and I'm your Romeo hero."

Yes, he was. She walked to the orchid section and plucked up a calypso orchid. "This variety is actually called Fairy slipper."

"See! There's magic everywhere, including in you. Rose, I wanted to ask you something. Come outside and let's toast. We got sidetracked."

She worried her lips together after picking up her flute and coat, hoping the lipstick she'd put on earlier hadn't smudged under her mask. Wanting to look good for a man shouldn't be this hard. The cold air was striking, but she'd undergo that and more to see Vinnie's face. Also, who couldn't appreciate the brilliance of the morning sunlight on the snow?

When he took off his mask, her breath caught. Every time she saw his face, she was a little more appreciative. His strong jaw and cheekbones were arresting, and his black hair curled as if angels had twined the locks from heaven. He'd always been the most handsome man in the world to her, but now when he was looking at her with those dark, intent eyes, she felt like she—Rose Fiorni—was the most beautiful woman in the world. It was a hell of a feeling.

"You gonna take your mask off?" he asked.

"No, I was going to drink through it. Try something new." But she'd told herself she'd be honest, hadn't she? So she admitted, "You should know I was mesmerized momentarily by your beauty, but I'm back now." She undid her mask and smiled at him.

A slow sexy smile broke across his face. "Every time I see you, it's like I'm seeing you for the first time. Rose, honey, you are one beautiful lady."

Under his gaze, she only felt confidence and peace, like

a part of City Rose was coming back. "Thank you, Vinnie."

"To your success—with your flower shop and everything else your heart desires."

Her heart desired him, and as she lifted her glass and drank, she made a special wish for their life together.

"Rose, I know you're upset about Al and his family coming for the holiday."

"My Covid test won't mean anything if I hang around them unsafely, and that's what they are. Unsafe. I don't want anything to happen to me or my parents, but if I can't figure out a way to get out of dinner and keep my mask on around them, then I'll need to take another test. With the upswelling of testing around the holidays, I'm not sure it will be back before New Year's. This whole thing is impossible, and I'm so angry I could hit something."

Any trace of his former good humor slipped away. "I know. In some ways you're lucky. Some people actually like their siblings and their families, and staying away from them for the holidays because of Covid is heartbreaking."

"You're right." She clenched her fists. "Vinnie, sometimes I feel like a terrible person for feeling this way about Al. But we've never gotten along. He was always jealous of my relationship with Papa, and because of it, he was always mean to me. I think that's why Mama babied him. To soften it. But he's not a good guy, and neither is his family. I don't want to hurt anyone, but I don't want to get sick either."

He put his hand over his heart. "If I could hold you right now, I would. Rose, you aren't a terrible person. Not even close."

Tears burned her eyes, and she lowered her face so he wouldn't see. "My parents and I are usually so easy with each other, but it's been tough around the house lately. We don't see eye to eye when it comes to Al."

"This is hard stuff for anyone to swallow, honey. Everyone seems to get bent out of shape over masks and safety. So...I got to thinking about how we could avoid hurting anyone and still stay safe, although nothing is one hundred percent. Rose, would you like to have Christmas Eve dinner with me? I get that it may be too soon to ask, and if you feel that way, I completely understand, but Hank would let us have it at the restaurant. We're closed on Christmas Eve. We should have our test results by then."

Her heart pressed against her ribs as it swelled. "Oh, Vinnie. I'd love that." *Please God, let them have their results back.*

He gestured to the house. "I thought your parents might feel better knowing we were spending it together. They like the idea of us dating. I think my mama will be good with it too. I'm still scared of putting her at risk by being around her without a mask on. Those days when she was on the respirator were the worst of my life. I'm never going there again."

Oh, what he must have gone through. Losing his aunt. Fearing for his mother. "This is where I wish I could wrap my arms around you."

He held them open. "I'll imagine it."

They gazed at each other for a quiet moment, taking occasional sips of champagne, and then she said, "You're quite simply the best, did you know that?" None of the other guys she'd dated had been this sweet. She'd always known no one could equal Vinnie. He'd been her gold standard. Now she knew every fantasy she'd harbored about him was true. Okay, well, not all of them. They still hadn't kissed or made love, something that was becoming harder with each passing day, and until they did, she would have to fall back on her fantasies.

"Let's go make your video and kick things off but good," Vinnie said.

They brought the champagne inside and got started.

Given the holidays would be winding down shortly, Rose had crafted a new year, new space idea for the videos. Vinnie ran with it with aplomb. She had a plant for everyone, and they ended up doing three videos, using the Romeoville concept for the first two.

In the first one, Romeo suggested plants for the romantic types looking for easy-to-grow options in small spaces, like the green and pink variety of Greenovia, which were called Mountain Rose for their shape. They resembled roses, the most romantic flower, he assured their target female audience.

The second was for the intrepid and featured a Staghorn Fern prized for its thick leaves that resembled animal horns, something a man about town like Romeo would appreciate.

The last one was for kids and featured one of her favorite succulents, *Monilaria obconica*, which had bunny ears in its early stages. They'd just gone with the Vinnie everyone loved at Two Sisters.

Vinnie changed outfits in between videos in her parents' house, and she tried not to think about that. Much. When he returned in the outfit he'd arrived in—pin-striped black pants, a black shirt, and red suspenders—her mouth went dry.

He was humming "Angelina," and when he caught her watching him, his eyes twinkled. "The next time you look at me like that, maybe I'll be able to take you into my arms and kiss you. Then we'll dance. I seem to remember you dancing with your papa at the church hall for Italian night back in the day."

The community used to come together for them a few times a year. There would be pans of lasagna, garlic bread, and salad, and they'd all dance to old classics people had brought in, played on Father Giuseppe's record player. "Maybe we can model one of our dates after those nights. I liked dressing up and twirling around to the music while people laughed and told jokes and tall tales in Italian."

"They were good times for sure." Vinnie shot her

a sexy wink. "We'll have a date like that. Count on it. Unfortunately, I need to get to work. You need anything else, you text me. Okay?"

She didn't want him to go, and from the reluctance in his voice, it was obvious he felt the same way. "I'll text you to say hello and see how your afternoon is going. You wearing a Santa hat today? I saw Alice posted a video of you wearing one behind the bar, singing a Louis Prima carol." The post had boasted over a thousand likes, with comments galore on Vinnie being hot and adorable. His star was surely rising.

"You know it. I'll bring you a candy cane. Rose..."

The soft way he said her name—so different than before—had her pressing her hands to her sides. "Yeah, Vinnie?"

"I like spending time with you. So much. I just wanted you to know. We don't banter as much as we used to, but I kinda like this better."

Because she wasn't pushing him to notice her or like her anymore. Because he made her feel like he really did see her and want her, just as she was. "I feel the same way. Vinnie, I wanted to give you something."

"You don't have to give me anything."

Picking up the small pot of Mountain Roses she'd used in the video, she held it out to him. "I wanted you to have something special and beautiful in your place."

"Something that reminds me of you." He blew her a kiss through his mask. "This is perfect. Thank you, sweetheart."

She set the pot down, and he stepped forward to take it. "I'll see you later, Vinnie."

They gazed at each other for a long moment before he finally turned and left the greenhouse. She gave in to fancy and twirled in place, feeling young and in love. Everything felt possible in that moment, and God, did it feel good.

She worked on editing the videos, savoring every word, every frame of Vinnie. She posted the first video, and satisfaction coursed through her. This was happening. She was doing it.

Next up, she was going to hone her design options for the boutonnières. She'd liked the pictures Vinnie had sent. The frosted greenery he'd mentioned was eucalyptus, paired with winterberry holly. Hank was all understated masculine, and the design she'd honed fit him perfectly. After sketching her designs, she pulled up her email to send the images to Hank and Alice.

Her heart quickened when she saw an email from a well-known grocery chain with pharmacy and healthcare capabilities. She'd applied for an entry-level marketing position there months ago. The interview had gone well, she'd thought, but she'd heard nothing. She opened the email and read:

We left you a voicemail, but we wanted to follow up and inform you that we would like to offer you the position of Marketing & Public Relations Assistant.

Her mouth dropped open as she read the rest. Her eyes zoomed in on the salary. It was thirty percent less than her former one, which was a kick to the gut. Not much to live on. The benefits were good, thank God. She'd have healthcare through them; right now, her parents were paying her COBRA, which was crazy expensive.

They wanted her to start immediately. At home. But move to their headquarters in Milwaukee, Wisconsin, in six months to a year, pending the Covid situation.

She slid into a chair as her legs went numb.

Milwaukee? She couldn't remember if it had mentioned relocating in the ad. She didn't want to leave New York. Especially when everything was here. Vinnie. Her parents. Orion. The city.

Her flowers.

She scrolled down and read the scope of work. Her heart sank. If she took the position, she would be doing marketing exclusively related to Covid offerings like new testing options and specialized urgent care.

Oh no. Not that. She'd been fighting depression hard. She'd even gotten a prescription to fight it halfway through lockdown, but she'd stopped taking the pills a couple of weeks ago.

She pushed away from the table and stood. Shock had her staring off into space. A job. She finally had a job offer. Only it wasn't at all what she wanted.

Pressing her hands into her face, she gave in to tears.

When she finished, she dried her face and sat down again, turning the chair to face her flowers. The timing of the offer couldn't be more ironic. If her grandmother were alive, she'd say fate was testing her heart. What did she really want? It came down to a choice between security and love. Neither seemed wrong.

One was practical, and the old Rose understood its power. She would have a job with health insurance and a guaranteed salary, even if it required her to take a few steps back and start at entry level. She wouldn't be a burden to her parents anymore, although it might be short-sighted to move out before she relocated.

Before she moved to Milwaukee.

How could she do this? After wanting Vinnie for her whole life, she finally had him. She wanted to keep it that way. Plus, she'd told him she was staying in Orion.

And what about her new business? The dream she was only just beginning to make a reality?

To abandon her plans so soon would hurt like hell. But she still wasn't completely sure she had that luxury.

CHAPTER 16

VINNIE COULDN'T SING "PUT A LITTLE LOVE IN YOUR Heart" loud enough as he closed up.

A former Two Sisters customer had left him three hundred-dollar bills as a thank you for keeping up his favorite restaurant's spirit at O'Connor's. Talk about generosity. He'd wanted to hug Mr. Marino, especially after the man had teared up about missing the chocolate ravioli his mama used to make around the holidays. Tips had been up with the holiday spirit, but this was something special. He couldn't wait to tell Mama. He also planned to buy Rose something a little nicer.

"Hank said you had a great night," Alice said, approaching the bar after exiting the back office. "Thank God for the holidays."

"Ain't that the truth. You want an espresso or something on the alcoholic side?"

She bounced in her barstool. "An espresso of yours always tops a mere pour of alcohol. Hank and I usually have a glass of something spirited when he gets home to wind down. It was so nice of that man from Two Sisters to do what he did. Has he been in before?"

Vinnie shook his head. "No, he apparently saw that video you posted of me singing a Louis Prima holiday song behind the bar and decided to give us a try. I used to sing Christmas songs at the old restaurant. Dance with the older ladies and little kids. You know... Good stuff."

"You should do that more here," Alice said, making a heart shape with her hands. "Clearly I'm not the only one who loves it. You dance socially distanced very well, as I can attest."

"You wanna dance now, sweetheart? I think I hear a favorite."

"All I Want For Christmas" was playing as he came out from behind the bar. They started to dance. One thing he appreciated about Alice was that she didn't do anything halfway. She gave him a happy wave and started to twist her hips, laughing. Vinnie matched her steps before doing a tight spin, ending on his tiptoes. They circled each other playfully, and he started singing. She threw the Swim at him and he responded with the Hitchhike.

When he did another turn, he caught Derrick videoing them and put some extra Elvis into his hips. Alice picked an air guitar. When the song ended, he held out his arms, his heart bursting with love and happiness.

"My best friend is the luckiest man in the world to have you, and that makes me lucky too. Alice Bailey, thanks for coming into our world."

"Amen," Hank said, crossing and taking his fiancée into his arms. "You looked pretty good out there, babe. Care to dance with a terrible dancer who loves you like crazy?"

She twined her arms around his neck, and they swayed for a few beats. "You dance just fine for me. But you could loosen up a little. Vinnie, do you give lessons?"

He laughed. "I've been trying to get this guy to loosen up on the dance floor since our first junior school dance. He was too embarrassed to ask the girls to dance, although he finally managed slow dancing, which the girls didn't mind much in high school. But at weddings, he's a lost cause when 'The Macarena' comes on."

"I love that dance!" she exclaimed.

Hank snorted, untangling her arms from around him. "Of course you do. Come on, dancing queen. Let's go home and slow dance in private."

"*Okay!*" Alice fluttered her fingers at Vinnie. "Derrick, if you send that video to me, I'll edit it and post it on O'Connor's' social media accounts. Hank, did you hear why that lovely man came in tonight? It was because he saw a video of Vinnie singing behind the bar like he used to at Two Sisters. Isn't that wonderful? And he tips well!"

Hank gave him a chin nod. "Vinnie being Vinnie is a draw in and of itself. Always has been. Which is why he's becoming a social media sensation. I can't wait to see those videos of you with Rose's plants."

"I can't say I'm a sensation, but I like helping people sell things and attract more customers," Vinnie said, aware of the pride lacing his voice. "Except that Lucia Tesoro. After what she said, I don't care if she decides to pay full price and hire us. You don't talk about people like that."

"She's always been hit or miss," Hank said. "Let it roll off your back. But I'll bet a whole lot of women wanted to see you in that gold Speedo she had in mind."

"I did!" Alice said. "Not in a weird way. I just thought it would be funny. I mean, who lays on a couch in a gold Speedo?"

"Someone who likes their junk squashed," Derrick said, making them all laugh. "Hey, Speedos hurt. Don't ask. Vinnie, we'd have had women flocking in here to see you. Wait! Maybe you shouldn't nix it. Be good for business. *Oh, Romeo!*"

Chef was downright smirking, and Vinnie dramatically opened his jacket. "I don't need a Speedo for women to find me irresistible."

"When you talk like that, we're outta here." Hank took

Alice's hand. "Seriously? Everyone ready to close up?"

"Yeah," he and Derrick said in tandem.

Vinnie grabbed his phone and jolted a little when he saw a text from the Covid clinic. His results were in. Heart pounding, he clicked on the link. "Negative! I'm negative."

"Don't fool yourself, Vinnie," Derrick said as he pulled on his coat. "You're the most positive person I know."

"My Covid test, you idiot!" He held up his phone. "Yes!" Had Rose gotten her results? God, he hoped so. He'd throw rocks at her window to wake her. Then he laughed at the idea. He was thinking like his troubadour character, not a twenty-first-century man. All he had to do was text her. He shot her one straightaway.

"I'm happy you're negative, Vinnie," Derrick said, "but doesn't it say something about the world when the highlight of your day is finding out you don't have the plague? I'm gonna go home and get drunk on that thought."

"Oh, don't think like that, Derrick," Alice said. "Not having Covid is a gift. Every day."

He rubbed the bridge of his nose. "Sorry. I know you lost your friend. Ignore me. I'm just feeling a little down with the holidays sneaking up. I know it was too risky to go see my dad, but that doesn't make it suck less. I'll catch you guys tomorrow."

They watched him walk out the front, and Vinnie sighed. "He's got that right. Feels different this year. I asked Rose to spend Christmas Eve with me since I didn't want to risk spending it with Mama and your dad. She likes having the meal at home, you know."

"We declined too, but we were going to ask you to join us so you wouldn't be alone," Hank said. "Then I got worried about how your mama would take it. I'm glad you have plans. It sucks that we have to make these calls."

He nodded. "I didn't think you'd mind if Rose and me had dinner here at the restaurant since my place doesn't have much of a kitchen. Al and his family are coming—"

"Jesus," Hank said. "No wonder you asked her. They're usually a shitshow on wheels. I can't imagine how they'd be with Covid."

"Rose says they post pictures of themselves in crowds, always without masks on. I looked online for myself, and yeah, it's about what you'd expect of Al and his wife. Cut from the same cloth, those two." He had a moment of feeling a little guilty for talking bad about them, but in this case, truth was truth.

"He was one of the biggest jerks in our class, Alice," Hank said. "From kindergarten to twelfth. A bully and a braggart."

"But Rose is so nice," she responded.

"Some siblings don't turn out like others," Hank said, rubbing her back. "I'm glad you asked her, Vinnie. If you want, we could meet you here for dessert?"

"Dessert sounds great, and we won't tell a soul. But only if you want to. You've got your new traditions to think of."

"Vinnie," Alice said, "I know I speak for Hank when I say spending Christmas with you would be a great part of our new tradition. Right, babe?"

They'd been friends too long for Vinnie not to know what his friend was thinking. They were both choked up. "Dessert. Socially distanced. Christmas Eve."

"I'll make it!" Alice said, bouncing on her heels. "You ever have *Bûche de Noël*? It's a rolled chocolate cake filled with chocolate whipped cream and covered in chocolate ganache. It's French, of course."

"Of course," Hank said, tousling her curly brown hair. "It sounds delicious. But don't work too hard, okay? You've been burning the candle at both ends."

"I echo that," Vinnie said. "Mama would always cook for days and then be exhausted by the time Christmas Eve rolled around. I don't want that—for any of us. I know I'm not much of a cook, but I'll do steaks for Rose and me to keep it simple. She's been working like crazy too."

Alice gasped. "But, Vinnie, don't you guys do the traditional *Il Cenone di Vigilia*?"

Hank gave him his *translate please* look, and he laughed. "Yes, we usually do the Feast of the Seven Fishes. Sometimes my mama served more than seven types of fish and shellfish, especially when it was a good year." His mouth watered as he thought of dishes like fried calamari, stuffed lobster, red snapper Livornese, and linguine with clams.

"You've never eaten the traditional meal at Vinnie's?" Alice asked Hank.

"No, we always did it with our families. Usually met up after midnight mass for a drink once we were in college."

"They couldn't send us to bed anymore by saying Santa would come," Vinnie joked. "Speaking of... You two get home. Let me check my phone and see if Rose got her test back."

There was no response, and he wondered if she was in her greenhouse or in bed. It was nearing eleven. He hadn't heard from her after leaving that morning, which was unusual. Usually she texted at some point during the day, and he'd text back when he had a break. But her silence hadn't made an impression because she'd posted the first video they'd made for The Dreamer's Flower Shoppe, and he'd felt like a proud papa hitting the heart button. So far it was doing well. Not velvet jacket well. But it was different content. Maybe Romeo needed to show a little skin to sell her plants in the beginning, until word got out about their quality. He'd do that for his girl.

"Any word?" Alice asked.

He grabbed his coat. "No. Let's go."

They walked together for a while but parted ways when Hank and Alice reached their street. He continued on and decided to walk by Rose's house. He could go to the fence and see if she was sitting in her usual spot in the greenhouse. Crunching through snow to reach it, he was disappointed by her absence. The rest of the house was dark too.

Something didn't feel right, but he couldn't put his finger on it. Had she told her parents about spending the holiday with him and it hadn't gone well? If so, he wanted to be there for her.

He continued walking. Loneliness wrapped its cold arms around him, and his heart started to ache. His dream was to come home to his woman after a long day. He used to daydream about what his wife would look like. What she'd be like.

He was starting to imagine her as Rose.

CHAPTER 17

S HE DIDN'T WANT TO GET OUT OF BED.
Not even her babies could tempt her. The bottom of her world had fallen out. Al and his family weren't just coming for the holidays—they were moving in with them.

Her parents had broken the news yesterday, when her papa came home for lunch. They'd held hands, tears in their eyes, and said her brother and his family were getting evicted for not paying back rent. Papa had said Al had finally agreed to learn the business and take over the barber shop, something he and Mama had always wanted but lost hope for.

The news was so shocking, so hurtful, she'd almost retched. Rose couldn't believe the timing. Al had never liked the shop, and they all knew it. Before she could speak, they'd assured her Al and his family understood they had to abide by certain safety guidelines due to the pandemic. They knew it wasn't going to be easy, but this was what family did. Rose and Al only needed to stay out of each other's way, and everything would be fine. She'd still have her own room. Al and Paulina would have his old one, and their girls would share the spare. After that, her parents had gone silent, clenching each other's hands.

She'd put a hand to her belly and reminded Papa how Al always said he was going to do the right thing and then didn't. How he'd always made fun of what Papa did for a living, swearing he'd never shave a man or cut his hair, like some servant.

Papa had shaken his head sadly and told her it didn't matter. This was the way it was going to be. When she'd looked at her mama, all she saw was the steel in her spine. She'd girded herself for what lay ahead, and Rose should too, from the hard look she'd given her. It was their house, after all. She'd never felt so alone.

Knowing there was nothing to discuss, she'd gone to her greenhouse and buried herself in preparing plants she might never sell to the public—anything to keep her from crying and screaming and losing it.

She was going to have to take the job.

Living here with Al and his family wasn't an option. The pandemic was stressful enough. She would break if she stayed.

Now she had to tell Vinnie. The news of his negative test should have been a reason to celebrate. She grabbed her phone after rolling out of bed. There were two texts waiting for her, and she read Vinnie's first.

Mornin', Rose! Didn't hear from you yesterday and something feels off. You okay? Need me to swing by before work?

She had to blink back tears. He knew her enough to know something was wrong.

She clicked on the text from the number she didn't recognize, and sure enough, it was the results of her Covid text. She clicked the link. *Negative.*

Something burst in her heart. They were free and clear to touch each other, and here she was, wondering if the possibility of what they could be had withered on the vine. No, she decided. If she was going to be here another six months at least, she wanted to spend every moment with him. She'd waited her whole life to be with him, and she'd be damned if she was going to miss a single second with him.

But he might think otherwise. He'd needed assurance she was staying in Orion before. He didn't want his heart broken. Neither of them did. If he said they'd be better off remaining friends, she'd find a way to live with it.

But a part of her would die inside.

She pressed her face into the pillow as hurt tumbled in her belly.

"Rosie!" Mama called through her door. "It's time for breakfast."

"I have work to do," she shouted back, knowing her mama wasn't going to leave her alone.

"You can do it after we eat. Rose, I know you're upset, but we all need to accept how it's going to be or go crazy. Now come on. Your papa is upset enough as it is. Do you want him to go to work with a heavy heart?"

What about *her* heart?

She rolled out of bed and shuffled to her dresser. Her hands didn't hesitate. She picked out pants and a shirt in all black.

When she reached the kitchen, her mama was worrying at her apron, and tears were already filling Papa's eyes.

"Sit down." Mama pointed to the table. "I made you something special."

She saw the traditional Easter bread in the center of the table. Tears slid down her face. "Mama—"

"Oh, Rose, you'll make me start crying along with you and your papa," she said, swiftly crossing with their cappuccinos. "We know this is hard, but we love you."

Papa took her hand. "So much, my Rosie. You know we can't just let Al and his family be put out on the street."

She nodded, her chest hurting. "But, Papa, you can't keep bailing them out either. How much do they owe this time with the rent and the credit cards?"

"Rosie!" Mama said.

"How much?"

"Twenty-six thousand dollars!" Mama said with an edge. "Does it make you feel better to know that your brother and his wife mismanage their money so badly?"

"They always have!" she responded, boggled by the amount. "Al is going to ruin your business, Papa. Mama just said he mismanages money. Have you thought about that?"

"He can't think like that," Mama said harshly. "His heart will break. This isn't a situation any of us want, but we'll find a way through it. We have to. You'll help me in the kitchen so I won't kill Paulina when she expects me to wait on her hand and foot, or raise my voice to my grandchildren when they run wild and break your grandmother's fine plates from Italy because their parents give them no discipline."

Rose only shook her head. It was going to be a nightmare, and she refused to be a part of it. Not even for her parents.

"We'll have to tighten our belts more since your papa will have to withdraw money from his retirement to help them, and I might try and find something too since Paulina isn't very employable or interested in working outside the home," Mama continued, "but the Fiornis have weathered hard times. We'll do it again. I mean, look at what you're doing. You're opening your flower shop. Your first video with Vinnie already had five hundred likes this morning."

Mama never checked things like that. Rose put her hand to her mouth. She had to say it. There was nothing else to do.

"I got a job," she said, softly because her throat was hoarse. "For a grocery store line that has health services and in-store pharmacies. I'll be moving out, and when Covid is over, I'll relocate to Milwaukee."

Her mother made the sign of the cross and murmured

what Rose imagined was a prayer.

Papa hung his head and started crying. "No, my Rose. Not when you just started your business. And not so far away."

She wiped under her nose and firmed her shoulders. "I don't see any other way, Papa."

"Is it a good job with a good salary?" Mama asked.

When Rose looked at her, she worried her lip. What could she say? Mama always knew if she was telling the truth. "It's less than I made before, but I knew it would be."

"How much less?"

"It's not important. It's a job." She had to remember that. Be grateful. Millions didn't have one. This way she could get out.

"But what will you be doing?" Mama asked.

She cleared her throat. "Helping the grocery store chain market expand Covid services."

"Oh, no, Rosie." Papa took her hand, his watery gaze breaking her heart. "It's important work, but not for you. You were already so depressed, and you're just coming out of it. Don't do it. Not for less money and not if you have to move to Milwaukee. You love New York. You love being close to your family and Orion."

Mama took Papa's other hand. "Joe, she knows what she loves. Rose, what about Vinnie?"

She only shook her head. Fresh tears rolled down Papa's face, but Mama nodded. She knew they had no chance if she moved. Vinnie's life was here. She'd have enough time to make good on her promise to help him stay in Orion. That was the only bright spot.

"I need to get going," she said, standing and kissing each of them on the cheek. "Thanks for making the bread for me. Maybe I'll be able to eat it later."

Her legs were shaky as she reached the doorway, but she made herself turn back. "I won't need the money you gave me, Papa. For my business. You can use it to help Al and his family. Take less from your retirement. Also, I'm spending Christmas Eve with Vinnie."

She walked down the hallway, and for once, Mama didn't call her to come back.

CHAPTER 18

WARREN WAS DRAWN TO AUNT GLADYS LIKE A BEE TO A flower.

Especially after hearing Amy was going to work for the woman. His wife had come home from a "get to know you" outing with their new town brimming with ideas for her new part-time consulting job. She'd even put on some Katy Perry and danced with him and the girls in the kitchen. He planned to keep encouraging this path, and this woman in the hot pink caftan was the key to his wife's transformation as much as a fount of knowledge about the town he was serving.

"You've lived here for decades, Aunt Gladys. Alice said you would give me the straight truth about any obstacles I might run into with the trust."

She picked up a pair of opera glasses from the counter and raised them to her eyes briefly. "You can see the bullshit pretty easy. Take Lucia Tesoro—"

"Antiques Anonymous." The woman reminded him of a pit bull.

"She's been bitching about paying for videos to highlight her store. She thinks I'm a crazy old bat for paying. Worse, she's bashing Vinnie and Rose by suggesting they're taking advantage of small business owners in dire straits. Not living up to the Friends & Neighbors motto we all agreed to. It's horseshit."

He couldn't agree more. "You perform a service, you get paid. This country was founded on capitalism. I don't expect she'd give a couch away for free if she found out the customer couldn't afford it."

"I'm going to use that," Aunt Gladys said, cackling. "People will bend anything to serve their purpose, and that's what Lucia's doing. She's got some others on her side, but in my opinion, they're being cheap and unkind."

Nodding, he said, "Can I be straight with you?"

"Of course! Good Lord, people tell me shit all the time running this shop. I've had men shop for their secret gay lovers, for heaven's sake. It's like a confessional in here even though I'm Jewish. Shoot!"

He had to smile at that. "They're jealous of your success. You've managed to make more money than they have in these times, and you've done it by being smarter than them. I'll bet you were one of the first to do a promotional video."

"Besides Alice and company, yes!" She peered at him through the opera glasses again. "But I'm screwy that way. Oh, here's Clifton. Hello, darling! On a break?"

The older man gave what could only be described as an elegant nod as he shrugged out of his tailored outerwear and hung it on the coatrack. "Yes, my love. Hello, Warren. I hope you and the family are doing well."

Warren wished he could look that cool. "We're great. Looking forward to Christmas. Amy is loving it here, and I have your fiancée to thank for it."

Her passion was back, and he was so there for it. They were rediscovering each other all over again over eggnog or spiced wine in front of the fireplace after the kids went to bed. Coming to Orion was like having a second honeymoon.

Plus, they weren't just talking about the kids or his work. She had plenty of ideas about how to help the town. It was like they were partners again on more than child-rearing, and he was loving it so hard.

"Your wife came in at the perfect time," the woman said, embracing Clifton as he joined her behind the counter. "I believe in timing. Don't I, Clifton?"

"You do, indeed."

"Warren was just asking what potholes he might need to avoid in town," Aunt Gladys said, brushing her hands down the man's velvet jacket. "This is the ship that launched five thousand likes so far for that video, Warren. Doesn't he wear it dashingly?"

"I'd date him," he said, knowing he could tease Clifton. "Talk about a brilliant marketing plan."

"And now your lovely wife is going to help me give my business another boost," Aunt Gladys said.

"She's good at taking photographs too," Warren said. "I know she's going to take your social media to a new level."

The woman raised her arms over her head. "I love it! I'm up to my elbows with the shipping."

"I have a solution for you on that front," Clifton said. "Which is why I came by. I mentioned it to Maria, and she said she would love the extra work."

She hugged him tightly. "You have the best instincts about people, Clifton. Warren, have you met Maria? Oh, of course you have. You've been to the chocolate house."

"Her Mexican hot chocolate is out of this world."

"So are her tamales, moles, and other dishes. She's a wonderful chef," Clifton said. "My love, we're having a small wedding—"

"Since you nixed a Zoom elopement," she shot back with a teasing wink. "Not that we've set a date yet."

"We will. I wondered if you would be open to Maria making the wedding meal for us. I would like to give her the work. Besides, I believe she would create an elegant meal for us given the dishes she brings in for Alice and me at lunch every once in a while."

"Pumpkin soup, Clifton?" she asked. "I remember when she brought some in for you last month. My God, that was heaven in a soup bowl."

"If she can do it, yes," he said. "We'll agree on the menu. She still hasn't shared her personal circumstances, being as she's the soul of professionalism, but I sense she has much on her plate."

"We all do," Aunt Gladys said, picking up her opera glasses again. "Fine. Tell her she's hired. Now we really need to set a date."

"In due time, but I will execute payments straightaway, don't worry."

"Of course you will. But, Clifton... We're too old to be living in sin much longer," she said with some snark.

Clifton merely lifted his brow in her direction.

Warren could barely contain his mirth, but he changed the subject because he believed in helping a guy out. "Anyone else I need to be concerned about?"

"Manny Romano can be a pain in the butt, and if he and Lucia join forces, they'll certainly make a nuisance of themselves. They could rally Fanny Janson, but if they do, I'll pay her a visit and threaten to short out her hooded hair dryers. She's afraid of me because I threatened to have one of my mob customers kill her after she left me under one of them for too long and turned my hair green before a cousin's wedding."

"Kill her?" Clifton asked, and Warren had to admit he was thinking it too.

"I was only kidding!" She pointed to her head. "Do you see me looking good with green hair? She was negligent. I had to make sure she'd never do that again. Trust me, she didn't."

New York, Alice would say, and colorful stories like these were why Amy was so excited to work with

Aunt Gladys. But Warren understood the deeper reason without having to ask. This woman wasn't afraid to voice her opinions or tell someone off. Amy had always folded under her mother's pressure, but perhaps she'd be able to steel herself under Aunt Gladys' tutelage. Warren certainly hoped so. And if she ended up threatening him with a mob hit courtesy of Aunt Gladys' connections because he forgot to take the trash out, he'd take it like a man.

"You are ever inventive," Clifton said. "When I was in Clara's employ, I might have threatened harm to one or two deserving parties."

She batted her eyelashes at him. "Oh, Clifton. That's so hot. You'll have to tell me all about it tonight."

Warren laughed. "I'm going to talk to Clara about adding an advertising budget for the town for some commercials. It would make sense for the town to have a social media account. Right now, the trust could run it."

"You won't get the local politicians to do it, let me tell you." She tapped her purple fingernail on the counter. "You thinking Amy might take the reins on that too?"

Warren shrugged. "I'm on the fence. I don't want there to be a conflict of interest. I'm managing the trust. Hiring my wife might be considered nepotism."

The door opened, and Warren glanced over his shoulder.

"Rose!" Aunt Gladys exclaimed. "Tell me you've met Warren."

"Hello," answered the woman, dressed all in black. "I... Oh heck. Aunt Gladys, may I speak to you alone for a moment?"

Aunt Gladys came around the counter. "Come, let's go back to my office."

The two wandered off, and Clifton folded his hands over his chest.

"That was Rose Fiorni, right?" Warren asked. "She's the one behind the camera with the videos."

Clifton looked off in the direction they'd gone. "Yes, that's her."

"She seemed out of sorts," he commented.

"She did indeed," Clifton said with his usual restraint.

Aunt Gladys reappeared, her brow knit with tension. "Clifton, how would you feel if I told anyone who dared ask me why I was buying condoms in the pharmacy that I was afraid I might get pregnant?"

Warren had to give the man credit. He didn't so much as blink when Warren almost fell off his chair.

"If anyone had the nerve to ask me about it, I would tell them we weren't ready to start a family," the older man replied with complete conviction. "We're not even married yet, after all."

Aunt Gladys hugged him. "Exactly what I thought. I need my purse. Clifton, do you have time to tend the store?"

"I can do it," Warren said. "Go on! I don't know anything about Italian fashion, but I've been selling soulless banking products for years."

Aunt Gladys laughed. "Then you'll be perfect. I won't be fifteen minutes. Clifton, we can walk together until you're back at the chocolate shop."

"Are you sure you don't want my help buying the requisite prophylactics?"

Aunt Gladys twined her arms around his neck. "You'd do that for me?"

"I would never want your reputation to be tarnished. We might be living in sin, but I fully intend to make an honest woman of you. I dare anyone to say otherwise."

She bumped him with her hip after she let go of him. "You're too good to me. Warren, Rose will stay holed up in my office. Even if you hear a scream, you are not to engage her. You get me?"

"I get you." He whistled softly, wondering what was afoot. "I'll sit back behind your counter, pick up a magazine, and look at all those handsome unaffected men you told me about."

Clifton shot him a quizzical glance.

"Your fiancée tells me she's immune to them. I'm still trying to break my habit."

Aunt Gladys barked out a laugh, but Clifton merely said, "From what I've heard, dressing up as a dinosaur is more your style."

God, what did that say about him? "Aunt Gladys, I expect to learn a lot by running your shop while you're out. Maybe I should volunteer to do this for a few of the other shop owners beyond the interviewing I've been doing to get more familiar with their current situations." He was hoping to start dispersing actual grants shortly, assuming the incorporation paperwork for the trust was approved by New York State. God, the red tape on helping people blew his mind sometimes.

"You would be most welcome at the House of Hope & Chocolate," Clifton said, helping Aunt Gladys with her coat before donning his own. "I believe Alice mentioned having you volunteer on occasion so you could work together like you did in the old days at your neighborhood chocolate stand."

"She did," Warren said with a smile. "Be good experience for me in terms of the trust. I can get a real sense of what's going on in the town."

Later he would tell Amy as firelight danced over her bare skin.

"By the time I'm done buying rubbers with Clifton in the local pharmacy, believe me, you're going to have a whole lot of 'sense.' Heck, I might even be surprised at the ripple effects from this outing. Come, darling. Our family planning adventure awaits."

As he watched them leave, Clifton agreeing to this ruse, his thoughts went to the philosophical. What lengths did one go to for love?

He knew he'd go to any.

CHAPTER 19

THE MOMENT VINNIE OPENED THE DOOR, ROSE RUSHED him.

She had her arms around him before he could blink. Then, whispered into his neck, he heard, "I'm negative too. Just please hold me and don't let go for a little bit. Okay?"

Usually her voice was strong, even playful. Today it was so soft it sounded like it had been worn down by sandpaper. He maneuvered them to close the door and cradled her against his chest. She'd buried her face against him. To hold her now, even this way, enveloped him with so much warmth and affection his throat clogged up.

"I've got you, honey. I just knew something was wrong when I didn't hear from you yesterday." He'd planned on swinging by her house on the way to work.

She tightened her arms around him and murmured, "In a minute."

When she suddenly started crying, his heart wrenched. He picked her up and carried her to the edge of his bed, putting her in his lap. She fit perfectly. "Oh, Rosie."

She curled into him, sobbing, and he nestled her close, tears filling his own eyes. God, whatever it was had ripped her heart out. Even as a little girl, he'd never heard her cry like this when she'd gotten hurt on the playground. Then again, this was no scraped knee or childish insult. This was grown-up stuff, the kind that could change your life. He understood this kind of gut-wrenching crying. He'd given into it when his mama and aunt got Covid and became so ill they had to be put on respirators. He'd cried when Aunt Alessa hadn't made it and he'd cried when Mama had. The night she'd decided to sell the restaurant, he'd bawled for what seemed like an hour.

He stroked her hair and kissed the top of her head, doing his best to comfort her. No one had been able to comfort him in his time of loss. Hank had stood by him while he mourned at Aunt Alessa's grave, but there'd been distance between them. Having someone hold you, comfort you in your worst moments was a powerful gift. He knew from growing up, and he wanted to give Rose every comfort he could.

When she finally quieted, she whispered, "I'm so sorry I lost it. I'd planned to be so strong. I had a speech and a plan. But do you have a tissue?"

He picked her up because he didn't want to break their connection. After so long, he was going to hold her every chance he got. "I'll do one better," he said, reaching into his top drawer for his favorite handkerchief. "My nonna handstitched this for me out of her father's favorite dress shirt from Rome. She said I got my singing voice from him. I've always treasured it."

"That's so nice," she said, sniffing as she took it. "Oh, God, I need to quit crying."

"But it feels like the end of the world," Vinnie said as he sat back down with her, his throat thick with emotion. "It's okay, Rosie. You don't have to try to be tough with me. We're making a go of this, remember?"

That sent her into a fresh round of tears, and his alarm bells started clanging. Why would that make her cry?

He told himself to be patient, but his stomach clenched, wondering what had hurt her so.

Moments later, she said, "I got a job offer."

He was glad he was sitting down. She was going to tell him she was leaving. That had to be it. "Why don't you start from the beginning?"

"Al and his family are moving in," she began, and he listened while she told him the rest.

His own reaction was like an aria, angry in places, sorrowful in others, and downright confused by the end of it. "Why would your parents do this? To themselves and you? I know he's family, but it's twenty-six thousand dollars of debt. Plus, the whole Covid angle."

"I know! I love them so much, and I know they love me. Mama even made me Easter bread this morning because it's my favorite."

Mrs. Fiorni must be feeling guilty all right. That bread took hours from start to finish, meaning she must have gotten up well before dawn to start. Plus, it was usually only made once a year. "Of course they love you. And sure, Al is their son, but I remember him making fun of your dad's profession in school. He was ashamed of him shaving men and cutting their hair."

"And sweeping the floors," Rose said. "Al used to point to the broom in the kitchen and say that was women's work. He's such an asshole. But, Vinnie, I don't see another way now. I can't live there."

"Of course you can't—"

"And I can't ask them to keep paying my health insurance and helping me out with my business, not when Al owes so much. They're having to take more money out of Papa's retirement. I can't be a burden."

He decided on the spot. "You'll stay here. I'll sleep on the couch at Hank's in the office."

She raised her head, her moss green eyes swimming with tears. "Don't talk crazy. I'll find a cheap place in

Yonkers."

"No way you're moving there," Vinnie said. "It's dangerous, especially if you're living by yourself."

"I'll be careful." She edged off his lap. "It's all I can afford with this new job."

He ran his hand through his hair. "Tell me more about it. Doesn't sound like it has a good salary if you need to live in Yonkers."

"It's entry-level," she said and laid it out for him.

By the end, his jaw was locked. She'd have to move to Wisconsin when the world got back to normal.

They'd never see each other if she did that, and they both knew it.

His heart was already breaking.

"I know what you're thinking," she said, taking his hand as she met his eyes. "I thought it too. Why do you think I started crying the moment I saw you? I had planned to charge in here, explain the situation with the job, tell you that I want to spend every moment with you until I have to move, and end by suggesting that we make love. Today. I even had Aunt Gladys buy me condoms just to be prepared in case you said yes."

His entire body went on alert. "You did *what*?"

She gestured at him, her long curly hair falling over her shoulder. "Well, I couldn't barge into the town pharmacy on my own, could I? I don't have a car, and after my talk with my parents, I couldn't very well walk back in and ask to use Mama's. She would have wanted to know why or, worse, insisted on coming along. God, this is when I miss the city! And either Aunt Gladys was having fun with me or she thinks we're going to have a lot of sex. See for yourself."

He was still reeling from her word bombs. She grabbed the bag she'd dropped by the front door and crossed to him. Unzipping it, she turned it upside down and dumped pack after pack of condoms onto his bed.

"Holy hell, Rose," he exclaimed. Aunt Gladys had likely

bought every product on the counter, given the wide variety of sizes, fits, and even colors. He flushed at the thought of Aunt Gladys having anything to do with this.

"We should be grateful the pharmacy doesn't sell the flavored kind," she joked, pushing some packs out of the way and sitting at the edge of his bed. "I still can't believe I did this. Or that she did."

His brain was totally fried. "But why Aunt Gladys?"

"Because I couldn't think of anyone else to ask," Rose said, hands on her knees. "I knew Alice would do it, but then she'd have to tell Hank—"

"I see your point." But he gestured to the pack of XXX on the bed. "But Aunt Gladys!" He still couldn't wrap his mind around it.

She started laughing. "She told me Clifton went to the pharmacy with her. They agreed that if anyone said a word they'd say they were being responsible in their family planning. Oh, I was so upset and shocked, that didn't hit me until just now. God, it's kinda funny."

"*Kinda*?" His lips twitched as her belly laughing continued. "It's madness, and yeah, it's epically funny. I would have paid money to see how people reacted in the pharmacy."

In a minute, he fully intended to circle back to her job and living circumstances, but he knew she needed to laugh. Sometimes it was the body's way of reminding a person that life wasn't all grief and sorrow. He laughed with her, pulling her close when she held up the extra-large pack and started guffawing.

"Clifton certainly is going to have some cred in town," Vinnie said, wondering whether he ought to thank the man. "Imagine that former butler walking into the pharmacy and doing this with Aunt Gladys."

"She said he was happy to do it," Rose said, wiping her eyes. "You know what else? She didn't even blink. I really appreciated that. But, Vinnie, if I'm going to be leaving town, then we need to think this through. In the beginning, you asked me if I was staying, and I told you I was. But now... I don't want to hurt you."

Too late. "What about you?"

"I've waited my whole life to be with you. I'm not going to let anything screw that up for me. Except if you want to call it off. Oh shit, I'll need to buy a used car so I can come visit you from Yonkers. What am I thinking? I can't afford that. Maybe there's a bus."

"A bus? Right. If you need to use a car, you use mine." He tipped up her chin. "But you aren't moving to Yonkers."

"Vinnie—"

"Don't argue with me, Rose. You'll stay here. I'd stay too, but you're a girl from the neighborhood. I can't do that to your rep. Now about this job... I need your honest answer. Do you want to take the job?"

Her already sallow coloring went gray. "I have to—"

"That's not what I asked," he said softly.

She looked away. "Vinnie, of course I don't want to take an entry-level job with a shitty salary that would require me to work on Covid and move almost a thousand miles from you and my hometown."

Then why the hell was she considering it? "You want to keep working at The Dreamer's Flower Shoppe, right? And working on our videos."

"I still plan to help you."

He fell for her even harder, then and there. "We're talking about you, Rose."

Standing, she walked over to his large-screen TV. "There's no other way. I can't take that money from my parents to start the business now, and I can't ask them to keep paying my COBRA. I had to cash in my 401K at a huge loss to pay for my apartment in the city when I was furloughed before my lease was up in July. Being furloughed, I didn't get unemployment—oh, it's so embarrassing to even admit I have it now, although I'm grateful. I don't have any savings. Vinnie, I have to take the job. Even if I don't want to. It will give me health insurance and a salary, even though it will be tight. I mean, I'm lucky. I actually got a job in this market. I should be jumping for joy."

He stood up and grabbed her to him before sitting back down on the bed, bringing her with him. "Be grateful then. Take it as a sign from heaven that you're still marketable. That there are people looking out for you. But, Rose, you told me not too long ago that I wouldn't be happy moving to Chicago to be a plumber. Don't make me say the same to you."

"But you have—"

"My place, which I'm giving to you."

Her eyes swam. "Vinnie—"

"Don't make me get tough with you," he said, his voice rough. "Dammit, Rose, this is what friends and neighbors do—they support each other—and now we're more than that. Did my best friend not pay for my salary from his savings? Let me do this for you."

"But I need to pay for COBRA, and it's almost one thousand a month. I have to take the job."

He didn't hesitate. "Those are your main concerns? That you need a place to live and health insurance?"

"Oh, come on, Vinnie. These are big ticket items."

Taking her hands, he met her gaze. "There's no way I'm losing you. Not when we've just started. I have a simple solution. Marry me. I have health insurance. Then we can live here together."

She shot to her feet. "*What?*"

He pulled her back down beside him, realizing he didn't feel anything but peace inside. "It's perfect. If we get married, you'll have health insurance, and no one will say a word about you living here with me. My great-great-grandparents had an arranged marriage in Verona when she lost her family in a fire, and they fell crazy in love afterward. This kind of thing is in the Scorsese blood."

Her eye roll didn't have its usual sangfroid. "This isn't last century, Vinnie. This whole idea is crazy!"

"Wouldn't it be a little nutso to tear your heart out and give up on your dream to move into some slumlord's apartment in Yonkers and then Milwaukee? Plus, how are you going to afford a car and car insurance when you can barely afford rent?"

"That's not fair—"

Her voice had cracked, which he took as a good sign. "Also, what better face for your business than your doting husband? Because, Rose Fiorni, I totally dote on you."

Her hand lifted to her heart, and he finally noticed she was wearing all black again. He couldn't let it happen. He couldn't let the vibrant, flower-loving Rose go into hibernation.

"Doting isn't love."

"You know, when I was walking home last night after I didn't hear from you, I started to imagine what it would be like to come home to you. I liked the thought. A lot. Rose, I'm not saying we love each other the way people usually do when they get married, but I'm at least on the way. I think you are too. We're going to get there. Only as married people."

"This truly is the craziest thing I have *ever* heard out of your mouth, Vinnie Scorsese," she said, her moss green eyes dark.

Yet her color was coming back, and she seemed to be feeling the same excitement stirring in him. She wanted this. She'd always wanted him.

"Are we not sitting on a bed covered in condoms bought by a couple old enough to be our grandparents? During a global pandemic? How could things get any crazier?"

"But we haven't even kissed—"

He covered her mouth with his own, gentling it immediately. This was their first kiss, a kiss they would remember for the rest of their lives.

He had to make it good enough to convince her to marry him.

CHAPTER 20

HIS LIPS WERE SO HOT.

And yet so soft after that first mad brush. It was as much caress as kiss, and her eyes fluttered shut, her heart beating faster. Her toes even curled in her boots.

She'd imagined kissing Vinnie Scorsese her whole life, but the reality was better than any fantasy.

Because she could, she threaded her fingers through his thick, curly black hair. He murmured against her mouth, and she opened for him. His tongue swept in, inviting her, and she joined him in the dance. His hand cupped her cheek as he changed the angle of their kiss, still so gentle, still so hot.

When he finally lifted his head, his dark eyes were mesmerizing. "Oh, Rosie, see how good we are together?"

She nodded and caressed his nape, studying his face. She'd had enough first kisses to know this one was special. If that wasn't enough, he only had eyes for her, his gaze so intent the gold rims of his irises burned as bright as sunshine.

"You are so beautiful," he said, kissing her softly again. "I'm so glad I don't have to block it out anymore."

"Me too." She slid her hands down his shoulders to his biceps. "I've been thinking about this for what seems like forever. Vinnie, it's more wonderful than I could have hoped. But I really can't accept your offer." The very thought was thrilling, but...it was insane, wasn't it?

His dark brows knit together. "You're being stubborn."

She threw her hands up in the air. "No, I'm being— Oh, I don't know what I'm being. It's an untenable situation. What if we got married, and it doesn't work out? Have you thought of that?"

He drew in a breath as if striving for patience. "You're right to think through every eventuality. Here's how I see it. We like each other a lot. Always have. We feel good around each other. Right?"

She stood up and took the chair in the corner to give herself a clearer head, but it didn't work because it gave her a view of the Mountain Roses she'd given him, perched on the windowsill by his bedside. "We do."

"I don't think we'd screw that up. We started out as friends. If we decide we're not going to make it as husband and wife, then we can call it and go back to being friends. Rose, I'm not a man to hold grudges, and even though I don't know anything about your time in the city, I know *you*. You're not the sort to hold them either. We would stay married until you could make it on your own and then divorce. I would look on it as helping a friend. If Hank were a girl, I'd do it for him. Understand?"

It wasn't the sexiest proposal, but his logic had merit. "Vinnie, it's a big deal. We can't pretend otherwise."

"Yet you can't get affordable health insurance unless you take a sucky job. I assume you looked into all the options."

"Healthcare is expensive, Vinnie. My COBRA had better coverage for the price if you can believe it. Especially for prescriptions. When I went on the health exchange to shop, I was shocked at the choices. I did some research and found out New York has the highest annual health insurance premiums in the country. How is it you have health insurance, anyway? The old policy?"

"No, Hank continued the policy for long-term employees his dad started. Got it way back for Marty and himself. Hank put me on it when Mama canceled the policy for Two Sisters."

"What a nice thing to have," Rose said. "Mr. O'Connor gets points for that. I didn't know."

"He's not the kind to advertise, but he got a good policy and the rates have stayed pretty reasonable. You know Hank. He likes to do right by people too. So he kept it. I believe in doing the right thing too, which is why you'll stay here, where you belong, and keep growing your dream business."

He put his hands on her shoulders, and after so long without being touched by anyone, let alone Vinnie, his presence was potent to her senses.

"Rose, it sucks that the only way for you to get health insurance and a safe place over your head is to take a soul-sucking job you don't want or marry someone, but as Derrick said the other night, we're in a plague. From my perspective, all regular bets are off."

"But marriage!" She put her hand on his chest. "This is a *big* deal."

"We don't need to make it one. I only see upsides. We'll get to hang out, without masks, I might add, and kiss and do more. If you want."

She very much wanted.

"And we'll help each other with our businesses. Because if you leave and take this job, you won't have time to help me. I'm not saying this to make you feel guilty, but if you go, then I'll end up moving to Chicago to take over my uncle's business."

The ache in her chest intensified. "Not that."

"You say that, and yet you would be doing the same.

You're no more a grocery chain Covid marketing assistant or whatever the hell they're calling it than I'm a plumber."

God, she could feel his words swaying her, encouraging her to take what she so badly wanted. "I never knew you could be this persuasive."

He traced her cheekbone. "Talking is what I'm good at. That's why I can persuade people to buy things. And you, sweetheart, are good at capturing it. But your greatest gift is with your flowers. Rose, I'm telling you. I just know your flower shop is going to be a success."

She did too, but she needed more time. When had marriage become the way for her to get it? "I can't believe I'm actually considering this."

His arms brought her to his chest, and she laid her cheek there, listening to the steady thumps of his heart. "Rose, I'm falling in love with you. I know it's not very romantic, but I think we have a good shot here. I promise to give it my all."

She would too. "It's not like the being with you part would be hard. I *want* to be with you. It's the longer-term stuff that worries me. Like, do we fit so well that we're going to want to share the rest of our lives together? Have kids together? Under different circumstances, we'd take more time to find out."

"Make a home together," he added, stroking her hair. "God, I love your hair. If you want to put it back straight, I would never tell you otherwise, but I love the feel of your thick, curly hair between my fingers."

"I feel the same way about yours," she said, looking up. Would their kids have curly hair like them? Probably. She wondered how many of them would have his singing voice. Oh, to hear them sing together... "Vinnie, maybe you should talk to Hank, and I should talk to—"

"Aunt Gladys? She does seem to be our matchmaker." He gestured to the bed and laughed. "Thank God my mama doesn't come over. Can you imagine the look on her face—"

They both started laughing. They kept their arms around each other as they laughed, and for some reason that helped her make up her mind. "If Aunt Gladys doesn't tell me I'm crazy, I'll go for it."

"I'll talk to Hank when I go to work, which I need to get to pretty soon, by the way. If he can't come up with a compelling argument against it, then we'll marry as soon as possible. In the meantime, you'll stay here. Do you want me to go to your parents' house and pack up your stuff?"

Thinking about her parents was nearly unbearable right now, but she couldn't let him do that. "No, I'll tell them in person. Vinnie, I'll still need to spend time in my greenhouse for my business."

He nodded crisply. "I don't trust Al not to be a jerk. When you're in the greenhouse, I want you to lock the door. You don't want him waltzing in without a mask on."

She could see him doing that all too easily. He'd always hated the greenhouse, complaining that he could have played soccer in the backyard if not for the space it took up. "There is no lock, but my parents said they laid down some rules. He's never listened to them before though, and I doubt he's going to start now."

His brow rose. "Then I'll put one on. Just to be safe."

"Vinnie, I'm so scared for my parents. They should get vaccinated early on because of their age, but—"

"We'll pray for them," he said, rubbing her arms as if to help her ward off a chill. "Next time I go to church, I'll light a candle."

She touched his chest. Because she could. She could do it whenever she wanted now. "I didn't know you went to church."

"Only to pray sometimes. I go at night or in the early morning when no one is around. For a while, it felt like the only tangible thing I could do for Mama. I lit a lot of candles during that horrible time, let me tell you. I might have prayed every prayer we learned in school. Being there usually gives me some peace."

"I'd like to go with you," Rose said, aware of how momentous it would be when they did. "We can light a candle together."

He lowered his head slowly and kissed her so softly, she sighed into him.

"We'll light one for us too." His mouth covered hers again. "And for your business." Another kiss punctuated that promise.

"And for you and your every dream," she said, cupping his beloved face. "You deserve everything you want too."

"Oh, Rose. This is why I know we have a chance. Right now, I have everything a man could ever want. You. A roof over my head. My mama healthy again. The best friend a man could ever ask for. Employment. And good neighbors like Aunt Gladys and Clifton."

Her mouth curved in a smile, hearing the warmth in his voice. In this moment, she felt like she had everything she needed too. That alone seemed insane after the day she'd had, but the feeling was only sweeter for it.

"Come on, let me kiss you a little more. This one time, Hank won't mind if I'm a few minutes late."

No, he wouldn't, but the burning question remained.

Would he think they were crazy?

The jury was out on what Aunt Gladys would say, but secretly, Rose couldn't wait to find out.

CHAPTER 21

HANK DIDN'T THINK HE WAS OUTRIGHT CRAZY.

But that was mostly because he was as pissed as Vinnie was about Al and the entire situation. "He's always been a jerk but this blows way past that to outright asshole," his friend ground out as they talked in Hank's office at break after the lunch hour. "How could he even think to put his parents and his sister in this position? As if Covid weren't bad enough. Oh, wait! I forgot. Because he's a narcissist. Alice loves that word."

Vinnie might have to start using it. "I'm trying to understand the family thing, and I'm sure Mr. Fiorni always had some secret hope his son would take over his shop."

Hank gestured to his place. "Yeah, my dad felt the same way."

Vinnie wished his mom had thought of it for him, but she was right. Their place had been about the food, first and foremost, and he wasn't a chef. "Still, it's not enough to explain this craziness to me. Mr. and Mrs. Fiorni are older and could get sick. And even if his business is doing okay, I doubt he has the kind of money to keep pulling Al out of debt. He'll never be able to retire."

"But that's what they've decided." Hank swore again. "Rose can't live with them. That's for sure."

"And she sure as hell can't move to Yonkers," Vinnie repeated.

"Hell no! Do you know how many bad things happen in Yonkers? One of my former servers lived there, and she said the police or fire sirens went off at least twice a day. Plus, she doesn't have a car. How can she afford that and car insurance?"

"That's what I said!" Vinnie gripped his knees. "She can't take this job just to get out and have health insurance. Don't get me started on the car situation. She said she'd take a bus from Yonkers to visit me."

Hank ran his hand through his hair. "Seriously? That's ridiculous! But marriage? I get your reasoning, but as someone who failed at it once, I can tell you that Rose is right. It *is* a big deal. You want to be in love with the woman. The entire shebang—another Alice word. God, I need a whiskey. Look, I can't tell you not to do it. Rose is wonderful, and I can see you two together. I only wish you didn't need to rush things. Fucking Covid. Fucking Al. Sorry, I'm swearing like a sailor."

"I cussed the whole way to work," Vinnie said. "She cried, Hank. Like 'sobbed on my chest' cried."

"Of course she did." Hank pinched the bridge of his nose. "It's a horrible situation."

"Do you think we should talk to Mr. Fiorni?" Vinnie asked.

Hank shook his head emphatically. "No. It's his business—literally—and his wife's. We can only take care of Rose. What if Alice and me gave her a loan? We would—"

"No way! You have two businesses you're trying to keep above water right now. She'd never take it anyway. I'd sell my car before that, but then we'd both have to take the bus."

"Not funny."

"Look, I know it's crazy, but this will allow me to help her as much as protect her. And I want to do that, almost as much as I want to live with her and enjoy all that goes with it."

Hank released a gusty sigh. "You mind if I call Alice and run this by her? I can't believe I'm this close to saying go for it."

"Call away." Vinnie gripped his knees as Hank called Alice and explained. It didn't take two minutes for Hank to hang up and tip his head back. "God help us, we're on board."

"You are?" He stood up slowly. Holy shit, he was getting married. To Rose Fiorni.

"Alice agrees that you two have a good shot of making it as a couple, and if it doesn't work out, then at least you've done something good for a friend. She said I'd do it for her and vice versa, and she's right. But she also mentioned that Warren is considering having the trust dispense grants to new businesses. She said she'll call him for a status update. I know he's still going through current applications as we speak, since he asked for a few more pieces of information from me."

"You think I should wait then? A loan for a new business wouldn't give Rose money to live on, would it?"

"No, but it would hopefully allow her to buy health insurance, although it's really expensive for a new small business owner. She'll have start-up costs, especially on the advertising side. Boosted social media videos aren't cheap."

He hadn't thought of that side of things. "Like how much? I haven't been involved in that part of the process."

"Depends on your budget, but it can be sizeable. We're talking thousands a month, Vinnie."

He muttered a swear word in Italian. "So good thing she won't need to spend money on rent, a car, and the insurance."

"Yeah." Hank stood as well. "What's the next step here? Is Rose talking to her parents?"

He wasn't looking forward to that conversation should it come to it. Despite everything, he respected them, but he didn't respect their decision. "No, she knew they couldn't be impartial. She's talking to Aunt Gladys."

Hank cleared his throat. "God, the condoms she and Clifton bought were for you and Rose, weren't they?"

Vinnie winced. "It's all over town already, huh? Terrific."

"They claimed they were for them, but everyone knew better. Clifton wouldn't even tell Alice the truth."

Vinnie wished he could ask his friend to keep her in the dark, but they were a couple. "We didn't have sex, Hank."

He put his hands over his ears. "You didn't have to tell me."

No, he hadn't, and that's why they were friends. "I wouldn't. Not when she's so worked up. But I'll be honest, I want Rose like crazy. The blinders are finally off, and all I can think about is how gorgeous and sexy she is."

"That's good," Hank said, shifting his weight. "It's the way things should be. Only...Vinnie, I don't want you to think a marriage is only about that. It has to go deeper."

"It's early yet, but I feel it stirring in my heart. Hank, when I listened to her cry earlier and thought about her leaving...it was like someone had taken an axe to my chest. I don't think I would have felt like that if my feelings weren't deep."

"It's good to understand how you're feeling right now. Sometimes bad news is like cold water and clears the head. But there's a lot you don't know about each other. What if you're not compatible enough to make it work?"

He faced his friend. "I know what I'm walking into as much as anyone does who gets married. Maybe more even."

His phone buzzed in his pocket. Taking it out, he read Rose's text.

Aunt Gladys doesn't see a negative given the circumstances. We're going into it with our eyes wide open. She said Warren was thinking about grants for new businesses, but she doesn't think it would be enough to live on and start up. Also, I can't wait. Al and his family are moving in tomorrow. Mama left me a voicemail.

He texted her back that Hank and Alice were both on board. Then he set the phone on Hank's desk so his friend could read the text. When he looked up, he read his friend's thoughts. "Don't be sad it's like this for me, Hank. I'm not. Be my best man and stand up for me."

"I'd shake your hand right now if I could," Hank said. "Looks like you're getting married before Alice and me, huh? I'll get right on those boutonnières."

Vinnie snorted out a laugh. "I've already submitted my ideas on yours to Rose."

"Can't wait to see them. Happy to return the favor."

They both gave a harsh laugh to cover their surging emotions.

"When are you moving Rose out?" Hank asked after clearing his throat. "Before Al arrives?"

"Let me text her and see." Moments later, he had her answer. "Yes, today. Let me tell her I plan to go to her parents' place with her. She shouldn't do it alone. Plus, I need to tell Mr. and Mrs. Fiorni I'll take care of her." He wouldn't feel guilty that he wouldn't be asking for her hand the traditional way. The circumstances were hardly traditional.

"They know you will, Vinnie," Hank said. "Alice and I will bring our SUVs over to help you guys. I'll gather up the boxes we have around here for her, and you can text me when you've finished talking to the Fiornis. If we move fast, we can get it done before the dinner rush."

Damn, but he had a good friend. "Thanks, man."

"You'll stay with Alice and me until the wedding, of course," Hank said.

"No! I'll sleep on the couch in here if that's okay. I can shower at my place when Rose isn't there."

Hank gave a full glower. "Bullshit. We have an en suite bedroom that opens to the back patio. You can come and go as you please. Don't make me set Alice on you. Also, your mama will feel better knowing you're living in a home and not on a couch in my office. She's going to have enough of a reaction when you tell her, I expect."

Yeah, he had no idea what his mama was going to say. "Got any pointers on that?"

Hank opened his arms. "I don't envy you, but you can tell her I'm on board. That should help some."

Vinnie nodded. "We can't both be idiots on this one, right? She always said you had a good head on your shoulders."

"So do you, which is why I know you're not rushing into this without having considered the implications."

Someone knocked on the door, and Hank called, "Come in."

His father stood in the doorway holding two envelopes. "Hope I'm not interrupting. I had something I wanted to give you both. Independent of Christmas." He stopped talking abruptly and regarded them with the same eagle-eyed scrutiny he'd used when they were kids. "You two okay?"

Vinnie lifted a shoulder and sent Hank a look before saying, "I'm getting married to Rose Fiorni. Just happened. I haven't told my mama yet, but I plan to share the news later. I'd be grateful if you didn't say anything to her until then."

"Of course," Mr. O'Connor said, inclining his chin. "Congratulations. She's a wonderful girl. I can see how you'd fit."

He did? "Thank you."

The man stared at his shoes for a beat before looking Vinnie straight in the eye. "Um...seeing as how we're talking about marriage, Vinnie, I'd like to ask for your blessing to marry your mother. I love her and she loves me, and neither one of us sees any reason to wait when we know what we want. Hank, I hope you'll give us your blessing too."

While it wasn't a surprise, Vinnie hadn't expected him to ask for their blessing. That was kind of touching. "You have it, Mr. O'Connor. You've made her happy, and that's all that matters to me."

"Dad, you have mine too," Hank said with a wry shake of his head. "You know Alice would say you're on the path of major transformation or something, right? Mom would be happy for you."

"Thank you, son." The older man coughed. "I talked to your mom about it when I visited her grave, and a cardinal landed on her tombstone. You remember how she loved to watch them from the kitchen window, especially in winter. I knew she was giving me her blessing."

Vinnie could barely speak over the sudden pressure in his chest. "That is a beautiful sign, Mr. O'Connor."

He cleared his throat again. "Well, I'm grateful to you boys for making that easy on an old man. I walked around the block three times before I could muster the courage to come inside. And me an old vet from 'Nam. Ah, never mind me. Vinnie, where do you and Rose plan on living?"

"At my current place, Mr. O'Connor."

"I see," the man said, tapping the envelopes against his thigh. "Well, I'll be asking your mother to marry me on Christmas Eve, just so you know. For now, I wanted to give you these. Should I lay them on the desk?"

Before Mr. O'Connor wouldn't have cared a whit about masks or social distancing, and Vinnie marveled again at the power of love to change someone. "Let me give you some room."

He stepped away from the desk, and the older man laid down the envelopes and stepped back to the doorway. He and Hank took turns picking them up. One glance at the paper in that envelope had Hank lifting his gaze to his father. "A thousand-dollar gift certificate to Old World Elegance? Dad!"

Vinnie opened his too. Sure enough, he had the same thing. "Mr. O'Connor, what are you thinking?"

"I'm thinking that my boy and his best man deserve new suits for his wedding." He shifted on his feet. "That was before I knew Vinnie was marrying Rose. Anyway, I know money is tight, and I wanted to do something for you two. Please don't fight me on this. It would mean a lot to me if you simply accepted it. Your wedding is a special occasion. Both of yours."

"But, Dad, it's a thousand dollars apiece!" Hank said, holding up the certificate.

"I asked Aunt Gladys how much a nice suit from her place would cost for a once-in-a-lifetime occasion and she laughed. Made me tell her what I had in mind. She said she could dress you both up right for this amount."

Hank had tears in his eyes. "Dad, I... Thank you. This means a lot. Alice will... Oh, hell, Alice will probably twirl around in a circle and talk about generosity being a subset of kindness or something."

"I owe that girl so much," Mr. O'Connor said. "And Vinnie, I know we have a long ways to go, but I want you to know you can count on me for anything. You and my boy have always been brothers in your minds. Now it's going to be official. I plan on treating you as another son from now on."

That choked the hell out of him. "Two Brothers. It has a nice ring to it. Mr. O'Connor, I'd shake your hand if I could. You keep doing good by my mama. That's all I need from you."

"I imagined you'd say that," he said, nodding. "Your

Rose is as much a part of things as Hank's Alice."

His heart clutched. Yeah, she was now, and it helped knowing they had another person on their side. "Not only friends and neighbors, but family."

The man's eyes smiled—they actually smiled. "It has a nice ring to it. On that note, I'll let you two get back to it. Thanks for making an old man happy today."

He left and closed the door, leaving Vinnie to sink into the chair in front of Hank's desk. "Holy cow! When I think of how much your dad has changed, it makes me believe anything is possible." Frankly, he needed that hope.

"Alice has me convinced." Hank held up the gift certificate. "Can you believe this? I couldn't say no. Not after what he said."

"He had tears in his eyes!" Vinnie exclaimed.

"We all did," Hank said. "Christ, I didn't expect any of this when I got up this morning. My dad coming here with these gifts, asking for a blessing to marry your mama. You getting engaged to Rose. Speaking of..."

He turned to the small filing cabinet in the corner and pulled something out of the bottom drawer and set it down on the desk.

"That's the application to add a spouse. Or a kid, for that matter. I assume you're going to be using the...ahem... supply Aunt Gladys got you for a while before you're ready to fill in that last part."

Vinnie eyed the folder, thinking about writing in the name of Mrs. Scorsese. The very thought did things to his heart. "Yeah, can't see us having kids for a while."

"Alice and I are in the same frame of mind," Hank said, nodding. "Kids are a big deal, even though we're both excited about the prospect."

Vinnie loved the idea of kids, but hell yeah, that had to be further down the line. "I'll need to figure out something simple for a ring since I can't afford much," he said. "No way I'm forgoing that."

"Well, you use that gift certificate to buy a suit for your wedding. You wear something old to mine. Got it?"

He stared at him. "Dammit, Hank."

"Since we're going to be brothers now, I'm telling you as your *older* brother."

"Crap, that got me, and you're only two months older." He finally shook his head. "All right. Only because money is tight. You were happy with where you bought Alice's ring, right?"

"Yeah," Hank said. "It's a simple engraved gold band. She loves it, but I hope to buy her something more when I can."

He would plan to do the same—should they get there—which he fully intended.

Negative thinking wasn't the way to start any new venture, least of all marriage.

CHAPTER 22

SHE WAS GETTING MARRIED.

Rose couldn't seem to take it in. Aunt Gladys had turned the store phone off and even pulled out a bottle of Nonino's Picolit grappa to toast her as much as bemoan the times they were in. At nearly three hundred dollars a bottle, Rose figured it was a hell of a way to seal her decision. She was so certain, in fact, she mentally started composing a rejection to the job offer while they were sitting there drinking grappa.

Either she and Vinnie weren't crazy or their friends were too. She was going to stop second-guessing. If they were doing this, she was giving it her all.

"I wish I could help you more, Rose," Aunt Gladys said, "but something tells me this is the kind of push you and Vinnie needed. I've watched your paths cross for a long time. Being back here and doing these videos together...you've done more than joined paths. You've laughed and flirted and found a connection worth risking everything for. Take it from an old lady. Sometimes impossible circumstances force truths in our hearts to make themselves known. You've always wanted Vinnie. Now he knows just how much he wants you."

Rose rocked in her chair. "God, I hope so."

Aunt Gladys' eyes twinkled over the canary yellow mask that matched her silk caftan. "Not everyone would think to offer marriage, Rose. And most wouldn't be brave enough to offer it."

She hadn't thought of that. God, she must be emotional because her eyes blurred.

"Here," Aunt Gladys said, pulling out a handkerchief from a drawer. "On the house. You can remember it as the day you and Vinnie decided to get married."

She took it and dabbed her eyes. "I want this to work so bad."

"Have you told him you love him yet?" she asked softly. "It helps ease people into a relationship. I was the first person to say it with my first two husbands. Italian men, as you know. Not as in touch with their feelings as Vinnie appears to be. But Clifton said it before I did, and I can attest to the power of hearing the words first."

"He doesn't love me yet," she said, folding the handkerchief. "But he cares."

"Of course he does. And you want each other. I believe I ran an errand for you earlier to that end. Not that we'll ever tell a soul. I've been getting calls that I plan to remember for some time. The funny things people say... You should get going and tell your parents. Do you need help moving?"

She gave the woman a smile she couldn't see. "You're a love to ask, but Vinnie is bringing me over there so we can break the news together. He's going to help me pack up, and Hank is coming too."

"You have a lot of friends in this town. I for one am glad to see you staying here. I would miss you something fierce if you had to move to Yonkers. Or Wisconsin. Now, go on, child. Time to gird yourself for the talk ahead."

"I wish I could hug you, Aunt Gladys," Rose said, holding out her arms.

"We'll do it like Alice does and put our hands over our hearts and close our eyes."

Rose joined her, her heart full to bursting. "I'd better go."

"You need me to talk to your parents, I will." She gave a deep sigh. "Hard to imagine what they must be going through. Al has never been liked in this neighborhood. He was a troublemaker growing up. Did some things people haven't forgotten. Your dad and mom have been covering for him for a long time. I hope this time will be different—for them and the rest of us. He was one angry boy."

Rose pressed the handkerchief to her eyes. She didn't want to think about Al, or the way he always ridiculed and hurt people. Ignored them until he needed them. She...she hated him. There, she'd let herself think it.

"Dry those tears," Aunt Gladys said. "You don't want people to see you coming out of my shop like this. The buttinskies will pepper you with questions you don't want to answer."

"You're right." She took some deep breaths.

The door chimed, and she turned around, hastily shoving the handkerchief behind her back. The sight of Vinnie nearly brought on more tears.

"I thought I'd walk with you," he said, his dark eyes never leaving hers. "Hello, Aunt Gladys."

"Hello, my boy," she said. "Your heart is as big as I always thought. Congratulations. When you feel like it, come back for some grappa. I opened the Nonino's Picolit."

"That's a nice grappa." He extended his hand to Rose. "We'll drink some when Hank and I come to buy our suits."

She laughed. "He gave you the gift certificates, did he? In all my years, I'd never have thought tough-as-nails Paddy O'Connor could turn into a model citizen. I hope it happens to more people. Al Fiorni comes to mind."

The thought depressed Rose. She couldn't imagine Al changing. "You'll have to tell me about it later, Vinnie."

"For sure. It was actually a bright spot. Come on, sweetheart."

She fluttered her fingers at Aunt Gladys and took Vinnie's hand. Outside, she said, "I'm so glad you're coming with me. Papa will be home on his lunch break. But I have to ask you one more time. Are you really sure?"

He took both her hands, steady as she'd ever seen him. "I'm completely sure."

With the lights of *Hope, Love,* and *Joy* shining on the hill outside the door, she decided this moment was as powerful as any to share the words in her heart. "Vinnie, I love you."

He let go of her hands and traced her cheek.

Before he could respond, she said, "I know it's early for you, so you wait to say anything. If...when you feel the same way, you tell me then. Okay? I only wanted you to know how I felt going into this."

She watched as he undid his mask and then her own. He lowered his head, his eyes gazing into hers, and pressed his mouth gently to hers. She felt herself fall. Complete surrender. She'd never imagined doing it, least of all feeling it.

Kissing her on the streets of their hometown, visible to their friends and neighbors, it was a public declaration if ever there was one. Even more so given Covid. This was his way of responding to her declaration, and it was as honest and sweet as it came.

When he lifted his mouth from hers, he touched her cheek briefly before raising their masks and taking her hand. "Come on."

On the way, he laid out his plan for moving her, and her heart overflowed when he told her that Alice had helped make the arrangements. Her mind must be shot by the shock of...well, everything. She'd forgotten about practical things like boxes and transportation.

At her house, she let them inside.

"Rosie! Is that you?"

Mama appeared in the hallway, Papa steps behind her. Anguish lit their eyes, and their faces were an overcast gray. "Yes, Vinnie and I have something to tell you."

Wiping her hands on her apron, Mama clapped her hands and said, "You two go into the parlor while I make us some coffee and a tray—"

"There isn't time for such things, Mama," Rose gently said. "Just take your apron off and sit with us." She wasn't going to do it standing up. Of all the times she'd imagined sharing the exciting news of her engagement, never had she foreseen this scenario.

Mama continued to stand, stricken, so Papa unfastened the apron for her and set it on a side table. Taking her hand, he led her into the parlor. Rose and Vinnie followed.

"Do you want us to put masks on?" Papa asked.

Oh, God, what to say here? It was their *home*.

"You probably should just in case, Mr. Fiorni," Vinnie answered. "We want you both to be safe."

Unlike Al. The thought lingered in the air like dust mites, burning her eyes.

Her parents found their masks, and soon they were sitting across from each other on the two gold couches that faced each other in the middle of the room.

Vinnie squeezed her hand. "First, Mr. Fiorni, I want to say that I regret not coming to you beforehand, but I hope you and Mrs. Fiorni will be happy to learn that Rose has agreed to be my wife. We would love to have your blessing."

"Yes, we would," she managed to squeeze out.

Her parents exchanged a timeless look before Mama said, "So soon? But you've barely started dating. What about the talk we had this morning? Rose, you didn't mention any of this."

She didn't want to talk about the reasons she and Vinnie had agreed to marry. Her parents would only feel guilty, and she wasn't sure whether they would give their blessing. She didn't need it, of course, but she wanted it something fierce.

"There was a lot going on," Rose said instead. "This is what Vinnie and I want. You know how I've always felt about Vinnie."

Mama uttered a dark, growly breath that suggested she had *many* more questions, but Papa patted her hand and said, "Of course we do, Rose. Does this mean you'll be keeping your flower shop then?"

She nodded, seeing the tears in his eyes. "Yes, Papa, and I hope it's okay for me to work in the greenhouse even though I'm moving into Vinnie's place."

"Of course you can!" Mama exclaimed. "It's your greenhouse as much as your papa's. Joe, tell your daughter."

"You know it's yours, Rosie, and it makes me proud to have you use it for your business."

She could tell he was forcing a smile behind his mask, but she couldn't bring herself to return it. "Thanks, Papa."

"I still want to know—"

"No, Carlotta," Papa said gently.

"But Joe!" She swung her head and gazed at him, gesturing to them.

He only shook his head. "Vinnie, thank you. You're a good boy, and my Rosie has always had her cap set on you. We welcome you to the family."

Mama sniffed and said, "Of course we welcome you! You're our son now, as much as—"

When her voice broke, Rose wanted to bury her face in Vinnie's shoulder. Mama knew why they'd hurried into an engagement.

"I'm going to pack up a few things now—"

"What do you mean?" Mama said, gesturing at them. "You can't live—"

"I'm staying with Hank and Alice until the wedding," Vinnie said. "Rose and I thought this would give her an opportunity to settle in with her stuff so we can make it home. You understand."

"You're getting married soon then?" Papa asked.

"Yes," Rose replied. "As soon as we can set a date. Weddings aren't the same this year anyway."

"You can still stand up for her, of course," Vinnie said. "We'll let you know as soon as we get it arranged."

She suddenly realized Al and his family would be at her parents' house by then. There was no way she was having them at their wedding. "It won't be a normal wedding, Mama. We only want you and Papa there and a few family members on Vinnie's side."

Mama inhaled harshly again like she was going to spew, but Papa said, "All right, Rosie. Do you need anything? Your mama and I want to pay—"

"Let's not talk about this right now," Rose said, her throat burning with emotion. "Money is tight all around, and we're keeping everything simple."

"But you need a dress." Mama threw her hands up as if the thought of getting married without a dress was crazy. "This is your wedding! A girl looks forward to this day her whole life."

"Mama, this is the time of Covid, and it's going to be different."

"Rose—"

"*Please, Mama.*" She put her hand to her heart. "Leave it alone for now. Okay?"

Papa slid his arm around her mama. "You go pack your things while I talk to your mama. When you're ready, I'll help you take them to Vinnie's."

"Hank and Alice are bringing boxes and their SUVs to help, Mr. Fiorni." Vinnie helped Rose to her feet and rubbed the small of her back. "No need for you to delay opening the barber shop."

Papa didn't answer, but Rose knew he probably couldn't, so she led Vinnie from the room. When they entered her bedroom, she closed the door. "I don't have much, but I don't know if you have enough space—"

"We can store anything you want at Mama's or Hank's. Of course, I need to tell Mama. That's after I get you settled."

She sat on the bed. "Vinnie, maybe you should tell her first. What if she's against it?"

"You let me talk to her," he said, looking around. "I like your room. I'm glad you didn't paint the walls black."

Moving off the bed, she punched his arm lightly. "That's a bad joke." And for a moment it had helped her forget, but only for a moment. "This just hurts so much, Vinnie."

He hugged her to him. "It's going to get easier. We're together. And we have so many people on our side. Even Hank's father, if you can believe it."

She lifted her head. "You mean it?"

Nodding, he kissed her lightly on the lips. "I do. Now, let's get going. I'm going to text Hank to bring the boxes. Alice can come once we're ready to haul things outside."

They worked quickly after that, getting everything ready to be boxed up. Toward the end, she needed some newspaper to wrap up a couple of curios, and she headed downstairs. When she reached the parlor, she stopped short. She craned her ear. Someone was sobbing. Her heart clutched, and she followed the sound. Her parents' bedroom door was closed, and from the pitch of the sound, Mama was inside.

Mama rarely cried like this.

Rose pressed her forehead to the door, tears streaming into her mask.

"We know why you're going, Rosie."

Turning around, she saw Papa standing in the hallway, a cup of her mama's favorite tea in his hand.

"Oh, Papa."

His eyes started to leak. "I'm sorry. We both are. Your mama and I can't say no to our boy. We're hoping the business will give him something he can be proud of and make his own. I know he's difficult to love, and we've prayed a lot because we don't want to feel that way. Or to wonder how we could have raised a son like him. Such thoughts weigh on me and your mama."

The teacup in his hand rattled, and everything within her ached as she met his eyes. "I know, Papa." She didn't understand, but she knew.

His mouth gave a glimmer of a smile. "You have a good heart, and I thank God that Vinnie is keeping you safe so you don't have to take a job you'd hate that would move you away from everything you love. And I'm going to pray to every saint who will listen to bless your marriage and your flower business. I've always trusted in your heart. It's like my own. That's why I'm not sobbing the way your mama is. Rosie, these are tears of joy."

She tore her mask off and crossed to him, kissing him on the cheek. Then she hurried back down the hallway before she started to sob herself.

CHAPTER 23

BEING NEW TO TOWN, AMY WASN'T EXPECTING TO HEAR A knock on the front door.

Warren looked over from making airplane sounds feeding Taylor dinner in the high chair as Madison said, "Who's at the door, Mommy?"

The questions continued, but since Amy was feeling better about herself and life—save that she didn't know Warren's size anymore and needed to return some of his Christmas presents—she discovered she didn't mind. "Why doesn't Mommy go and see? Daddy's got a good airplane routine going. Keep up the good work, Captain."

He saluted her with the spoon, making Taylor clap and Madison giggle. "Aye, aye, miss."

"She's Mommy, not miss," Madison corrected as she left the kitchen.

Looking through the side windows to the front door, she spied Aunt Gladys in a full-length black fur next to Clifton Hargreaves. She turned on the porch light and opened the door. "Well, hello. This is a surprise."

"Sorry to be calling around dinnertime but we came after closing the stores," Aunt Gladys said.

"I suppose we could have called, but we were hoping to have a moment of Warren's time," Clifton said. "Out here is fine."

"Of course," she said, curious. "Let me get him for you."

When she reentered the kitchen, Madison was sitting on Warren's lap, eating her chicken. "Clifton and Aunt Gladys are outside. They wanted to speak to you."

His face tensed. "Nothing's wrong with Alice or Hank, right?"

She hadn't thought of that. "They didn't seem super distressed. Let me take over here." When Madison tried to run after him, she called to her daughter, "Come help Mommy with Taylor. Then we can take a bubble bath. What color do you want tonight?"

Her big eyes brightened. "Blue!"

She undid Taylor from the high chair and took her to the sink. The squirming began as she used a wet cloth to wipe her face, but they got it cleaned. As she took the girls past the front door to the stairs, she could hear Warren and the others talking on the front porch.

"What's Daddy doing outside, Mommy?" Madison asked, stopping at the bottom of the steps.

"Talking to some of our new friends," she replied. "The lady out there is named Aunt Gladys, and Mommy's helping her with her business. The man helps run the chocolate shop with Aunt Alice."

"I hope he brought chocolates," Madison said, but she raced up the stairs after her.

She had the kids bathed and ready for bed by the time Warren joined her, and when he kissed Madison, she squealed. "Cold, Daddy."

"Oh, sorry, pumpkin." He rubbed his hands together to warm them. "Let me try that again. How about a story? *Somebody Loves You, Mr. Hatch* sounds like a good choice."

He'd read that book to her after they first got engaged.

The story about how an accidental note of kindness to a lonely man changed his life was a further embodiment of Warren's philosophy. Kindness and inclusion were the Holy Grail to her husband, and he'd seen them work wonders time and again at his childhood chocolate stand with Alice and Sarah.

Tonight, as he read it with his usual flair, she noticed that his voice was deeper and filled with great emotion. Soon he would tell her why, but in the meantime, she'd lie next to their two daughters and listen to a sweet story about the power of love and kindness.

After they put the girls to bed, Warren took her downstairs and poured them glasses of wine. Their new post-kid routine was to snuggle in the window seat in their bedroom and talk and more. Tonight he sat on the couch, patting the cushion next to him.

"Uh-oh," she said, sinking down beside him.

"Not uh-oh," he said with a wry look. "I just need to get my head around whether it's feasible to issue grants to new small businesses."

"The trust isn't official yet and you haven't even finished with the current businesses," Amy said. "Why the rush? What did Aunt Gladys and Clifton say?"

"They told me a story about someone in town—a new small business owner—who could use help. She needs health insurance and more. They didn't want to be indiscreet so they didn't share her name, but I'd say it's Rose Fiorni."

"She's the one doing the videos with Vinnie." Amy had already started to work for Aunt Gladys, commenting on the current posts that were up and running. They'd agreed she could kick into full gear with new content after the holidays.

"Clifton thought Clara would be supportive of greenlighting the new business grants, but wisely, he didn't feel it was right to call her about Rose's issue. I know Rose and a few others like her could use the help, but I have to get my thoughts together on what kind of parameters we'd need to set to make it work. It's even more high risk than offering support to the current stores in this climate, and I want to be a good steward of Clara's money."

She cuddled against his chest, and he put his arm around her. "And Christmas is right around the corner."

"When we got married, I promised you I wouldn't work on Christmas or New Year's," Warren said. "I don't want to break my promise to you or the girls. This is our time, and we're still settling in. I feel like we've been in reactive mode all year."

When they weren't bored out of their minds. "You didn't express any worries about me working a little on Aunt Gladys' social media."

"Liking and responding to comments isn't as work-intensive as creating loan parameters." He jostled her a little. "No offense."

She nudged him in the ribs. "Do I look offended? I know it's not the same. But if you need to work on this, you do it. If people are in trouble—"

"When it comes to giving out loans or grants, Amy, someone is always in trouble. I know I don't always leave work at work, but I can't save the world. I learned that a long time ago. You do good where you can, and you take care of the people you love."

That struck a chord. "Warren, I love you," she whispered. "And I've been feeling guilty about something."

He shifted so he could see her face. "What?"

She pressed her lips together in frustration. "I didn't know your chest size anymore. Aunt Gladys had to tell me. I feel like the worst wife ever."

"Seriously, babe? With everything going on in the world, you're going to feel bad about this? Come on. It's just a coat size."

Giving herself some room, she put her hand on his

thigh. "No, it's not. It's about knowing your body and seeing you as you are right now. I should have noticed you lost weight from the stress this year. I'm sorry that I stopped noticing the small things. I'm going to do better, Warren. I promise."

She watched as he swallowed a couple times before saying, "Babe, it's been a tough year for all of us. I know there are things I haven't noticed about you and the girls. A couple of months ago Madison asked me why you were wearing your shirt backward. I hadn't even noticed. You want me to wear a bad husband sticker for that? I felt horrible for a week."

Her mouth gaped. "Why didn't you say anything?"

"Because I didn't know what to say, and that worried me even more. Were you tired that day? Or did you put it on like that and didn't have enough energy to turn it around? Heck, I wondered if you might not have noticed yourself."

"I didn't! I don't even remember this. Why didn't Madison tell me?"

He set his wine aside. "I told her you were on a secret mission, and it was part of your undercover persona. I also told her you needed extra hugs to complete your assignment."

Now she did remember a few days where Madison had hugged her every time she turned around. Even in the bathroom. "Oh, Warren, that was sweet of you. But why not ask me about it?"

Taking her hand, he said, "I was afraid of hearing your answer to a problem I didn't have a solution for yet. Every day, I thank God that one appeared. Moving here has changed things for us. I haven't seen you go all day with your shirt on backward once, even after a quickie when the girls are napping, and frankly I don't expect to."

She sputtered out a laugh. "If I did, Aunt Gladys would tell me."

"I would too this time." He took her wineglass and set it aside. "Amy, we've both been paddling hard to stay afloat this year, but I plan to stop fighting the tide and go with the current more. With you, the girls, and this new job. But you guys are first. Always."

She leaned in and kissed him softly. "How about this? We'll take thirty minutes after the kids go to bed to work on things over the holidays, except on Christmas and New Year's."

"Eve *and* day," he said, his mouth tipping up at the right. "And only because our friends and neighbors need help."

She thought of her conversation with Baker about believing in people helping people. Damn if it didn't feel good. "Deal."

"And starting now, we'll let go of any guilt we've been carrying in our relationship and clean slate everything. That would be the best Christmas present you could give me, honey. I only want you to feel good. Never guilty. Besides, at the rate I'm eating chocolate, I'll probably be back to my old size in no time."

She narrowed her eyes at him before smiling. "All right. Clean slate. And I won't return your presents."

"Babe, I didn't know monster onesies came in men's sizes." He tickled her ribs.

"A monster onesie, huh?" Of course he would want that. "That's all you want for Christmas?" There was no way it would arrive in time, but she would see if she could find one later.

"Besides you and the girls, heck yeah, that's all."

As he kissed her, she couldn't help but think how good he was going to look in the red velvet jacket she'd ordered from Aunt Gladys.

He could wear the monster onesie for the girls.

CHAPTER 24

SEEING ROSE SITTING AMIDST HER BOXES IN HIS PLACE—
their place—felt right.

Now he needed to explain the situation to his mother. She'd opened her window as Hank and Alice drove up. "What's going on? Why aren't you all at work?"

He'd said he'd tell her after they finished unloading, and while she clearly hadn't liked it, she'd nodded and shut the window. Moments later, Mr. O'Connor had come out and helped them carry up the remaining boxes. The way everyone had pitched in, even though they had to take turns helping, was a memory Vinnie would always cherish.

Then the others left, and it was just the two of them and Rose's things.

She'd only brought a few of the plants from her room, and he'd asked why.

"I don't want to turn our home into a jungle," she joked weakly. "Besides, I can visit my babies in the greenhouse with their new friends."

He'd oddly felt a little sad about that, wanting her to be surrounded by everything she loved in their home.

Their home.

His chest was so full he swore he might pop a rib, so he started to sing "Ain't That A Kick In the Head" by Dean Martin quietly. When Rose joined in, he stopped packing his bag to take to Hank and Alice's place and crossed to her. She was staring into an open box. He put his hands over hers and leaned in to kiss her. She tipped her face up to meet his mouth more fully, and the sweetness of their connection rocked him back on his heels.

"I need to talk to my mama." He traced her cheek. "I can do it alone or you can come with me. Don't feel like you need to take on more today. You've had plenty."

Plus, Mr. Connor's help had been reassuring, as if he were offering his support for their arrangement. After all these years, the man was finally showing up, and it was much appreciated.

"I want to go with you." She rose when he helped her to her feet. "Vinnie, I want this to work. Even if it's unconventional."

"Me too." He raised her hand to his mouth and kissed it, wanting to assure her he felt the same. "Let's go."

When they arrived at Mama's back door, she already had her mask on, as did Mr. O'Connor. "Come on in."

They journeyed to the parlor and took seats on opposite couches. That she'd included Hank's dad confirmed that she considered him family, even if they hadn't made it official yet. Mr. O'Connor would ask her soon, and she'd say yes. He nodded to the older man, and they shared a silent moment of understanding.

Mama patted her knee nervously. "Rose, it's good to see you. I hear you're starting a flower business. I wish you every success. No one knows better than I do how tough it is to start a business—certainly when you're a woman. I was lucky to have my sister, God bless her in heaven. And a wonderful man supporting me if I ever needed anything, God rest him too."

As an opener, it was encouraging. He'd been afraid

she was going to bust his balls straight off before asking questions. "What am I? Chopped liver?"

"You weren't old enough in the early years to do anything but gurgle and sing from your high chair. Even as a baby, he was musical. His dad loved the classics, and they'd sing together at dinner."

Good memories, those. Man, Vinnie missed his father right now. He'd been gone ten years, but Vinnie would always miss him. He'd have to visit his grave to tell him about Rose. He knew Papa would be pleased.

Rose glanced his way, and the softness in her dark green eyes made his heart knock harder against his ribs. "Somehow it doesn't surprise me to hear that. I love hearing Vinnie sing."

His mama nodded crisply, pulling out a handkerchief from her pocket and worrying it between her fingers. "You have something to tell me, I imagine. I know my boy is a good man and wouldn't be moving you into his place without a promise. Did you two elope?"

He appreciated that she trusted in his honor, and he reached for Rose's hand. "We are getting married, Mama, and we would love your blessing. Rose is making herself at home a little early because her brother and his family are moving in with the Fiornis."

She wasn't a woman to show her shock, but her dark eyes shot to her hairline. "But your parents' safety... Oh, I shouldn't say anything. It's not my business."

Rose's eyes were suddenly wet. "No, you can say it. The situation is pretty horrible, but he's family."

"True, but he's a delinquent." Mama clucked her tongue. "Always stirring up trouble when he was younger. Breaking windows playing streetball. Kicking flowerpots and holiday decorations downtown."

Vinnie also remembered him stuffing the toilets at school with paper to flood the bathroom and throwing rocks and sticks at other kids. Always a bully, Al.

He was going to hit the hardware store before going to buy a padlock for Rose's greenhouse, no question.

"Poor Joe and Carlotta." Mama crossed herself. "They have suffered much over that boy, but you're right. He's their son. God knows Joe's wanted to give him the business. There isn't much you wouldn't do for family, even when they're a trial. Hope the grandchildren might be different. Given that, I'm glad you're moving in early, Rose. Vinnie, you'll stay here."

"Hank and Alice are having me stay with them. They have an en suite bedroom that I can come and go from that has its own exit."

She shot him a fiery look. "Vinnie—"

"No, Mama, we agreed to keep a safe distance, what with me working at the restaurant. It's better this way. Plus, it's only temporary. Rose and I will be getting married as soon as we can arrange it. You don't need to worry none."

The hand fingering the handkerchief clenched. "Not worry? Vinnie, my boy, don't tell your mama what to do. What can I do to help for the wedding? Rose, I imagine your parents have offered—"

"They aren't in a position to help, Mama, given the times." He pleaded with his eyes that she wouldn't ask more. "It's going to be very small. Her parents. You and Mr. O'Connor and Hank and Alice."

Mama paused a moment before saying, "Not her brother and his family?"

"No," Rose answered before he could.

Silence permeated the room like garlic before Mama said, "I see. Well, you two let me know if I can help you. Of course, you have my blessing. I can't say I'm surprised by anything but the timing. Your aunt Alessa and I always wondered if Rose Fiorni would finally make my boy notice her." She smiled softly. "You used to give him flowers when you were a little girl. It was dear."

"You and Aunt Alessa talked about it?" Vinnie asked,

his heart tearing a little at the thought. He wished she were here too.

Mama waved her hand. "Yes, and that's all I'll say about it."

He didn't need to hear any more. His mother had given her blessing. That was all that mattered. "I need to go to work," Vinnie said. "Thank you, Mama."

"Yes, thank you, Mama Gia," Rose said softly.

"You need anything, especially while my boy is at Hank's, you knock on the door. I know his place isn't very large, but if I can help make it cozier with a lamp or some curtains or pillows, you let me know. I haven't gotten out the sewing machine in a long time, but I imagine I can still whip something up if need be."

She'd whipped up all the tablecloths, napkins, and curtains at the restaurant to save money, Vinnie remembered. Those treasures were in boxes in her basement. She'd found the gumption to sell the restaurant, to Alice and Clifton, in fact, but she hadn't been able to let those go yet.

"We appreciate it," Vinnie said. "Come on, Rose."

"Congratulations, you two," Mr. O'Connor finally said. "I know you'll be very happy together."

"Thanks for helping with my things," Rose said, taking Vinnie's hand as they stood.

"I'm here to help you too," Mr. O'Connor said, his words an echo of what he'd said earlier.

"We'll see you later." Vinnie nodded to them both and led Rose out of the parlor.

They'd reached the front door when his mama called him back, just like he'd thought she might. Rose lifted her eyes to his. "Go. I'll be fine."

He found his mama in the kitchen, spooning leftover pasta into a plastic container. "I don't imagine you have dinner for Rose. Here, it's simple but good."

Taking the container, he faced her across the butcher

block in the middle. "You want to ask me something, Mama?"

She worried a breath, letting it rattle around in her throat like she did when she was gathering her thoughts. "What about Uncle Angelo's business? I won't ask about the rush to marry. You know your own heart and what it demands of you as much as I know mine, and I expect the situation with Rose's parents played a part in your decision. But a wife and a family are a big commitment, Vinnie."

"I'm aware of that, Mama." He set his hands on the butcher block for purchase. "I'm giving the videos three months to take off. Then I'll see where things stand." The same thought had occurred to him while he carefully packed his cologne bottle to take with him to Hank's. He still intended for his new venture to succeed, but it didn't hurt to keep his options open. Mama was right. He would have a wife to think about.

"But Rose's business is here," Mama said, pointing at the floor.

He could see where this was going. "She doesn't have a storefront, Mama. Selling them out of her home gives her freedom. Plants are easy to move. But I'm hoping it doesn't come to that. I don't want to leave Orion. You and Hank are here, and so are my friends and neighbors. Rose's ties are here too." Still. It would be hard for her to stand by and watch Al wreak havoc on her parents, wouldn't it? He'd need to think about that.

"I'll delay your uncle for now." She included a few holiday cookies in a baggie. "But, Vinnie, you're not just thinking about your own prospects anymore. Rose is a good match, from a good family—even though her brother's a hooligan. You take good care of her because she's going to do the same for you. Of that I have no doubt." She raised his hand as if to cup his cheek, then set it down. "Your papa would be happy for you. Surely he's smiling down on us from heaven. Now go off to work. Tell my other son I miss him. These times are hard on visits."

"Someday soon we will all be together again."

"I'll miss you on Christmas Eve," Mama said, tears filling her eyes. "But I understand."

"We'll still have a chat. Next year we'll eat together. Don't worry."

Her pause caught him unawares, and he knew she was thinking about the illness that had nearly taken her life and had struck Aunt Alessa down. For a time, he had thought he might be alone for every holiday.

"I pray for that and more every day," she said finally. "Wait a moment. I have something for you."

When she returned, she set a ring on the butcher block. He recognized it immediately. She'd worn that wedding ring every day until Papa died. Then she'd placed it in her jewelry box and packed up his things in the room they'd shared.

"I don't imagine you have the money for a ring right now. You don't have to use mine, of course. I only offer it to help, and because it's from a marriage that made me happy for a very long time. I would wish that for you and Rose. I still have Papa's ring too, should Rose wish to give it to you. They might need to be resized, but they'll work. I'll let you ask her."

He dried his eyes on his sleeves. "Thank you, Mama. I'm going to go before my eyes are so blurry I won't be able to walk to work."

She extended her hand before pressing it hard to her chest. "I love you, Vinnie."

Fighting his own emotion, he finally managed to say, "I love you too, Mama. So much."

Picking up the ring and the food she'd packed up, he journeyed back to find Rose. Setting the food down, he held up the ring. "It's Mama's, and I'd love to give this to you for now if that's all right. It doubles as an engagement ring and a wedding band."

She gasped. "She gave you her wedding ring?" Reaching out, she touched it. "It's beautiful. I think there's something strong and enduring about a simple gold band. It's like saying, 'I don't need to broadcast to the world how I feel about you because we know how we are.'"

Hearing that she felt as he did only added to the rightness of it all. "Yeah, and she offered Papa's to me too. If you'd like to use it. Money is tight, and we can always get new rings when we're better off."

"I love the idea of wearing your parents' rings. They always seemed so happy. I remember your papa singing to your mama and dancing with her after the restaurant was closed. That's how I hope we might be."

Holding her hand, he slid it on.

He took it as another sign that it fit perfectly.

CHAPTER 25

A S A FIRST OFFICIAL DATE, CHRISTMAS EVE WAS PRETTY spectacular.

Rose smoothed down her purple sweater and made sure her black velvet skirt's seams were running along the outside of her thighs. She fingered her new ring. She'd decided to wear it as an engagement ring because it gave her happiness to see it on her hand. They had a wedding date now, after going online and filling in the application and paying the fee—December 28. Hank had said they could have their wedding at the restaurant, and Monday was perfect since it was closed. If things had been different, she would have preferred to hold the ceremony in the greenhouse, but not with Al and his family around.

She didn't care that the wedding was on a Monday. Not when it meant Vinnie would be joining her in this little place she was starting to think of as home. The succulents she'd brought with her were sitting in the window facing east, and when she'd awoken in his bed, she'd imagined she could smell Vinnie on the sheets.

There was a knock on the door, and she glanced at the small mirror on the wall for one last look at herself. Her hair might not be straight, but she was starting to embrace the wildness. Vinnie loved it, and through his eyes, she was starting to see the appeal.

Striding to the door and cracking it open, she was surprised to see a masked Mr. O'Connor on the other side. In the porch light, he lifted his hand in greeting. In his other hand, he held two black garment bags.

"Merry Christmas. You settling in all right?"

"I am. Hang on. Let me get my mask."

She closed the door to keep the cold out. After retrieving her coat and mask, she returned to open it. It felt rude not to ask him inside, but there was so little space it seemed best to talk to him from the doorway.

When she pulled it open, his shoulders seemed to tense. "Gia wanted me to bring you these two wedding dresses in case you might want to wear them. One was hers and the others was Alessa's. Her lungs are still sensitive to the cold, or she'd have come herself."

"Oh. That's very sweet of her." She'd been fussing over what to wear since every formal dress she owned was in black. Her mama must have been so caught up that she hadn't even offered hers for Rose to wear. She'd been thinking of asking Aunt Gladys if she could borrow something.

"Both were handmade from Venetian lace that their grandmother brought over when she came to America. Gia said she could make any alterations on her sewing machine. Of course, she also said you shouldn't feel pressured to wear one of them, but she knows money is tight. It's her way of saying she's behind you both one hundred percent."

The history of the wedding gowns touched her as much as the show of support. "Please tell her thank you. Just leave them on the stair rail. Let me look at them and see."

He nodded. "You need anything else, you let me know. Vinnie too. Well, I won't keep you out in the cold any longer."

After he headed down the stairs, she brought them inside and set them on the bed. Unzipping the first one, she exclaimed, "Oh, it's beautiful."

The prized Venetian lacework was soft and fine. The sleeves and the top of the scoop neck bodice were solely lace, while the rest of the lace fitted over a silky underbody. She loved it immediately. The other was equally beautiful, but Rose preferred the first. She could already see herself in it.

Did she have time to try it on? Oh, who cared? She couldn't wait. Stripping quickly, she worked on the buttons on the bodice. Cloth-covered, they wouldn't be easy to button herself, but at least she could gauge the fit. The dress flowed like water over her as she drew it on, and she hugged herself when she realized it was going to work. The sleeves were a little long, but that was such a small thing.

She picked up the small train to go to the mirror. Her breath caught. My God, she looked like a bride. A beautiful one. Her grandmother used to say lace always enhanced a woman's beauty, which was why Italian women wore it to their weddings and to cover their hair going to church or to the market. Rose could see the appeal in a new way. She looked and felt like a woman.

She could already imagine the flowers she was going to bring in for their wedding. Special roses topped the list, but she daydreamed about amaryllis, hydrangea, cockscomb, anemone, scabiosa, and maybe even Japanese Lisianthus. She'd have to see what she could find at the flower market to pair with what she had from her greenhouse, but oh, the possibilities. Rose Fiorni was finally getting married, and she was going to have the flowers she'd always dreamed about.

Another knock sounded at the door. It had to be Vinnie this time. "Don't come in!" He didn't normally barge in unannounced, but she wasn't going to chance it. "I need a couple of minutes."

"Take your time," he called through the door.

As she changed back into her date clothes, she could hear him singing through the door. Oh, how she loved this man. Quickly putting the dress back in its garment bag, she hung both gowns up and walked to the door. When she opened it, she launched herself at him. His coat was cold, but his lips were warm, and after catching her, he gave her an enthusiastic kiss before setting her back on her feet. His grin was dear and tempting. "You make me forget my mama might be watching from the window, but I suppose we're engaged so she won't shout at me to take it inside."

"Vinnie, I'm so happy right now I could dance in a circle."

He picked her up off the floor and closed the door. "I promised you we'd dance. Now seems like a good time."

She laid her cheek on his coat, and he started singing, "I've Got The World On A String," leading her in a close-embrace shuffle over the small space in what would be their home. Her heart floated in her chest as his voice washed over her, and her skin felt impossibly sensitive where his hands gripped her. This was heaven.

When he finished that song, he ran his hand up her back and into her hair. She tipped her head back, and his eyes were there on his face, as if he'd been waiting for her. "I'm happy too. I sang the whole way here because I knew I was coming home to you. Christmas lights were shining and blinking, and the cold was almost welcoming in its crispness. Rose, I must have been the most thickheaded guy in the world to have waited this long to be with you, but I've gotten smarter, thank God. I'm never letting you go."

His mouth lowered, and this time it was a tender meeting of lips. But soon, she opened her mouth to him, wanting more. His tongue swept in to dance, and they both murmured their passion. "Oh, Vinnie, I love you, and boy, do I want you."

He cupped her face and kissed her one last time. "I

want you too, but I want to do things right. We don't need to rush other things just because we're getting married. As far as I'm concerned, we're going to act like we're still dating until we feel married."

She couldn't help saying, "What exactly do you mean by that? Are you thinking we're going to live together, sleep in that small bed, and not have sex until some magic moment happens? Vinnie, I hate to tell you, but *this* is a magic moment. As far as I'm concerned, every time we're together is magic, and if you think I'm going to wait until we feel married—whatever that means—you're crazy." She threw her hands up as she said it.

He bit the side of his lip. "I haven't see Rosie the Riveter in a while. You know, I kinda miss her. You look pretty gorgeous when you're calling me out and shaking your hands at me like I'm an idiot. Just like old times, except now it feels a lot like foreplay."

"*Foreplay*? You were just talking about not having sex! How did you think I'd react?"

"I'm convinced you want it," he said, pointing to the drawer with the condoms. "You brought those, after all. I only wanted to make sure you didn't think I expected everything else to go out of order because of the wedding. We're being a little unorthodox, Rose. Give me a break."

"Give me a break," she mumbled, realizing it did feel good to fire off at him a little.

He cozied up to her, pulling her to his large chest. "Maybe when you start shouting at me, I'll grab you and kiss you like my papa always did to my mama. He used to say it was the Italian way."

Her parents were like that too, and she loved watching them smile or laugh at each other afterward. "You'd better kiss me good then."

He pressed his mouth to hers in another slow, deep kiss that made her toes curl in her shoes.

"Still feeling feisty?" he asked.

If he was going to ask, she knew how she'd respond every time. "Yes." Another kiss had her sighing into his mouth. "You'd better keep this up for a while. You're lucky you don't have a rolling pin in here because I might be feeling vexed enough to chase you with it." Her nonna had teasingly done that to her husband once, when she was making pasta, and Rose had thought it was so funny and sweet when he'd caught her and kissed her, both of them laughing.

This time *she* kissed *him* to make her point, and he gave her the lead. She indulged in his mouth, in running her fingers through his thick hair. He was the one who gave a deep groan, and she lifted her mouth, triumphant.

"You can chase me any time you like if that's how you're going to kiss me." He traced her cheekbone. "But back to what I was saying. You understand where I'm coming from, right?"

He held her gaze, and she finally nodded. Yeah, she knew he was being a good guy, letting her know he had no intention to rush her. "I get it. But, Vinnie, I want to make love with you."

"I want that too," he said in a deep voice. "But I also want to wake up with you, and that's not going to happen until after we're married."

He was right. "It's only a few days," she said with a nod. "But if I burn through my wedding dress, I'm blaming you."

His delicious mouth twitched. "Thankfully it won't be a long ceremony—or in church. That could have been awkward. But at least the holy water would have been close by to hose you down with."

They both started laughing, and she loved how they kept touching as they did so—his hand on her hips. "Hose me down! What a photo that would be for our wedding album."

"I'd frame it and put it on the wall."

He wisely wrapped her up and kissed her again before

she could playfully swat at him.

"You have any feelings about flowers for our wedding?" she asked when he released her mouth.

"That's your department, so you do whatever you want." He pulled out his money clip and handed her some bills.

"No, I have some money for this. Vinnie, I want to bring this to our wedding. If you can do a little for the food..."

"Mama told me she'd like to make lasagna, if that's okay. She remembered that you love it."

His mother was being more generous than she'd expected. "I do love it. She's been so kind."

Did she tell him about the dress? No, she would wait. For now, it would be her secret with his mama, although she wondered whose dress she had chosen: Gia's or Alessa's.

"She's the best," he said. "Hank is giving me a couple days off, whenever I want it. Given how angry you got at me earlier, should I request them around our wedding?"

"I want to make love on our wedding night, Vinnie."

"Me too," he said, kissing her again. "I hadn't expected our first time to be on our wedding day, but I kinda like that it's turned out that way. I guess I am a little traditional, because it feels like a good way to start our life together. Rose, I'd like to go to the church before our wedding. To bless things. Would you come?"

"Yes, I'd like that," she said, already seeing them standing there. She still wanted to light a candle for her parents too. "Does it bother you that we're not getting married in a church?"

He lifted his shoulder. "A little, but I'm considering our marriage sealed the same way."

"Me too." She hugged him. "Vinnie, I know you're doing this to help me, and I'm so grateful, but I want you to know that I'm going to mean every vow."

His arms nestled her to his body. "So will I."

She thought of Aunt Gladys saying Vinnie hadn't

needed to suggest marriage. The truth of that only gave Rose more faith in their future together.

"We should go before I kiss you more," Vinnie said.

But they did kiss, and because they couldn't seem to get enough of each other, they did a little more. When they finally left, she took his hand. "Can we stop at the greenhouse? I have my first order going out tomorrow, and I need to pick up the shipping labels. Thought I could fill them out at our place and have them ready to go." She'd decided it might be better to only spend as much time at the greenhouse as needed in the early days of Al living there. Packing the plants would take a little extra time to make sure they were nestled into her special plant-shipping containers, but she planned to be in and out as quickly as she could.

"I'm glad I can go with you," Vinnie said as they walked toward her parents' house. "I'll come with you before and after work for a while to send a message."

But that left the time in between, and Rose needed to figure that out. "The lock you installed should be enough. I'm not scared of Al. He has a way of being very unpleasant is all. I can manage."

"He never listened to me in school, but I'll talk to him if I have to," Vinnie said as they arrived in front of the house. "I can't imagine he would be happy I'm marrying you."

She spied their car in the driveway and stopped short. "When did he get a Range Rover?" Sure, he was a mechanic, but even used they weren't cheap.

"You probably don't want to know," Vinnie said, putting his hand to her back as they crossed to the backyard and let themselves in through the gate.

Moments after they arrived in the greenhouse, Al appeared and let himself in at the other end. "Heard you'd cozied up to my sister and broken my mama's heart, Scorsese. I don't like you causing trouble in my family." He wasn't wearing a mask, of course.

They'd always borne a resemblance, she and Al, but his features were mean and hard.

"You're the one who's causing trouble," she said, putting her hand on Vinnie's arm. "I'm happy to be marrying Vinnie. And I'd appreciate you staying out of the greenhouse. This is my place of business now."

"It's Papa's greenhouse," he said with an edge. "You put on airs in the city, coming back, claiming all this. I'm entitled to what's in here as much as you."

She blinked in shock. Entitled?

"Not according to Mr. Fiorni," Vinnie said. "You can ask him with me as witness anytime. Also, you step wrong with your sister, and Hank and I will pay you a visit. You hear me?"

"Like I was ever worried about you and that moron. You come anywhere near me, you can expect a visit from me and Tony Grasiaca and his boys. I've already had a beer with him. He said you two are still acting like homos and playing at sainthood."

Rose clenched her fists. "Shut up, Al."

"No, it's fine, Rose." Vinnie made a rude noise. "Al, we don't need to have any contact. My concern here is for Rose. This is her place. Not yours. You stick to the house and your papa's barber shop."

He started forward. "Like I'm going to let you tell me where to go."

"Enough!" Rose called, feeling Vinnie tense. "You go back to the house, Al. I don't want to stir up trouble, but you damn well know Mama and Papa don't want you out here bothering me."

"My mom told me you got tubby, and it looks like she was right."

Rose spied Al's eleven-year-old daughter in the doorway, also maskless. Her niece might have been nicknamed Angel for Angelica, but she was anything but.

"Hi, Angel," Rose said tightly.

"I saw you in that stupid video with the jacket," she said with a smirk in Vinnie's direction. "I can't believe so many people liked it."

Vinnie's jaw locked, and Rose knew he hadn't expected this kind of behavior from a kid.

"But they did like it, and the store sold out of jackets," Rose said. "Al, I don't want anyone in this greenhouse. Are we clear?"

"This place is stupid, and so are your plants." Angel kicked at the end of one of the tables holding her ferns.

"Stop that, little girl." Rose strode forward. "You go inside."

"Don't talk to my daughter like that," Al shouted.

"Enough of this! Al, I don't like you being here any more than you do. That's between you and Mama and Papa, but I won't take your abuse. You stay out of my way, and I'll stay out of yours."

Al grunted. "Still think you're Papa's favorite, huh? He's always given you everything and me nothing. I heard he was even giving you money for your stupid business. But that's all changing now. I'm going to have his shop, and I'm going to have this place too."

Her stomach sickened. "You don't even like flowers."

He pushed over a newly potted maidenhead fern. "Who cares? You do."

With that, he gave an eerie wave and walked Angel and himself out. Rose was shaking from their confrontation, and Vinnie put his arm around her. They were still visible, or she would have buried her face against his coat. "Don't say anything yet. Let me get what I came for, and then let's go."

She grabbed the labels from the drawer of office supplies and tucked them into her purse. When she turned around, Vinnie was repotting the fern like she'd taught him. No, she couldn't rage or cry now.

"Tell me something good as we leave here, Rose,"

Vinnie said, wiping his hands off on a nearby rag and pulling his gloves back on. "How many orders do you have so far?"

She knew he was trying to distract her so she could hold it together. Still, she told him as she walked through the greenhouse to join him. She'd sold ten plants so far, and even though it wasn't much yet, she continued to see mountains of flowers being shipped at her request when she closed her eyes at night.

He put his arms on her shoulders, his dark eyes steady. "And when are you going to release the next video I did for The Dreamer's Flower Shoppe?"

"After Christmas," she answered, unable to feel her earlier excitement about it. "Aunt Gladys offered me a take-over post on her social media accounts, something Amy suggested."

"I like her," Vinnie said. "She came into O'Connor's the other day for lunch. She and Warren fit. What plant are you going to share?"

His calm demeanor was reassuring, but she could see the tension in his muscles. "A few more decorative plants like the staghorn fern we featured in one of the videos."

"I like that one," he said. "When we have a bigger place, we should put it in the family room."

He was boosting her spirits with every word, and she rubbed his shoulders briefly to offset the boulders she expected they were carrying. "I have an idea for another one we can use. You know, Aunt Gladys said I could sell some plants out of her store."

"That's great," he said with extra enthusiasm. "Today I had an offer from a men's hair and body care line to highlight their products. Seems they love my hair..."

He told her more about it as she let them out of the greenhouse. She glanced at the house and noticed her Mama and Papa standing in front of the patio window, holding hands and looking so alone. In the background, Al had his arm slung around Paulina, who was sitting on his lap on the couch. Their three girls were running around, and even through the windows, Rose could hear them squealing at each other.

Her parents' house had turned into hell. There was no other word for it.

She waved to them, sorrow burning in her throat. Vinnie did the same and then took her hand. Through her thick throat, she managed to tell him about the larger specimen plants she was planning to showcase at Old World Elegance, including her fabulous Red Congo plant in the philodendron family, prized for its big lush green leaves with the long red stems. She was also going to include one of Mr. Palladino's lemon tree babies once they rooted enough. Aunt Gladys had plenty of Italian customers who might enjoy the story.

"I love that lemon tree, Rose. You bring the one I asked for Mama home to take root, okay? It would make me happy to see it there."

They fell into silence as they walked together, and Rose reasoned it was shock. She was aware of feeling colder than she had before, walking the streets. Only he didn't take her straight to O'Connor's for dinner. Instead, he led her to the church. She clutched his hand, knowing what he planned.

The way he held the door for her made her feel another surge of emotion. It really felt like they were a couple, here to anoint their union. Inside, the faint scent of incense touched her nose. There was no holy water, she realized. Only hand sanitizer, and her heart seemed to tear all the more. Midnight mass would be in a few hours, and the earlier service had wrapped up, so the church was mostly quiet.

She caught sight of the candles as they walked farther in, and her vision immediately began to blur. Vinnie had his hand to her back as they genuflected and entered a pew. She knelt down next to him. He passed her a handkerchief and put his arms around her as he bowed his head to pray.

She fought the urge to cry, zeroing in on the spotlit faces of Mary and Jesus in the nativity scene to the right of the altar. It was surrounded by white lights, and as she gazed at the angels watching over the little infant, she prayed they would also watch over Mama and Papa, and her and Vinnie, and everyone else in the world.

The quiet of the place calmed her as much as Vinnie's presence beside her and the few others praying in the church with them. Some were kneeling. Some were sitting. All were masked.

Even though Covid had been around for what seemed like forever, it just didn't feel right for it to touch this place. How did God feel about not seeing their faces anymore? Then, because she had doubts, she wondered how he had ever let any of this happen.

Her spirts plummeted again, and her conversation with her brother replayed in her head. It had especially hurt to hear such cruelty from his daughter, who was only eleven years old. How had it come to this?

Vinnie touched her back, and she looked over to see him standing up. She followed. When they reached the candles, she noticed the box that usually sat out for donations was gone. Covid again. He took a lighter and then put her hand over his as he lit two candles. The flames flickered, and her heart hurt from the pressure of all the sadness it carried. Then Vinnie put his arm around her back again and leaned in to whisper, "I don't know how it's going to be all right, but it is. Somehow."

She looked into his dark eyes, brighter than the candles in front of them. Love and devotion welled in them. Not just because of this place, she realized. But because of her.

When he took her hand, she understood what he meant. They were together, and that was why it would be all right somehow.

As they left the church, she started to believe it.

CHAPTER 26

THEIR WEDDING DAY WASN'T GOING TO BE CONVENTIONAL.

But when Vinnie saw Rose walking into O'Connor's with her parents, all he could think about was her. She was stunning. No, beyond stunning—more radiant than the crush of eye-popping flowers around them. "You wore my mama's wedding dress."

The words tumbled out of his mouth in a hoarse rush. He stared at the gown, one he knew by heart after having seen it every day in his parents' wedding photo, hung by the front door of his mama's house.

Her green eyes glowed like the candles they'd lit at church the other day, a moment when he'd felt their commitment deepen in their hearts. That night, she'd become his in a new way, and today they would go further still. "She was kind enough to offer me either hers or your aunt Alessa's, and I fell in love with this one. I decided to surprise you."

His heart seemed to rise in his chest as if on a tide coming into the beach, and he glanced over at his mama. She was holding Mr. O'Connor's hand, her dark gaze steady and warm. She hadn't told him about her engagement, nor did she wear a ring, but something had changed in the air between her and Hank's dad. He expected she was waiting to tell him until after his own wedding.

"It was nothing," Mama said, greeting Rose's parents. "You look beautiful, Rose. Doesn't she make a lovely bride? And the flowers she created for her own wedding are incredible."

Everyone murmured, and he sent Rose a wink. No surprise, she'd wanted loads of flowers to celebrate their union, and he thought their cheeriness extra special, as was the individually wrapped *confetti* Rose's mama brought forward on a silver platter. Each guest ate five almonds to wish the couple good health, wealth, happiness, children, and a long life. Vinnie was touched by the traditional gesture. Aunt Gladys finally stepped forward and opened her arms. "Are you two ready?"

They'd asked her to be their officiant last-minute after Alice had shown them how easy it was for someone to become certified online. She knew because she'd arranged for Warren to officiate her wedding to Hank. Helpful as always, Alice had practically filled out the form for Aunt Gladys.

"More than," Vinnie said, sensing Hank behind him.

The presence of his friend had always been something he could count on, and he never appreciated it more than today. He had the best friend in the world, and that made him a lucky man.

Now he would have the most wonderful wife, and while their courtship hadn't been traditional, he knew they were going to be good together. Happy. He'd known it to his soul when they'd knelt beside each other in church, and he could have sworn he'd heard Aunt Alessa's voice telling him everything was going to work out. Those were the words he'd shared with Rose, and a new peace had settled between them.

Rose approached him, her smile radiant. "You look

more handsome than I've ever seen you, Vinnie."

He felt a powerful, primal sense of being a man. He couldn't wait to share it with her once they were alone. Tonight was the night, and they'd both looked forward to it these last days in every glance, every kiss, every touch.

"And I will never forget how beautiful you are today." He traced the sweeping arch of her cheekbone. "Alice, you got your camera ready?"

"I've been taking pictures left and right," she said, wagging her phone in the air. "You two look incredible. You make my job easy."

"Speaking of jobs," Rose said, lifting her bouquet and unpinning something. "Will you hold this?"

Alice took the bouquet, leaving Rose with a small boutonnière.

"You chose red roses for us."

And they weren't just any red rose. They were the richest red he'd ever seen. The table arrangements were all simple white flowers, some roses and a couple of others he didn't recognize.

"They symbolize love and passion," she said, "plus, they're my favorite. This variety is called 'Thinking of You,' and I want you to remember that I'll always be thinking of you. Every day for the rest of my life. I thought you'd prefer a simple boutonnière because you mentioned the way you used to slip a rose into your lapel at Two Sisters. This rose is called 'Precious Time,' and its significance is to remind us of all that's come before, what we have now, and all that's ahead."

God, she was going to slay him before they even said their vows. As she pinned it to his new suit, she began to chuckle. "I didn't realize this was the same jacket you wore in the video."

He leaned close to her ear. "You loved it, and velvet jackets are all the rage for winter weddings. Plus, I can wear it at home." Aunt Gladys had thought it a brilliant idea, assisting him in selecting the wine-colored bow tie, tuxedo shirt, and black dress pants to complement it.

"I can't wait," she whispered in a sexy voice that seemed to caress his skin. "Oh, I'm so happy."

"Me too," he said, lifting her hand to his mouth and kissing it. "Let's get married."

He was grinning as they began the ceremony. Aunt Gladys' sparkle was potent as she stood in front of them in an emerald green dress. "I'd like to think I had something to do with this, but having lived in this neighborhood since you two were born, I know your connection started a long time ago. Everyone knew Rose loved Vinnie. She followed him around everywhere he went. Gave him flowers. Asked her parents to go to Two Sisters to see him. Vinnie, being a good guy in the neighborhood, treated Rose with respect and affection—until he finally saw her as the woman she'd become."

Rose shot him an amused glance, and he sent her a wink. Okay, so it had taken him a while. But he'd more than caught up.

"Respect and friendship matter as much as passion in a marriage, which is why I know you two will live a life like fine wine, improving with each year."

He nodded at her allusion to a time-honored Italian wedding blessing. Then he took Rose's hands as Aunt Gladys instructed them to say their vows. As they started, Vinnie realized he hadn't told Rose he loved her, and he was about to vow to do so for the rest of their lives. He didn't want the first time to be this way. He cleared his throat. "Aunt Gladys, can we have a moment?"

Her eyes narrowed. "*Now?*"

Rose's hands clenched around his, and he squeezed them to reassure her. "I need to tell Rose something right now. We'll be back in a minute."

Their friends and family shot them concerned looks as he led her outside. Only Hank wasn't worried, but then again, he knew Vinnie best.

The weather was a balmy thirty-two degrees, and he took off his jacket to place it around her shoulders.

"What in the world are you doing?" she asked, her face stricken.

"I needed to tell you something before we got to our vows," he said quickly to assure her, bringing her hand to his heart. "I love you, Rose."

Tears filled her eyes. "Oh, Vinnie. I didn't expect this. Not today."

"What better time than our wedding day?" He pressed her palm to his chest, so she'd feel that his heart beat for her. "I wanted to say it to you and only you before I vowed to love you before witnesses. I needed you to know that I mean it. Rose, I'm so glad we're getting married. Everything feels so right with you."

She traced his jaw. "For me too. Vinnie, I'm so glad you brought me out here. I was telling myself this morning that it was okay you didn't feel that way about me yet, but...I hoped you would. Let's go back in and seal it forever."

"Tell me again," he said, cupping her face in his hands.

"I love you." Her voice and eyes were steady.

"And I love you," he said, kissing her softly on the lips.

He had to kiss her, and by the time he lifted his head, it felt like they were both floating in the clouds. Hand in hand, they went back inside and got married.

After the short ceremony and their first kiss as husband and wife, he took her hand again and turned to face their friends and family. "Thank you so much for joining us today. I have something planned for my bride, if you'll sit down."

Everyone took to their individual tables, and Hank brought out a chair for Rose. He gave Alice the cue, and the song he'd chosen began to play over the speakers. "I Only Have Eyes For You" had struck the right chord with him, and from the way her face glowed as he serenaded her,

Romeo from Romeoville once more, he'd picked a winner. As he brought the song home, he drew her out of the chair and dipped her before kissing her again. Applause sounded in his ears but it couldn't compete with the beating of their hearts.

Hank popped the Prosecco he'd offered for the reception and poured everyone a glass, which Alice and Clifton helped distribute. "To my best friend and the best girl in the neighborhood. Vinnie. Rose. May your life together be filled with everything you could ever want, good friends and neighbors and something to laugh about together every day. *Slainte!*"

Everyone lifted their glasses, but Rose's parents had elected to wear their masks at all times given Al and his family's unsafe habits, so they didn't drink it. Vinnie told himself it wasn't bad luck, and to keep Rose from dwelling on it, he twined their arms together. They drank the toast laughing.

Mama had made a feast of their favorite dishes: garlic bread, salad, and lasagna, followed by a slice of tangy lemon wedding cake, known as *Delizia al Limone.* They'd intentionally kept things simple, and Vinnie found he was enjoying the gentle flow of the afternoon. At the weddings he'd attended, there had been a lot of duties and guests for the bride and groom to attend to. Not today. He and Rose could sit together and have fun, although he was aware of her watching her parents, huddled and masked at their corner table. Only one thing he could do about it. Patting his full belly, Vinnie took his bride's hand. "Care to dance?"

She smiled at him, and he started up the song he'd chosen, then spun her into the center of the restaurant. He joined Dean in singing "You'll Always Be The One I Love" as he swayed with Rose in a close embrace. He liked the way her body fit against him, and the lacework teased him with the promise of her soft golden skin.

When the song finished, she tipped her head back, her

eyes dancing. "I love dancing with you, Vinnie Scorsese."

"I love dancing with you," he murmured and took the opportunity to kiss her again.

"The next song is mine," she said, grinning. "You're going to have to broaden your musical range because this band is one of my favorites."

Walking to his phone in the docking station, she found what she wanted and turned around with a triumphant glow as male vocalists began to sing.

Alice hooted and cried, "Yes! You go, Rose."

"Grab Hank and dance!" She linked her wrists behind Vinnie's head as he put his hands on her waist and, sure enough, Alice pulled Hank onto their makeshift dance floor.

"You know this one?" Rose asked him.

"Not a clue," he said, his shoulders shaking. "But from now on, I'd like to be your number one male vocalist."

"I can get on board with that," she said, pressing her hips deliciously into him as she swayed. "But prepare yourself to listen to a lot of Boyz II Men. This is 'The Color of Love.'"

Picking up the melody, he started humming to the music. "If you love it, I'll learn it."

"How do you feel about Pink?" she asked.

"I don't mind wearing it. I'm comfortable in my manhood."

Laughing, she pressed back and spun in a circle. "Not the color. The singer, silly."

"This song's about colors, Rose. It was an easy mistake." And he liked that they could tease each other and laugh about it.

He had another piece of cake, feeding Rose a few bites, and afterward they crossed to tell his mama how delicious everything had been.

She held hands with Mr. O'Connor, and the look she wore was the one his papa had described as her "all is well with Gia's world" look. He had a moment, missing his papa, but he knew the man was smiling down at them from heaven with his aunt Alessa, God rest them both.

"You look beautiful, Mama," he said. "More radiant than ever."

"Your happy day with Rose lightens my heart." She turned to smile at Mr. O'Connor. "As does this man."

"I love seeing you happy, Mama."

"Thank you again for letting me wear your dress," Rose said, pressing her hand to her heart.

"It's your dress now, my child," Mama said. "Maybe someday your daughters will wear it. Today I feel like anything is possible again. You have no idea how precious that is to me. Thank you!"

Vinnie got tears in his eyes and coughed to clear his throat, as much at the thought of his future daughters as his mother's renewed hope. Rose was also wiping her eyes, and he pulled her to his side. "We love you, Mama. Would you come dance with me? Alice and I dance swing six feet apart all the time quite successfully."

He waited to see if she would express concern about her lungs, but she didn't say a word. Only stood and held out her hand. As he led her to the dance floor, he glanced over at Mr. Fiorni. Traditionally, he and Rose would have had a father-daughter dance, but he suspected his father-in-law hadn't thought it possible due to social distancing. Hopefully he might see Vinnie with his mama and give it a go with Rose. He imagined her heart was hurting over the situation.

He selected his mama's favorite Louis Prima song, and they started moving their hips to "Buona Sera." Always a good dancer, his mama followed his moves and improvised her own. Alice was dancing around Hank with her usual gusto, and his friend sent him an exaggerated eye roll. Afterward, Mama surprised them by asking Hank if he would give her a whirl, and Vinnie matched Alice's wacky moves to "Oh Marie" as Aunt Gladys led Clifton onto the dance floor.

Out of the corner of his eye, he saw Mrs. Fiorni push Mr. Fiorni gently from his chair. The older man straightened his tie and then crossed to Rose, who wiped away tears as she waved goodbye to her current dance partner, Mr. O'Connor, to join her papa. Vinnie went over to ask Mrs. Fiorni to dance. Her solemnness shifted as she smiled with her eyes, and they swayed to "I've Got My Love To Keep Me Warm."

When the song ended, Mrs. Fiorni pressed her hands to her middle. "Thank you for taking care of our Rosie. We should be getting back, but Joe and I left something for you on the table. I'll go say goodbye to Rose now."

He noted the time and wondered if she was expected to cook dinner for Al and his family. Anger surged, but he reminded himself it wasn't his business. Instead, he crossed to put his hands on Rose's shoulders as she said goodbye to her parents. Gone were the days when they could embrace, and he could feel the pain radiating from all of them as they said their goodbyes.

Shortly afterward, his mama and Mr. O'Connor also paid their respects, noting they'd left something on the table too. Mama said not to read it until they were alone, and he wondered what that meant. The goodbyes continued as Aunt Gladys and Clifton departed, and soon they were left with only Hank and Alice. Suddenly he could see how the four of them would be as time passed—the best of friends, spending cherished time alone, even after a large party.

"It was a wonderful day!" Alice said, her big brown eyes bright. "Who said weddings during Covid couldn't be awesome? Hank, I can't wait for ours. I'm totally adding some Louis Prima and Dean Martin to my wedding playlist."

"So long as you have Dropkick Murphys too," Hank said, hooking his arm around her.

"So long as you understand that playing the theme song from *The Departed* at a wedding isn't an obvious choice for most people. Which is why I'm your perfect partner. You need me to remind you."

He snorted. "You're one to talk, given how you're probably planning on playing song after song from *Pulp Fiction*. Also a mob movie."

"Oh my God! You're so right. But it's a great soundtrack. Right, Vinnie?"

"Right, sweetheart." He took Rose's hand, feeling the pull to be alone with her. "Let's clean up and close up shop. Thanks again for letting us have our wedding here, Hank."

"Yes, thank you," Rose said.

"Please!" Hank waved a hand. "This is your home, and it's what friends do. We have a little gift for you two."

"Come on, you did enough letting us get married here," Vinnie said as his friend set an envelope down on the bar.

"Vinnie, be a good friend and take it or Hank might get upset," Alice said, crossing her arms. "We love you both and want to celebrate you."

He picked up the envelope and gave it to Rose to open, standing behind her to read it, all the better to smell her subtle perfume. He thought about his cologne bottle and discarded the thought. This wasn't the time to think about the bargain he'd made with himself about getting his life back on track. Marrying Rose was only the beginning. He knew his luck was more than turning, and now that they were together, the possibilities were endless.

"It's a gift certificate for an overnight stay at the Ai Fiorni Hotel in the city," Rose said with a gasp. "I used to go there for drinks to see the flowers. Oh my!"

"We wanted to give you the option of when use it," Alice said. "I liked that the name of the hotel means 'among the flowers' in Italian. Seemed perfect. No shock you've been there, Rose. Plus, the food is supposed to be so good."

Clever of them to leave the timing open-ended. Vinnie

and Rose had decided to spend their first night together at his place, where they would be living. Some of it was because of money concerns, sure, but the rest was about cementing their commitment together in their new home.

"This is way too much," Rose said, "but thank you!"

"Yes, thank you," Vinnie said, his heart full. "I love you guys."

"We love you too!" Alice said, linking her arm through Hank's. "You two gather your things and then go on home. Hank and I will clean up."

"But—"

"Not on your life," Hank said, pointing to the door. "Out!"

"Fine!" Vinnie said, taking Rose's hand. "We won't say no. Thank you, guys. So much! Rose, I'm going to turn the car on so you'll be warm. Be right back."

They collected everything they needed, Rose touching the roses in her bouquet as they walked to his car. The quiet between them was different, perhaps because they both knew what came next. This anticipation felt different than anything he'd experienced with anyone else. It felt... reverent. After helping her inside, he went around the hood and settled into the driver's seat. She loved seeing the back seat filled with flowers from their wedding.

"You were sweet to warm the car up for me," she said softly. "Vinnie, it was the best day ever. I'll never forget it."

He leaned over and kissed her tenderly. "The day's not over yet."

His entire universe lit up when she only smiled.

CHAPTER 27

THEY WERE GOING TO HAVE SEX.

She and Vinnie Scorsese. As he closed the door to their new home after helping her bring in the flowers, she didn't know what to do with herself. Sitting on the bed seemed too obvious so she remained standing in front of the big-screen TV. Oh, God, she was suddenly nervous. And this after asking Aunt Gladys to buy condoms for her.

"You okay, sweetheart?" Vinnie asked, shrugging out of his coat.

"I'm good, yes." Prim, Rose, she thought. "It really was the best of days."

"You want some Prosecco?" He held up the open bottle he'd brought home. "When I was pouring this the other day, I discovered another reason to love it. There's a 'rose' in Prosecco. After the *P* and before the two *C*s. Did you know?"

She shook her head, mesmerized as he undid his bow tie and slid it from his collar.

"Every time I drink it from now on, I'm going to imagine I'm drinking you in a glass," he said, undoing the top black-studded buttons of his shirt.

Drink her? Her mouth went dry. This man, *her husband*, was temptation incarnate.

"What can I do to make you more comfortable?" he asked, setting her glass in her hand. "To us being us. Rose, we're pretty damn wonderful from where I'm standing."

She set the Prosecco flute down and put a hand on his chest. "Yeah, we sure as heck are. Vinnie, I want you to kiss me. And don't stop."

He gave her a downright wicked smile. "You got over your nerves quick. Then again, you always did. I *am* going to kiss you, Rose, and I don't plan to stop until you call out my name."

That wasn't going to be hard. Her belly was tight with desire, and she wanted him with a need she'd never experienced before. Lifting her hand to his jaw, she met his gaze. "Vinnie Scorsese, I have wanted you my whole adult life. Make love to me."

"It will be my pleasure, my beautiful bride," he said, setting his flute down too.

He lowered his head and kissed her, sipping at her mouth as if he had nothing but time. She couldn't wait, the longstanding need for him surging to life within her. Her mouth opened, and he took the kiss deeper, his tongue dancing with hers. She made a sound in her throat, her hands starting to undo the remaining buttons on his shirt.

"You in a hurry, honey?"

Should she admit it? "Yes, actually. I'm burning up. I want you."

"We have all night," he said, taking her hands. "We'll drink some Prosecco, listen to some music, maybe dance some more, and kiss each other until we're breathless. I'll even throw some rose petals on the bed."

Every relationship expert said you had to ask for what you wanted, especially in the beginning. She stepped away, scooped up some rose petals, and sprinkled them on the comforter. "What if I want to kick off the breathless part right now and then intersperse more breathlessness in between all those other things you just mentioned?"

His chuckle was rich and deep. "Then I'd say I truly am the luckiest man in the world. Come here. I'll give you what you need."

Music to her ears. "I want you so much."

He joined her by the bed. "I want you too. I was trying to hold back. Take some time."

"Holding back is crazy sometimes," Rose said, loving how his hand was caressing her leg as he lifted her wedding gown up to reveal more of her thigh-high stockings. "Moments like this come to mind."

"You're wearing a garter," he said, whistling. "Normally I would have taken this off you and thrown it to the single guys at the reception."

"I'm kinda glad we didn't do that," she said, not wanting just now to tell him it was her mother's. She'd almost cried when Mama had given it to her before they left for the wedding. "I always thought that ritual was embarrassing. I need your hands on me, Vinnie."

He slid those strong, capable hands behind her knees, making her jolt with desire. "All right, love, settle back and let me show you just how well your husband plans to take care of you from now on."

Sliding the rest of her skirt up her legs, he gathered it at her waist with one hand and touched her where she needed him with the other. Her head arched into the bed as he slipped his fingers around her underwear and boldly caressed her. She came in a rush, crying out and panting. "Oh, God."

"That's right, baby. Come more for me."

He slipped a finger inside her, and she went higher. Sparkles of color as bright as her flowers appeared behind her closed eyes as she moved against him. Her body started to peak again, and she knew she was on a new path of desire. She'd never been this responsive, although it was no wonder it would be like this with Vinnie.

She leaned up for a kiss, and he took her mouth harder, moaning with her. "God, babe," he whispered when he pulled back, shock and desire in his expression.

She was too turned on to be embarrassed. Then again, why should she be? She wanted him. Wasn't this how it *should* be?

"Kiss me again," she urged, undoing the rest of his tuxedo buttons.

He leaned back and stripped off his jacket and then his shirt. "You should know I would normally hang this up, but I can't wait for that either."

She laid her hand on the golden muscles of his chest as he settled back over her to kiss her thoroughly, the pace urgent between them. "Yes," she whispered, her body rising to meet his growing passion.

"Let's get this off you," he said, turning her away from him, his lips on her nape as he undid the cloth buttons of the gown. "Usually I appreciate old-school buttons like this, but now I'm thinking a good pair of scissors might be necessary if it's going to take much longer to get them undone."

She'd had a hard time with them herself, but her fingers were smaller. "Let me. You finish undressing."

"Ordering me around already, huh?" He shot her a sexy wink. "Do it some more."

Oh, yeah, they were going to be so good together. "Gladly," she said. "I want your pants off right now." She wanted to see him naked. All her life she'd wondered how beautiful he would be.

When they slid to the floor, her breath caught. He was even more gorgeous than she'd imagined, his strong build shaped by thick muscles crafted by weightlifting. And he wanted her very badly, she was delighted to see.

"Satisfactory?" He was grinning, preening even. Well, she had come a few times in little more than a few minutes, and he'd barely even touched her. He had a reason to preen.

"More than," she said, unbuttoning the last button. She removed her arms from the sleeves and slid it down her waist and to the floor. Stepping out of it, she laid it over the back of the chair—it was his mama's dress—and stood before him in her strapless white bra and panties. She hadn't splurged on a wedding set, but it was sexy anyway, and it looked good with the thigh-highs.

"I'm a bit curvier than I used to be," she said, forcing herself to stand tall as his gaze took in every detail. "But I meant what I said the other day. I fully intend to lose the weight."

"You're perfect. Don't be talking like that. I love your body, and I'm about to show you just how much."

He closed the short distance between them and put his large hands on her hips. They were hot, and when they slid down her curves, her flesh caught fire.

"You're so beautiful, Rose." He slid his hands up to her breasts then. "I'm never going to get enough of you."

As he undid her bra and set his mouth to her breasts, he more than proved his point. She'd known Vinnie was a thorough man, but she learned there was no end to how thorough he could be when it came to loving her. He caressed every line of flesh, every lush curve, sometimes giving one area his sole focus. Other times, he touched her slowly, never taking his eyes off hers. It was hot and sexy and she came again when he laid his mouth to her most sensitive curves.

"I love how you are with me," he said, rolling away for a moment to pull open the bedside drawer. "Now I want to see what it's like when we become one."

She helped him with the condom because the act felt important. Then she lay back and opened herself to him as he slid into her body and covered her. She moaned, feeling him fill her, settling into her core.

He took her hands in his on the pillow. "Look at me."

She fought the urge to close her eyes. Sweat was beading on his temple, and the pulse in his neck was knocking against the skin. He wanted her, but the emotion in his gaze was what made her breath catch.

"I love you, Rose," he whispered, and his words sounded like the vows he'd made to her earlier.

"I love you too," she whispered back, caressing the wedding ring on his left hand.

He pressed forward, causing her to moan. "This is me loving you."

She tightened her hands around his and opened to him, loving him back in this timeless expression between two people. "Put your legs around me," he urged, thrusting deeply into her.

She could feel the passion gathering inside her again, swirling in her belly. He was about to take her to an edge she'd never reached before, and she was afraid she was going to scream. She clenched his hands, trying to hold it all back, but he kept up the deep thrusts, his pace quickening.

"Come with me." His hoarse pleading had her straining against him. "Come on, Rose."

He pressed fast and hard, and she lifted up to meet him. Her entire body started to shake like she was going to break apart, and then she was crying out, pulsing around him as he called her name and shook in her arms with a force that took her higher.

They were both moaning brokenly, panting, and clutching each other when he pressed his forehead to hers. He was sweaty, but so was she, and God, coming apart with Vinnie—and then coming back together with him— was the most perfect feeling in the world. After a while, his mouth found hers in the most delicious and loving way. She'd never had a kiss like that, and she touched his jaw to ensure it went on for as long as possible.

There'd been so much tenderness in that kiss. So much love and peace.

When he finally lifted his head, he was smiling, warmth in every line of his face. She swept his damp curls from his forehead and ran her fingers down the back of his head, happiness filling her every pore along with the scent of crushed rose petals. Oh, how she would always savor this moment.

"I don't know that I have words to describe what we just did, but all I know is that I've never felt anything to equal it." He gave her some room and took care of the condom. "But if this is what making love and being married is like, I can see why it caught on thousands of years ago."

"I don't have words for it either," she said as he tucked her close to his body. "All I know is that I love you and I love making love with you."

He kissed her and reached for their warm Prosecco. "Rose, my love, here's to being married and loving every minute of it."

They loved every minute of it that night and into the morning. When growling stomachs finally made them leave the bed and make breakfast, he held up a couple of envelopes as she made them eggs.

"My mama said to read her note when we were alone. You mind if I read it out loud?"

"Please do," she said, luxuriating in her body as she did something as simple as stir scrambled eggs. My God, she'd never see sex or her body the same way after last night, and she loved knowing Vinnie felt that way too. He began to read.

Dear Vinnie,

It's hard to adequately express how happy I am for you and Rose. As someone who was happily married for almost twenty-five years, I know what it takes every day. Friendship. Respect. Love. Laughter. Loyalty. Generosity. Passion. You and Rose have all of these, and they will deepen with the years as you build your home together.

It's because I know what it takes that I have agreed to marry Paddy O'Connor. It may be a surprise in terms of speed, but as you obviously know, time has little to do with the heart. I loved him when I was young, and he loved me. But things happened, as you know, and we had different lives, him with his beloved Kathleen and me with your beloved papa. Both of us cherish them and our time together, but now we plan to cherish each other. We're grateful for this second chance to spend what time we have left together.

I hope you—and Hank—will give us your blessing. Paddy and I have remarked on how you two have always been brothers, and when I was praying the other day, I wondered if that wasn't a sign of the love between our families being ever present.

Family is ever important, and so is something else: having a home. With me marrying Paddy, I want to give you and Rose the house you grew up in to live in together. You and Rose can keep it as long as it makes you happy. I'll be signing the title over to you shortly, and Paddy and I plan to marry not long after Hank and Alice.

We wanted to give you children your days in the sun, and we eagerly look forward to you sharing our celebration with you come late January. Afterward, it will make me very happy to think of you and Rose in this house that has seen so many happy moments, knowing such happiness will continue.

All my love,
Mama

Vinnie wiped at the tears spilling down his cheeks. "I never thought..."

Rose was crying too, and she turned off the stove and crossed to him. "Oh, your mama... Your sweet mama."

He pulled her to him, and she hugged her tight. They both took some time to settle. When she finally pulled back, he was shaking his head. "She's the best. Rose, are you good with this? I mean, I know it's not your home."

"But it's your home, the place you grew up," she said. "Vinnie, I would be so happy and grateful to live there. Only I feel a little guilty. It's so much."

Kissing her softly, he tucked her to his chest. "Mama wouldn't offer it unless she wanted us to have it. Rose, I love everything about this house. I love the land too, and the garage under us where I keep my car. Every room is full of good memories, and I want to make more of them here with you."

She kissed the center of his chest, where his heart beat. "I want to make them here with you too. We have to thank her. Congratulate her. Do you think Hank knows she's getting married?"

He chuckled. "Mr. O'Connor asked both of us for our blessing before you and I got engaged. I wasn't supposed to say anything."

"Of course!" She put her hands to the sides of her face. "I think I'm in shock."

"Then I should probably open the rest of these," he said, holding up the next one. He pulled out the note and smiled. "It's from Aunt Gladys and Clifton. Oh, she shouldn't have. I have another jacket on the house waiting for me, per your pleasure. She signed it with a winky face."

"She's incredible. I can't wait to see you bare under the next one. But this one is perfect for kicking off our first morning together."

He'd pulled on the midnight blue velvet jacket over his bare chest and wore nothing else but loose gray flannel pants. So hot.

"Do you want to open the next one?" he asked. "I think it's from your parents."

She pursed her lip, fighting emotion. "Please read it."

He slit the envelope open and pulled out the card. Inside, he pulled out a check. Her heart tore. His eyes widened before he started to read the note out loud.

Our dearest Rose and Vinnie,
We celebrate your marriage with great joy and will
pray for your health, happiness, and success every day.
Rose, we know you want to return the gift we gave you for
your business, but please don't hurt us by sending it back.
This additional money isn't as much as we'd imagined
giving you and your husband, but it's given with all the
love we have for you. Please don't fight us on this. It would
make us so happy to know we can help you and Vinnie
start your life together, much like our parents and our
parents' parents did for their children. This is what family
does, and we cherish having the two of you in ours. We
love you both.
Always,
Mama & Papa

She sank into a chair and pressed her face into her hands, not even looking at the check. The amount didn't matter. They didn't have that kind of money, especially not when they'd agreed to help Al and his family.

"We can't take it," she said, lifting her face. "I'm sorry. I didn't mean to speak for you. Vinnie, I can't—"

"Of course we can't," Vinnie said, wiping her tears. "Mama's gift is different. She's moving to a new house, and this one will be vacant. Besides, your greenhouse is the biggest gift of all, right? Don't worry, Rose. We'll figure out a way to tell them no."

"I don't want to hurt them, but all I see is hurt right now." She blew out a long breath. "Yesterday I wondered when I would be able to hug them again. I couldn't even ask Mama to help me button up my wedding dress."

"Rose, I know it hurts, and I'm sorry it's like this. All we can do is be there if they need us."

"And light a candle for them." She shook her head.

"I didn't want to get upset like this. I wanted today to be about us. About being happy together."

"We can feel both," he said, caressing her cheek. "That's life, I guess. Since the eggs are cold, why don't you let me help you feel better another way?"

Making love with him this time opened her up to another powerful truth: being with him could be both passionate and comforting all at once.

Marriage was all she'd hoped for and more, and the roots anchoring her heart to Vinnie, to Orion, were starting to deepen and spread like the most long-lasting of plants.

CHAPTER 28

"EXCUSE ME. HAVE YOU, OR HAVE YOU NOT, GOTTEN MY messages?"

Warren had always believed in community engagement. From the early days of running the neighborhood chocolate stand, he'd gotten darn good at talking to people about their hopes, dreams, and concerns.

But Lucia Tesoro was perhaps his toughest cookie yet.

Warren had been excited to bring Amy to the Coffee Roastery while Alice watched the kids. And they'd had a few nice moments—greeting Baker and ordering their coffees, saying hello to Maria Sanchez, who was arranging some chocolate boxes from the House of Hope & Chocolate in the window in a cross-promotional display. That kind of community collaboration was going to get Orion back on track. But then Lucia had stormed in and confronted him. It was pretty clear she hadn't come in for coffee.

He turned to face the woman and prayed for patience.

"I *did* get your messages, Lucia," he said calmly. "And I appreciate that you have a view on the new business grants the trust is considering."

"Then I ask again," she said, her dark eyes blazing

over her red mask. "Why haven't you talked to *me* about it yet? Gladys Green isn't the only one with views in this town, even though I know how cozy you've gotten with her, especially now that your wife is in her employ."

Before Warren could step in, Amy said, "Lucia, I'm working with Aunt Gladys because it's a good match for both of us. Warren hasn't spoken to you yet because he's still doing what Warren does best. Researching models, honing a successful plan, and yes, talking to people in the community. It's the holidays so he's not doing full-on meetings yet, but I am sure he'll be speaking to you sometime soon."

The woman looked down her nose at them even though she stood barely over five feet. Despite her diminutive size, she resembled a scary warrior in black, dripping with silver necklaces with teeth-like links, likely antique relics from a time when people wore the trophies of their victims. "Well, I'm working full-time to keep my business open, even over the holidays, so if I can do it, so can Warren."

"Lucia," Baker said from behind the counter, "they only just moved here. They have kids. Let them settle in some. Welcome them to the community a little more, huh?"

She turned her attention to Baker, which had probably been Baker's intention, bless him. "Like I don't know your leanings on this topic. We can't start letting outsiders infiltrate Orion and take up all of our storefronts."

Warren saw Maria glance quickly over her shoulder, her hands stilling from arranging the truffle boxes.

"Why not, Lucia?" Baker shot back. "More businesses attract more foot traffic. We need to fill those empty spots. They're like missing teeth."

"We need to put existing Orion businesses first." She made a fist and knocked it into her other hand. "Those of us who have had businesses here for decades deserve more help. Bigger grants. We're the town's foundation. I'm not the only one who wants to deter upstarts who washed out in the city from coming to Orion and starting a competing business. Why should they get money from the trust? I'm a proven quantity, from this community."

Warren held up his hand to stop Baker from replying. "The trust is designed to help Orion, and as you know from receiving your loan only last week, its goal is to create a business climate for your business and others to thrive. Empty storefronts are any town's worst nightmare, and your business sector is down thirty percent. I can provide you with the research I've compiled so far, but supporting the business sector involves helping established businesses *and* attracting new ones. You will be gaining business owners who believe in the Friends & Neighbors motto. They will want to support Orion as much as you do."

Again, he watched as Maria nodded in agreement.

"You can't know they'll support Orion," Lucia snapped. "They might just want a free handout to start a business."

"Come on," Baker said with an edge. "Running a business is hard work, even more so now. Anyone who has the guts to jump in the deep end right now gets my applause."

Warren wanted to clap, but that would have been rude. Given his position within the community, he had to at least act like a neutral party.

"Also..." Baker picked up a stirring stick and tapped it on the counter. "Like with the grants for established businesses, yours and mine included, I imagine Warren will have strict parameters for newcomers to follow. Wouldn't you support Rose Fiorni receiving a grant so she could open a florist shop on Main Street instead of just doing it out of her parents' greenhouse?"

"After the rest of us are taken care of," Lucia said with emphasis. "Plus, Rose is from Orion. Mr. Palladino would be thrilled to see her make a business from the greenhouse and plants he originally gave Joe. He was a good customer to me as well."

"I didn't know that," Baker said. "People speak well of him."

"Yes, and of course Joe and Carlotta are good people too. But that girl is going to need all the help she can get with her brother being back in town. He broke a lamp in my store once."

Warren was hoping they didn't cross paths. The guy sounded like a nightmare.

"Sure, Joe ended up paying for it," Lucia continued, "but now that Al's back and possibly taking over Joe's store someday—God help the men who let him cut their hair or shave them—we're going to need at least one sane Fiorni with a storefront on Main Street. Joe and Carlotta have lost their minds if you ask me."

Baker leaned his elbow on the counter. "Here I'd heard you were pretty rough on Rose—and Vinnie—about charging for their videos."

She threw up her hands. "Maybe so, but these are tough times. I was shocked to hear how much a video like that cost."

Warren bit his lip as Baker said, "Haven't you gone online and checked, Lucia? Trust me, three hundred is a bargain from what I've seen. Maybe you should do a little more research before you take shots at good people and hurt their pride."

Her dark eyes sparked before she made an exasperated sound. "Fine, Baker. You're right. I'm wrong. Now let's get back to these new grants. I still have concerns."

She was like a dog with a bone. Warren continued to take mental notes, knowing Lucia was one of the strongest opponents to the new grants he was considering. Baker seemed to be doing a fine job of bandying with the woman, however, and he decided to sit back and let them duel.

"And we've heard them." Baker pointed to the words on his T-shirt: *We're All in This Together*. "We can't start picking favorites or keeping some people out and letting others in. If someone has a great business idea and wants to start it in this town, I'll be the first one to greet them with a cup of coffee and support."

Maria turned fully around, facing the group. Her eyes were intent, and again, Warren found himself wondering about her perspective. Alice couldn't say enough about how much she valued Maria's judgment.

"You can't do this willy-nilly," Lucia declared. "What if someone from Brooklyn wants to open up a new boutique furniture store? They'd be a direct competitor to me."

"Then you'll have to make sure you do your part to make your store succeed—just like you always have, just like the rest of us do," Baker said. "No one should have a monopoly."

No, they shouldn't, and he shot a look at Amy, knowing she agreed.

"You saying you would be fine with Warren giving some hotshot barista from Soho a loan to start a coffee shop next door?" Lucia asked, drilling her finger into her palm.

"You bet, and I'll tell you why." Baker gestured to his store. "Because I stand by my product. I roast the best coffee in town, and I make it better than anyone else too. That's why no one has opened another coffee shop. Bad idea when another one has all the business, especially in a small town. If he or she can do better than me, taking away customers, then it would be a sign I need to up my game. Competition is good for the market, Lucia. It's why our town can have three gas stations and all can thrive."

Maria nodded her head emphatically, and Warren almost asked her to join their group. Solidarity mattered in moments like this one.

Lucia gave an indelicate snort. "You're young, Baker. Maybe not a spring chicken, but you're still far away from your sell-by date. Competition doesn't look so good when you get older. Plus, I'm tired. This year has been unimaginable."

Baker shook his head. "Yeah, it has. That's why we need to stick together. Here. Have a coffee on the house. I believe in our friends and neighbors mission."

Warren held his breath, wondering what she'd do.

A lengthy sigh gusted out before she said, "You're the kind who kills with kindness, but you're honest and direct, and I respect that." She turned to Warren. "All I'm asking is that you consider my side before you roll this out. People like me and Manny Romano have other ideas, and we'd like to be heard."

"I fully intend to listen to everyone, Lucia," Warren said.

"He means that," Amy said. "Warren is the best listener I know, and he's good at what he does."

Lucia reached for the coffee that Baker had set on the counter. "Good, because we need the trust to weather this damn pandemic. Thank you for the coffee, Baker."

With that, she let herself out of the coffee shop, the wind as much as her force hurling the door closed. The truffle boxes Maria had carefully arranged into a tower fell over onto the table. *"Por Dios."*

"Well, that was fun," Baker said, gripping the counter.

"But you did good with her," Maria said softly.

"Yes, you did," Warren said, and Amy nodded. "Kindness. It doesn't defuse every bomb—"

"But some of them," Baker said, laughing. "Sorry you had to be here for that, Maria. I guess it was bad timing for the display."

"There is no such thing," Maria said. "I've worked in Orion since Mama Gia hired me at sixteen to work at Two Sisters. I know there are very different feelings in this town. You can sense it as you walk by people's stores."

Warren rubbed his forehead. "Well, I listened to what she had to say. Didn't agree. But I listened."

"Some people don't want to listen back," Amy said, glancing in the direction she'd left. "She reminded me of my mother."

"Mine too," Baker said with a harsh laugh. "Lucia's a tough woman, and I'm sure she got hard for a reason, but she's wrong about regulating new businesses."

"There are always some business owners who bark," Warren said, having gone through a few rounds with some of them. "I appreciate you stepping in and playing devil's advocate. It's good to know Lucia would support Rose getting a loan but not a stranger. Some small towns make it mandatory for someone to live in a town for a certain amount of time before they receive a loan. Like a residency requirement."

"But who can afford to move here months or years before they start their business?" Amy asked. "No one I know of. Alice came with her capital, remember? And so did Clifton."

Warren nodded. She was right.

"Many people can't afford to live and work here," Maria said, stepping forward. "I'm one of them. But that doesn't mean I don't believe in this community and its new motto."

"The residency requirement isn't the only way," Warren said, pleased she was sharing. "There are also models where the person puts up some percentage of their own money, not only as investment capital but good faith. How does that strike you, Maria?"

"Fair." Her golden brown eyes were glowing. "The heart isn't the only key to a successful business. One must bring start-up money, a plan, a good product, even a good location. There are many factors, ones I've learned from working at Two Sisters and now the House of Hope & Chocolate."

Baker came around the counter. "Have you thought about opening your own place, Maria? No one makes better hot chocolate, and I expect you made some of the dishes that I loved at Two Sisters. I'd support you. What do you have in mind?"

She clasped her hands as if trying to still them. "A real Mexican restaurant. With tortillas being made in the window. Moles bubbling on the stoves in the back. Hot peppers hanging on the walls, waiting to be roasted in the fire dancing in the wood oven."

Baker put his hand on his heart. "I want to eat there *right now*. Maria, you need to do it."

Her eyes crinkled over her white mask. "You are kind. I have been saving money and learning from wonderful women how to run a business. Someday it will happen if it is meant to be."

Warren smiled for the first time since Lucia had interrupted him, and Amy nudged him in the side as if to encourage him to say what he already intended to say. "When you know it's time, you find me. Even if I can't help you through the trust—I still have some legwork to do in terms of figuring out our approach for new business loans—I'll help you apply for a loan somewhere else. I know when I meet someone if their business will take off. Not only do I know yours will, I want to bring my family there to eat."

"I can already see the tortillas being made in the window," Amy said, gesturing to where the woman was standing. "Smell the roasted peppers."

She put a hand to her heart. "Thank you. See, Baker, there is no bad timing."

He nodded, the tension in his shoulders apparent. "Perhaps I need to have a little more faith."

"You are finding it," Maria said gently. "Now, if you will excuse me, I will finish this display and go back to work. Clifton must be wondering where I am."

"You tell him I started talking your ear off," Warren said. "I guess I managed to tie up two of his favorite people. Alice volunteered to babysit while the girls napped so we could have an outing."

"She is good like that." The woman smiled with her eyes, quickly finished the display, and left with a wave.

"I wish there were more people like Maria," Baker said, following her progress across the street. "We need to attract new businesses. I'll talk to some of the other owners. People will feel more comfortable if the newbies, as Lucia called them, bring some capital to the table."

"I agree. You, babe?"

Amy shook her head, also gazing after Maria. "Seems like a good way to counter some hard feelings. Yet not everyone can do it."

Didn't he know it? "But would they bark less?" Warren asked, almost rhetorically.

"Lucia's always going to bark," Baker said as he set their coffees on the counter. "While I believe people can change, I also believe people become so entrenched in their beliefs that some of them simply won't. Even if it's in their best interest. Even if it's making them miserable."

Amy lifted her coffee in the air. "To the closet cynic in you as much as the openhearted rebel."

"Ha," Baker said, lifting his water bottle. "Some days I'm not sure who's winning. People like Lucia bring out my inner cynic, even though I'm dogged about killing them with kindness, as she said."

"Sometimes it's the only place to start." Warren picked up his coffee. "Otherwise, the anger and other stuff wins. Personally, I think she brings out the openhearted rebel more. If you were a complete cynic, you wouldn't give a—"

"No, I wouldn't." He patted his T-shirt. "I do believe we're all in this together. That's why I want new businesses to come in. That's why I try and talk sense into Lucia even though I want to bash my head in afterward sometimes. We need each other. Maybe the next new business to come into town will make all the difference. That's how I see the House of Hope & Chocolate. Alice, Clifton, and Sarah— God rest her soul—came in at the right time. They helped this town come together when we needed it most."

Amy took Warren's hand, sensing he was choked up.

"Words like that keep me going," he said. "They make me more determined to see things through."

"Me too," Amy said. "Seems the Friends & Neighbors motto still hasn't fully caught on. We've got some work to do."

"The optimist in me wonders what the next catalyst will be to anchor it in more. It's not only words on a sign to me," Baker said. "When I order more store bags, I'm going to put the logo on them."

They weren't just words to Warren either, and he knew Amy felt the same way. "Alice said if Paddy O'Connor can embrace it, anyone can. Let's hope she's right."

"Maybe I'll ask Paddy to visit Lucia," Baker said. Grinning, he added, "Oh, to be a fly on the wall. Speaking of, did you hear about Vinnie's mother giving him and Rose her house? Now that's the kind of love and support that gets me right here."

Warren pressed his hand to his breastbone in comradery. "Yeah, it's an incredible gesture. Alice said Hank got so choked up he could barely string together a sentence. He loves Mama Gia hard, and even though I haven't met her, I already halfway love her too." Especially after hearing how the woman had been a mentor to Maria.

"It's nice to hear about mothers being kind to their children," Amy said with a thread of softness in her voice.

They'd gotten through a holiday FaceTime with her mother, but it had required her to grit her teeth occasionally. She'd suggested they paint the house neutral again. Amy had responded they were going with hot pink flamingos, making her mother sputter.

"Well, I'm going to go work with Aunt Gladys like the newbie I am and show Lucia Tesoro just how much innovation an outsider can bring to an established business," Amy said.

Baker laughed. "When you finish, can you show me? I'm stuck. I can only afford a few hours a week, but I'm more tech savvy than Aunt Gladys. I can do a lot of the online stuff. It's the higher-level thinking I'm missing at the moment."

Amy's eyes sparkled, much like they had after another passionate night in their new bedroom. God, she looked more beautiful than ever. This town was helping her blossom. Before, she never would have spoken back to someone like Lucia. But she had today. Progress.

"My first suggestion would be to start taking selfies in your T-shirts, with a featured coffee, of course," Amy said. "People need to hear those messages right now."

"Some people find them annoying," Baker said with a wry glance. "Lucia comes to mind."

"They're not your audience. You have good stories and you care about people. It's not just about coffee. You're also supporting other businesses, like the chocolate shop. You might talk about why you believe we're in this together."

"I can do that," Baker said, looking calmer now. "It's always been about more than coffee."

The best businesses always were. And that was why Warren would always consider the Bakers of the world more successful than the Lucias.

But they all still deserved support, and it was his job to give it. He left Amy with Baker to talk about social media and headed down to Manny Romano's deli to hear his concerns.

He would do his part to live up to the Friends & Neighbors motto in this town.

CHAPTER 29

VINNIE WAS PURE MAGIC.
In their home.
In their bed.
In the greenhouse.
In the videos.

This was the click Aunt Gladys had talked about, the one that happened when two perfectly suited people came together. She and Vinnie had clicked but good.

He had told her about his morning routine, red at the collar with embarrassment, but she had embraced it. Now they sang their hearts out together to Frank, the Chairman of the Board, as Vinnie called him, after they drank their espresso every morning.

She'd included him in talking to her babies—the Mountain Roses, succulents, and the baby lemon tree she'd cut for his mama. He'd started talking to them too, and she'd fallen even more in love with him.

The start of the new year was a breath of fresh air. They'd agreed to keep focused on the things they were grateful for—each other at the top of the list—and keep track of their successes: plants sold, video requests and views, product sponsorship, and the like. She'd decided Romeoville only worked for some posts and had broadened her range since Vinnie's range was broadening too as he sponsored more products and found his online voice.

Today they were feeling euphoric over The Dreamer's Flower Shoppe's first viral video, an homage to Christopher Walken's hilarious *Saturday Night Live* skit about the man who put googly eyes on his plants because he was scared of them. Vinnie pulled off an impressive Walken accent and look, courtesy of a bad wig they'd bought online and an outfit from the vintage store, and he'd showcased a new collection of cacti, ferns, bromeliads, and banana plants she wanted to sell, googly eyes optional. People were liking it and commenting on it and sharing it, but better yet, she'd also gotten over a hundred orders, most of them asking for googly eyes for their plants.

"You've got a lot of shipping to do, babe," Vinnie said, kissing the top of her head as they looked at the post. "You sure you don't need me to help you carry Hank and Alice's wedding flowers from their house to the greenhouse?"

"No, I've got it. Thanks again for letting me drive your car into the city yesterday." Her quick trip to the flower market had been fantastic, and a few of the shop owners had even shared her Walken-inspired post with their followers. That kind of outreach and support was completely unexpected, and it had made her feel supported beyond Orion.

"I'm so happy, Vinnie." She threw her arms around him. "I finally believe this is going to work."

The only thing that still worried her was Al. While she hadn't seen him in the greenhouse again, she'd smelled pot around it a few mornings. Maybe she was being paranoid, but it felt like he was trying to send her a message that he was still around. She always kept the door locked during her visits, but last night, she'd decided to keep it locked at all times. That had made her throat thick with sadness, but she'd gone home feeling better.

"Everything is working out," Vinnie said, caressing her hair in the slow, sexy way he had that always felt both arousing and comforting. "My heart is so full I sometimes don't think it will fit in my chest anymore. In fact, I think I'm going to bust these shirt buttons. You want to help me save them?"

She edged back, already grinning at the twinkle in his eyes. "Maybe we can replace them with googly eyes."

He laughed and pulled her hips to his. "Maybe. But I like the thought of my wife saving me so much more."

"I thought we'd agreed that we'd get going once we'd dressed and finished our morning routine." But she started to unbutton his shirt and then his pants anyway because she couldn't help herself. "You're going to be late for work."

"I plan to be on time," Vinnie said with a gleam. "It's going to be good but quick. I just can't go to work without having you again. I want you all the time."

She shimmied her hips in happiness as much as to shuck off her pants. "I want you all the time too. When I was working in the greenhouse the other day, I was thinking about how hot we are together, and I swear my *Monstera Deliciosa* started to wilt."

He picked her up and carried her effortlessly to the small counter in the kitchen. "Delicious monster?"

Opening her legs to him, she moaned as he rolled on another condom from their Aunt Gladys stash and pressed in deep. Both of them were pretty pleased that they'd gone through over half of it already. "Your Italian will only bring you so far with that name. It's a Split-lead...Philodendron. Oh, God yes. Right there."

"I know I have your full attention when you stop talking about plants," Vinnie joked, pumping his hips in a rhythm that had her clutching his back.

"I could still recite all the Latin names of my cacti," she whispered, her belly taut with desire. "Want me to?"

"Shut up, Rose," he teased gently, taking her mouth in

a deep kiss.

When they were both gasping from their orgasms, she tickled his ribs, a ticklish spot she'd discovered the other night in bed. He gave a high-pitched giggle, making her laugh, before catching her hands. "Funny. Now tell me the cacti names. It's either that or I'm putting on more church music. I already want you again, and I really do have to go to work."

They needed a honeymoon. Rose had never fully realized the brilliance of the idea. Before she'd thought it was a vacation, somewhere to go to after the stress of putting on a wedding. Even a time for the couple to settle into their married couple rhythm. Now she realized it was also for sex, so a couple could have it twenty-four seven if they wanted. Like she and Vinnie wanted.

"I'm trying to remind myself I'm grateful we both have jobs," Vinnie said, putting the church music on anyway.

"Cacti names weren't going to be enough this morning?"

He didn't answer, but she heard him muttering a *Hail Mary* under his breath. The poor guy.

"I feel you," she said, fanning herself. "Get dressed and get out. As fast as you can. Before I text Hank and beg him to be a pal and give you an extra hour this morning."

"He'd do it, but it's not fair to him," Vinnie said, turning his back and buttoning up. "Okay, my beautiful wife. I am out of here." Turning back to look at her, his eyes mischievous, he said, "I will blow you a kiss because just the thought of that luscious mouth is making me hard again."

He was out the door without putting his coat on, and she went to their small fridge and pulled out a soda bottle and pressed it between her breasts. Oh, what a life! Even in their small space, where she sometimes turned around and ran into him—usually because he liked to be close to her— she couldn't imagine wanting more.

Moving into his mom's house was going to be a blessing,

but she would always be grateful for this time.

She began to pack her bag. Yesterday she'd gone into the city for flowers for Alice and Hank's wedding, which was tomorrow. Today she would make the bride's bouquet, the flower arrangements for the tables, and the boutonnières. As she walked down the stairs, Mr. O'Connor emerged from the main house.

"Hi, Rose," he said, tucking his bare hands into his pockets to stave off the cold. "I hear you're heading to Alice's to pick up the flowers in her fridge. Want some help carrying them? I figure two sets of hands are better than one."

She wondered if Vinnie had said something on his way out. Either way, it was a sweet offer, the kind she wouldn't refuse. "I'd love the help. Thanks."

"Let me grab my coat," he said, and then he was off.

Mama Gia came to the window and opened it. "Rose, you need any help with the flowers for tomorrow, you let me know. I can follow directions. I know you have a lot of shipping to do for your new orders. I can help with that too."

"I'm good, Mama Gia," she called, delighted by the offer. "Mr. O'Connor is going to be my helper today."

She supposed she could take Vinnie's car—his silver '86 Alfa Romeo Spider was a dream to drive and especially dear as a symbol of trust—but Alice and Hank lived close to her parents, and she liked to walk. Her figure looked and felt better to her. She didn't know if she'd lost weight—Vinnie had no scale—but her figure didn't feel overly full anymore. She felt downright perfect, just like Vinnie told her every day.

When Mr. O'Connor came back down, she gave a wave to her mother-in-law and they set off. There was a crisp wind, but the sky was bright blue, the clouds were splashes of white, and the sun was bright and shiny. Like she was on the inside.

"You mind explaining why those flowers are in Alice and Hank's fridge?" he asked.

"Flowers need to be kept chilled," she said, crossing the snow-shoveled path to the gate to the back of Hank and Alice's home. "I don't have a commercial cooler yet. This way, I can keep the flowers their optimum temperature to stay fresh."

"That kind of cooler expensive?" He opened the gate for her and let her precede him. "Or is it a matter of space?"

"Both, I suppose." She didn't want to mention her hesitation about storing a future cooler at the greenhouse. When she could afford it, she would keep it at their new house. Perhaps even in their old space. Vinnie had suggested she use it as an office so she wouldn't have to spend so much time at the greenhouse. Being there wasn't the same anymore. She was in and out, doing her best to avert her eyes from the windows, where she might catch glimpses of her mama or Al and his family. Often she could hear the yelling, and sometimes even one of the younger girls crying, but she kept her head down. What was going on in there was not her business.

She had to remember that.

Still, when she and Mr. O'Connor arrived at the greenhouse, the first thing she saw was the broken lock. Her brother had broken it? She rushed inside, her eyes zeroing in on the ashtray resting beside her newly potted ogre ear succulents. The smell of pot was strong in the air. Her stomach clenched. There were two joint tips in the ashes, and one had lipstick on it. Paulina had been smoking in here too.

She glanced around casually to check if anything else was out of place and breathed a shallow sigh of relief that it looked the way she'd left it.

"The lock is broken," Mr. O'Connor commented. "That's concerning. Where do you want me to put the flowers, Rose?"

When she glanced over, his eyes were on the ashtray. Shame and anger boiled up through her. "Those aren't mine or Vinnie's."

"I know that," Mr. O'Connor said, shifting his weight as he looked around. "I remember your brother and that Grasiaca punk smoking pot in my parking lot, looking for trouble. Do you want me to talk to him?"

"It won't do any good," she said, futility lacing her voice like cobwebs. "He almost came to blows with Vinnie. I…I'm doing my best to stay in my lane."

"Bullies don't like that," Mr. O'Connor said, rubbing the back of his head. "I've had my bullying days, so I'd know. They like to push. Provoke. You were smart to keep this place locked, but he made a statement breaking it."

Tears filled her eyes, and she turned away. The greenhouse had been her most sacred place, a sanctuary. Now she couldn't walk in without fearing she'd see some new "statement" left by Al.

"Well, well, well," she heard him say.

She turned around. Al stood in the doorway in jeans and a black sweatshirt. He'd left the door wide open, which wasn't good for her plants. She thought of telling him to get out and close it, but his mouth curled with such hatred she was afraid she'd start a fight by doing so.

"I never imagined seeing you on Fiorni property," he said, his mouth twisting. "Rose, you might bring Vinnie back here, but I won't stand for this. I remember how you used to talk to me when I hung around your parking lot. Now it's my turn. You get the hell out of here, O'Connor."

Rose fisted her hands at her sides. "Don't be rude. He's helping me. It's Hank and Alice's wedding tomorrow."

"Like I give a fuck about his do-gooding son and that chocolate bitch. Heard she was as looney as fruitcake. You know, I always thought you were an asshole, Mr. O'Connor, but even you've fallen under her spell. Makes a guy wonder if that chocolate bitch has more charms than are apparent through her shop window."

"You watch your mouth," Mr. O'Connor said harshly, setting his weight. "That's my family you're talking about. Now, Rose has work to do."

"You moving me along?" Al ambled farther into the greenhouse, angling his thumbs into his pockets. "This is my own house. Who the f—"

"It's my house as much as it is yours," Rose said, quivering. "This greenhouse is my place of business. Al, I told you not to come in here. Don't make me talk to Mama and Papa about this."

"Like you hold any sway in this family anymore," Al said. "You moved out, remember? Ran away from what I hear. Big bad brother came back to town, and little Rose had to be rescued. Now you're doing real fine, and your business is taking off. From where I'm standing, you owe me."

She gaped at him. "I *what*?"

"If I hadn't come back, Vinnie would never have married you." He spat on her floor. "He didn't once look at you. Not once. You convinced him with your poor-little-me act, just like you did Mama and Papa, even though you've gotten fat. You think *I'm* pathetic? Please, you're worse."

Her response burned to ash in her mouth. She knew better than to engage. Her mama had always said so. It had only ever encouraged him.

Al looked around, as if surveying his property. "You might need to start paying rent for this place, Rose."

"When hell freezes over," she shot back.

"We'll see." He spat again and finally strolled out, leaving the greenhouse door open. She hurried forward to close it. During his short visit, he'd dropped the temperature inside by twenty degrees. Nothing damaging, but still, her plants didn't like it. She wondered if he'd left it open while smoking in here.

"He's as pleasant as ever," Mr. O'Connor said with a

muttered curse. "Sorry. Until today, I haven't had any inclination to pick up my old ways, but he tested me, sure as hell he did. And he knew it. I wanted to punch him. He knew that too. It seems I'm not as reformed as I thought."

His shoulders slumped, and Rose walked over to him. "He insulted you *and* your family. I wanted to punch him too, but I knew that's what he wanted. Mr. O'Connor, wanting to hit my brother doesn't make you a bad man. It makes you normal."

He sighed heartily. "I want to believe I can be a good man. The kind Hank and Gia need me to be. I don't want to screw things up. Rose, I came close to throwing him out of this greenhouse like he was a loud-mouthed punk in my pub back in the day. Maybe I need to wait longer to see if I'm changed. For Gia especially."

That he would start to doubt himself was crushing. Even more so since it was because of her brother. "Stop that. You're doing great. Don't let him get to you. But I understand. He's getting to me. It's getting harder to come here."

"Al broke a few locks back in the day if I'm remembering right," Mr. O'Connor said tightly. "Broke into a few cars too. I couldn't prove it, but once I thought he and a few of his friends broke into my kitchen and smashed the food in the cooler around St. Patrick's Day."

Rose remembered him calling it a mick holiday. She'd never liked hearing talk like that. "Did my parents know?" she asked.

"They fixed a few windows when he was a kid, but nothing stuck as he got older." Mr. O'Connor glanced toward the house. "He's a mean cuss, but he's clever. Why don't I go to the hardware store and buy you a better lock? Do you want me to talk to Joe?"

Her heart broke at the thought. "I'll talk to Papa. In fact, I'll walk with you to Main Street."

"When you're done, I'll walk you back here, install the

lock, and stay while you work," Mr. O'Connor said. "I've got nothing to do but sit with my thoughts and feel frogs jump in this old belly of mine about tomorrow. I know I don't have to do anything at the wedding, but I still want to stand up well for Hank and Alice. They deserve the best, and I want them to have it. My boy didn't get the kind of father he deserved before. I have a lot to make up for."

Her heart ached, hearing him talk like that, another wound on top of what she'd learned about Al. "From where I'm standing, you're pretty incredible."

He snorted. "You didn't think I was a mean son of a bitch before?"

She couldn't lie. "You aren't anymore. I'm glad for it. I'm glad you're..."

Searching for the right word, she settled on the one displayed on the store windows downtown.

"I'm glad you're my friend."

His eyes gleamed before he wiped them. "No better word than that, I've discovered recently. Come on. We have some things to see to, and then it's back to the wedding flowers."

They parted ways at the hardware store, and she walked past a few more stores to her papa's barber shop. When she looked inside, she spotted him with a green stocking hat on. He never wore a hat inside. Normally she would never interrupt him while he was cutting a client's hair, but she could make it quick. Something wasn't right.

Opening the door, she said, "Papa, do you have a moment?"

He looked over sharply and murmured something to his client before setting his clippers down and joining her on the street. "What is it, Rose?"

"Papa, why are you wearing a hat?"

He put his hand to the back of his head. "Don't ask me this, Rosie. Are you okay? Your mama and me miss seeing you."

Tears were burning her eyes. "Papa, tell me about the cap."

He gestured with frustration. "Your brother needs to learn how to cut hair, and like the first haircuts I gave, it didn't turn out so well. I had to shave it. Don't shame me on the street by making me show you."

She moved to put her hand on his arm and realized she couldn't anymore. "Oh, Papa. It couldn't be that bad."

"It doesn't matter," Papa said hoarsely. "Tell me how you are. Is Vinnie treating you good? He seems happy when he waves to me on his way to work. I can hear him whistling or singing through the window."

"We're very happy, Papa." She couldn't speak over the emotion in her throat for a moment. "Papa, I'm sorry to tell you, but Al isn't staying out of the greenhouse. I don't know how he got inside—"

"You shouldn't have put a lock on it. I didn't know until his youngest told me. She wanted me to show her the pretty flowers. I couldn't get inside, so I broke it. Rose, that greenhouse might be mostly yours, but it still belongs to this family. I won't have it locked."

He'd broken it? She clutched her stomach as pain radiated through her. Before the wedding, he'd told her it was hers now, for her business. How could he be saying this? "Papa, it's my place of business. He's been smoking pot in there. And he turned one of the pots over before. So did Angel."

"I don't want to hear this, Rose," Papa said, making a slicing motion with his hand. "You work in the greenhouse, but you keep it open. I'll tell your brother to stay out of it, but if my grandchildren want me to show them the plants, I'm going to. Understand? They're children."

"Angel insulted me to my face, Papa."

"No," he said harshly. "I don't want to hear this. I know you and Al don't like each other, and they can be difficult, but I will not tolerate this kind of ugliness in our family.

You be nice and stick to the greenhouse. Stay out of each other's way, and it will all be fine. Now, I have to go back to my client. You know better than to interrupt your papa when he's working."

That he would give her a set-down like that shocked her to the core. "Why isn't Al working today, Papa?"

He paused as he clutched the door handle. "He didn't feel good, so he stayed home. Your mama will take care of him. He and his family have been stressed. It's taken a toll. Now, leave me be. I have to work."

Opening the door, he left her standing on the street, hurt rolling over her like ocean waves. *Stay out of each other's way.* He'd always said that growing up. Only it hadn't been fine then. Just like it wasn't now.

She walked away from the shop so he couldn't see her anymore. Curling over in the alley, she pressed her hand to her heart and fought tears. He'd closed himself off like he always did when Al was home. She'd forgotten how hard her father could be. How single-minded he could be about work in tough times.

This wasn't the Papa who'd taken her to the flower market or sung songs to her while they worked in the greenhouse planting seeds.

The greenhouse.

What was she going to do? He'd forbidden her to lock it. She had to abide by his wishes. Straightening her spine, she went to find Mr. O'Connor and stop him from buying the lock.

She had no choice but to keep it open and pray everything would be all right like Papa had said.

CHAPTER 30

HIS BEST FRIEND WAS GETTING MARRIED TODAY.

Since marrying Rose, Vinnie sang "What A Wonderful World" more often than ever before. But today, he was looking forward to singing a really special song for the bride and groom: "Love and Marriage." He had more of a perspective on it now that he was a married man.

"I like this one," Rose said as she pinned the boutonnière she'd made to his lapel. "You outshine my flowers. I know I've said it a half dozen times—"

"With a half dozen sighs," he said, kissing her softly on the cheek.

"Stop, I don't want to stick you." But she kissed his chest before she secured the pin. "There, that looks excellent."

He waltzed her over to the small mirror in their place. "Perfect. I like that you combined one of my ideas with your own. Feels more special that way, like we're both wrapping our friends up with our best intentions."

"I love it when you talk like that," she said, cuddling close to him. "We need to get going. Mr. O'Connor told me to text him when we're ready so he can bring the flowers. He was so nice to let me put them in his fridge. He thought it might be a nice surprise if Alice and Hank saw them for the first time on their wedding day and not when they were reaching inside the refrigerator for dinner."

"Mama said he stayed with you for most of the day while you worked in the greenhouse," Vinnie said. "That was nice of him."

"After the trouble with Al and my talk with Papa, he told me he'd feel better staying around." She patted his chest, almost nervously. "I appreciated it."

"I'll go and talk with your papa tomorrow, Rose," Vinnie said, trying not to glower. "It's not fair what he said to you. I'll tell him he can have a key to the greenhouse—it is his, after all—but I don't feel comfortable with you being there if it's left open. Would he leave his barber shop unlocked? I don't think so."

"Let's not talk about it," Rose said, kissing him quickly on the mouth. "I'm only going to get upset again, and today is a happy day. It's my first wedding with my flowers. Other than ours, of course."

"And soon you'll have Aunt Gladys and Clifton's to add to your portfolio." He framed her face with his hands. "And my mama's and Mr. O'Connor's."

They'd asked for her help too, and he knew she was over the moon excited, although she still felt guilty taking money for her work.

"You're gonna have more wedding business in no time."

"Not sure that it will bring much money in," she said. "Weddings aren't the same right now."

"Seems like a great opportunity to start out small." He sent her a wink. "You can get your feet wet without too much pressure."

"I like that kind of positive outlook. Speaking of, Lucia Tesoro finally gave in and settled on our price for a video. She said she was impressed with the Christopher Walken homage. Wanted to know if we could do something funny with a nod to *Downton Abbey*. I had to give her credit for coming up with it."

"That would be funny," Vinnie said, puffing his chest out and doing his best Earl of Grantham impression. "These antiques used to be in my elegant English estate. Now they can be in your home."

"We'll have to work on that. But I see what you're going for, and I like it."

He tapped his temple. "Of course you do. We're partners. Alas, your carriage awaits, my lady."

She curtsied, making him laugh, and picked up the back of her dress like a train. "Very good, very good."

He was grinning as they waited for Mr. O'Connor to pull up in the driveway. When they spied his car, they grabbed their coats and took off down the stairs.

"Fine day for a wedding," the older man called as Mama came out the front door.

Before Vinnie could make a move to help her down the sidewalk, Mr. O'Connor was hurrying over to her. She kissed his cheek before putting on her mask and righting his. "It's going to be a grand day for a wedding."

The moment they stepped foot into the House of Hope & Chocolate, Alice squealed when she saw the bouquet of red, white, and purple ranunculi dotted with a few roses of the same color. She looked beautiful in her white sheath-style dress.

Hank joked about ruptured eardrums as Alice pinned on his boutonnière, but he claimed he was squealing on the inside, and Vinnie almost believed it because they really were that nice. He cast a glance at Rose, who was beaming as she and Mr. O'Connor placed the flower arrangements around the Chocolate Bar.

Alice introduced them to the other guests: her matron of honor, Francesca, and her husband, Quinn. Warren also introduced his wife, Amy, and their sweet young girls. They all laughed when Madison threw some rose petals on the floor well before her cue, but Warren took it as a sign and assembled the bride and groom to begin the ceremony. Sure enough, Rose had found him a water-squirting boutonnière.

"Having this wedding in the House of Hope & Chocolate is one of the best ideas I've come across in a while. When I got to thinking about it, a good marriage needs hope as much as love, and it also needs sweetness. As we bless Alice and Hank's union, let's all imagine those ingredients filling the lives they're about to join together."

Vinnie bowed his head and said a prayer for their marriage, overflowing with his warm wishes for them as the scent of jasmine enveloped them. With images of their two families coming together for years to come. He took Rose's hand as their friends said their vows and exchanged rings.

After the simple ceremony, the bride and groom kissed. Vinnie whistled, and Alice beamed as Hank stole another kiss. Because Alice was Alice, she immediately started the music, playing "How Sweet It Is (To Be Loved by You)" by James Taylor.

"Warren!" Alice called as she took Hank's hands and started to dance. "It's like you read my mind about sweetness and love."

He made the shape of a heart over his chest, and everyone nestled in close to their loved ones as the couple danced their first dance. Then "Yeah" started to play by Usher, which made Rose laugh and Vinnie bite his lip at Hank's incredulous expression.

"You told me I could pick the music," Alice said, crooking her finger at their guests. "Let's party!"

Everyone started to dance except for Vinnie's mama and Mr. O'Connor. Even Aunt Gladys strutted around Clifton, who seemed to be laughing behind his mask. But the next song was "I Love You for Sentimental Reasons" by Nat King Cole, and Mr. O'Connor immediately took Mama in his arms, making Vinnie smile. His mama did like to sway to the old classics.

When it came time for Vinnie to give his toast as best man, he kicked it off by singing "Love and Marriage," which made both Hank and Alice tear up. Then he lifted his champagne flute and looked at his good friends. "They say a person's life is measured by those they love. Seeing you two together, I can't help but think that love is pretty great. Enduring. Happy. Supportive. Here's to two of the best people I've ever known and to a marriage that I have no doubt will grow stronger and happier as the days go on. To Hank and Alice."

"To Hank and Alice," everyone echoed.

The couple rose and joined hands. "We want to thank you for celebrating with us today and making our day so happy," Hank said.

"We can't wait to have a giant party as soon as it's possible," Alice added, "but in the meantime, we're going to party like it's 1999. Hit it, Warren."

Sure enough, Prince's iconic song began to play. There was more dancing, and then they enjoyed the meal Mama had made, followed by more dancing. Vinnie and Alice got down to "Jungle Boogie," and then Warren took over for the next song, doing an interpretive dance to the lyrics of "I Will Always Love You" by Whitney Houston, which was an absolute riot. Even Quinn Merriam was laughing by then. Hank pretended to walk out when Alice started "The Macarena," and Vinnie couldn't help but laugh until he cried as his friend tried yet again to dance a dance he would never master.

Madison and Taylor danced the chicken dance with Warren, Alice, and Amy when it came on, with Alice shouting out that it was a Midwest wedding staple. Hank had had enough dancing by then. Vinnie was still game and even convinced Rose to flap her arms like the others, and they were soon laughing so hard they had to hold each other up. Hank told him he was crazy but that the chicken dance looked good on him, and Vinnie sent him a rude Italian gesture that had his mama clucking her tongue. Mr. O'Connor burst out laughing.

Then "Hakuna Matata" from *The Lion King* began to play, and Vinnie started singing with Alice. Madison came over as if she wanted to dance with them, and he told her to follow his actions as he sang the song, keeping her socially distanced yet still having fun. She was laughing by the end and followed him by spinning in a circle.

"You're a sweetheart," he told her and blew her a kiss, making Amy and Warren blow him one too in thanks.

When the festivities finished, Vinnie inclined his chin at Hank, who returned the gesture. They didn't need to say anything else. They'd always been able to read each other's minds.

"Do you want to bring the flowers arrangements home with you?" Rose asked. "We can put them in your car."

Alice danced in place, making her bell-shaped dress sway. "That would be terrific. Thank you so much for the flowers, Rose. For everything. Oh, this is one of the best days of my life. I'm so grateful to all of you."

"Me too, babe," Hank said, taking her hand. "Let's load the car, and then we can get going."

Everyone cheered as the couple drove off moments later. Clifton and Aunt Gladys volunteered to clean and lock up, so Vinnie and Rose said their goodbyes to everyone else and headed home themselves. Back inside their home, Vinnie undressed himself and Rose, and they settled under the covers.

Propped up on his elbow, he looked down at her, taking in her glorious black curls and her cat eyes. "When I used to come back from weddings," he said, "I'd imagine what it would be like to come home with my wife."

She touched his jaw. "I used to feel lonely after weddings too. I was never the type to hook up with someone from the reception, although I understood why people did it."

"When I wasn't so damn happy for Hank and Alice today," he told her, "I was thinking about being with you later. Rose, you give me so much joy. And you dance pretty good like a chicken. I think I fell a little more in love with you because of that."

Her snort made him chuckle. "And I think I fell a little more in love with you when you danced with Madison." She snuggled closer. "You're going to be a great father. I've always known it."

So she was starting to think like that, was she?

Yeah, he was too.

"Now that I've seen the chicken dancing side of you, I'm sure you're going to be a good mother."

Her finger nudged his rib, but she laughed. "Silly dancing is essential, although we have a while before we can think about having kids. Because we are going to have them, Vinnie."

He liked that she was saying how it was going to be. "We are. Got any names in mind for our little cherubs?"

"Cherubs?" She laughed. "How about flower names?"

"I'm not fond of Cactus for a girl," he teased.

"Oh, for goodness' sake, I wouldn't name our kid after a prickly plant."

"Roses have thorns," he said, wrapping his arms around her to keep from getting poked.

"Good point." She kissed his chest. "Cactus Scorsese, it is."

"I can't wait to tell Hank and Alice about their future godchild's name." He could see the horror on their faces already. "He might believe me."

"For a second, maybe," Rose said. "I like thinking about them being godparents to our kids."

"We'll be the same to theirs," Vinnie told her. "Hank and I have talked about having BBQs to watch the Jets on Sunday and letting the kids run around in the yard together. Knowing you, they'll have flowers in their hair like you did when you were younger. Happy days."

"The more I think about it, the happier I get," Rose said, kissing his chest. "Who knows what our lives might be like by then? I might have a physical location on Main Street."

He spotted his cologne bottle on the side table beside the bed, the remaining liquid like sand in an hourglass. Helping Rose with her business gave him joy. Would he be happy greeting the customers who came into her store? Would that and the videos be enough to fulfill him?

He still didn't have all the answers, but he was trusting in the process. Focusing on the positives continued to produce good results for him, and he was going to keep doing it.

Good luck attracted better luck, and a man could control his fate by making his own luck, his papa always said. Vinnie had always believed it. The wisdom was serving him now, and he sent a prayer of thanks to his papa for teaching it to him. He would pass the lesson on to his children, their children, and their family line would continue to thrive. They would look back on this time— one of hardship, loss, and new beginnings—with gratitude. These times had brought him and Rose together, after all. He would always be grateful for that.

"Come, wife, let's make love," he said, leaning in and finding her mouth.

The joy of their shared life seemed to infuse their lovemaking. Every kiss, every caress only anchored in more of this feeling of rightness. Her sigh expanded his heart as much as his own passion did, and when she called out his name and clutched him to her in bliss, he was a phoenix reborn by her love.

Afterward, their heads together, he caressed her back until she softened into sleep. "I love you," he whispered as he did every night. Those words would always be the last ones she heard before waking again in his arms. He nodded off to sleep, warm and content.

He shot out of bed, his heart pounding.

Rose jerked awake. "What the—"

Someone was pounding on the door. Groggy with sleep, Vinnie reached for the lamp beside the bed and knocked something to the floor. The pungent scent of his cologne touched his nose. He fumbled for the lamp again and found the switch.

"It's after four," Rose said, shoving out of bed and reaching for a robe.

"Let me get it," Vinnie said, pulling on his pants.

They shared a look. Her face was knit with worry, and his own belly felt tight. Part of him didn't want to open the door. He crossed to it and pulled it open anyway.

"It's horrible," Mrs. Fiorni said, standing in nothing but her nightgown and slippers, her teeth chattering.

"*Mama!*" Rose called, rushing forward.

Vinnie grabbed her before she could go to the woman. She looked wild, and she didn't have a mask on. "What happened?"

She pulled at the sides of her hair. "Some boys destroyed the greenhouse."

"Oh, my God!" Rose cried. "No!"

"They broke the windows. Kicked over the pots. Rose, they killed our lemon tree." Her voice broke.

"No, Mama, no!" Rose called hoarsely.

Not this, Vinnie thought, hands clenching. Not that tree. Not any of it.

"Your papa is in there— *Please*, I don't know what to do."

He resisted the urge to put his hands on her mama's shoulders to comfort her because, of course, he couldn't. "Rose, grab my coat. Have you called the police?"

She shook her head. "I ran here when I saw it. There was this awful breaking sound outside. It all happened so fast."

"Here, put my coat on." He handed it to her. "Rose and I will get dressed and come with you."

She was already tugging on her clothes, and he noticed she'd chosen a black sweater. He didn't say anything but pulled on something warm. When they left their place masked, his mama was standing in the soft light in front of the open window.

"What's going on?" she shouted, clutching her robe.

"Someone vandalized the greenhouse," Vinnie called out, feeling numb. "We'll be back in a while."

He wanted to hustle down the street, but Mrs. Fiorni couldn't keep up so he slowed his pace and took Rose's hand. What he could see of her face was white under the streetlamps. Shock. Yeah, that hazy feeling was settling over him too.

The lights were on in the surrounding neighbors' houses, and a few of the men were out in their yards in heavy coats.

"It's horrible, Vinnie," one of them called out. "I can't believe anyone would do this."

He led Rose to the gate. She made a pained sound when they reached the backyard, and he had to bite the inside of his jaw as he took in the scene. The greenhouse windows had been systematically destroyed, the broken glass shining in shards on the floor. Dirt was strewn across the floor from overturned plants. Mr. Fiorni was crouching by a large broken pot, his hands clutching pieces of Mr. Palladino's lemon tree.

"Imagine someone hurting plants like this," Vinnie heard someone say.

He turned to face Al, who stood by the back door next to his smirking wife.

"You know something about this, Al?" Vinnie asked, wanting to stalk forward and tear him apart.

Rose clutched his back as if she sensed the violence he

was fighting.

"I was asleep in bed with my wife here," Al said. "You can ask Mama and Papa. We were as surprised as they were when we heard the glass breaking. Chased off the three boys who were doing it."

Vinnie tasted blood in his mouth and realized he'd bitten his cheek. There was no way some random boys had decided to destroy this greenhouse. Not now.

"Oh, Vinnie, it's all gone." Rose pressed her hand to her mouth. "Everything."

He didn't know what to say to her. He could only pull her to his side.

"Jesus, Mary, and Joseph," he heard from behind him.

Turning, he saw Mr. O'Connor. They shared a long look before Vinnie nodded.

He pulled his phone out of his pocket and called the police.

CHAPTER 31

HER DREAM WAS GONE.

Because without these plants, her business was dead.

Rose numbly heard Vinnie explain the details and give their address before pocketing his phone. The police were coming. She glanced over at her brother, and he smiled. That son of a bitch smiled! She was two steps closer to him when Vinnie stepped in front of her.

"I know what you want to do here." He put his hands on her shoulders. "Me too. But it won't help anything. Plus Covid. So, let's see what we can salvage before everything dies."

The winter temperatures weren't the only problem, Rose knew. When they reached the structure, shattered glass lined the ground, and dirt and plant material were mixed in with it. Some of the lights overhead had been taken out, her grow lights were dark, and the fans weren't turning, but there was enough light from the back porch fixtures for her to understand the truth. Her sanctuary, her business, was beyond help.

"Oh, Rosie," Papa cried. "I should never have gotten

rid of that lock. They destroyed everything. They even cut up Mr. Palladino's lemon tree. How could anyone do such a thing?"

How could he ask that? He'd broken the lock and let the monsters in. Tears began to rain down her face. She saw the rabbit ear succulents she'd potted up only yesterday squished on the floor.

"There's glass everywhere," Vinnie said, his hand on her arm. "Maybe you should—"

"No, it's my greenhouse too. My plants." *Her business.*

"Perhaps we can salvage some of them," Mr. O'Connor said as he stepped carefully inside, glass crunching under his boots.

When Rose knelt down to pick up a bromeliad, she knew it was hopeless. "Even if we could pot them back up, we'd need to use new potting soil. There's glass in the dirt, and I don't have enough in the bags in the drawers."

"I have some in my garage," Mr. O'Connor said, "and I imagine others do too. That should give us a start until Home Depot opens. Then I can make a trip, and we can buy more. You make a list."

"There's no point," she said, setting the bromeliad aside. "I can't do it all in time. I don't even know if it would be worth it. The shock alone would kill them, but the temperatures..."

Hank's father crouched down six feet from her. "If there's one thing I learned in Vietnam, it was how to set up triage before more help could come in. I was damn good at it too. I know who has the best yards in town. I'll go door to door and ask for help. Rose, you have friends and neighbors. Let us help you."

Vinnie crossed to her potting drawers and pulled out two pairs of her best leather gloves. He helped her stand and fitted one of the pairs on her. "I agree with Mr. O'Connor. These plants are too precious for us to let them all go without a fight. You sift through them—carefully—and see what can be saved. We'll sort them and then pot them up."

"I will help you," Papa said, his eyes puffy and red from tears. "We will not let this go, my Rosie."

"I'm going for the potting soil then," Mr. O'Connor said, standing up. "We'll need to set up tables for assembly. I'll see to it."

"It's too cold to keep them out here for long," Rose said, hugging herself. "We're fighting time. The tropicals—"

"You can store them in my house until you're ready to pot them." Mr. O'Connor met her eyes. "And we can bring heat lamps from O'Connor's to help. Rose, we'll make this work."

Vinnie tugged his gardening gloves on. "I'm going to start with the cacti since I know them. Hard to miss. Anyone have a box? We can wrap them in newspaper for now."

"I'll grab some from inside," Papa said as the police sirens tore through the night, growing closer. "Is that the police?"

"I called them," Vinnie said. "Someone is going to pay for this. But that'll take time. Right now, we have a lot of work to do. Come on, Rose. I'll be right beside you."

"Me too," Papa said, his posture righting. "After I talk to the police."

As he left the greenhouse, Rose looked at Vinnie. "Do you really think we can salvage this?"

"We have to try," he said, his eyes widening as Hank and Alice walked into the greenhouse.

"Oh, not on your wedding night," Rose said, pressing a hand to her heart.

"You were in trouble," Hank said after looking around. "It's what friends do. Jesus. I'm glad my dad called. I can't believe—"

"Yes, you can," Vinnie said angrily.

He glanced back at the house. "Right. How can we help? I heard you needed heat lamps. Tables. I'll run to the restaurant for them."

Alice brushed away tears. "You can have mine too. I'll ask Clifton to bring them."

"Holy shit," Baker said as he stepped inside. "I heard it was bad, but this— Rose, I'm here to help. I used to plant coffee when I was Peace Corps in Guatemala. I once faced frost, and I know how fast it works. We're not going to let you go down without a fight."

They were right. She had to try. She looked at her friends and wiped her nose with her sleeve. "Let's start with the tropicals."

And so they got down to work. She sorted the plants she thought might make it, pulling off damaged leaves and setting them aside to be repotted. More neighbors showed up with Mr. O'Connor, carrying garden soil bags, some half open and others not yet touched, while others brought used pots and cardboard carriers.

In addition to her parents and her friends, she spotted Lucia Tesoro, Fanny Janson, Aunt Gladys, and Manny Romano, among the others. Clifton conferred with Mr. O'Connor before stepping inside to outline an assembly line that would maximize time and efficiency. Baker was going to lead the potting at the tables.

Alice glanced at Rose after he left, saying, "Clifton is a master at organization. With his direction, we'll have this done in no time."

She didn't look up until she noticed her shadow covering the tiny succulent plants she was sifting through. They were so fragile that most of them had broken when their pots were tipped over. When she picked up one googly eye in the soil, her heart clutched. She had felt so victorious after getting all those orders. Now she wasn't certain she could fulfill any of them. Who wanted to pay for a damaged plant?

"Have some coffee and a roll," Vinnie said, crouching down beside her. "Neighbors are keeping the coffee going and handing out treats."

"What time is it?" she asked, suddenly feeling the cold on her cheeks.

"It's about ten," Vinnie said, putting his hand on her back. "You're doing great, babe."

"But you have to go to work soon," Rose protested, looking over at the other downtown shopkeepers who were still potting up plants with Baker. "You all do."

"Clifton, Aunt Gladys, Maria, and Warren are opening up the shops for everyone. Store triage, Mr. O'Connor called it. If there's a customer, they'll help them as best they can. People are staying until we finish this, Rose. It makes my heart swell to see everyone helping."

Everyone except Al and his family, she'd noticed. Not that she wanted his help anyway. Had Mama and Papa realized they weren't helping? She glanced over to where they were working, sorting the flowering trees and vines like the clematis and jasmines. They had to suspect her brother had something to do with it. She wanted to scream at him, hurl dirt and glass shards at him until he confessed.

"What did the police say?" she asked Vinnie instead.

"They took a few statements, but there were no prints. It's winter, so gloves. Your brother is insisting it was boys, but your parents didn't see them, so it's the only lead. They'll follow up when they have more. Don't think about that now. Here, let me take that poor plant from you. I'll take good care of her."

He kissed the top of her head after gently taking the French lavender from her. Her eyes filled with tears again, and she had to blink rapidly so she could see well enough to continue.

She went into autopilot after that, careful not to look at her growing rubbish pile of plants too broken to be saved. Clifton came to report that their friends and neighbors were going to take home a selection of her plants in the meantime to give them light and care.

He didn't have to mention the unspoken ghost circling her in the broken greenhouse. She had nowhere to store the plants they'd saved.

When Vinnie knelt beside her again in mid-afternoon, she was going through the final corner of the greenhouse. Her roses. She'd saved them for last because their root balls were sturdy and could wait. But she'd also delayed it because the person responsible for this destruction had made it personal.

They were her favorite, her namesake, after all.

The climbing roses she'd so lovingly trained upright had been destroyed with pruning shears, like the lemon tree, their beautiful branches eviscerated, along with the rare flowers she was able to coax to bloom in winter. The harsh cuts at the base were so severe she wasn't sure they would come back.

"I feel like whoever did this was trying to cut me," she said as she held up all that was left of the eight-foot-tall climber. "This is the *Rosa odorata Mutabilis*, and it's called the monthly rose for good reason. It starts to bloom in bright coral in the warmer months before changing to a dark pink as the weather gets cooler. I bought this plant for my sixteenth birthday with money I'd made that summer helping Papa at the shop. It came to me bareroot. Over time, it grew taller than me, in that corner trellis beside our prize lemon tree. It hurts, Vinnie. It hurts so much. It's like they've killed a part of me."

She couldn't deny the truth anymore or hold back the tears, and he pulled her to his chest. She curled into him and unleashed the torrent, knowing The Dreamer's Flower Shoppe had been killed before it could grow deep enough roots to survive.

CHAPTER 32

LUCIA TESORO HAD DIRT ON HER FOREHEAD AND A determined glint in her eye.

Warren cleared his throat and stepped out of her doorway. "You had a couple of sales. A lamp and a silver cat. Receipts are on the counter. I used your credit card machine with no problem."

"Thank you," she said, her voice unusually soft. "I know we got off on the wrong foot. I don't like admitting I'm wrong, but you need to help Rose. If that wasn't enough, Mr. Palladino would be rolling in his grave. Thank God he isn't here to see what was done to his beautiful greenhouse. I'm still in shock like everyone else."

So was Warren, frankly, and he was new to the community. When Alice's number had popped up on his phone shortly after dawn, he'd answered with a pounding heart, knowing nothing good could have happened. She'd just gotten married, for goodness' sake. Then she'd shared the news about the greenhouse. Only a mean son of a bitch could do such damage to a bunch of beautiful flowers. To hear the police were looking for kids was even worse, although Alice was certain Rose's brother was behind it, whether or not he'd held the shears. Time would tell, Warren supposed, but that didn't help Rose.

"You don't need to admit anything to me, Lucia. Let's focus on agreeing Rose needs help. I plan on drilling into how the trust can help her."

"All of us are passing the hat, so to speak, but it won't be enough to cover all she's lost. Paddy got to thinking about creating an emergency fund for any business that suffers a catastrophic loss like this. Insurance companies take their sweet time paying out claims, as some of us know. Not that insurance is on the table here."

"Because her greenhouse wasn't insured," Warren said, shaking his head. "Of course not."

"Joe never saw the need, and it costs an arm and a leg, so Rose probably wasn't at a point where she could consider it. You think about what can be done, Warren. We're all behind you."

If only it hadn't taken this kind of destruction to make it happen. "I'm glad to hear it. Maybe I should swing over there and talk to her."

"You might give it a while," Lucia said, rubbing the dirt on her forehead. "She was sobbing in Vinnie's arms when we finally quit. Hard to imagine seeing all that hard work and love be destroyed like that. Years of care gone in an instant. Mr. Palladino's lemon tree... I can't imagine what she must be feeling, especially since we all know her asshole brother was likely behind it. He and his wife just smoked and smiled in the shadows while we worked. That son of a bitch. God, I need a drink. Want one?"

Normally he didn't partake with clients during the day, but hell, Lucia Tesoro had just become a human being and an ally. He was going to make an exception. Amy would understand.

After having a very fine negroni from ingredients she kept in an antique bar behind the counter he'd noticed earlier, he headed over to the Fiornis', following directions from Lucia. He called Amy on the way to check in. When he arrived, he spotted a man smoking on the front steps, and Lucia's description immediately came to mind.

"Hey, aren't you the moneybags for the trust?" the guy asked, stubbing out the cigarette and throwing it in the bushes.

That simple act was as good as putting on a nametag—Warren *knew* it was Al. "I work for the trust, yes. I'm Warren Anderson."

"Al Fiorni."

He approached without a mask on, and Warren stepped back and held up a hand to stop him.

His lip curled. "I ain't scared of Covid."

Interesting response. "Well, I am, and I have a family I care about, so let's keep our distance, okay?"

"Fine," the man said testily. "I hear you're thinking about giving new businesses grants. I have a few ideas of my own. I'd like to apply when you're taking applications. You should forget about helping Rose if that's why you're here. There's nothing much salvageable. They did a thorough job, those bastards."

Warren had to fight the urge to clench his fists as anger surged through him. "I'm still working out the criteria for new business grants, but when I finish, it will be public and open to everyone. Excuse me. I'm here to see how I might help your sister. Everyone in town is very upset over what happened."

"Of course they are," Al said, spitting on the ground as Warren walked to the backyard.

What an asshole.

He stopped short when he reached the gate. "*Jesus.*"

The greenhouse was bigger than he'd imagined, and the broken windows were holding on to dangerous shards. Dirt and glass still covered the ground, and the mound of broken plants and pots was astounding.

Mr. O'Connor looked over from the collapsible tables he

was breaking up. "Heard you were doing good downtown."

"Heard you were doing good over here." Alice had filled him in on the man's transformation. Warren wasn't surprised. That girl always worked miracles with people.

"You come to help?" the older man asked, walking over. "Vinnie took Rose home since we'd finished saving all the plants we could salvage. Her dad's inside. Not sure how many are going to make it, but we had to try. You have any idea how much a new greenhouse costs?"

Warren shook his head, still taking in the damage. "None."

"This one was top-shelf, and Rose and her father have cared for it well." Mr. O'Connor took off his stocking hat and rubbed his head. "I don't imagine a loan would cover the cost to fix it. I counted the panels. They broke thirty-six of them. Only missed a few overhead."

Warren didn't like to be a naysayer right off the bat, but he couldn't lie either. "I was thinking business grants for new owners would be small. Like five to ten thousand max."

"Makes sense," Mr. O'Connor said. "We took up a neighborhood collection, but times being what they are, it's only a thousand. That's a lot for everyone, and Rose cried her heart out when I gave it to her. But it won't be enough for her to start over or fix what's broken. Whoever did this knew what to take out. I didn't see it at first, but the fan wires and lights were cut, and the main panels that control the windows' opening were bent."

Son of a bitch. "Not mere vandalism."

"No, sir." He inclined his head toward the house. "It's all been done way too smart. No way mere boys did this. But I doubt the police will find a way to tie it to the real culprit."

"No," Warren said. "And it wasn't insured."

"Who would have thought it needed it?" Mr. O'Connor said harshly. "It was a greenhouse filled with plants. Even now, we're fighting the clock on helping Rose reestablish her business."

Warren knew it took time to recover from a disaster. He'd visited restaurants that had been flooded. Businesses that had been hit by tornadoes. The sorting and sifting of the ruins took time, and then there was the damage to repair. Even for an established business, it was touch and go for the first six months. Few came back stronger. Some didn't make it at all.

Depression settled over him. He'd come to help, and dammit, he didn't like being put on the bench this early.

"How much of her old stock survived?" he asked. "And how much space would she need, do you think, to rebuild?"

Mr. O'Connor shrugged. "I'm no expert, but given the extent of the damage and what she was able to get repotted, I'd say she needs about half the space. I'd been thinking about calling in a special glass guy and an electrician to see about fixing it, but it's not safe for her to work here anymore, dammit."

No, he couldn't imagine it would be. Not with the guy he'd met out front.

"I might have an idea," he said to the older man.

CHAPTER 33

ROSE WAS DRESSED ENTIRELY IN BLACK WHEN HE returned.

His mama had stopped him to ask for news and to give him some lasagna. Rose had gone ahead to their apartment after accepting his mama's condolences.

They were all acting like there was no hope, and Vinnie couldn't accept that.

"Come eat, *cara mia*," he said, setting the food on the counter.

She sat on the bed with her back to him, something he *really* didn't like. He could feel her slipping away.

"Why didn't you bring home some more plants for us to take care of, Rose?" He sat in front of her and took her hands.

Lowering her head, she lifted a shoulder. "I don't know. Maybe I didn't want to watch them die."

"Come on, Rosie," he said, ducking to meet her gaze. "I know it hurts. I can't even imagine how much. But we have to try to save them. At least you have a baby lemon tree from Mr. Palladino's. That's something, right?"

"Papa wouldn't bring any of the plants inside with him.

Because he knows there's no hope."

"Maybe he didn't want Al to kill them inside his own home," Vinnie shot back. "Don't you dare let your brother win."

"He was always jealous of me," Rose said, her dark eyes red with anger and tears. "Of the greenhouse and my bond with Papa. But how could he have gone this far? He set this up, I know he did. The damage was too targeted for it to have been anyone else. Vinnie, I will never understand it. I don't want to ever walk by that house again."

He knew she was starting to get worked up. "I want to hit him as much as anyone does, but we need to focus on your business right now. Fuck your brother."

She pulled away from him and stood up. "The business is over," she said flatly. "I can't fulfill the orders I've gotten. Most of the plants are too damaged."

Oh shit.

"And I already invested the money from the orders on online ads. Thank God our friends and neighbors took up a collection to help, or I'd really be in the hole."

It wasn't just her—it was them—and he had to help her remember that.

"You have so many people rooting for you, Rose." He pushed off the bed and cupped her face. "You focus on that. We'll figure out the rest."

"No, it's time to be practical," she said hoarsely. "I'm going to start applying for jobs again. In the meantime, I'm going to do videos to help us. Help you."

He gestured at her. "So you're giving up, but I'm supposed to keep dreaming? Where did you put the cologne bottle I broke this morning?"

"I know what it meant to you," she said in a small voice. "Everything seems to be breaking."

He could still smell its scent—a pungent reminder that his time was up. "I told you that when that bottle was empty, it was time for me to have figured things out. Well, today's the day."

"What are you talking about? It broke before it was finished."

"So what?" He gestured in the direction of her parents' house. "Your greenhouse broke too. We're both at a crossroads. If you're going to give up on your flower shop, then I'm going to give up on the videos."

Except he couldn't allow her to give up. He wouldn't.

"How about we just move to Chicago?" He took her by the shoulders. "I can take up my uncle's business, even if it's just for the next ten years. You can relaunch your flower business there. I'll have more money to help you than I do now. Rose, it kills me that I can't write you a check for a new greenhouse and everything you lost."

She pushed at him. "Write me a check? It's my problem, Vinnie. I don't expect you to pay for anything."

"I'm your husband." He pointed at his chest. "I'm supposed to take care of you."

"Don't be an idiot!" Tears started raining down her cheeks. "You do take care of me. You were there with me every step of the way today. Vinnie, you have no idea what that meant to me."

"Then let's leave Orion," Vinnie said, the words ripping his heart clean open. Because he'd imagined them living here, in his mama's house. He'd imagined watching those football games with Hank while their kids played together. But his wife was hurting, and it was more important for him to be there for her. "You just said you don't ever want to walk by your parents' house again. Do you really want to stay here and watch Al destroy your parents the rest of the way? Because, God help us, what will he do next?"

Her lips started to quiver. "They didn't throw him out. And he smiled at me, Vinnie! He *smiled*. Oh, why won't Mama and Papa see what he's really like?"

"He's their son, and they aren't going to stop supporting him and his family. They see it as doing their duty, and if they didn't stop today, they won't ever."

She hung her head. "I don't want to leave town, but you're right. I'm afraid to stay here and see what happens next. To them. To me. Or you. Vinnie, what if I'd been there?"

His blood went cold at the thought. Yes, maybe it made sense to leave. He wanted her safe and happy again. It couldn't happen here in their neighborhood.

"Leaving is our best option," he said, pulling her toward his chest. "Even though it's hard. I can sell the business after a while. We'll come back someday."

Maybe, he thought. Surely Al wouldn't be here forever.

"I came back home after living in the city," Rose said, clutching his back.

"Hank did too," he said hoarsely, wondering how he was going to leave his friend.

"Are you sure?" She pressed back, her eyes swimming with tears.

He cupped her face. "There's a successful business waiting for me in Chicago. I can still do the promo videos to support your business."

"And to grow your following." Because she didn't want him to give up everything for her, and because it would help them come back sooner. "Oh, Vinnie, I love you," she said, starting to cry.

He grabbed her to him. "I love you too. All that matters is that we're together."

CHAPTER 34

THE KNOCK ON THE DOOR MADE ROSE WANT TO PULL THE pillows over her head.

Vinnie stopped singing his morning Frank song, sighed as he slid his mask into place, and shuffled over to see who it was. *Don't answer it.*

Still, she peeked from her position in bed to see who it was. Hank and Alice were in the doorway, both holding gifts from the chocolate shop. The numbness coating her started to slide off, and her heart burned with both hurt and warmth. They were newlyweds, but they'd come to the greenhouse to help them. And they were here now.

"We thought we'd bring by some hot chocolate and truffles since they always cheer Rose up," Alice said, holding up her robin's egg blue bag while Hank extended the beverage tray.

"Thanks," Vinnie said, closing the door partially to shield her. "Rose, come see."

She pulled her black shrug around her, along with her mask, and joined them at the door. "It was really nice of you to bring something, but you didn't need to."

"Need to, shmeed to," Alice said with her trademark

humor. "I can't imagine how tough it was waking up this morning and remembering what happened. Been there. We thought we'd remind you of how much you're loved. That's always helped me get out of bed in bad times."

Tears filled her eyes, and Vinnie reached for her hand. Leaving these two was going to hurt. She would miss them, and it would hurt even worse knowing how much Vinnie longed for the company of his best friend.

"We're taking care of the plants we have," Hank said, clearing his throat. "Don't worry. My dad said they're the kind that didn't need much help."

Her babies.

"Cacti," Alice said. "That was all I felt comfortable with. Now, Hank and I were thinking of doing a video with a GoFundMe to help you rebuild. I know Warren's looking into what the trust might do—"

"Let me stop you right there." She couldn't listen to this. "It's really wonderful what everyone did and wants to do, but it's over. There's no rebuilding after yesterday. Vinnie and I— Do you want to tell them, or should I?"

Her beautiful husband turned his head, tears brimming in his eyes. "You."

He could barely manage that one word. "We talked about it last night, and with everything that's happened, we're going to move to Chicago—"

"*What*?" Hank put his hands on his hips. "Fuck that."

She started trembling. "Vinnie's going to take over his uncle's business for a while until he can sell it, and I'll start my new flower business there." Just the thought of starting over made her ill. "He'll still help with videos, and we'll—"

"Vinnie, seriously, what the hell?" Hank asked. "We talked about this. Man, I know what happened yesterday was gut-wrenching, but this is your home. Our kids are supposed to grow up together. Mama Gia gave you her house."

"I need to take care of my family," Vinnie said. "And

Rose needs time away from hers. We don't see another way."

"You'd let Al drive you out?" Hank put his hands on his hips. "I'll take him apart myself before I let him run my best friends out of town."

"Hank, we both know I can't work at O'Connor's forever," Vinnie said. "It's not my place like Two Sisters was. And if I take over my uncle's business, we'll be in a better financial position. Rose can have her dream. I'll still get to help with the videos, and maybe I'll even sing to her customers when she has a floral shop. We'll make the best of things."

"Bull—"

"Hank," Alice said softly, touching his arm. "Stop, babe. You know this isn't easy for them."

He wiped his eyes, making Rose do the same as the hurt spilled down her cheeks. Vinnie tightened his grip on her hand, and she knew he was close to losing it too.

"Can I ask you both something?" Alice's eyes were bright with tears in the morning sunlight.

Rose could only nod.

"You don't believe you can both have your dream, right?"

"Sometimes you have to make adjustments," Vinnie said, clearing his throat. "Yesterday changed things. It isn't fair, but it forced us to be realistic. Hank, Rose was talking about taking some shitty job. I couldn't let her do that."

"Of course you couldn't," Hank said hoarsely, "but dammit, Vinnie. Being a plumber is pretty shitty too."

"If you make a toilet joke right now..." Alice said.

"I don't have it in me," Hank said. "What about your parents, Rose? Are they really going to stick with Al after yesterday? Didn't they notice that he and his family didn't lift a finger to help? Trust me, everyone else did."

"They want to believe he had nothing to do with it," she said. "He was smart, having someone else do it for him."

Hank cursed. "My money is on Grasiaca and his boys. Dammit, I don't like this. I don't want you two to leave."

Vinnie brushed his eyes with his sleeve. "Neither do we. But we don't have much of a choice."

"You're in shock," Alice said. "I remember feeling like that when Sarah died. For a few days, when I didn't want to get out of bed, I thought about forgetting about the chocolate shop and going back to work for Francesca."

"I didn't know that," Hank said, putting his arm around her.

She gazed at Rose then. "You're wearing all black again, and I understand it. I know it's not the same—your place of work was destroyed, and you feel physically unsafe. But I still get it. Because I was afraid I couldn't take living here without Sarah. But do you know what I concluded? I'd rather be around friends and follow my dream than give up and move away. Especially because I knew there'd be plenty of good people here to surround me and lift me up."

Vinnie put his other hand over his heart. "This isn't just because of what happened with the greenhouse, Alice. I need to figure out something for myself too. A career. I gave myself some time, and my time's up."

Hank looked at him. "Vinnie—"

"Give it a few days," Alice interrupted. "Sorry, babe. I know you want to argue with him, but it's not helping. Is it, Vinnie?"

Rose felt a sinking sensation in her stomach. "Hank, do you think I want him to take over his uncle's business?" She held out her hand. "I'm going to do everything I can to help him gain enough influencer cred that he can walk away from it as fast as possible. I feel guilty enough as it is that he wants to support my dream at the expense of his own."

"*Cara*, I don't even know what my dream is," Vinnie said. "Not like you know yours. And my time to figure it out got moved up to yesterday."

"Well, I think I know what you want," Alice said. "Give things a few days to settle. *Please*. For the people that love you."

"For me," Hank said, tapping his chest. "For all the years we've been friends."

"You'd call in that marker?" Vinnie asked.

"You're damn right I would." Hank stuck out his chin. "You'd do the same if the situation were reversed. If I was telling you that I wanted to do something like... Hell, join the circus."

Vinnie snorted. "The circus? You're reaching, O'Connor. You hate the circus. I remember the field trip where you put your hand over your eyes because you were terrified the tightrope walker was going to fall to his death."

"Fine, forget the circus. How about—"

"Honey, he gets what you're saying," Alice said. "Come on. We have some thinking to do. My suggestion for you two is to sit tight and let your friends help you. See if we can figure something out. Can you do that?"

"Please." Hank's voice was desperate.

She felt desperate too. God, she wanted to say yes, and when Vinnie's hand started to tremble in Rose's, she knew he did too. She could tell he was close to breaking down, so she nodded for both of them.

"Thank you," Alice said. "Now, warm up your hot chocolate and sit back."

"I need to go to work," Vinnie protested.

"You stay here," Hank said, pointing into their place. "Eat chocolate. Let us...do something."

"Dammit, you just got married," Vinnie said.

"Then let this be your bonus wedding present to us," Hank ground out. "Stop being stubborn."

"Fine," Vinnie said, gesturing. "But I'm going back to work tonight."

Rose was going to have to figure out something to keep her occupied or she'd go crazy, and it sounded like the same was true of Vinnie.

"All right," Hank said. "Hopefully we'll have some ideas by then. Alice, I'm trusting your record for coming up with good ideas and hope."

Frankly, so was Rose.

Chapter 35

The O'Connor's sign was gone.

Vinnie stopped short, and Rose gripped his hand. When Alice had texted them both to come to the restaurant at five, he hadn't thought anything was wrong. He'd figured they'd wanted Rose to hang out at the bar, or whatever, so she wasn't alone. Since he'd had no intention of leaving her by herself anyway, he'd been fine with that.

"You don't think someone vandalized their sign, do you?" she asked worriedly.

He tugged her forward, fearing the worst. When they opened the door to the restaurant, Hank and Alice glanced over from where they were sitting at the bar. He was aware of others sitting at the tables in the restaurant, but his sole focus was on his friends.

"You two okay?" Vinnie asked.

"Other than being tied up all day, thinking about losing my best friend to plumbing, I'm great," Hank shot back.

"He's wondering why the sign is gone," Alice said, hopping off the barstool. "We've got good news. I think we have a working plan if you're willing to give it a try. We thought we'd gather together some of your other friends and neighbors to help convince you to stay. Who wants to go first?"

He turned his head finally and spotted Mr. O'Connor sitting there with his mama, along with many more from their neighborhood—Aunt Gladys, Clifton, Baker, Lucia, Warren—but before he could take in more, Hank stomped his foot and shoved his hands into his pockets, commanding his attention.

"I'm up. Vinnie, I want you to hear me out. I know you like to talk more than me, but this time let me do the talking. *Capisce?*"

His mouth actually twitched into a smile when he heard his friend use Italian. "Your accent is terrible."

"And my head is about as thick as yours, or I would have come up with this sooner." He gestured to the bar. "Alice diagrammed everything you love about working here and doing the videos. I'm not sure I will be able to look at cartoon bubbles the same way ever again. But you love greeting people. Making them feel like a restaurant is home. Hamming it up. Being you."

Vinnie nodded as he felt Rose's hand touch his back.

"So why not do that here?" Hank asked. "With me. Be my partner. In a new restaurant we run together. Alice... The sign please."

He stared at his friend in shock as Alice reached behind the bar and held up a hand-painted sign.

"*Two Brothers?*"

"Isn't that what we are?" Hank came and stood in front of him. "Don't make me go all Hallmark on you. Vinnie, I don't want to do this without you. Since you started working here, everything has been better. Let's make it our place. You loved doing Two Sisters. Do Two Brothers. With me."

"Oh, Hank..." he heard Rose whisper.

"But it's your livelihood," Vinnie said. "You have a family."

"You're my family, dammit! And there's something special about a family restaurant. You said it yourself. Didn't you and Mama Gia and Aunt Alessa, God rest her soul, all do great at Two Sisters? We're already doing better, what with you bringing in old customers and Derrick rocking the food. We can do better still. Vinnie, people loved hearing why Mama Gia and her sister started their restaurant."

"He's right," he heard his mama call out. "We put it on the menu, remember? People always commented about it. Your and Hank's story is one that will touch people's hearts."

He turned to where she was sitting at a corner table, next to Mr. O'Connor. "But, Mama, you always said the heart of a restaurant was in the kitchen."

She opened her hands on the table as if uncertain before saying, "The heart of Two Sisters, I thought, was me and Alessa, bless her. I couldn't think about cooking without her. Not even if you were still up front doing your part. Vinnie, I'm sorry I didn't praise your role enough. You were just as important to our success."

He wiped at the tears. "It's okay. I didn't do it for that."

"I know, but still... Forgive your mama."

Their eyes held, and he nodded.

Then she pointed to Hank. "Listen to your brother. I know I encouraged you to take over your uncle's business. But Hank is your family too, and when you have a chance like this, one that fires your heart, you take hold of it with both hands. You do everything in your power to make it work. I know restaurants, and from where I'm sitting, you two working together is a recipe for great success."

"She's right, boys," Mr. O'Connor said. "You two have the best friendship I know, plus this is a great new direction for the pub. You're sitting on a winner."

"Thank you, Mama." He blew her a kiss. "Thank you, Hank. I..."

"Vinnie," Rose whispered, turning him toward her.

"Do it. I want you to be happy. I'll find a job that will make me happy somehow—"

"Oh, we have you covered too," Alice said, crooking her finger to someone in the other corner.

"We didn't make cartoon bubbles for you," Warren said, "but your dream was already taking root. Someone tried to rip it out."

"We weren't about to let that happen," Paddy said, standing up.

Vinnie gripped Rose's hand as the two men walked toward them.

Mr. O'Connor said, "We can't guarantee the police will catch the people who destroyed your greenhouse or that your family will stop standing by their son, although as a parent I understand their dilemma."

He looked over his shoulder at Hank before continuing. "It's tough to turn your back on family or bear the weight of knowing those bonds might be broken. Drives a man to do incredible things. In my case, it helped me change, and I'll be forever grateful for it. But, Rose, you have a new family. In Vinnie, and in Hank and Alice, and in me and Gia. *This family* wants you to stay and start over, and we found a new greenhouse for you so you can do just that. You have your pick of three, in fact."

"*You what?*" Rose squeaked out before Vinnie could say anything.

"The power of Craigslist is never to be underestimated," Warren said, holding up his phone.

Displayed on the screen was a freaking greenhouse! Warren swiped over and another appeared and then another.

Vinnie couldn't believe his eyes. They were all so beautiful, and their friends had gone to so much effort to help her. "Oh, Rose!"

"The trust has a new emergency fund for cases like this," Warren said. "You can thank Lucia Tesoro for suggesting it.

And Clara for agreeing without blinking an eye. Also, there are a lot of garden nurseries going out of business, I was depressed to see, but that meant there was an opportunity for someone looking to pick up a greenhouse for a song. The same is true for floral coolers, I might add. It's just the way the market works."

Rose let go of his hand and pressed her hands to the sides of her head. "This can't be happening."

"*It's happening*," Alice drawled.

"Depending on what you want," Warren said, "between the money our incredible friends and neighbors raised for you, Alice's awesome GoFundMe campaign, Mr. O'Connor's volunteer labor to transport and install the greenhouse with security cameras, I might add, and the first emergency loan, I believe we will have you back in business in three days. In a few weeks, I'll hopefully have a new business grant to give you to help more. If you agree..."

"If I agree?" Rose said, turning to him and gripping his coat. "Oh, Vinnie."

He already knew her answer. "To The Dreamer's Flower Shoppe rising again," he said, "and to Orion's new restaurant, Two Brothers."

Alice gave a cheer, and everyone started to clap. He pulled Rose to him and rocked her in his arms. They were staying. She'd have her dream, and he'd have his. And all because of their friends and neighbors. Their *family*. He glanced over at Hank, who had his arm around Alice, and they inclined their chins to each other.

Still hugging Rose tight, Vinnie then put his hand to his heart and nodded to Warren and Mr. O'Connor. He blew Alice a kiss before turning and blowing one to his mama. Aunt Gladys waved to him, and Clifton gave an elegant nod. Baker made a power-to-the-people fist, and Lucia Tesoro gave an Italian gesture for good fortune.

Good fortune is right, he thought.

Walking over to the bar, he plugged in his phone,

knowing the exact song he wanted to commemorate this moment.

"Ten bucks it's Louis Prima," Baker called out.

"No," Hank answered. "I'd know that Dean Martin glow anywhere."

"It's totally going to be Dean," Alice said with a laugh.

"Ten bucks I can name the song," Rose said.

Vinnie paused before playing his selection, meeting his wife's beautiful moss green eyes. They hadn't had a regular courtship, and certainly they'd decided to marry for unusual reasons, but he didn't doubt that he'd be playing this song at their fiftieth wedding anniversary someday.

"Ten bucks?" Vinnie asked. "How about I get to name our firstborn? I'm really worried about you choosing some errant flower name."

"I thought we already picked Cactus Scorsese?" She laughed.

"Cactus Scorsese!" Mama Gia exclaimed. "Who's naming my grandbaby Cactus? Wait, are you two expecting?"

"Hell, no!" Vinnie said, shaking his head. "Not for a while yet, but it always pays to plan early. Right, Rose?"

"Right." She walked toward him, her gait back to being a little saucy, the way he liked it.

"Name that tune," he said, "and I'll give you whatever you want. You can even name our firstborn Carnation."

Because he would always give her everything.

"It's the classic 'You're Nobody Till Somebody Loves You,' of course." She raised her brow as he acknowledged her victory. "I'll take my win in kisses. For the rest of our lives."

He hit the song, came around the bar, and took her in his arms as Dean started to sing. Others joined in, singing and dancing, but Vinnie only had eyes for his wife as he shared the words in his heart.

"When our children are born..."

"You mean Cactus and Schefflera?" she shot back with a twinkle.

He shuddered. "As I was saying, when they're born, I'm going to tell them that their old man knows one of the greatest secrets to life."

"What is that?" she asked.

"To find somebody to love," he said, pressing her closer. "Because once you do, the world really is a better place."

"You bet it is," Rose said, her eyes smiling. "Want to know what I'll tell them?"

His heart warmed in his chest at the joy and love in her eyes. "Always." He could already see her brushing their children's hair and sharing her wisdom alongside him after bath time.

"You'll know who to entrust your heart to because that person will do anything to make your dreams come true. That's who you want to love. I knew that even as a little girl. Every time I gave you a flower, I was sharing my dream."

"I can't wait for you to start giving me flowers again," he said, envisioning her among the plants in her new greenhouse. "But my favorite will always be roses. Because you're my rose."

"And roses mean love," she said softly, only for his ears. "I'm glad it makes our world go 'round. We're so loved, Vinnie."

They both looked around at their friends and neighbors before meeting each other's eyes again. Somehow, he knew they were both thinking the same thing.

Their roots were here with these people in this place, and they would thrive here. Hardship might have touched them, just as it would surely touch them again, but it hadn't broken them. It wouldn't.

Because love heals all and brings good fortune, and they were chock-full of it and would be for the rest of their lives.

CHAPTER 36

THE DAY HER NEW GREENHOUSE ARRIVED, ROSE WORE A yellow dress, as much to remind herself of sunshine on a winter day as to bless her plants with what they needed to grow.

Under this glass, they would reach toward the sun, and her heart would always reach for her babies and all the joy they'd bring to her and others.

After Mr. O'Connor and a few other handymen helped set up fans and lights—and her new floral cooler, oh my!—all the neighbors came out socially distanced to bring the plants they'd lovingly cared for over the past week. Rose couldn't help but cry, tears seeping into her mask as she thanked them.

"You guys are so wonderful," she said, facing them, her hand in Vinnie's. "This has been one of the worst years, but in a strange way it's also been the best. It's made me realize how wonderful this community is. Thank you for your help. For everything!"

"We love you, Rose," Baker shouted, pumping his fist into the air.

"Hear, hear," Clifton said, as Aunt Gladys winked.

Alice and Hank appeared from behind the house, carrying a large package wrapped in butcher paper. "We have something for you."

Vinnie held it so she could step forward and unwrap it. Inside was a simple sign.

This greenhouse is protected by Friends & Neighbors.

"Oh, man," Vinnie said, putting his hand to his forehead. "You're going to make me cry now."

"Like that's hard," his mama called. "It's not just a sign, now. Paddy's going to put up video cameras inside and out too. We're all going to keep an eye on it. Rose, your greenhouse is safe. Don't you worry."

The police hadn't found any suspects in the vandalism at her parents' house, and she and Vinnie had concluded they likely never would. They knew who was responsible for it, however, and she had worried about Al trying to repeat his attack. But the community was making a stand. With her.

"Thank you," she said, her heart pressing against her ribs. "You can't know how much this means."

"Sure we do," Lucia Tesoro said, stepping forward. "We have businesses here. We know how much courage it takes to start a business and keep it going. To rebuild when you get kicked in the teeth. We're behind you, and I know Mr. Palladino is backing you from heaven, and we've all made sure everyone in town knows it. Rose, I also wanted to give you a table and a few chairs for your greenhouse. They're in my truck."

A feather could have blown her away. Lucia hadn't exactly been on her side in the beginning, but she'd more than come around. Funny how troubles often brought people together, along with the shared love of an old friend like Mr. Palladino. "Thank you, Lucia."

Others started to bring forward gifts. Baker, a coffee box set and a T-shirt that said *Kindness Matters*. Lala, some brightly colored pillows for Lucia's chairs. New pruning shears and gardening hoses from Tom Kelly's hardware store. Aunt Gladys gifted her some long and supple leather gardening gloves. Others, like Manny Romano, said she and Vinnie had a lunch coming on him, while the owner of the Merry Widow offered up a couple vases for her business. Clifton surprised her with his favorite flamenco CD, and Alice gave her a Boyz II Men compilation.

But it was their joint gift that had Vinnie rubbing her back—a set of truffles decorated with flowers, part of the House of Hope & Chocolate's upcoming spring collection, inspired by The Dreamer's Flower Shoppe.

"We're going to tell everyone we know about your business, Rose," Alice said.

"We all are," Lucia said, nodding to her. "Amy is even going to help me spread the word."

Rose glanced over to where Amy and Warren stood with their two little girls. He'd gotten her the emergency funds, with the promise of helping with more. Even more exciting, with the business owners' support, Amy was going to work directly with the trust, both to showcase current stores and to attract new businesses to town.

Their little girls were peeking from behind Warren's tall legs, and Rose remembered what it was like to be that age. The whole world lay ahead, and everything was possible. While she knew she needed to heal, she was grateful for everyone who'd helped her reconnect with that side of herself. With the dreamer.

She glanced up and met Vinnie's warm gaze. It had all started with him, when her dream of marrying him had come true. She squeezed his hand, then looked at the people surrounding them, their friends and neighbors. Her parents stood at the edge of the gathering. She knew they were here to show their love and support, and even though she was hurt by the decisions they'd made, she understood that life sometimes presented choices that weren't easy, solutions that weren't perfect.

She wasn't going to let that hurt she felt come between the love. When her mom and dad brought forward one of her favorite hydrangeas, the Annabelle, she knew what they were saying. A Japanese emperor had given them to people as a way of asking their forgiveness, her father had told her as a child.

They both were crying as she nodded her response. Of course she would forgive them. Vinnie pressed his handkerchief into her hand as he took the plant from her.

Flowers. They all meant something. They were like people, just like Papa had always told her. She glanced back at her new greenhouse standing proudly in the yard of their new home, the one Mama Gia had given them.

Most of the plants nestled inside of it had taken a beating, much like everyone this year. Some were already showing new growth after being cut back. If there was one great piece of wisdom she'd learned about gardening, it was that a hard pruning—while seemingly harsh and painful—often led to a stronger plant and even stronger flowers. Take a few of her amaryllis plants. They'd shot up new stalks and blooms, thriving from the pruning and the less-than-ideal conditions they'd borne this week. One in particular had turned into a beauty.

She squeezed Vinnie's hand before walking toward that blooming red stalk. It boasted two flowers, and she knew just who to give it to. Somehow it felt like coming back full circle.

Using her new pruning shears, she cut the stem and then headed to the Anderson girls. Six feet away, she stopped and knelt down to their level. "Do you like flowers?"

Taylor gave a shriek while Madison nodded shyly. "Why is it red?" she asked.

Rose laughed as Warren and Amy exchanged a look. "All flowers choose a color to be. This flower wanted to be red."

"I like purple," Madison said. "Do you have any purple

flowers?"

She thought of the restocking she'd be doing, possible because Clara Merriam Hale had decided to help their community come through these times stronger. She sent her a prayer of thanks. When she had a truly spectacular plant to send, she was going to send it to her. Something bold and generous and elegant, like the woman herself.

In the meantime, she felt the push to inspire these little girls with the magic of flowers. "I do. In fact, purple is one of my favorite colors too. You'll have to come to the greenhouse when they bloom so you and your sister can see them."

Madison danced in place as she showed Taylor the flower, both of them touching the blooms carefully.

Rose wrapped her arms around herself as she took it all in. Her greenhouse. Their soon-to-be new home. Her friends and neighbors.

And Vinnie.

"Babe," she called out, gesturing like her old self. "Where's the music? I know you have something ready." She'd decided to surprise him with a new cologne bottle as soon as she had a little more income from her business. This time, it would only be cologne to make him smell sexy, not some sort of hourglass. He more than had his life figured out.

"Of course I do. This is one special day." He blew her a kiss, then grabbed the lapels of his coat and started singing "The Days of Wine and Roses" a cappella, much to her and their neighbors' delight. The sound of his voice and those joining in to sing brought more joy into her heart.

This was the rest of her life.

After today, she was going to tell everyone she met to keep dreaming—everyone from her children to her customers. Because dreams did come true. Love brought them into existence.

She was living proof of it.

EPILOGUE

CLIFTON HAD COME TO ORION TO FIND HOPE AND FOLLOW A new dream.

What he'd found had exceeded his wildest expectations.

He imagined marriage would do the same.

"You ready to get hitched?" Gladys called from their bedroom.

Eyeing himself in the full-length mirror in his walk-in closet, he gave a final inspection of his wedding attire. The tuxedo with tails pleased him, as did his silver vest and perfectly tied bow tie.

A groom needed a touch more than his usual *sprezzatura*, so he'd added an antique pocket watch he'd bought from Lucia Tesoro, whom he now enjoyed sipping negronis with whenever she brought in new items of interest. Since helping Rose, Lucia had been more supportive of others in the community, and it had bridged some relationships with longtime neighbors, Gladys included, as well as newcomers like himself.

"Come on, Clifton," Gladys called. "It's not bad luck to see the bride before the wedding. Not when the bride is as old as I am."

He thrust open the closet door and went utterly still. She was resplendent in a creamy fitted gown of lace and tulle with a short train that hinted of the 1920s. The feather fascinator with the silver clip in her hair added another dash of old-world elegance.

"You are breathtaking normally, but today you nearly robbed me of all speech."

She laughed gustily. "Tough to say your vows that way, but since you did the same to me, I vote in favor of giving the officiant a thumbs-up if the temporary silence strikes us both again."

He couldn't help but chuckle. "I doubt Clara will be conversant in the thumbs-up gesture."

"You might be surprised," Gladys said, crossing to him and adjusting his bow tie a mere fraction.

He did not need to look in the mirror to see that it was brilliant perfection now. She was a master, after all. "Aren't you glad we didn't marry over Zoom?" he murmured, taking her by her waist.

"Oh, it would have been a grand story," she said, running her hands down his lapels. "But aren't you glad we decided to wait until this damn Covid stuff was over? Now we can have a real wedding with a real party."

"With all of our friends and neighbors around us," Clifton added. "That was the only reason I agreed to wait, you might remember."

She cocked a thin brow in his direction. "Living together helped, of course. Oh, Clifton, did you ever imagine getting married at this age? I was thinking last night that I might be the luckiest woman in the world."

"I confess to toasting my good luck last night as I contemplated our wedding and the years ahead."

"Your reflections often lead to some good thinking," she said, taking his arm. "Care to share as we drive to the church? Once we get to the church, it's going to be a conga line from start to finish, not that I'd want it any other way."

He kissed her cheek. "On that we agree, but yes, I'm grateful to have some time for just us."

"I'm driving." She stared him down as if daring him to challenge her. But this was their wedding day, and to please her, he wouldn't insist on being the gentleman.

Still, he opened her car door for her, pleased he'd ensured her cherry red 1953 Buick Skylark had been detailed for the occasion. Arthur also had an old convertible, one he and Clara had driven off in for their honeymoon. He wondered what Gladys had in mind. "Please tell me you don't plan to pop the top today."

She was already hitting the button. "You worried about your hair? Clifton, it's a glorious day. Live a little."

She sounded so much like Arthur when he teased Clara that he had to smile. Clara was marrying them, and Arthur would stand up with him as his best man. The youngest Merriams, Flynn and Annie's girls, would be flower girls alongside Warren and Amy's little ones. Gladys had instructed Rose to give all five girls buckets of rose petals, saying they wanted to leave the church on a carpet of flower petals to lighten their steps into married life. She wasn't always poetic, but she had her moments, and Clifton had loved the sentiment.

The wind teased them as they slowly drove down Main Street. "My heart warms every time I see those Friends & Neighbors signs, you know," he said.

"It's wonderful to see it on new store windows too," Gladys replied, gesturing to Rose's shop as they passed. "Her aesthetic is stunning, don't you think, Clifton? I especially love the baby lemon trees on the cake stand in the window. Mr. Palladino would have loved that Rose was inspired to find new ones to share with people."

"She's ahead of her timetable already, businesswise," Clifton said. "After everything she went through, it's good to see her thriving."

"She's hiring Amy to help her on social media too,"

Gladys said. "That girl has eight clients now, including me and you and Alice. Last I heard, Vinnie and Hank are thinking about hiring her too, although Vinnie and Derrick's posting strategies have been impressive."

"Two Brothers is packed every night," Clifton said. "It's wonderful to see."

"A blessing," Gladys said. "And people are starting to buy formal wear again. Still, some tell me they miss working from home and the slower days."

Clifton sent her a wry glance. "There is always greener grass elsewhere if one decides to look, I suppose. The one thing I'm grateful for is that the pandemic nudged me to envision a new life for myself and take the risks needed to achieve it."

"And I'm grateful it brought you to me," Gladys said, sending him a sweet smile. "I'll always remember that hope came to Orion in the form of a chocolate shop and our community decided to put down its foot in the face of Covid and other struggles and put friends and neighbors first. I pray it continues."

"As do I," Clifton said, "but I have faith in the people in our community, new and old."

"It's good to have new people coming in," Gladys said as she passed the wellness store that had opened last month.

"And to have new businesses from old friends," he said. "I am excited for Maria to open her restaurant in a few months. Baker has promised to be back from his coffee trip to Kenya in time for the opening. We will miss her at the shop, but she has waited a long time for her dream to become a reality. Much like I have waited to find and marry my soulmate."

"Do I know her?" Gladys quipped.

He shot her a look. "Will you please take a right at the next street? And then a left."

She gave an answering grunt as she gunned the engine and made the turn, forcing him to clasp the armrest to keep his seat. Of course she laughed, that loud, gusty laugh of hers. He closed his eyes and savored the sound as the sun touched his face.

After all, today was his wedding day.

"Stop here, please," he said as they reached Rose and Vinnie's house. "You can park in the driveway."

"Clifton, we need to be at the church in thirty minutes."

"We'll be on time," he said, coming around to help her out of the car.

"For someone who bemoaned overtightening the crown of his Swiss timepiece, you're playing very fast and loose today." She twined her arms around his neck and kissed him. "I like it."

"Let this be an indication that I'm loosening up more as we prepare to wed," he said, taking her hand when she laughed and leading her to the backyard.

The greenhouse Warren and Mr. O'Connor had found Rose was actually better than her former one. She'd admitted as much to him yesterday, while she was preparing their wedding flowers. He knew it had been hard for her to confess, out of loyalty to her parents as much as the memory of the greenhouse she'd first loved.

He didn't envy the pulls in her heart. Her brother and his family were still living with her parents, and he wasn't working at the barber shop as originally agreed. No, he was often seen drinking with Mr. Grasiaca and others of his ilk, thankfully in surrounding towns.

While their relationship was strained, her parents visited Rose and Vinnie's new house, the one Gia had lovingly given to them. Sometimes Joe was even seen working in the greenhouse beside his daughter, it was said by their neighbors, and he always walked home as if he were Sisyphus reincarnated.

"Are we picking up flowers?" Gladys asked as Clifton entered the code to the greenhouse door, an act of trust from Rose he hadn't taken lightly.

"No, they are all at the church and the reception area," he said as they walked inside. "I have a special surprise for you."

"I take it the surprise is that potted plant with the gold bow, right?" She put her hand on his arm. "You got me a plant, Clifton?"

Her touch was pleasing, just as he knew it always would be. Already he planned to savor the sensation of her sliding his wedding ring on his finger, a new delightful weight after eighty years bare. "Not any plant. This is named after you. It's called a Gladys rose."

She barked out a laugh. "Clifton, I might not be a gardening guru like Rose, but even I know the difference between a rose and a rhododendron."

"Indeed," he said, touching the leaves. "But that is its name. I thought it might be nice to plant something together to commemorate our wedding. I liked the idea of looking out the back windows and seeing a plant named after you."

"The creamy blossoms are elegant," she said, nestling close to him. "You are always so thoughtful, Clifton. It's one of the things I most treasure about you."

"Yet I know it sometimes amuses you too." He raised his brow.

"Only sometimes, and because I like to laugh." She kissed him again, which pleased him greatly. "But, Clifton, you missed something important. I don't want to look outside the window and see a plant named after me."

He studied her.

"I want to look outside at a plant named after *you*."

"Quite." He found his lips were twitching. "I do not know if there is a plant named Clifton. I don't imagine plants are often named after men."

"An incredible oversight by the plant-naming people." She linked arms with him. "Still, we can ask Rose when we go to the church, which we need to do. Right now, dear."

"I thought we'd plant it now," he said, just to tease her.

She pulled him along, which was really the only response necessary. When they reached the church, his heart expanded. All of the Merriams were gathered outside, along with Arthur and Clara and their Orion friends and neighbors.

"I still think you should have had Alice give you away," Gladys said as they exited the car. "Take a good look, Clifton. In fact, I want to take a picture of all of our loved ones waiting for us. Usually they take a picture of the bride and groom on their wedding day, but I want to have one of everyone who came to support us."

He thought about Vinnie playing the Dean Martin song, "You're Nobody till Somebody Loves You" those many months ago when everyone had banded together to support the young couple's dreams.

When he'd heard the song in the past, he had thought it missed out on the importance of loving oneself, but he'd come to appreciate its wisdom. Before, he had loved himself and been quite alone, save for his friendship with Clara. Now his circle had grown to extraordinary proportions. He loved many people—yes, loved—because there were many forms of love.

His world was a richer place for it, and he knew theirs was too. So he knew the power of finding people to love.

They were all in front of them, in fact.

Everyone cheered and waved as he took Gladys' hand and they started walking to the church.

He started to hum the song and was delighted when Gladys joined in.

Hours later, Gladys laughed quite nosily when Rose informed them there was an entire species of plants named after Clifton, known by the common name of Clifton's Eremogone. Known as both a flower and an herb, it boasted elegant white flowers enhanced by pink accents, and while it was extremely uncommon and unique, it thrived wherever it was planted and pleased who knew it.

Once she heard its description, Gladys gave him a sly look and said she thought they must have named it after him without him knowing, since it described him perfectly to her mind.

He was quite delighted to agree, if only to please her.

Of course he pleased her again later when he played his guitar and sang "At Last" by Etta James to her, with Vinnie providing backup. After all, he might be uncommon and unique, but his soulmate was the rarest of the rare. He had waited eighty-one years to find her, and he had every intention of riding off into the sunset with her like in all the great love stories.

What's Next?

You're invited to take a trip to Ireland with Ava
to kick off her enchanting new series,
The Unexpected Prince Charming.

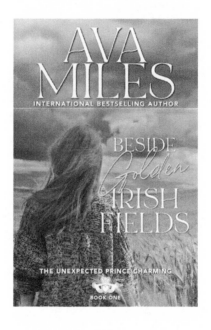

BESIDE GOLDEN IRISH FIELDS

~

Order it now.

ABOUT THE AUTHOR

Ava Miles is the international bestselling author of powerful books about love, happiness, and transformation. As a former conflict expert, Ava rebuilt warzones in places like Lebanon, Colombia, and the Congo to foster peaceful and prosperous communities. While rewarding, Ava recognized she could affect more positive change in the world by addressing the real roots of conflict and unhappiness. In becoming an author, she realized her best life: healing the world through books. Her novels have received praise and accolades from USA Today, Publishers Weekly, and Women's World Magazine in addition to being chosen as Best Books of the Year and Top Editor's picks. However, Ava's strongest praise comes directly from her readers, who call her books life changing.

Made in the USA
Monee, IL
19 July 2021

73913547R00204